REINCARNATE

MCKAY  MERTZ

www.mascotbooks.com

For more information, please contact:
Mascot Books
620 Herndon Parkway, Suite 320
Herndon, VA 20170
info@mascotbooks.com

Library of Congress Control Number: 2019908480

CPSIA Code: PRV1019A
ISBN-13: 978-1-64543-095-7

Printed in the United States

To my wife, Jessica. For her love, support, and patience.

Most people's lives have a single beginning and a single ending. Not mine. Will I be able to forget this one? Or will it just blur together with the rest?

Glasses clink, chefs call out orders, and dozens of smells fill the busy kitchen. A waiter brushes past me carrying a tray full of steaming food. It's pure, organized chaos. Have I really gotten so used to my current life already? When did this place stop feeling so overwhelming? Jill's body must…

No. Stay focused. I have a mission. A purpose. Camden Louis. That's why I'm here. But why a restaurant of all places? Does it even matter? I guess there are worse places to die than Le Lac Caché.

Would a three- or four-star restaurant be worse?

"Bluefin is almost ready, Jill. Here's the sirloin."

The male chef—what was his name again?—deposits a full dish on my black serving tray. I smile thanks to the young man. His floppy hat nearly tumbles off his curls as he smiles back. The chef's eyes linger on me for a moment as they usually do before he hastily readjusts his hat and returns to his station. Did he have a thing for Jill? Or can he not keep his eyes off me because Jill's black button-up and matching skirt expose a little too much skin? It is too much? Or just more than I'd feel comfortable with if I were wearing something similar on my own body? Why is it still difficult for me not to care about things like modesty? It's not *my* body.

Why did my handlers decide this body was perfect for me to use for Louis' murder? Was it just because Jill was single? Easier to make the switch?

At least Jill's lack of attachments has made the past week easier than most…

"Hey, Jill. Have a nice weekend?"

I flinch.

Olivia drops her purse on the counter next to my tray. I glance at a clock on the wall. She's late to her shift again.

"Hey, Liv. My weekend was pretty chill. How 'bout yours?"

Olivia smiles back at me. The dimple in her cheek is just like my own. No. Not mine…Jill's.

"Not bad. Except I broke up with Marcus. The SOB. I caught him cheating—again."

How would Jill respond to such news? She was Olivia's friend…so she probably would've supported Olivia's decision to break up with Marcus. Right?

"Have anyone you can set me up with?" Olivia's curly black hair bounces slightly as she speaks.

Olivia is practically in Jill's face. Her perfume smells like orchids. "Well, do you?"

Maybe if I look busy Olivia will drop it.

"What about Camden Louis?" Olivia's tone matches her wry smile and she leans against the counter.

I ignore her and prepare the small glass vial inside my black apron. I'm holding Louis's death between Jill's polished fingernails.

"Look, Jill, I know he's asked you out before and I know you turned him down. A decision I *still* don't understand, seeing as he's handsome *and* loaded. So since you're not interested…"

The blonde female sous chef deposits a second plate on the white cloth table, and I continue to ignore Olivia. With practiced fingers I place some cilantro on Louis' plate of steaming food. Why is Olivia still trying to chat with me when she hasn't even clocked in?

"Uh, hello? Earth to Jill. If *you're* not interested in a rich hottie, do you think you could at least introduce me to him? Maybe even let me wait his table for once?"

I finger the vial's stopper. My knuckles rub against the inside of Jill's apron and I finally meet Olivia's eyes.

"Jill, what's your problem today?"

Say something. Jill wasn't this remote, or cold. Plus, Olivia's attention needs to be away from me and away from my hands.

"I'm sorry, I'm just…you're right. Camden *did* take me out…of the city actually. I went with him on one of his business trips."

Olivia's eyes widen.

"So *that's* where you were a week ago! I *knew* you weren't sick."

"Yeah…"

One of Jill's fingernails snags a thread in her apron. I fumble with the vial as the tiny white crystals tumble out across the bluefin.

"What are you adding? Is that part of the recipe?"

Damn.

I maintain a neutral expression as I slip the vial back in my apron. I'm an idiot. Could I wave Olivia off and lie about how Louis requested extra salt or something? Maybe, but that's a weak excuse. I need another distraction.

"I had a nice weekend with Cam, but I ended things with him as soon as we got back. He's not my type. Plus, the sex wasn't that great."

Olivia covers her mouth with a hand and grins. Her eyes are practically popping out of her head.

"Oh. *Snap.* Girl, I can't believe you! This is *too* good. Give me a minute. I've got to go clock in, but you need to tell me all the gory details."

Olivia winks at me before she finally scurries toward the back of the kitchen. No doubt she's also off to spread the juicy news that Jill hooked up with one of her regulars. It certainly won't be the worst thing people will remember about Jill Thomas after tonight.

I place Louis' plate next to the sirloin, balance the tray on my right shoulder, and make my way out of the kitchen.

It won't be long now. The small, deadly white crystals have already dissolved into his food. Even a small dosage will kill him in less than a minute.

By then, I'll be long gone. At least, I'd better be long gone. Jill's body will have served its purpose.

On my way out of the kitchen, I pass a small window. It's late. Later than Louis' normal dining hours. The moon is bright, like the first time I died. If all goes well, I might die again tonight. Maybe for the last time. Er... second to last?

Why do my handlers want me to kill Louis tonight? I was supposed to have another week.

Have they learned what they needed from the tapped conversations I've managed to get between Louis and the man he's been meeting with at Le Lac? Now they want to cut him loose? Early?

With each step I take, Louis' life gets closer to ending. At least I only have to poison Louis. Should I count myself lucky that I don't have to shoot, drown, stab, or strangle him? No. Nothing about my existence is lucky.

Louis' private table is only two doors away.

Soon, this will all be over. Just one more target...

The steam rising from Louis' food smells good to this body. I grit my teeth and Jill's mouth waters. *I* hate fish...but it smells *amazing*.

A fellow waiter passes me, and he nods politely in my direction. I reply with a quick smile. Jill was always quick to smile.

I retrieve a foldable table, and the silverware rattles a little as I place Louis' tray of food on top.

He's ordered two entrees. He must be meeting with the politician again. Are my handlers aware of this?

I knock on the door to Louis' private room. A second later, the heavy wooden door slides open, and I enter.

Something's wrong.

Louis is seated to my left at the round table. He's wearing a khaki blazer with a white shirt that's unbuttoned at the collar. His hair is styled, and his short beard looks like it was recently trimmed. Louis' large, muscular bodyguard stands like a silent shadow next to him. The politician, whose pallid face I know but whose name I don't, is seated to my right.

All three men are staring at me. Unblinking.

Fine hairs on the back of Jill's neck stand on end. Her palms get clammy. Her body wants me to run. To flee.

"Good evening, gentlemen." I keep my voice level, but Jill's hands tremble as I place their individual orders on the table.

"Jill, so good to see you again." Louis' voice is soft, and something is off in his tone. His cold blue eyes stare at me unblinking.

"Would you believe me, Senator, if I told you Jill is the best waitress I've ever had? This is before the Border Shutdowns too, mind you."

The senator eyes me with a hint of a smile as I set his plate in front of him. The urge to cringe is almost unbearable.

"I missed you when you were gone last week, Jill. One of your coworkers mentioned you might be ill? I'm glad to see you've...recovered."

I nod but remain silent. Louis' eyes continue boring holes into me like a hawk with its prey. The senator continues glowering at me from across the table.

"The senator and I were just discussing a concerning development."

I refill their wine glasses. Not daring to meet Louis' penetrating gaze.

"You might find this alarming, but I've just been told someone wants to kill me. Can you believe that?"

Louis taps a knife against his plate. The senator adjusts his tie and leans back in his seat. His face is smug. He's looking at me like he can see right through my false body.

They definitely know.

This has never happened before.

I need to leave. Jill's body had the right idea.

Perhaps Louis won't know his food is poisoned even if he somehow knows someone at Le Lac wants him dead. I can't fail in my mission, but I can't risk exposing the people who sent me. The latter would be worse than failure.

My options are limited. If I leave, it would only worsen my situation. It would look far too suspicious. Maybe I can talk my way out of this situation. Should I pretend Louis is joking with me? Yes. That could work...

"That *is* concerning, Mr. Louis. Shall I bring a bottle of Cheval? My mother always told me life is too short to drink cheap wine."

I wink at Louis. He hesitates, and his expression betrays a hint of doubt. I seize my opening.

"One bottle of Cheval Blanc it is! I'll be right back."

Clutching Louis' empty wine bottle in my hands, I turn to leave.

Louis' hulking bodyguard is blocking my way. His arms are folded across his massive chest, and his feet are spread slightly apart.

I'm in trouble.

Jill's body isn't the strongest, even though I've been exercising it regularly for the past week. Do I risk a physical altercation with these men? Do I have a choice? Jill's heart rate sure doesn't think so...

"I'm afraid I won't be ordering any more meals from you, Jill. Or wine for that matter." Louis' voice is so low it's barely a whisper. He stands and frowns as if he's disappointed, but confirmation dances behind his eyes. How. Does. He. Know?

The bodyguard's hand grips my left shoulder. My stomach sinks.

Before Louis' bodyguard has a chance to react, I whip around and throw two of my fingers into his left eye. Jill's long fingernails act like mini-spearheads. The bodyguard howls. I drop the heavyset man with a swift kick to his groin. Spinning, I launch myself at Louis. His eyes widen and Louis fumbles inside his suit jacket. He only gets his gun halfway out before I collide with him. The force of my tackle sends him tumbling back onto the table. Silverware, wine, and food go flying in all directions.

Louis' death won't look like an accident now. But I have no choice.

Leveraging my weight against his, I seize a knife from the table and attempt to plunge it into his right eye. Louis manages to move at the last second, and all I get is his ear. He screams in pain, but the second time—I don't miss. The knife slides easily through his eye and stops at the back of his skull with a dull squelch.

Louis' hands go limp against Jill's body. I step away, covered in thick, warm blood.

Mere seconds have passed, and the senator has remained motionless, sitting on the opposite side of the large round table. His eyes bulge and his mouth hangs open.

I turn to leave. They didn't tell me to kill the senator. Getting to the safe house is my only priority now. My handlers will have questions for me. Questions I won't be able to answer. Like how Louis knew I was coming. Should I interrogate the senator?

No.

My cover is blown, and I can't risk being caught.

The door opens silently as I turn to leave, but the senator's trembling voice stops me from taking another step.

"Who...who...*are* you?"

A bitter laugh almost escapes Jill's lips. He'd be better off asking *what* I am, not *who* I am.

"I'm Divest."

The name I've given myself will mean nothing to him. Not even my handlers know what I call myself.

Leaving the senator behind, I flee into the safety of night. The sound of Enforcer sirens heralds the success of my mission. I keep running. This has to be the final nightmare, the last murder, the last body. *It has to...*

"The body wasn't the problem. Right now, my best guess is it was actually Senator Andrews who somehow knew and tipped Louis off."

"At least she still killed him. Perhaps we should've had her kill the Senator too."

"That was your call."

"And it was yours *to have her try poisoning him!"*

"We can argue all night long. Point is, someone knew."

"I'm not worried about that. Her next target won't know about us. Even if the Americans have somehow learned who we are…he won't believe them if they go public."

"Her next target? I thought you said this was her last mission?"

"It was *her last mission. Things have changed."*

"I don't know how many more transplants her brain can handle."

"Good thing that's Doctor Powell's area of expertise—not yours. Just make it work. Make her *work. I'm a man of my word; perhaps you can remind her of that."*

"Anything else?"

"No. I'm sending you the mission overview right now."

"Very good, Director."

Why am I not allowed to shower? It's not like a shower could wash away the guilt and pain, but feeling *physically* clean would be nice.

At least they gave me a fresh change of clothes. The light T-shirt fits well, and the jeans are my favorite shade of blue. Jeremy always told me to look on the bright side...

The room they're holding me in is small, and the walls are bare. There are no windows. The only illumination comes from a bright industrial light set into the ceiling. I trace the seams of the leather couch I'm sitting on with Jill's index finger. It's difficult, but I keep my eyes locked on the gray cement floor to avoid looking at the small mirror lying in the corner of the room. Did my handlers put a mirror in here for the sole purpose of torturing me? Do they even know about my paranoia? Powell might...he seems to know my brain better than I do myself.

Surely my handlers won't punish me. When I gave my report their voices weren't happy, but they didn't blame me. After all, I did what they asked.

A strand of Jill's wavy blonde hair falls across my eyes again, and I brush it aside. It took nearly thirty minutes to clean my...*Jill's*...hands. To scrape the blood from under her fingernails. I shudder.

Blood. So much blood. Is that why I'm here? Because my real body has such a special blood type? No. Stop it. Answers aren't going to come. They haven't since day one. Why would day five hundred and thirty-one...or is it thirty-two...be any different?

It's been at least an hour since I gave my handlers my initial report. I bite the inside of Jill's cheek to stay awake. How much longer are they going to make me wait? Jill's eyelids are like lead.

Do they have my real body stored here? Will I finally get it back, and will they release Jeremy?

My handlers didn't *expressly* say so, but didn't they imply this might have been the last assignment before they'd release me?

Tracing the seams of the leather couch begins to bore me, and I start pacing back and forth within my small room. My "room" is more like a prison, seeing as I can't leave.

As I cross the length of the room for the fifth time, the door to my comfortable cell opens.

Doctor Powell enters the room flanked by two massive men in tactical gear. His two companions dwarf him in size, even though Powell is of average height. Powell's blond, receding hair line is even thinner than the last time I saw him. Is going bald a side effect of working too many long hours for murderers?

He's probably as much a pawn in this organization as I am. At least he's honest with me. Is that why I trust him? Even though I hate him? He *is* my attending physician, after all…

The men behind Powell carry sidearms with built-in Tasers. Smart-guns. The weapons serve to remind me I cannot escape—and what will happen if I try. But their added presence is just for show. Large, intimidating mercenaries with guns don't keep me in line. The fact that my handlers have Jeremy as their hostage does.

I wait for Powell to speak and try to read his face for any sign of emotions but am once again reminded—he doesn't have any.

"Anything to report?" Powell's eyes do not meet mine. Unblinking, he stares through his thick glasses at the blueish glow of the tablet held between his pale, bony fingers. His words are monotone. Detached. I catch myself wondering for the hundredth time if Powell is either anti-social or a sociopath.

"No. This body didn't have any issues. Although…like the last body, I still had severe headaches during early morning and late evening."

As if on cue, my head throbs.

The ache is dull and perfectly in sync with Jill's heartbeat.

"The headaches were worse this time too. And last time, you said the headaches would go away with a new body."

Powell nods absentmindedly as he glances at his tablet. The faint light from the screen reflects off his glasses and makes him look like an insect. An insect that would feel great to crush beneath my heel.

"Headaches again, hmm? How would you describe your pain on a scale of one to ten? Ten being the most painful."

I frown. He acts like I'm sitting in a clinic with an earache. Not living a hell no scale can describe.

"Four or five."

Powell taps at his tablet, still not meeting my eyes. "How long did they last this time?"

"I don't know…longer than the last body."

Powell mumbles something to himself. Then he turns his tablet toward me. He's pulled up a multi-colored image of a brain. "Point to where you think the pain is concentrated."

I regard the glowing image and point to an area somewhere in the middle.

Powell nods. Did he expect me to point where I did?

"What does it mean, Doctor?"

He ignores me. I ball my fists and frown. My brain is the only thing I have left, and I don't know if something is wrong with it or if the pain is just…in my head.

"Anything else?" Powell finally meets my eyes.

"When do I get my body back? My *real* body."

"You know I don't have anything to do with that."

"They told me this was my last mission."

"Did they?" Powell is mocking me. I could probably punch him in the face at least twice before his guards could…no. They'd hurt Jeremy.

"Can I rest now, Doctor? Or do you need to ask your experiment anything else?"

"I'll address the headaches you've been experiencing during your next assignment."

I grind my teeth and take a step toward the doctor. He doesn't notice, but the two guards do. They put their hands on their side arms. I hesitate.

"My *next* assignment?" I can't keep the anger out of my voice. "When are they going to tell me I'm done?"

Powell shrugs and turns to leave.

I'm supposed to follow him.

I refuse to move.

Following Powell means one nightmare will end and another will begin. I have no choice.

The guards take me roughly by Jill's arms and walk me to the door.

No.

I kick one mercenary in the knee and elbow the other in his ribs. The guards grunt in pain. Good.

Before I can swing another fist, one of them hits me hard in my lower back, just above my kidneys. The second guard slams a heavy, steel-toed boot to my left foot. I gasp and fall to the ground hard. The cement floor is cold against Jill's cheek. I squeeze my eyes shut. I shouldn't have tried to hurt them. Divest doesn't lose control of her emotions on a whim. What was I thinking?

I remain limp and silent as the mercenaries kick me. Over and over.

When they're through, the mercenaries grip my arms again and haul me out of the room. Have they broken Jill's foot? It hurts more than it should.

They know they can hurt me. This body won't be needed anymore. Injuring my head is off limits, but everything else is fair game.

The guards tow Jill's limp body through the door, trailing behind Powell toward his lab. Toward my next mission.

The lab door at the end of the hall is just a normal, everyday white door with a silver handle. Who knew hell's gate looked so ordinary? So deceivingly average? The only thing missing are the flames. Or a three-headed dog.

Jill's back tenses and her heart begins to beat faster. I swear each body I use has a mind of its own.

Get a grip. I've been in Powell's lab plenty of times before. This is nothing new. All they'll do is sedate me…then proceed to remove my brain from this body.

Jill's body continues to tremble. With concentration, I manage to calm myself until all I feel is resignation. This is my fate. My way of ensuring they'll let Jeremy go and give me my real body back. I just have to cooperate and do what they tell me. No more emotion. No more mistakes…

Powell approaches the door to his lab and keeps walking. Why aren't we going to his lab?

My guards follow him, pulling me along, my feet half dragging on the cold, hard floor.

"Where are we going?"

"For a ride." Powell doesn't turn around when he speaks.

Did he just answer my question? Powell never answers my questions…

"Your next body is waiting for us in San Diego."

What? California? The furthest my handlers have sent me is southern Florida. Most of my targets have been on or near the East Coast. Why would they suddenly transfer me to the West Coast?

"Who's my target this time?"

We're approaching an exit. A repeated thumping sound, like rotating helicopter blades, echoes through the empty hallway. Surely we aren't taking a helicopter to California, are we?

"You'll know in due time. Rest assured this man deserves to die."

Will he deserve to die? Not all of the men or women I've been sent to kill were evil people. Some of them definitely were. But did any of them really deserve to die? Even the bad ones?

Before, I only killed to defend my comrades, my country, and those I loved back home. At least as a soldier I *knew* the men who were giving me orders. Now, I kill for evil, twisted, unseen people with their own agenda. I kill to get Jeremy back. I kill so Jeremy will hold me, *the real me*, in his arms again.

The door to the exit opens and we're on a roof. The thumping sound *does* belong to a helicopter. It's small, black, and has no doors. My two guards force me to duck and tow me across the landing pad. Wind whips Jill's hair across my face, partially blinding me, but my hands are still held by my guards, so I can't do anything about it.

I'm lifted up by my forearms and placed roughly into a back seat of the helicopter. The guards are callous with me as they strap me in. They're particularly careful to remind me they've broken Jill's foot. I have to fight back tears from the pain. Does Powell notice the treatment I'm receiving? He doesn't do or say anything to stop them. He never does.

Someone shoves a pair of headphones over my ears. A crackly voice asks if we're ready to take off. Powell speaks into his own headset and tells the pilots he's ready to go. After the two mercenaries climb into the back and buckle in, we begin to lift off the ground.

I shiver violently.

Winter is dying slowly, holding on just a little longer every year. I glance at Powell's long black coat. My thin shirt does next to nothing to keep me from the sharp bite of the cold wind. The sun is rising in the distance, which warms me a little. We must be a dozen miles out from the city. Morning light glints off the few buildings that manage to rise above the smog. Willis Tower peeks through the gray blanket that covers the city. I won't miss Chicago.

Roads, like black snakes, weave themselves through run-down neighborhoods below us. I could stay up here forever, flying above the world with its filth and corruption. Is this what freedom used to feel like? Soon we exchange the tops of buildings for the tops of skeletal trees. A thin airstrip soon comes into view, and a small jet pulls lazily out of a hangar onto the solitary runway.

Why didn't Powell just remove my brain back at his lab for transport? Maybe my handlers are in a hurry?

No.

They must need me to learn about my next body, my next identity, *before* making the switch. Like Samantha. It's the most logical explanation for what's going on, but who am I kidding? I should stop trying to guess what's going on.

What new horrors have my handlers planned for me this time? Will I be someone in a position of power? A devoted spouse? A mistress? Or will I be someone like Jill whose closest relationships were with her coworkers? Someone no one notices or expects would be a murderer.

Jill's body shivers when a fresh gust of air rushes over her exposed arms. We descend straight down until we reach the tarmac. The asphalt looks freshly shoveled of the sickly gray snow that covers the surrounding ground and trees.

A voice over my headset tells Powell and I to unbuckle and exit to the right. The pair of mercenaries don't handcuff me as I disembark the helicopter. They don't even point a gun at me.

Head bowed, I dutifully limp away from the helicopter, following Powell toward the plane. Twin engines hug the tail, leaving the wings sleek and unencumbered. Its white fuselage is stark against the sharp, black winglets.

A second pair of men in body armor wave us toward them and the plane. Powell quickens his pace, and I try to do the same, gritting my teeth from the pain shooting up Jill's leg. The beating I had coming, but why did they have to break bones? At least now the sun is higher and it's not quite as cold. It should be even warmer where we're supposedly heading. That's at least *something* to look forward to, I suppose.

They have a ramp lined up against the small plane. Powell reaches the top quickly and steps into the plane before I'm even halfway up.

Pain throbs up Jill's leg with each step, even though I'm using the railings to avoid putting too much pressure on Jill's foot. I grimace but manage to make it to the top and in through the open gate.

The interior of the plane is more spacious than I'd thought it would be. There are several leather recliners and even a small couch.

I claim the couch. My body is exhausted, in more ways than one, and sleep would be amazing. Will they will allow this one mercy?

I stretch my legs out, being careful with my broken foot, which is throbbing and has noticeable swelling now. I remove my socks and shoes, something Jeremy always said never to do on a plane, and find a pillow to rest my foot on. Elevating Jill's broken foot might help with the pain. Right?

Other men enter the plane. None of them bother me as they head toward the back, giving Powell and me some distance. Powell is seated opposite me. He pulls out a tablet and a computer from one of his bags and sets them on the table in front of him. The man is either an insect or a machine. Which is the better analogy? Have I ever seen him rest or even eat?

The plane begins to move. Small buildings flash past my window, and I struggle to keep my eyes open. Suddenly, the horizon tilts, and we're flying.

Wishing I had a blanket, and some major pain killers, I close Jill's eyes and try to find solace in my own mind.

Why don't I dream anymore? I haven't since becoming Divest. Should I even be complaining? If I *did* have dreams…they'd probably be stained with blood.

"How much do they know?"

"They know there's an assassin or *assassins*, but that's the extent of their knowledge."

"That's it?"

"As far as we know. My contact still has limited clearance within the Agency itself, but he says a team has managed to connect three of McKenzie's murders, including her most recent. We think Louis was the link the CIA needed to connect some of the others."

"Does the CIA know about the nature of our assassin?"

"Not according to Dominguez. He says the CIA is still trying to put together a profile for the murderer or murderers. Which should prove impossible for them, seeing as McKenzie has had eight 'profiles' in the last year alone."

"Anything else?"

"Powell again. He says her brain is exhibiting increased degeneration. But he's been wrong before."

"I'll deal with Powell. Tell him to send me the latest test results."

"Right away, Director."

Someone taps my shoulder.

A flight from Chicago to San Diego can't be more than a few hours, but are we already there?

Powell nudges me again with the corner of his tablet. I blink and rub Jill's eyes.

"We've landed. Get ready to leave."

I nod and twist Jill's body to sit up. A throbbing migraine pulses across my forehead and I wince.

"I have a headache. Can you give me something for the pain?"

Powell ignores me. Typical. Was it even worth the try?

Something else is aching. It's not my head, it's…Jill's foot.

It's purple in a few places and throbbing with an acute pain that shoots up Jill's leg with each beat of her heart. I grimace. I'm fine. I'm okay. This isn't the worst injury I've ever dealt with, but it still hurts—a lot.

Powell notices my swollen foot, but makes no comment. Didn't he have to swear some kind of oath to help people when he became a doctor?

I get shakily to Jill's feet, putting all her weight on her good leg, and catch a quick glimpse outside the window. To the west, green palm trees contrast sharply with red clay roofs. Are we near some kind of suburb? I can almost smell the warm ocean breeze. The sun is suspended so high it's out of sight.

We've landed on a thin strip of tarmac. No other planes, or people, are in sight. Just a few closed hangars. The men in black body armor are busy pulling their bags from the overhead compartments. Powell orders me to start walking toward the front of the plane.

I obey.

The plane door slowly opens outward as I approach. The bright California sun instantly blinds me as I step out and descend the few short steps onto the black tarmac.

Rough hands grip my upper arms, and I'm pushed in the direction of a waiting vehicle. It's a black Suburban with windows so tinted they might as well be mirrors. Don't look at them…

One of the guards opens a back door to the vehicle, and I get stuffed inside. A solid barrier separates the front and back seats. I feel like a piece of luggage.

"Put this on."

The mercenary tosses me a black cloth bag then shuts my door loud-ly. I sigh.

Powell approaches the Suburban and takes the front passenger seat. Muf-fled words are exchanged; it sounds like an argument. Seconds later, Powell exits and climbs into the back of the vehicle across from me. He's frowning as he buckles himself into his seat.

I grin. Looks like someone isn't as entitled as he thinks.

Powell glances at me sharply. I wipe the grin off my face, but it's too late. His face turns red, and he slaps me. Hard.

My cheek smarts and I cringe.

Powell's never personally assaulted me before. Never. Only refrained from helping when others have done so. Even *Powell* is abusing me now...

Why?

Jill's lower lip trembles. I fight the urge to retaliate and rest my head against the door of the car. Stinging tears begin to well in Jill's eyes. My cheek continues to burn.

The black canvas is thick and rough as I slip it over Jill's head just as a single tear makes its way down my cheek. I swallow hard. I will *not* cry. I'm Divest. I'm in control of my emotions...

A few bumps and stops are the only way I know we're even moving at all. Our drive lasts at least thirty minutes. Where are they taking me? An abandoned warehouse like Chicago? A beach house? Disneyland?

Why me?

Why am I *here*?

Will asking the question for the hundredth time change the answer? Why didn't I just die the first time like I was supposed to?

My first death should've been my last. Did my handlers plan all of it? Or were they just lucky things worked out for them? Why couldn't American Special Forces retrieve my body before my handlers? Did my handlers kidnap

Jeremy the same day they took me? I'm told he's kept frozen and stable in cryogenics—same with my real body, which they've promised has been healed.

Have my memories surrounding the first time I died always been this hazy? My team and I were closing in on a terrorist cell. They were supposed to be responsible for the terror strikes on Washington. We were ambushed, outnumbered. There was lots of shouting. I was afraid. Soldiers aren't supposed to be afraid...

Why didn't the terrorists think to shoot me in my head rather than... wherever else they hit me? It could only have been about six minutes from when I went down to when my handlers recovered my body. Otherwise, my brain would have ceased functioning. But thanks to those six minutes, my life has never been the same. Time is a bitch.

When we stop for the seventh time, my car door opens.

Arms remove me roughly from the car, and a gruff voice tells me to start walking forward. The ground beneath my feet is uneven and shifts with each step. Gravel. A guard keeps a hand on Jill's arm and stops me after I've taken several steps. His fingers dig into Jill's skin, and I wince.

I'm pulled forward, nearly stumbling over a small step.

The air is suddenly much cooler. We must be inside a building.

Light blinds me as the bag over my head is removed, and I pause.

We're in some kind of...mansion. Fancy paintings hang on the walls. There's even a Rembrandt. Jeremy appreciated fine art and used to take me to exhibits all the time.

"Keep walking."

The carpet appears hand woven. The furniture looks brand new and expensive.

"I said keep walking. Now!" The mercenary shoves me. He has a buzz cut and a mean scar across his cleft chin. He looks like a stereotypical bad-guy mercenary straight out of a James Bond movie. The guard behind him looks pretty similar. Where do my handlers find these guys? Film sets?

Why don't my handlers or the mercenaries they employ ever call me by my given name? Because doing so would humanize me...?

I've been divested of my name too.

I'm nudged a few paces down a hallway lined with single-pane windows until we stop at an unmarked door. Mercenary number two swipes a key card, and a light near the handle turns green. The door slides open automatically.

Metal stairs lead down into a dimly lit basement cellar. Tweedledee leads the way, and Tweedledum pushes me forward by digging his elbow into my back.

The handrail helps me take Jill's weight off her right foot. I make it to the bottom and stop. This is no ordinary cellar. The air is thick and smells of antiseptic. A single operating table rests in the center of the room. Directly above the table, Meridian lasers hang from the ceiling like the legs of a spider.

"Over here." Tweedledee points, and I walk over to the operating table. "Sit."

Do they have my next body somewhere in this lab? Possibly frozen in a cryogenic chamber?

As soon as I'm seated on the table, Tweedledum approaches me carrying a tablet. "This is a double-body operation. Your first body will allow you to get close to the second, which belongs to the person you'll use to kill the target. Understand?"

I lock my jaw and manage a curt nod so he knows I'm listening.

Not again.

A *second* double-body operation?

Bile rises in my throat.

Will it be like the first? How long did I pose as Samantha Demeter's assistant? Was it five or six weeks? I worked for Samantha, interacted with her, entered an existing *relationship* with her. Then I became her. At least Sam and her husband had a rocky marriage. I only had to sleep with him once before I killed him. Or was it twice?

Then I helped my handlers stage Sam's suicide…

I refocus my attention as Tweedledum pulls up an image of a mature Hispanic woman on his tablet.

"This is your first body. Her name was Maria Antonio. She was a maid for the woman you need to study. Maria was unmarried. She had family, but they live out of the country and she didn't speak with them often. Maria didn't have any major social commitments except for her local religious congregation that meets every Sunday. You should be able to skip these reunions without raising suspicions."

The mercenary hands me his tablet, and I scan through the data he's pulled up, memorizing as much of it as I can.

If my time spent as Divest has taught me anything about myself, it's that I'm very good at becoming someone other than myself.

It takes me less than three minutes to read the information they've given me on Maria. I focus on the basics like date and place of birth, names of her closest family members, work history, et cetera. It's like I'm reading an obituary. I hand Tweedledum back his tablet when I'm finished.

"Now." He pulls up a second image. "*This* will be your second body. Her name is Tahira Collins. She's an only child and lives with her ailing mother. Mehar Collins is Indian-American. Tahira's father, John Collins, was also American. The pair divorced when Tahira was ten years old. Only Tahira's mother, Mehar, is still alive, but the woman has early onset Alzheimer's and her life expectancy is down to three or four months."

I nod. If there's no family around to fact check me, I won't have to memorize as much information.

I study the image of Tahira Collins. She's an extremely beautiful young woman. Probably somewhere in her mid-twenties. Only one or two years younger than myself...my *real* self. Tahira has long black hair that matches her eyes. Her skin is more brown than I'd have guessed, knowing her father was Caucasian. Based on the car she's seen standing next to in the image, Tahira Collins also looks to be about my same height. No...not my height... *Jill's* height.

Why does Tahira Collins' name sound so familiar? Maybe she's an actress or something?

"When she was healthy, Mehar Collins was very religious. Hindu by tradition. John Collins allowed his ex-wife to raise Tahira with Hindu beliefs as well. The reason you're being told this now is because Tahira Collins is secretly engaged to Deval Abdul Kapoor—this is the man you will kill."

Tweedledum shows me the image of an Indian man. I've seen this man before. But where? Maybe I've seen his face in the news somewhere? Social media? His skin is even darker than Tahira's, but his hair, which curls slightly at the ends, is a lighter, chocolate color.

One of Powell's orderlies approaches me and rubs an alcohol wipe on Jill's right arm. The woman inserts a small needle just below the bicep. I cringe. Jill's body is especially sensitive to pain. Tweedledum drops his tablet but keeps talking, ignoring the masked orderly.

"Kapoor is Indian, also Hindu by tradition. Deval's family consists of his mother and two younger sisters. Deval's mother never married. We believe all three children came from a single sperm donor. Now, this is important—the engagement between Deval Kapoor and Tahira Collins is part of an arranged marriage. As far as we know, Collins and Kapoor have never met in person. Their contact has been limited to a few supervised video conferences. Questions?"

I shake Jill's head. Even if Tahira's supposed relationship with her fiancé is as formal as it sounds, this doesn't make what I'll have to do any easier for me. I'll still be part of not one but three murders. First Maria, then Tahira, and finally, if I do as my handlers say…Deval Kapoor will die too.

Why would an American family agree to an arranged marriage with foreigners? Since the Terror Strikes, and especially after the United States closed borders, feelings toward foreigners have been distrustful, hostile, or at least unfriendly. Right?

"You don't need to know anything else at this juncture. You'll be provided with more information as your mission requires. Maria works over forty hours a week, but her schedule should still give you enough time to learn everything you need to about Tahira Collins before you leave for India."

"India?"

The mercenary nods. "Collins and Kapoor are set to be married ninety days from today. In Bengaluru."

Tweedledum turns his back to me and leaves. Is he going to find Powell?

The information they've given me is minimal—but what's new? Do they get some sort of sick pleasure by leading me along little by little? Only giving me more intel as it becomes relevant to my situation? Maybe they do it to keep me from forming my own opinions of what's going on. Do they think I'm easier to control that way?

I close Jill's eyes, steeling myself.

The surgeries are painless. I'll be fine. It's like I'm a machine just having my components moved around. It's like my brain is a computer hard drive.

Or maybe it's more like a CPU?

Either way, with every transplant, as my brain is taken from one body and shuffled to the next, I lose a bit of who I am each time. Is it because I spend so much time acting the part of someone else's personality? Do I even have my own personality anymore? Playing musical chairs with other people's bodies is disorienting…

Did I really just use musical chairs as an analogy?

How much more personality decay can I handle? This *has* to be my last mission. So I don't lose myself. So that when I'm reunited with Jeremy I'm not just an empty shell of the woman I used to be. How much of the real me is even left at this point?

Steps approach, and I open my eyes. Powell emerges from shadow and tells me to lie down.

He towers over me. Insectoid eyes staring down at me like *I'm* an insect he's about to dissect.

Metal squeaks as one of Powell's masked orderlies wheels a cylindrical cryochamber next to me. If I reached for it, I could touch it. The condensation and dark blue liquid of the chamber blur the silhouette of the body held within. My next body…

I shiver.

How is creating someone, or some*thing*, like me even possible? It's been over a year. How is it that I still know virtually nothing about the science that makes this all possible—that makes *me* possible?

I can't be sure, but I'm fairly confident the injections Powell gives me are just as essential as the cryogenic chambers. Are the injections what's keeping my host bodies from attacking my brain? Do they somehow help in repairing the severed nerve tissue? Or do they have some other purpose I can't even fathom?

Powell puts a mask connected to a clear, plastic tube over my mouth and orders me to inhale. The gas smells weird. I close Jill's eyes again and begin to count.

One...two...three...four...five...

The next time I open my eyes...I'll have a new body.

A new life.

A new mission.

A new nightmare.

My mind is on a precipice.

Thousands of feet below, the desert stretches endlessly in all directions. White sands slope up to meet my cliff.

The sky is nothing more than a dark void. It never changes. Shapes materialize on the edge of my awareness then disappear just as quickly, too indistinct to separate from the swirling void.

There's no horizon.

This impossible space isn't real. It can't be.

My awareness compels me to find a rational explanation for this illusion. Why? I've been here dozens of times, but...there *has* to be an end to this wasteland.

The landscape beneath me tilts somehow. My disembodied consciousness shudders, and my vision swims. Please. Not again. Can't I stay here? Even just a little longer?

What would happen if I didn't fall? Why can't I ever decide whether I stay or leave? Why *must* I fall?

Pressure builds within me until I cannot hold it back any longer. I struggle. But like an ocean wave which builds and builds until it breaks, the plunge is inevitable. My consciousness drifts forward. I'm helpless to resist.

I reach the edge. The pressure inside me releases its grip.

I plunge toward the desert below.

If I had a voice, would I scream?

Sand rushes toward me on all sides. The desert's mouth opens wide to consume me. The swirling darkness above me collapses.

The void is me, and I am the void.

When we collide with the desert floor we're obliterated.

Darkness explodes in all directions, mixing with the pale white sands of the desert. Flashes of light blind my awareness. Pain sears my mind. Energy courses through me. I'm ripped apart. Fragmented. Shattered.

My consciousness lies broken, staring upward. Above me there's only whiteness. Gone is the swirling dark void. Slowly the desert pulls me beneath the sand with its cold embrace. I gasp for air. But I can't move. I'm powerless to keep from suffocating.

I inhale sharply.

My eyes snap open. No, not my eyes. *Maria's* eyes.

I'm staring at a fan rotating on the ceiling above me. The blades spin in lazy circles. I follow them until I get dizzy.

Bachata music plays softly from a radio that sits on a small nightstand. I'm in a bed. It's neatly made, and I'm lying on top of the comforter. This must be Maria's apartment…

When did I arrive here? They must have brought me while I was still unconscious. Why didn't I wake up in Powell's lab? He must have run his tests before they took me here.

I flex my…Maria's…fingers and bring them up to her eyes.

The skin is brown and much darker than my last body's. Her fingers are old and worn like they're used to working and cleaning.

Using my new hands, I reach up and explore the sides and back of Maria's skull. There. The scarring is nearly imperceptible. The only evidence of Powell's lasers. The scars of Divest. I also find the faint scarring at the base of my... Maria's...neck. There are no stitches and almost no trace of the surgery itself. Even so, I suppose it helps to be female because having longer hair covers the faint scarring left behind from my transplants.

Maria's hair only falls to my...her...shoulders, so it's not as long as Jill's was, but it does the job.

The walls of Maria's room are painted an earthy, reddish color. Like the red-rock canyons Jeremy and I hiked before we were married. He loved getting me to try new things with him. Our life was one big adventure.

A tall wooden cabinet lines the wall to my right, and next to it...

A mirror.

My reflection.

No.

I turn my head, averting my eyes, but it's too late. I've already looked. I squeeze my eyes shut and bite my lip.

My body is short. Shorter than most bodies I've had.

Please no, no, no, no.

My face is plain but has a mature wisdom to its features.

My breathing becomes shallow. Rapid.

My eyebrows are slender. So are my small lips. I have a few wrinkles which speak to my age too.

My lungs are on fire.

I shake my head.

"No! Stop!" My voice is hoarse.

It's just the mirror. A reflection. I'm *not* my body. This body is *Maria's*. *Not* mine!

I need a blanket. A towel. Anything.

There's a *serape* at the end of the bed. Yes. That will work.

I slide off the bed. I keep my...*Maria's*...eyes on the ground. With shaking hands, I throw the *serape* over the top of the mirror.

There.

Cautiously, I remove Maria's wrinkled hands. The blanket starts to slip a little so I readjust it. With quivering fingers, I lift the mirror and rotate it until it faces the corner—where it can't find me.

I can breathe again.

I'm not Maria...

I'm wearing a corpse. No. A shell. Wearing a corpse seems more accurate, but slipping into an empty shell is easier to swallow. Let's stick with shell...a fifty-year-old shell...

What am I thinking? Does age really apply to me anymore? I was twenty-six when I became Divest, but with all the transplants and brief periods in cryogenics, my current age has certainly broken the normal rules. Is age based on one's brain? One's body? Both?

Either way, on the outside—I've just aged about thirty years. So much for aging well...

At least Maria took care of herself. Wearing a healthy body is always a plus.

The modest apartment is tidy and very clean. A few photos with smiling faces lie here and there. The mercenary who debriefed me in Powell's lab told me Maria had family in Mexico, so the faces in the photos are probably her siblings.

Maria was a big fan of crafts. She has handmade blankets, pottery, and even some jewelry. All free from dust and arranged in a very organized manner. My fingers touch each of these items with respect, knowing I'm a stranger here, even though my body isn't.

The apartment has only two windows. I approach the one that gives light to the small living room and peer outside.

The street below is dirty and lined with a few yellow palm trees. Maria's apartment is on the third story of the building. Young children kick a soccer ball around in an alleyway, and there are a few men talking in front of a vehicle with its engine exposed. The men are smoking and laughing about something. My Spanish isn't strong enough to understand them and certainly not enough to pass as a native speaker. I really hope it's true that Maria doesn't have any social groups. Or I'll have a big *problema*.

Maria's stomach growls. Her body is starving. Powell still hasn't given me a good explanation why my bodies are always famished when I first come to. I wander to Maria's kitchen and poke around. Substituting bread for a wheat tortilla, I make a sandwich and wolf everything down with a glass of juice. While eating, I scan the walls of Maria's apartment for any sign of the cameras I'm sure my handlers have placed to keep an eye on me.

An obnoxious buzzing distracts me from my search, and I turn to find a phone vibrating on one of the small coffee tables. The caller ID simply says *Unknown*.

"This is Maria." My voice still has a bit of an accent. That's a first.

"Status?"

The modulated electronic voice belongs to one of my handlers. Unrecognizable and likely untraceable.

"Body is fine. I have full motor control."

This is all they care about. They don't care about my emotional status, just my physical status.

"Good. Go to the bedside dresser, and on the top, you'll see the tablet we've left for you. On the tablet is more information on Maria Antonio. We've also left you Maria's phone, where you'll find her work calendar detailing her daily and weekly routines. Maria's calendar is usually updated once a week by Tahira. You have until early tomorrow morning before Maria is expected at the Collins home."

"Understood."

"Do everything we tell you and we give you our word, this mission will be the last thing we ask of you. After this is all over, we will return your body to you. Totally healed and in perfect condition."

"You're forgetting something else of mine."

"Of course. Jeremy will be released to you as well—unharmed."

My hate is as cold as ice. In the beginning, when I awoke in my first new body, divested of everything I loved in life—the hate I felt was like a burning fire. Hatred raged inside me, and like a real fire, it nearly consumed me.

I've since learned to channel my anger, for Jeremy's sake.

If I fail or if I'm tempted to exact revenge on my tormentors, they will kill him. Then…I'll truly lose everything. They've made it abundantly clear to me if I step out of line, Jeremy will die because of me.

"If anything changes, we will contact you using Maria's phone. We've encrypted it, but do not lose it. Do not let the tablet leave the apartment. You are to return

it to the safe under the bed after use. The combination is your date of birth. Do you understand?"

"I understand." Covering your ass is always a necessity.

The phone goes silent.

Sighing, I return to Maria's small bedroom to retrieve the tablet my handlers have left for me.

Most of the data is in text format, but there are a few recorded phone conversations to help me learn her voice's unique tones and inflections. Her accent makes her English a little tricky. I practice speaking for about an hour. The tablet also has a few videos that help me see how Maria moved in her own body. How did my handlers get these videos? They must have been watching Maria long before I entered the equation.

I can do this. I can pass as Maria. If I'm going to be a maid to a wealthy woman, this shouldn't be difficult. The rich tend to ignore the non-rich. Even the ones they employ.

I set the tablet aside and glance at a clock. It's late. Why am I not sleepy yet?

I study a bit more about Tahira Collins and review the basics, like date and place of birth and other significant life events, before I can't keep my eyes open any longer. I yawn.

My new schedule starts at 5:30 the next morning, so I have a few hours to try to sleep. Maria's eyes are heavy as I slip under the sheets of her small single-size bed. I keep the fan on. But the battle it's having with the humid heat permeating the air is hopeless. Still, this body seems to cope with warmer weather better than other bodies I've had. Why are some of my bodies more or less sensitive to certain climates? Powell might know...but he'd never tell me if I asked.

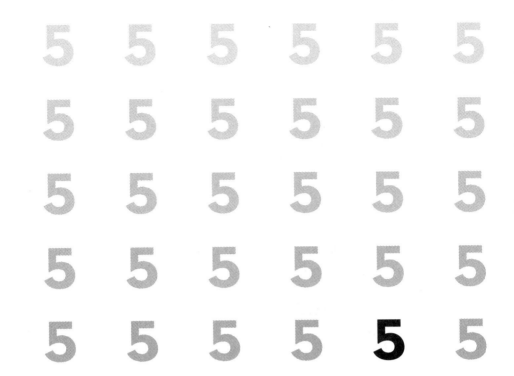

Maria takes a half-hour bus ride to the Collins neighborhood, which is part of a gated community called Las Colinas.

Most of the other people on the dirty bus look as tired as I feel. Has the recession worsened? Everyone seems to be dragging themselves to wherever it is they're going.

Like me.

I'd gladly trade places with any one of the sad faces I pass…

A few people on my bus get off for a connection downtown, but I remain seated and continue up into a more residential area of the city.

I get off at the last stop the bus makes and walk a short distance to a set of tall metal gates next to an artistic sign with the words *Las Colinas*.

Maria's face and ID badge get me through the gates. The young Latino guard seems to recognize me, even without my ID. He waves at me when I enter, and I wave back.

The sun isn't up yet, and a sliver of the moon is still visible. The blinking white and red lights of an airplane streak across the early morning sky as I make my way up the hill toward the Collins' home.

I turn a corner on the private drive, and the massive home finally comes into view.

It's about two stories tall and looks like it was converted from a Catholic mission into a modern mansion. The walls are a pale white stucco, and the roof is made from red clay tiles. They've even kept three large metal bells that look original to the mission.

The cobbled driveway curves around a gorgeous fountain lit by small lights that glow underwater. I avoid looking too closely at the water.

Bodies of water are just as bad as mirrors.

There should be a door on the side of the building toward the back that I can use to get inside. Isn't that what my handlers' info said? The Collins' home has a large perimeter fence, but it's discreet and looks like it's mostly for decoration. There's a large detached garage and a pool in the backyard. Eventually I find a door with a blinking red light next to the door handle. I swipe Maria's ID over the door, and the light above the frame turns green. The wrought iron handle twists smoothly when I reach for it, and I slip inside.

Automatic lights spring to life as I enter, bathing the small mud room with soft yellow light. The air smells like a mix of antiseptics and some kind of wood…maybe pine? Reddish cabinets line the walls above a few coat hangers. I slip out of Maria's light jacket and hang it on the rack.

Maria's uniform is stiff and a little uncomfortable, even though it fits her small frame perfectly. The simple pale blue dress comes complete with a white apron.

Unless something has changed within the last twenty-four hours, the only residents of the home should be Tahira Collins and her ailing mother. The home is silent, and I make my way to the kitchen as quietly as I can. The only noise comes from Maria's rubber heels against the hard wood flooring.

Hallways are lit by small rectangular lights set low in the walls. I navigate my way through an extravagant living room, surrounded by wide, open archways that grant access to a spacious interior courtyard.

Finding the kitchen takes me less time than I expected. Now I have to worry about breakfast. Great. When was the last time I cooked for anyone besides myself? Technically, *Maria* is supposed to cook breakfast. I can do this. But…am I expected to prepare food on demand, or is there a set schedule?

I pull out Maria's phone and…yes. I find a meal routine entered into the calendar. According to Maria's phone, she prepares breakfast for both Mehar and Tahira and delivers their meals to their bedrooms by 7:00 sharp. Maria's schedule even lists recipes.

This will be easy—I'm good at following orders.

I find eggs in the large refrigerator and pick the vegetables fresh from the garden outside. As I whip the eggs I wonder how my handlers will ask me to kill Tahira's betrothed. A special poison, to make it look like an accident? A weapon, to make it look like a homicide? A blow to the head, to make it look like self-defense from domestic abuse? Or will they ask me to simply make him disappear? They usually don't tell me until the last minute. Sometimes literally…the last minute.

The sound of a door closing startles me. I almost spill egg all over my front. That'd be a *great* way to start my first day. Footsteps approach the kitchen.

I continue with my work and only glance up when the person enters the kitchen.

She's taller than Maria by a solid ten or twelve inches. Her long, raven-black hair is pulled back into a smooth ponytail, and she's sweating like she's just been for a run. Her bright yellow sports bra and matching pair of tights help confirm my theory.

Tahira Collins removes her Bluetooth headphones and taps the smartwatch she's wearing on her left wrist.

Maria's heart rate increases. Why am I so nervous? I've done this before.

Should I say something? Is she going to say anything to me first? Surely she'd at least acknowledge my presence. My mouth opens to say good morning, but I hesitate. It's like I'm not even here. I'm invisible.

Tahira Collins goes to the fridge and retrieves a protein drink from the door. Maria's eyes follow her as she exits the kitchen and passes through the living room out into the courtyard. I don't stop working as I watch Tahira. Already I'm noticing everything I can about how she holds herself, how she moves.

The young woman stretches and goes through a series of yoga exercises. With the rising sun, the courtyard outside is soon bathed in a golden light. The light reflects off Tahira's smooth, brown skin. She's fit, if not overly muscular, and very flexible. Eventually Tahira finishes with her yoga and disappears up a flight of stairs. It's getting close to seven now, so I hurry to finish preparing the meals.

It takes me a second, but I find a tray for the food and even a small trolley. It's like I'm Jill the waitress again...

A small elevator takes me up to the second floor.

According to Maria's schedule, I'm supposed to deliver breakfast to Tahira first then see to Mehar's extensive needs. I locate Tahira's room both by what I memorized of the floor plan and the sound of the shower. Tahira's door opens with a light push, and I slip inside.

Why do I feel uncomfortable? I've entered plenty of strangers' bedrooms. The trolley wheels squeak a little as I roll it across the textured carpet. I begin making Tahira's bed. The circular mattress gives me trouble. Who has a mattress in the shape of a circle? Honestly.

The sound of running water cuts off, and I quickly place Tahira's tray of food on her coffee table. I turn to leave.

"Don't forget I'll be leaving at noon to meet with my lawyer. Susan can't make it today, so you'll have to help Mother once Kodye leaves."

Tahira has a red towel wrapped around her wet body with a second towel tied around her hair. I avert my eyes, but she's not even looking at me. Tahira's attention is on the phone in her hands.

"Yes, Miss Collins."

She ignores me, and I take my cue to leave.

Susan and Kodye are Mehar's nurses. If one is gone I guess my first day on the job will be getting to know Tahira's mom even better. Yay...

Tahira's mother's room is only a few doors down the hall. I can't just leave her meal for her like I did Tahira's. I really hope Susan being gone today is just an anomaly.

How long will I have to take care of Mehar before I'm part of the murder of her only daughter? Is that only my second morbid thought of the day? Usually I'm up to three or four by now. As soon as I enter Mehar's room and take a look at the frail old woman, I understand what my handlers meant when they told me she only has weeks to live.

Mehar Collins looks like a skeleton with flesh. Her pale wrinkles hang loose on her bones, and her eyes dart around like she's lost. Which, due to the terrible effects of Alzheimer's, she probably *does* feel lost.

"*Buenos días*, Maria!"

I blink. Did Mehar just *speak*?

I push the door open further to find a second woman sitting crosslegged in a leather chair where the door was blocking my view. She's dressed in pale green scrubs and looks like she's listening to music. Kodye pops out one of her earbuds and smiles at me. She looks young, maybe even fresh out of nursing school. She also looks Latina. I freeze. If Kodye is used to speaking with Maria in Spanish, then…

"Sorry to bail on you, Maria. I've got to be at the hospital in an hour for a mandatory training. You've got my number though, right? Call me if she needs anything."

Kodye flashes me one more smile, slings a backpack over her left shoulder, and exits the room.

Phew. No Spanish. Does everyone treat Maria with such…abruptness?

Mehar seems to recognize me as I approach. She's mumbling something incomprehensible. I set the trolley of food next to her bedside, where a small dresser is overflowing with medications. On the edge of the dresser is a hand-written note from Kodye detailing pills to give to Mehar and at what times. Reading the labels is difficult. I have to hold them away from me at arm's length. Even then, the words still feel harder to read.

"Again?"

Mehar's voice is so weak I almost don't hear her the first time. Her eyes are lucid for a moment, and Mehar frowns when she sees what I'm doing.

"Yes, ma'am." I hold the pills out so she can see them. I help her with a glass of water, and she chokes down the two white capsules.

Mehar becomes distracted by something unseen, and I have to coax her attention back to me and help her with a spoonful of yogurt. At least the old woman seems to trust the body I'm wearing. She doesn't fight me as I slowly help her through her breakfast. This is the worst…

"Good morning, Mother."

Tahira's voice startles me, and I whip around to find her standing near the foot of the bed, her attention on her phone. How did I not hear her enter the room? Usually I'm extremely aware of my surroundings. Maybe I can blame my aging body.

Tahira's dressed in tight-fitting business attire and has her hair pulled back in a simple braid. Her makeup is subtle.

As soon as Mehar notices Tahira, she starts talking about something that probably happened a long time ago as if it were happening today. I hold back a grimace. It's sad to watch.

"Uh-huh, sure, Mom. We can stop by the bookstore after the park if you want. I'd love to have you read to me again…"

Mehar continues talking nonsense, and Tahira just listens and nods occasionally. Tahira's expression is filled with a soft spoken pain. Maybe she feels just as uncomfortable being around her mother as I do.

"I have to go now, Mom. But I promise I'll be back soon, and we can go for a walk, okay?" Tahira finally puts down her phone and looks right at her mother.

Tahira's eyes betray more sadness. There's something else too…*loneliness*. Is that why she avoids looking directly at her mother? Perhaps doing so reminds Tahira that the woman she knew as her mother isn't really here anymore?

My eyes linger in the empty space between the frail old woman and her daughter.

Oh my God. Mehar…is my *opposite*. While she's here in body, her *mind* is elsewhere. While I'm here in mind, my *body* is elsewhere.

I shiver slightly, disturbed.

"Call me if she needs anything?"

My cheeks flush as I glace up at Tahira, and I nod in reply.

"Good. I'll be back in a couple of hours. Don't bother making lunch for me."

Tahira leaves after one final glance at her mother, who is now distracted by something outside her windows. A tiny butterfly.

When Mehar is finished with her medications, and most of her food, I begin to clean up. Through Mehar's windows, a black sports car with the top down peels out of the main drive. Tahira drives out onto the street and disappears from view.

I retrieve the dirty dishes from Tahira's room and return everything to the kitchen. After I place the dishes and silverware into the dishwasher, I begin to explore the house.

I start in Tahira's bedroom.

It's larger than Maria's entire apartment. But the furnishings are surprisingly simple. There's the bed, a large carved cabinet, a desk with an expensive computer, a coffee table, a full-size bathroom, and a walk-in closet. There's also a balcony overlooking the backyard.

After my cursory walkthrough, I approach Tahira's desk. I memorize the exact position of everything she has placed on her desk so I can put everything back when I'm done. Out of habit, I also don a pair of leather gloves.

Everything on Tahira's desk looks normal, but what seems to be *missing* from it?

Tahira doesn't have a single picture of her betrothed. Why? Surely she'd at least have something even though it's all part of an arranged marriage, right? But no, there's nothing to remind her of Deval Abdul Kapoor. Perhaps she has something on her computer? I tap the spacebar. Tahira's screen saver is just a relaxing image of a lake.

Had Tahira even been wearing a ring when she left? No, she hadn't. I open a small drawer under the desk and strike gold—her engagement ring.

She doesn't even have it locked away in a safe. It lies, still in its box, seemingly forgotten.

How does this information help me? Obviously, Tahira Collins must not be too excited at the prospect of her marriage, otherwise, she'd be flaunting these massive diamonds instead of letting them sit abandoned in her desk. Right?

The ring Jeremy gave me was far less extravagant than Tahira's. It was nothing more than a simple gold band. But I'd worn it every day since he proposed. Was I wearing it when I died…?

Tahira keeps a small physical copy of a religious Hindu text on her desk. The Vedas. Dry pages rustle as I turn a few. The main body of text is in a foreign language, next to a translation in English. Maybe I should eventually read some Hindu literature. That might be important.

There's a small sticker on a corner of the desk, hidden under an empty phone case. The sticker is a simple red S with the silhouette of pine tree on top. It's a Stanford University logo, the school Tahira attended to get her bachelor's in international relations. What did she do after graduating again? Did she start working for her father's company? I need to check on that tonight.

Next to the Stanford sticker I find a bracelet. The band is leather and holds a simple rhombus symbol. Its weight hints at its value. Silver maybe?

Light catches the polished metal, and I turn it over in my hands. Have I seen something this before? I make a mental note of the design. Maybe it's something significant. Or maybe Tahira just likes trendy jewelry?

Placing everything I've moved back the way I found it, I glance around the room. The closet is calling me next.

Tahira Collins' wardrobe is full of simple yet modern clothing. Do Tahira's religious beliefs have anything to do with her clothing choices? It's hard to tell because for the most part it looks like she wears normal clothes. Lots of jeans and T-shirts.

Among Tahira's things I find a few formal pieces, like dresses and suits, that are all hung on wooden hangers. Some even still have the tags. Tucked in a corner of the closet are what have to be traditional Indian garments. All are made with bright colors. Some have small beads sewn into some of the seams. They're incredibly soft beneath Maria's fingers. I trace some of the stitching and try to imagine Tahira wearing something so exotic.

I explore the bathroom but don't find much I didn't already expect to come across.

Before I leave the second level I poke my head into Mehar's room to make sure she's alright. Her eyes are closed, but her chest rises and falls faintly.

The steps creak a little beneath Maria's feet as I descend the flight of stairs to the main floor. I sigh and begin to meander through the living room.

Suddenly, a four-legged visitor makes its way out from under one of the couches. The cat is an orange tabby, and it meows as I bend over to pet it.

The small animal has a collar bedazzled with tiny rhinestones. Since when do the Collins have a cat? My handlers must have thought a minor detail like this didn't have bearing on my mission...

"I told Tahira that thing would just keep coming back if she fed it."

I nearly jump out of my skin...I mean...Maria's skin. Which is stupid because I do that all the time, literally. Is that my third morbid thought for today?

"Sorry to startle you, Señora Maria."

The man is a foot and a half taller than Maria. The edges of his eyes crinkle slightly as he smiles. He's wearing a dark long-sleeve shirt and gray dress pants. His salt and pepper hair is more salt than pepper, and he looks to be in his mid to late fifties. Gary Ryan. What did I read about him last night? He's a long time family friend of the Collins. He's also supposedly employed by the family. He's been somewhat of a mentor to Tahira too. Stepping in to help with the Collins estate when her father, John Collins, died.

I smile at him.

"I noticed Tahira took the R8. Did she mention where she was going?"

R8? Oh, yeah, the sports car.

"Miss Collins left for her lawyer's office. She said she would be back later." My voice is Maria's, and Gary has absolutely no suspicions. My response elicits a slow head nod from Gary. His eyes narrow and he furrows his brow.

"Tahira wasn't scheduled to meet with Yolanda until tomorrow...I was supposed to go with her."

Gary strokes at the gray stubble on his chin. "I'm worried about what's going to happen to us after the wedding, Maria, but I'm even more worried about Tahira."

You have no *idea* how worried you should be, Gary.

There it is…my fourth morbid thought of the day.

"I don't think the girl really knows what she wants."

I nod. Agreeing with what he's saying seems like the easiest thing to do right now. Gary is distracted and isn't too focused on me at the moment anyway. It's like he's just thinking out loud.

"I've tried talking with her, but she's starting to shut me out. I can't help thinking she partially blames me for trying to, well…Mehar doesn't have much time. Do you think you could talk to her, Maria?"

Er…I doubt Tahira would listen to Maria's advice on anything. Let alone…whatever Gary wants Maria to speak with her about.

"I just think Tahira needs some guidance, some support. And you're one of the wisest, most supportive people I know."

Gary smiles again and squeezes my shoulder in a tender, compassionate way. What kind of relationship did Gary have with Maria?

The right words elude me, so I just nod. That seems to be enough for Gary, and he smiles one last time before turning on his heels leaving me alone in the living room.

He's halfway to the front door when Gary stops.

"Oh, and Maria!" Gary turns the door handle and looks back over his shoulder. "Deval Kapoor has a video conference scheduled with Tahira tonight after dinner. Do you mind sitting in for me? I have to be at my niece's baptism later."

"Yes, Mr. Ryan, sir. I'm happy to."

"Thanks, Maria. And since when did you start calling me sir?"

Crap.

A small mistake to be sure, but one I should've avoided.

"Anyway, I'm off to see if I can catch Tahira at Yolanda's office. There are a few more details regarding long-term care of Mehar we still have to sort out. Assuming she still needs professional care after the wedding…I'll see you tomorrow, Maria!"

Gary departs. The soft *click* of the front door closing behind him echoes slightly in the empty entryway. Once again, I have the house to myself. Well... and the visiting cat.

I prepare Mehar's lunch, help her take more medications, then I'm back to learning whatever else will help me when the time comes for me to take Tahira's body.

Photographs and keepsakes help fill gaps in my handlers' info on the Collins family. Numerous household items give me hints into the kind of relationship Tahira shared with her mother before the Alzheimer's. They traveled a lot together. Before the border shutdowns at least. Photos often tell false narratives, but I think Tahira had a very good relationship with her mother.

As I continue searching the Collins mansion, I'm surprised that despite the divorce, Mehar still has a lot of her ex-husband's stuff. But maybe that's Tahira's doing?

My handlers' tablet said John Collins died of a brain tumor about nine years ago.

In one of the mud rooms I find a pair of baseball gloves with initials—*J.C.* and *T.C.* A picture of Tahira playing a board game with her father rests atop a cabinet filled with a collection of old-timey board games. Tahira seems to have maintained a deep connection with her late father.

After three more minutes of exploring, I find John Collins himself.

His name is etched into a small gold plaque on the gray stone of the urn.

It sits atop the mantle of a large fireplace inside one of the two living rooms. Fresh flowers lay next to it, jasmine—I think. Why was John Collins cremated? After all, he was born American and obviously had enough money that the family could afford a traditional burial. But John's ex-wife and daughter *are* Hindu, so perhaps cremation was a tradition they kept, even after the death of their ex-husband and father? Still, it seems strange Mehar would hold onto her ex-husband's remains. But what do I know?

It's after 5:30 P.M. before Tahira finally returns. Her headlights momentarily blind me through the kitchen windows as her car approaches the house and pulls around back to the detached garage.

A few moments later, Tahira enters the house from the back.

I'm still invisible as she passes me working in the kitchen. Tahira's footsteps recede up the stairs to the second floor. Maria's small watch tells me it's almost dinner time for the Collins household. I serve up the alfredo chicken I've made for Tahira on a square glass plate and set it out on the dining table.

Mehar's meal is far simpler. Some applesauce and a few pieces of chicken I've cut into manageable portions.

Before I'm even finished setting out the silverware on the table, Tahira reappears. She's changed into a form-fitting dress that falls down to her ankles. The dress has a seam that runs scandalously high on her right leg. That dress was *definitely* not in her closet when I searched it.

Tahira finally acknowledges my existence.

"I guess I should've given you a heads up. I'm going out with some friends tonight."

"No, you're not." Gary emerges from the shadows of the hall. His arms are crossed, and he doesn't look pleased.

Tahira crosses her own arms and stares Gary down. If looks could kill.

"I can do as I please, Gary." Tahira's voice is low, almost a whisper.

"You have an obligation tonight…to your betrothed. Friends can wait."

"We spoke yesterday. Can't he…?"

"Deval wants to get to know you as much as he can before the wedding. I know he'd be here in person if he could. He wants to love you, Tahira, truly."

Tahira looks torn. Her eyes fall to her feet, her head bowed.

Tahira *does* care about her fiancé, but the relationship is definitely complicated. She runs her fingers through her long black hair, and Tahira's shoulders relax a little.

"And by the way, I don't appreciate you lying to me about your meeting with Yolanda. By the time I got there, Yolanda said you'd already come and…"

"You're not my father, Gary. You never have been. My decisions are my own; I can make them without you."

"I know. And you're making a series of very *noble* decisions. I just want to help with…"

"With what? You've already done enough for this family, Gary. I'll be married soon and won't have any use for you. I'm sorry, but it's the truth."

Gary frowns and bows his head.

"Gary I…I didn't mean it like that. It's just…I'm leaving to India, and you have your own family here…"

"Just…remember there are a lot of people who care about you, Tahira. We want what's best for you."

Tahira says something under her breath I don't quite catch and storms off. Gary sighs deeply before turning toward me.

"I'd still appreciate it if you could find a time to talk with her, Maria. Tahira's prideful, but she may listen to you."

The thought makes me sick to my stomach. No way will I do as Gary has requested. How can I? I'm being forced to learn about Tahira and how she lives her life, not develop a personal relationship with her.

Gary checks his watch. "I apologize, I have to go. I'm already late. Good luck, Maria. I don't know what we'd do without you."

I wave goodbye, and now I'm all alone with a plate of food in my hands.

An alarm on Maria's phone reminds me Mehar needs her medication, so I hurry and get the food on a tray and carry it all up the stairs to her room.

I'm cleaning up after Mehar when Tahira yells at me from downstairs.

"Maria! I'm guessing Gary asked you to play chaperone with me and Deval. You've got less than a minute before he's supposed to be calling."

Yes. This is exactly what I need. Thank you, Gary's niece…

After helping Mehar, I hurry down the stairs and only stop long enough to dump the tray on the kitchen's granite countertop.

I walk into the living room to find Tahira has changed clothes again. Now, she's wearing a pair of blue jeans and a red crop top. She's seated on a couch in the living room with a remote in her hands. She's also put her engagement ring on her left hand.

Interesting.

The large flat television hanging above the fireplace is displaying an incoming video chat request.

I settle into a chair somewhat adjacent to Tahira and prepare myself. This is crucial. I *need* to understand how to act around Tahira's betrothed…when *I'm* the one wearing her ring.

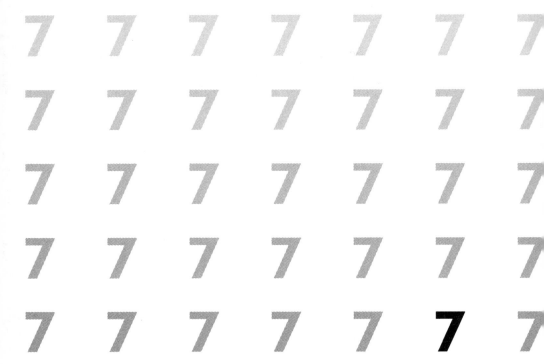

A man's face fills the screen.

Deval Abdul Kapoor looks very similar to the image my handlers gave me. He has a dark brown complexion and curly chocolate hair. His eyes light up as soon as the video is established on his end. Tahira's expression flushes a little, but she smiles back. Was that embarrassment? Shyness? What's Tahira feeling?

"Shubh prabhaat, Tahira. Or rather—good evening." Deval chuckles. His voice is strong and resonant, only a faint hint of an accent. *"I suppose it's silly of me, but I still forget we're calling each other from opposite sides of the world."*

"Hello, Deval. It's good to see you."

"You don't have to be so formal, Tahira. We're getting married, after all." Deval winks.

Tahira's smile fades slightly, but Deval doesn't seem to notice. His grin is just as big as when he first started speaking.

"How was your day?" Deval asks after Tahira doesn't say anything. *"How did the meeting with your lawyer go?"*

"It was fine."

Is Tahira referring to how her day was or how the meeting went? From his expression, Deval probably doesn't know either.

"Did the merger alterations look…"

"From what I've read, so far everything looks fine. Yolanda and her team are also looking over the full contract tomorrow and the day after. The meeting today was mostly to ensure my mother is properly cared for until…"

Deval nods. Now it's his turn to look a little uncomfortable. What's this about a contract? A merger?

"How is your mother?" Deval's tone softens at the mention of Mehar.

"The same. She still forgets what year it is, forgets I'm not a little girl anymore."

"Maaf kijiye. I'm sorry, Tahira. If there was any way she could live with us here, I…"

"It'll be fine, Dev." Tahira finally betrays some emotion in her tone. "Yolanda and Susan will see that she's taken care of if she lives past our wedding day."

"We can change the timing of things if we need to, Tahira. If even a few weeks would make things easier for you, I can…"

"No. I'm still willing to…go through with it all. The date is fine."

A trace amount of frost enters the conversation. Deval looks a little pained but manages not to show it too badly.

Deval tries to change the subject and asks about Tahira's running. It's as much a hobby to her as a way to exercise. Tahira doesn't seem in any mood to ask questions of her own, so Deval asks how Tahira's enjoyed driving the car he sent her as an engagement present. Tahira finally shows a hint of real excitement in the smile she gives him. This sparks a big grin from Deval.

They're both car people. The couple talks about Tahira's new Audi for a while, and I try to memorize each detail they discuss.

Because Tahira doesn't ask any of her own questions, the rest of the conversation is mostly directed by Deval and whatever he can think to ask her. Mostly, Deval asks things one would ask on a first or second date. What have they talked about in their previous video conferences if they're just now discussing each other's favorite movies?

Deval asks Tahira what kind of music she likes.

"Everything."

Deval's questions are only eliciting one-word answers from Tahira. She's making things more difficult for me. Deval, however, doesn't seem to care. He just looks happy Tahira is communicating with him at all.

How do arranged marriages even work? Are couples *supposed* to be awkward around each other? The relationship between Tahira and Deval seems so formal it could be dressed in a tuxedo.

I glance at my watch. It's nearly 9:00. Does Maria get paid overtime?

"Well Tahira, I know it's getting late for you and you probably want to go for another run before bed, so I'll get going. As always, it's an honor to speak with you…even if I'm just a flat screen television."

Tahira actually laughs a little. That wasn't even very funny. What does Tahira really think about Deval Kapoor? She has so many conflicting emotions I can't get anything straight…yet.

Deval touches his fingers to his lips and pretends to blow Tahira a kiss. A very American gesture. Someone on Deval's end says something to him that I can't make out, and he looks at Tahira a little guiltily.

Tahira waves goodbye without returning Deval's gesture, and the video chat ends.

Without even glancing at me, Tahira leaves the living room without a word and heads upstairs.

I should bug her room. My handlers will probably order me to eventually anyway. I'll need to see how Tahira reacts to conversations with Deval when she thinks no one is watching. Surely my handlers could get me a camera to put in her room. They've already bugged Maria's apartment so they can keep an eye on me.

Before I leave for the night, I wait in Mehar's room until Kodye returns for the night shift. Tonight, she's wearing bright pink scrubs. We exchange brief pleasantries, and I report on all the medications I gave Mehar.

As I'm heading down the hallway back downstairs to leave for the night, a sound coming from Tahira's room gives me pause.

Sobbing?

Is Tahira crying?

Yes. She's talking too. Not to herself, surely…perhaps on the phone?

"...don't know, okay? You wouldn't understand."

I press my ear up to the door, trying to hear more.

"I have to go. I'll see you later. I...I know you do. Bye."

Tahira's room is silent for a moment before her muffled sobbing starts up again. Damn. Who was she talking to? What has her so distraught? Is she upset because of her call with Deval? This girl's emotions are all over the board.

Quickly and silently, I retreat downstairs and clean up the kitchen. I turn off most of the lights and leave through the mudroom door.

There's still plenty of time for me to learn who Tahira Collins really is as a person. Still plenty of time before she's murdered. Plenty of time before I become Tahira Collins.

On the bus ride from Las Colinas, three armed men dressed in blue government uniforms enter the bus brandishing tablets. Enforcers. They're checking public transit now? Is this some expansion of the Border Protection Act? Is everyone really still afraid of international terrorists? It's been over three years since the last Strikes.

I should have expected this.

Random citizenry checks must be pretty common since we're so close to the Mexican border. Maria...you'd better be legal...

Without a single word, the armed men begin scanning people's fingerprints by holding out their tablets and waiting for each passenger to place his or her right hand flat against the screens.

A squat, slightly overweight Enforcer holds his tablet out to the young man in the row in front of me. The young man puts his hand on the tablet and the screen flashes green.

When it's my turn, I place Maria's small hand onto the surface of the Enforcer's tablet. A light at the top flashes yellow. Half-citizen. Thank God.

Before he leaves, the Enforcer frowns at me and spits. His saliva lands on my left shoe. I bow my head, and the Enforcer moves to the next passenger.

The man sitting across from me is dressed in a white collared shirt that contrasts sharply with his skin. He's brown but not Latino. Maybe Arabic.

Or possibly Indian. He's got to be in his mid-thirties. A gold band wraps around his left ring finger.

The man calmly places his palm on the Enforcer's tablet when he's prompted. The tablet flashes red. Uh oh…

"Sir, I'm going to ask you to stand up and disembark."

The Enforcer's voice is low. Dangerous.

"But I'm a full US citizen." The panic in the man's voice is unmistakable.

"Sir, stand up now, or you'll be removed by force."

"I can prove my citizenry! Here, scan me again, I…"

The Enforcer's fist sends the man's head snapping back against the bus seat. He slumps forward, and a pair of Enforcers drag him toward the exit. No one helps. No one intervenes. It's over in an instant.

The remaining Enforcer doesn't even bother scanning the rest of the bus. Once he's gone, the bus pulls silently away from the curb. I watch as the Enforcers deposit their quarry into the back of their cruiser. Everyone knows the rumors. Despite what the government says, you're *lucky* if you get deported.

"We're still looking into it."

"*Well look faster. And I want to know why Dominguez is just now discovering we're not the only ones with embedded agents in the CIA. Can he confirm if they are Unitas or not?*"

"No. But if he discovers anything I'll alert you immediately."

"*Fine. Anything else?*"

"McKenzie requested a few pieces of surveillance equipment. I can forward you the full list or…"

"*Give her whatever she needs. She knows what she's doing. But be sure she gets us access to the Collins' security hub too.*"

"Affirmative, and…Director? There's something else, it's regarding McKenzie. She um…well she may be having a…problem."

"*What do you mean* a problem?"

"Powell analyzed data from the past three body transfers. Including her most recent. He wanted me to make it clear this data goes beyond what I had him send you in Chicago. He's worried the injections are having a decreasing effect on her brain's ability to handle new bodies."

"Okay. So…what? What does that mean?"

"He isn't sure yet."

"Is there a worst-case scenario?"

"No."

"What do you mean, no? Does he know anything*?"*

"This is unexplored territory. New science. None of what we're putting her through has ever been done before. She's the first to have made it this far. Like I said—there is no worst-case scenario."

"So guess."

"You'll have to bring that up with Powell."

"Did Powell at least say anything about how this affects our time frame for the current mission?"

"…he said we should be fine. She should still be able to handle what's required of her for her current mission."

"You can tell Powell it's his neck that's on the line if she isn't."

Day two as Maria confirms what I could only guess yesterday. Tahira Collins doesn't like me.

Why doesn't she like me…or, *Maria*? Aside from the fact that I'm a Divest assassin sent to kill her fiancé, I'm very pleasant. When she's not ignoring me, Tahira treats Maria like she has no feelings whatsoever. She's only being rude to Maria's body and the persona I'm imitating, but still…it's hard not to take it personally.

I'm cooking breakfast when she arrives. The scene plays out the same as the day before. Tahira jogs into the kitchen, sweaty from a long run, and in no mood to talk. At least not politely.

"Did you get those organic eggs like I asked? Because last time you messed up even *that* simple task."

I glance at the carton of eggs I'm using. They *do* say they're organic. Maria must have bought these before she died. Thanks, Maria.

"And don't forget to clean the pool. I'm having some friends over later and need it cleaned before then. *Tú comprendes?*"

I remain subservient, head bowed. Tahira's expecting me to answer, though, so I simply nod in reply.

"Good."

Tahira spins on her heels and returns to the interior courtyard like she did yesterday to stretch.

The rest of my morning follows mostly the same routine as the day before. I deliver breakfast to Tahira while she's in the shower, make her bed—faster this time—then help Mehar with her breakfast. I listen to her mumbled stories while she takes her medication.

Kodye said Mehar's other nurse Susan should be here soon, which should give me more time for…cleaning the pool. Great.

I'm folding some of Tahira's laundry when there's a solid knock at the front door. I open the door to a young woman, probably in her thirties, dressed in dark blue scrubs. Susan. She's carrying a duffel bag with the Caduceus sewn into the sides. She's on her phone when I open the door, but her eyes are friendly when she greets me.

"Morning, Maria! Or should I say *buenos días*, ha-ha! Sorry I'm a little late today. Traffic was a nightmare."

I step aside so Susan can enter.

"How's Mehar?"

"She's doing okay. I've given Mrs. Collins her medications, and she's been eating well."

"Maybe they should just hire you on as the maid *and* the nurse." Susan throws her head back a little and laughs at her own joke.

I smile politely as Susan heads up the stairs to the second floor to check on Mehar.

As I close the front door, an engine roars, and Tahira, behind the wheel of her black sports car, peels around the house and off down the street.

Where does she go every day?

Maybe on Maria's day off I should follow her on one of her outings to see where she goes. I also need to find out who she was talking to over the phone last night in between her sobs, after she'd just had a video chat with her fiancé.

Once I hear the bathwater running in Mehar's room, I make my way upstairs. Susan should be distracted with Mehar for at least the next thirty minutes, so I sneak into Tahira's room to plant the hidden camera my handlers left on Maria's doorstep for me this morning.

Tahira's room is much the same as it was the day before.

I have to stand on a chair to place the camera right above her doorframe. This will give me a good view of the entire room. This is so wrong. So intrusive. But not as intrusive as having your brain transplanted into someone else's body...

Why can't my handlers just bug people's rooms for me?

Who am I kidding? I know why. They want as little contact with me, and the targets they send me to kill, as possible. That has to be part of the reason why I exist in the first place. It's times like these I wonder if the people behind my torment were exposed, would they turn out to be powerful people in government? Or would they be highly dangerous, highly sophisticated criminals with their own agenda? Is there a difference these days?

Despite being forced to observe previous targets like I am with Tahira—I still hate doing it. The spying. The elimination of privacy. It all feels so wrong to me. But to accomplish my mission I have to get to know Tahira so intimately no one will question me when I'm in her body. I need to know everything about the way she acts. Even when she's alone.

Sometimes I wonder if I'm becoming slightly insane. As Divest I try to rationalize things that cannot, or should not, be rationalized. Is worrying I'm becoming insane evidence that I'm doing just that? I hope not.

This is my living nightmare. One I cannot escape from...it won't truly be over until I have Jeremy and my real body back. I haven't allowed myself to think what will happen when that day finally comes, how I'll move on from all this. I'll worry about that when I get there. For now, I just have to focus on saving Jeremy, on doing what I'm told so they'll let him go.

With the tiny camera securely positioned in Tahira's room, I go back downstairs to locate the Collins' security hub. After some searching, I find it in the basement inside a utility closet. There are three different consoles. Just like my handlers said, a large gray one with blinking lights rests on a shelf at about eye level. I reach into Maria's apron to take out the small black device that's no bigger than a starburst—Jeremy's favorite candy—to attach to the

Collins' security hub. It snaps onto the surface of the console with a click. Is that it? That's all they told me to do, right?

Once I finish with my handlers' chores I go back upstairs and continue with Maria's chores.

I nearly forget about cleaning the stupid pool.

Just as the sun is starting to set, Tahira's "friends" start to arrive.

They all drive expensive-looking cars, and a lot of them seem like they're friends from Tahira's college days.

I set Tahira's preferred selection of drinks and snacks out on some tables. Her friends are the only ones who drink while Tahira just wanders around poolside, chatting with the three or four groups of friends she's invited.

At first, everyone seems to be relaxed and enjoying their individual conversations. After about twenty minutes, once most everyone has had a few drinks, someone starts playing music. Is this crap popular nowadays?

"Turn it up!"

"Yeah, dog! Whooo!"

Tahira's friends are complete idiots.

Are Tahira's neighbors close enough to be bothered by the noise? The mansions of Las Colinas are far enough apart it might be fine. Plus, the music might not carry very far past the tall trees that surround the Collins' property. Still…the music is annoyingly loud. After a while I get a ringing in my ears that won't go away.

Someone either gets pushed or falls into the pool, and everyone starts laughing. A few more of Tahira's drunk friends join the one that's fallen into the pool without even bothering to remove any of their clothes first.

Before Tahira can order me to, I find a large stack of towels and set them on a table outside. Should I be depressed or impressed at how easily I've slipped into the role of Maria Antonio? In another life I would make a killer maid…

A killer maid? Did I really just think that? I've lost track of how many morbid thoughts I've already had today…

Surely some of Tahira's friends are going to drown themselves. Did Maria know CPR? More splashes accompany the sound of poolside laughter. It's so dark I almost don't notice the pair of bodies that slip into the house using a small, rarely used back door.

I quickly scan the backyard.

Tahira has vanished.

Curiosity battles with concern as I slip inside the house using the same door. Who was Tahira with? Why the sneaking around?

The door leads into the home via a mudroom filled with shelves and cabinets for storage. I pass through another door and find myself in a hallway that leads into one of the two living rooms.

Soft footsteps move quickly across the hardwood floors of the house. Sticking to the shadows myself, I slowly follow the sound of footsteps.

I reach a wide hallway with three doors to choose from, the one at the end of the hallway leads to a large guest bedroom. The door is ajar, and I peek inside.

Nope.

Even though it's dark, Tahira is definitely *not* one of the pair in the bed. Moans mix with the sound of my quiet footsteps as I retreat to the main living room with its tall, arching windows. Where is Tahira?

She's still nowhere to be seen.

Before I can step back outside, I pause when I hear someone coming down the stairs. Was Tahira upstairs this whole time? Nope. Wrong again.

"Another party?" Susan nods at the group of Tahira's friends outside.

I nod and shrug my shoulders.

Susan shakes her head like she's Tahira's disapproving aunt or something. "That girl...ever since the engagement it's like she's a completely different person."

Rather than comment, I simply return my gaze outside. Some of Tahira's friends look like they're about to pass out. One of them is already sprawled out in a lawn chair. Should I be calling for cars?

"I'm going to head out, but Kodye just texted me, and she says she's coming up the hill now. I'll be back in the morning, hopefully on time this time. Anything I can do for you, Señora Maria?"

I like Susan. Officially. I tell her I'm fine and to have a nice night, and she departs.

Maria's shift is technically supposed to end soon. I'm already getting sick of the thirty- to forty-minute bus ride home every night, so I collect my meager belongings and prepare to leave.

As I'm putting on Maria's jacket, voices drift down from upstairs. I can't make out what they're saying, but one of the voices definitely belongs to Tahira.

The voices are coming from her bedroom. The camera I put in Tahira's room had better work…

I wait for Kodye to arrive before leaving through a back door. There's still one chore left on my list for the day.

I sneak into the Collins' garage, locate the R8 among the four other vehicles, and attach a magnetic GPS tracker to the undercarriage.

The night air is very warm. Maria's apartment is going to be stifling.

The Latino night guard who mans the gates to Las Colinas waves at me as I make my way past his little guardhouse. I wave back.

"*Comó estás, Señora María?*"

Oh no.

I pretend I don't hear him and keep walking.

"*Espera! Tengo tu libro!*"

What do I do? I don't speak freaking Spanish!

I pick up my pace.

"*Señora!*"

Footsteps approach me from behind. I stop and turn. The guard is dressed in a blue security uniform. His silver name tag says *Alfonso* in black letters. He's only a few inches taller than Maria, not including his hat.

"*Quería retornar tu libro. Me gustó el final. No pensé que terminaría así. Gracias por prestármelo.*"

Crap. Crap. Crap.

I meet Alfonso's dark eyes as he extends a small paperback novel to me. I reach for it; it's a copy of *Don Quixote*.

What was he saying? He said *gracias*…is this book mine? Or…Maria's? How do you say "you're welcome"?

"Er…*de nada*."

Alfonso smiles and tips his hat toward me. "*Nos vemos, ya? Cuídate, Señora.*"

I nod and smile. "*Nos vemos.*"

Turning, I walk as quickly as I can the rest of the way to my bus stop without looking back. I need to avoid any more interactions with Alfonso…

Maria's body is exhausted. My muscles are sore, and my knees feel like they're on fire. I hate being old.

After I unlock the door to Maria's apartment I stop in the kitchen long enough to grab something quick to eat before retreating to Maria's bedroom. The safe unlocks with a soft click, and I pull out the tablet.

My handlers' tablet scans Maria's retinas, and I pull up the app that will allow me to connect to the camera in Tahira's room. I take another bite of my makeshift taco and settle into an armchair for my sick entertainment this evening.

The image of Tahira's room on the tablet screen is bathed in a pale green light. I'm seeing everything in real time. Tahira's still form lies unmoving beneath her sheets. She's alone. That's good…I think.

It takes me only a few seconds to rewind the footage until I find the moment I want.

The time matches when I noticed Tahira missing from her own party. From the camera's perspective, the door to Tahira's room opens, and she enters—hand in hand with a man.

The camera doesn't offer a view of the man's face as she turns toward him. He shuts the door behind him without turning around. I have to adjust the audio on the tablet a little so I can hear them.

"*…don't know what I want.*" Tahira sounds upset.

"*Then stay. If you go, you may never figure out if this is right or not. By then it will be too late.*" The man's voice is steady, and his tone is filled with concern.

"*It's what my father would've wanted. It's what's best for the company and our two countries. This is what's best for the world.*"

"But what's best for you, Tahira?"

Silence.

Is this just another one of Tahira's "friends" that she's confiding in, or is he something else? Something more? The way he's holding her hand gives me a pretty solid hint.

"Look…I've already made my decision. It was fun while it lasted, but you should go."

"Why did you invite me here tonight then, Tahira? Huh? Was it just so you could tell me to leave?"

"I care about you, but I can't be with you. I don't think…I don't think you're good for me. I'm sorry."

"Tahira, come on. Don't say that, I still want to be with…"

"You should go…"

"I'm not giving up, Tahira. Even if you are."

The sliver of light on Tahira's cheek gets brushed away by the man's hand. The couple embraces.

The man reaches a hand up and touches her face.

Tahira recoils, but the man pulls her close and kisses her face.

"I'm sorry, I had to, I…"

"You need to go. Now." Tahira's voice trembles. She's angry and sad at the same time. A second trail of light falls from her eyes.

The man hesitates. Is he going to say something else? No. He turns to leave, and I finally see his face. He has pale skin, dark eyes, and long blond hair.

Once he's gone, Tahira shuts the door behind him and starts weeping openly. She falls to her knees, and only the top of her head is visible as her sobs echo through the tablet's speakers.

Tahira, an engaged woman, has broken up with someone. Someone special to her, special enough that she wanted to see them again even though it was just to say goodbye. Watching this has broken new boundaries inside of me. There's a lump in my throat, no, *Maria's* throat. What I've just witnessed is important for my mission to become Tahira. But personally…I want to turn off the tablet and break it against the far wall.

Is the constant struggle to hold onto what little sanity or morals I may or may not have really worth it?

The video feed tells me Tahira eventually disappears into her closet and returns wearing sweats and a loose T-shirt. She spends some time in the bathroom before returning to curl up on her bed. Her chest moves slightly with each sob. I watch her until she falls asleep. I can't tear my eyes away from the poor girl's form.

I shake my head and turn off the tablet. I'm doing this to get my old body back. I need to hold Jeremy again. We can still get our life back. I have to save us…

"I don't know."

"*You don't know!? Doctor Powell, you're the only one who* can *know.*"

"With all due respect, Director, the human brain is the most complex entity in the world, maybe even the universe. We can study the brain, but in the end, even the most intelligent neuroscientists have to admit, we don't always know why the brain does what it does."

"*But you made this possible.*"

"I had a theory, I experimented with it, and it worked. That doesn't mean I'm all-knowing."

"*Well…tell me then, Doctor…will it* keep *working?*"

"The last time I conducted tests the results were…mostly normal. But it's possible that her brain is starting to exhibit symptoms commonly related to many degenerative disorders, possibly even some diseases."

"*Like what?*"

"Hard to say at this stage…dementia, Alzheimer's, Parkinson's, possibly even a kind of motor neuron disease…"

"*Why would this be happening now? She's lasted far longer than…*"

"It's possible her brain could slowly be rejecting the astrocyte treatments between transplants…Then again, because we're dealing with the most complex structure in the world—I could be completely wrong. The data only shows hints."

"But her symptoms, her head pain…"

"She may just be experiencing the occasional normal headache you and I get from time to time, but again, like I told Haight this is unexplored territory."

"Can you help her? If her brain really is at risk, can you fix these problems before they develop further?"

"Your guess is as good as mine."

"Don't get cute with me, Powell. If she dies…you're next."

"There may be something I can do if her condition worsens. But for now, I can only observe. It's strange…the last few transfers have necessitated neither the expansion nor contraction of her brain's gyri or sulci. Nor have the surgeries taken longer than normal. The cryogenic chambers have always kept her detached brain sufficiently oxygenated, but perhaps…"

"Just don't let her die, Powell. Not when we're so close."

"I will do my best."

My headaches are back. So soon?

I send a message to my handlers' ghost number using Maria's phone to let them know my symptoms. The pain isn't as bad as it had been the last few days I was Jill Thomas…but the aches are annoying. Worrying.

Maria's little apartment is already stifling, and the sun isn't even up yet. Willing the fan to put up more of a fight, I pull up Tahira's files on my handlers' tablet and start reading. I've already read most everything, but I settle on a report about Tahira's father's company.

WorldFuse is apparently one of the largest communications companies in North America. Why haven't I ever heard of it before?

It's a challenge to keep my eyes from glazing over WorldFuse's annual reports, SEC filings, and other financial data. I've always hated accounting and finances. I keep reading until I find something interesting.

Apparently, just before he died, John Collins named his daughter an honorary board member of WorldFuse and left Tahira with majority control of the company itself. Since her father's death, however, Tahira has had little to do with WorldFuse, and the company has mostly run itself.

I review data on Tahira's childhood and read through her high school graduation before settling on some papers she published shortly after graduating from Stanford.

Her writing seems to have involved a lot of political theory. The papers she wrote are addressed simply to: *The World*. Her writing talks a lot about positive outcomes that would be realized if people and governments across the world cooperated more with one another. Perhaps Tahira was just going through a Kumbaya phase for a while? There are only a few such papers, but Tahira's words are so…passionate. Sincere. Engaging. If also a bit too idealistic. Governments don't cooperate. Many country borders are still *completely* closed.

The motives behind Tahira and Deval Kapoor's arranged marriage now seem even more…what exactly? Mysterious? Confusing? Absurd? I'll need to do additional research on Deval Kapoor later this week. The pieces to this puzzle are slowly coming into view…even if I'm still a long way away from understanding how they all fit together.

By the time I leave for the Collins' home, the sun is barely peeking over the horizon.

I have to run a little to catch my bus. Of all the bodies I've worn, Maria's is the least athletic. Morbid thought or not, I'm already getting sick of it.

Susan is at the Collins house by the time I arrive. I catch her coming down the stairs from the second story.

"Mehar had a stroke last night." She rushes past me without another word. "I'll be right back. Just grabbing something from my car."

A stroke?

With Mehar's condition already tenuous, what does a stroke mean for the old woman? How should I react? What should I do? Cautiously, I make my way up the stairs into Mehar's bedroom.

The stillness of Mehar's room makes the air seem thick, heavy—dead. The door creaks slightly on its hinges as I push on it further.

Mehar is hooked up to more machines than usual. She's breathing, but only because one of the screen monitors says so. If she wasn't already, Mehar Collins is definitely on her death bed.

"It's about time you got here."

I jump a little. Tahira smirks at me from across the room. She's sitting in a chair next to her mother's frail form. Her eyes fall back to the book she's holding in her lap.

"My apologies, Miss Collins. Is there…anything in particular I can get you?"

"Protein shake and some toast."

"And…for Mrs. Collins?"

"Susan's taking care of her."

I hesitate in the doorframe for a moment. Tahira doesn't look up from her book so I retreat out of the room and back down the stairs to the kitchen. I'm eager to get away from both Collins women. Tahira is rude and annoys me. Mehar just makes me nauseous…

After I bring Tahira her meal, I go back outside to retrieve the mail. It takes me about a minute to walk to the edge of the property, where the circular drive meets the road. The Collins' mailbox is a large stone sculpture of a pioneer. One of Maria's keys allows me to unlock the back of the mailbox and pull out the stack of papers inside.

I take my time walking back to the house so I can sort through the mail to see if there's anything interesting. Mostly it's just magazines that I doubt Tahira or her mother even read anymore. Who buys physical magazines these days anyway?

What will happen when Mehar finally dies? With her gone…it will just be me and Tahira…and possibly Gary. But the relationship between Gary and Tahira is strained to say the least. Will we both be out of a job?

As if my thoughts have somehow summoned him, the crunch of tires on gravel signals an approaching car. Gary's silver SUV pull into the Collins property.

He waves at me as he drives past the fountain.

Gary parks his car on the side of the house in some shade and gets out of his vehicle.

I smile at him as we approach each other.

"Good morning, Señora. How are you?"

"Very good, Señor Gary. And you?"

"I'll be better once I figure out how Mehar's doing. She's stable now?"

I nod.

"Miss Susan is seeing to her right now."

"Tahira texted me last night. She told me about what happened and said she had to call 911. As soon as I got her texts I was about to drive over here, but she told me paramedics had already come and gone."

Gary frowns. "I know this is stupid of me to think, but it hurts that she didn't let me know what was going on until it was all over. I don't know, Maria. I think I'm losing any connection I used to have with her, you know?"

I nod my head as if I agree with him.

"Speaking of which, have you had a chance to talk with her? One on one? I realize it's a lot to ask of you, but..."

"*Lo siento*, Señor Gary. I have not had a chance to speak with Miss Collins. Last night, I was planning to find a moment, but the party Miss Collins had with her friends...and today, well, I still have much to clean..."

If only Tahira Collins had to clean her own stupid pool.

"Another party? I can't say that I blame her." Gary shakes his head slowly. "An arranged marriage...it has to feel daunting. Maybe even restricting. Even if the whole thing was mostly *her* idea."

Say what?

Her idea?

So Tahira's engagement isn't the product of controlling parents? Isn't that how arranged marriages usually go? Of course, there's also the idea of some kind of merger...

Gary's intel gives me a lot more to think about. I need to understand what is motivating Tahira...all decisions are motivated by *something*. Once I understand what that something is for a person, I understand *them*. But Tahira's motivations are so...nebulous.

Perhaps my handlers aren't even aware that the Collins and Kapoor wedding isn't as arranged as they think. Still, there's something about the engagement that seems forced...at least on Tahira's part. Even if it was "her idea."

"Anyway, I'm going up to check on Mehar. Are you coming inside, Señora?"

"Not right away. The pool needs my attention." This evokes a sympathetic smile from Gary, and he offers to take in the mail for me.

Small buds are forming on a few plants growing along the sides of the house. Once they've bloomed, this part of the yard will be absolutely gorgeous. Jeremy took me to a botanical garden near our home once. We used to spend a lot of time outdoors together...

I round the corner of the house and sigh. The pool area is a disaster.

Cans litter the deck, and there are even a few floating in the pool itself. The lawn furniture is in total disarray. A few discarded shirts and more than a few socks litter the grass too. Would Tahira have invited so many people because she knew the mess it would create for Maria? I wouldn't put such a petty thing past her.

I exhale deeply then start to pick things up.

It takes me about an hour to clean the entire pool area and get it back the way it was looking before Tahira's idiot friends trashed the place.

Jeremy always teased me that I wasn't a fast cleaner...if I ever got around to cleaning things in the first place. If only he could see me now. No. He can never see me as Divest. As a monster...

On my way back into the house, the sound of a door slamming rings in my ears. Tahira stalks from the house away toward the garage. Her shoulders are tight. She brushes back a lock of hair to reveal a deep frown. What's got her panties in a wad?

I watch from the shadows of the house as Tahira drives off. Where the heck is she...? I almost slap myself. The GPS tracker. Why haven't I checked it yet? Tonight. Tonight I'll see where she goes in her fancy engagement car. It better not be her ex-boyfriend's place or something...

Once I'm back inside, I find Gary pacing back and forth in the living room. He looks up when the door clicks shut behind me.

"Did she leave?" Gary's eyebrows are furrowed, and he doesn't look very happy.

I nod.

"That girl…I told her she needs to be prepared. Mehar she…she doesn't have long. Tahira refuses to let me handle funeral plans by myself, says she'll do it when she's ready but…"

Gary runs his hands through his short, graying hair.

"I care about this family too much to do nothing, Maria. I can't sit idly by without…it's going to happen. Whether Tahira is ready for it or not. Susan says with the stroke she just had…Mehar is probably down to less than a month now."

Gary's voice is filled with sincerity. He certainly cares deeply about the Collins family.

Maria probably wouldn't just keep standing here like an unfeeling statue. I walk up to Gary and take his right hand in both of mine. He smiles at my gesture and squeezes my…Maria's…shoulder in return.

"It kills me to say this, Maria, but Tahira is technically my boss, and she may let me go sooner than later. You'll be all she'll have left if I'm gone and Mehar is…gone too."

What can I say?

"I'll take care of Miss Collins." The words nearly choke in Maria's throat as I say them.

Gary smiles warmly at Maria. "I know you will."

Have I ever felt like more of a fraud than I do at this moment?

No Enforcers stop the bus on my way back to Maria's place after work

Maria's front door slides open with a faint squeak. After downing a quick glass of water, I retrieve my handlers' tablet to find out where Tahira Collins goes every day.

I blink. Weird.

For the past few days, Tahira has driven to the exact same place.

It's a lake. A private one by the looks of the satellite images. There are no buildings or homes for miles. Only hills and forest surround the tiny lake. A small structure, possibly a cabin or lake house, is situated right next to where my GPS locator shows Tahira parks every time she visits.

This seems like something too significant to ignore. I need to know what goes on at this mysterious lake. The next chance I get, I'll follow her.

Before I go to sleep, I send Powell another update on my symptoms. My headaches are bothering me in the evenings now too. Still not as sharp or as painful as previous bodies I've had, but it feels like they're just getting started.

I tell him I want answers for why my heads are aching, not just ibuprofen. Neither of which I've been receiving.

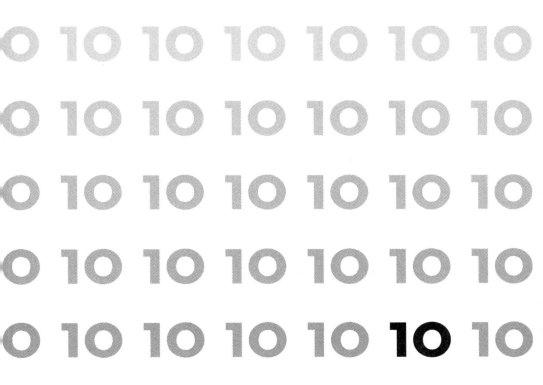

Water from the tap rushes over the head of lettuce and wets Maria's arms. What is Tahira's deal with organic everything? Honestly.

I drop the lettuce into the sink and remove Maria's watch. The small face flashes the time…and the date.

I blink. Two weeks. No. Have I really been Maria for two weeks now?

Why am I surprised? Every day is the same. Every. Single. Day.

Nothing changes. Bus ride. Breakfast. Cleaning. Lunch. More cleaning. Groceries. Errands. Yard work. Repeat.

At least Mehar's deteriorating condition lets me know time really is passing. Which one will fail faster? Her body or her mind?

Does Maria's deferential, humble personality have anything to do with why time just seems to slide along? I'll be a maid in the Collins home forever. It's never going to end.

What is motivating Tahira to marry Deval? Love *may* be a tiny factor… but there's something bigger going on here. Otherwise, my handlers wouldn't have selected Deval as a target. Can it be because of this supposed merger?

My handlers haven't said anything to me about stopping it. Do I really know so little about what's going on?

It's Tahira's fault. There's never anything suspicious or revealing. Even when she's alone in her room. She's just always on her phone. She also meditates. A lot.

It's fine. I still have over a month before I'm expected to become Tahira Collins. I don't need all the answers yet. There's still time.

At least I know Tahira Collins well enough now that, when the time comes, I can become her. Right?

Yes…and no.

I don't want Tahira Collins' life.

Sometimes, when I look in her eyes, I wonder if she feels the same way about her own life—that it's not worth living.

Her life is a sad one. Pitiful really.

But…isn't my life even more pitiful?

Still, Tahira's life is well worth living. Despite the fact that she grew up in a broken household. Even though her father is dead and her mother's health is failing, even though Tahira faces a looming marriage motivated by…something besides love…no life is such that it should end prematurely. Except maybe the lives of evil men or women.

I finish washing the lettuce and set it aside to dry. I reach for some tomatoes when someone knocks at the front door.

Who could be visiting in the middle of the day? Did Gary not update his biometrics with the security system, or something? He's stopped by less and less. Has he come to terms with the apparent fact that Tahira doesn't want him in her life anymore?

I dry my hands on Maria's apron and exit the kitchen.

The door swings wide, and I'm greeted by the sight of a young man. His blond ponytail contrasts sharply with his dark, brown eyes. He has a short beard, and most would probably consider him handsome. He's dressed like I always picture salespeople, with a pale blue dress shirt unbuttoned at the collar and a navy blazer. I've seen this man before…

His expression falls when he sees me.

He's carrying something in his right hand. It's an unmarked envelope, and he's holding it close to his chest like it's filled with a stack of hundred-dollar bills or something.

He glances nervously over Maria's shoulder.

I clear my throat and fold my arms. "Can I help you, sir?"

"Uh, yeah…Is Tahira home?"

"No. She's left for the day."

"Do you know where she's gone?"

Technically, I do. Tahira is at her mystery lake house today. Maria's responsibilities around the home have been such I haven't had a chance to follow Tahira yet. My handlers have me reading up on a bunch of legal documents pertaining to WorldFuse and a company called Jarrius Incorporated in Maria's spare time. There's no such thing as a day off as Divest.

Maria's lips frown, almost of their own accord.

"I am sorry, sir. I don't know where Miss Collins has gone for the day."

He sighs. "Can you give her this for me…when she gets back?"

He hands me the envelope he's carrying. It's not heavy. By the weight of it, I'm guessing it's just a letter or note.

The man starts like he's about to leave, but hesitates. He removes a slender, beaded bracelet from his left arm and hands it to me as well.

"If you could give that to her too…"

That does it. This guy is definitely Tahira's ex-lover. The man Tahira broke up with in her bedroom not too long ago. What's he doing back here?

He looks over my shoulder into the house one last time before turning to go. I close the door behind him but find a window so I can watch him get in his car. He takes his time, maybe hoping Tahira will magically appear. She doesn't, obviously, and after another minute or so, the man starts his car and drives away.

I've finished with most of Maria's chores, and Tahira likely won't be home for at least another hour or two. Susan is probably busy with Mehar up in her room, and I haven't seen Gary for a few days, so I figure I have a while to myself.

I can't resist. The envelope is calling me. Begging me to open it. Tahira's ex-lover's envelope may or may not be mission critical, but I'm bored... and curious.

Thanks to my handlers training, opening and resealing an envelope should be a breeze. It isn't even sealed all the way.

The first thing I do is start a pot of boiling water. Once the steam is thick enough I hold the envelope in a pair of tongs over the pot and allow the heated water vapor to soften the bond that's keeping the envelope sealed. I'm careful not to let the envelope curl from the moisture. Next, I set the envelope on the granite countertop and take up a small butter knife, which I slide carefully under the flap of the envelope.

The top lifts off easily, and I withdraw the two sheets of paper within.

The writing isn't Shakespeare, but it's handwritten and seems sincere even if, to me, the content is a bit vague.

Tahira,

I can't let you leave without telling you how I feel.

You didn't exactly give me the chance when you ended things. And because you won't answer any of my calls or texts I have to resort to this letter.

I get that you want to help the world.

Hell, it's your selflessness, your vision, and your drive that make you so attractive to me. But this isn't the way to accomplish your goals. The world won't follow your example, Tahira, not like you think it will. You can't sacrifice your own happiness like this. I know you don't love him. You might be able to lie to yourself and maybe do have some feelings for him, but I know you don't love him. Not like you loved me.

You may hate me for what I'm going to do, but I love you too much to let you do this to yourself. Perhaps this will help you see what a mistake you're making.

I'm sorry...

—Liam

I reread the letter two more times before I have it memorized. The letter slides easily back into its envelope, and I reseal the flaps. I set the envelope and bracelet at the end of the dining table where Tahira will see them when she gets back.

Should I make mention of the envelope and its contents to my handlers? Maybe not. After all, if they keep me in the dark, I can keep them in the dark too. In the end, though, I'll do anything and everything my handlers tell me to…anything to keep Jeremy alive…

Clear water spews forth from my water pail. The air outside is hot, but the shade of the Collins home makes it bearable. An insect makes a buzzing noise as it zips through the air, and I swat at it.

I continue watering. A different buzzing comes from Maria's phone. I pull it out of my apron and am surprised to see Tahira has texted me. Her message is short.

Calling Deval tonight. Gary's out of town.

Is Gary really out of town, or did Tahira just not tell him about the video conference tonight? Ever since Mehar's stroke, Gary hasn't really been by the house. Did Tahira fire him? It's not like Tahira would tell Maria if she let Gary go. For all I know, Gary *could* be out of town.

As I'm finishing watering the last few potted flowers that surround the large Collins property Maria's vision begins to swim.

I have to place a hand on a wall to keep from stumbling. My balance is off. Something is wrong with me.

Both of Maria's hands begin to shake, and I drop the garden pail I'm holding. Water spills into the cracks of the stone walkway.

A throbbing pain courses through my head. My heartbeat slows.

My stomach heaves, and I feel like throwing up.

I watch helplessly as Maria's arms do little to keep me from crashing head first into a clay plant holder.

Blood.

Metallic and thick, it coats my tongue. No. Maria's tongue.

I've cut my lower lip, probably on the shards of clay that lay scattered around my face…I mean…Maria's face. I'm still Maria…right?

Where am I? Why is it so hot? The air smells like fertilizer and dirt. That's right, I was watering plants…

How did I end up on the ground?

Did someone attack me? No. I passed out.

Have I been unconscious for long? The sun hasn't moved much, has it?

This is bad. Something is definitely wrong with me, and Powell will be pissed when he learns I've hit my head and put his precious experiment in harm's way. Should I avoid telling him?

I've been abundantly clear in my reports to Powell about my concerns regarding my bodies' health. He *must* be aware something is wrong with me, but he hasn't answered any of my questions. Maybe if I tell him I passed out then my report will finally spur some feedback.

Getting to my feet brings a fresh wave of nausea. I push the feeling aside. My head hurts where I hit it, but after exploring Maria's scalp with her hands, I don't find any open wounds. The only bleeding is coming from my split lip.

I find a broom and clean up as much of the broken pot as I can.

Once I'm back inside the Collins mansion, I take a washcloth and dab at the blood on my face. I don't have much time to worry about myself or Maria's face. Tahira will probably be home soon. Once I'm finished in the bathroom I return to the kitchen and start preparing dinner.

I make a special meal for Mehar and enough Spanish rice for both Susan and Tahira. I'll probably eat whatever is left over. Maria's body doesn't get hungry as often as Jill's did…

When Tahira returns, she's aloof and distant, which is an improvement to rude and hostile.

She walks into the kitchen, and her eyes immediately find the envelope and bracelet on the dining room table. Tahira reverently picks up the bracelet first. Her emotions are well hidden behind her eyes, so I can't tell how she's feeling. She slips the bracelet into the back pocket of her jeans before picking up the envelope. She freezes when she finally notices that I'm watching her. Is she embarrassed? The moment is gone, and Tahira looks away. She quickly collects the envelope and heads upstairs to her room.

Tahira returns about thirty minutes later than normal to the dinner I've laid out for her. I expect to see signs of crying, like the night she broke up with Liam, but her face tells a different story. Whatever the impact Liam's words have had on Tahira, sadness wasn't a result. Instead, Tahira looks resolute, determined, sure of herself.

When Deval calls, Tahira is much more engaged in their conversation than the last time I acted as her chaperone. The change in Tahira's attitude is bizarre.

Most of what they talk about is…still unhelpful. I'm no closer to understanding Tahira's motivations for marrying Deval than I was before.

Deval asks Tahira about her mom, and she gives him a detailed answer. Mehar's Alzheimer's is progressing faster than her doctors anticipated. Tahira says her mother's heart is failing too. Her voice is steady, but Deval still does his best to console Tahira and ask if there's anything he can do for either her or her mother.

"Your texts are more than enough, Dev. They help. A lot."

Texts?

They've been texting each other?

Deval's mother disapproves of her son having one-on-one interactions with women, but texting is okay? Maybe it has something to do with her culture? Or maybe it's somehow political?

I'll have to see if my handlers have access to Tahira's phone. Those texts might be critical in helping me portray an accurate Tahira Collins. Especially when I'm with Deval.

"I know there's a lot going on right now, Tahira, with your mother especially. And the merger and the politics of course. But I want you to know I'm looking forward to being with you soon."

Another mention of "the merger." What are they chances my handlers already know what's going on but haven't deemed it necessary to inform me yet?

"I look forward to being with you too, Dev. Really. I'm glad the merger is happening, and I'm glad that…*we're* happening."

Tahira's words are genuine. She's definitely being sincere. Deval smiles broadly.

"I got in trouble for the way I said goodbye last time, so I'll just say goodbye like normal."

Tahira laughs a little as Deval rolls his eyes.

"Goodbye, Tahira."

"Bye, Dev."

Just before the video chat ends, Deval raises his hand in a small wave goodbye. I catch the gleam of something silver on his right middle finger. It's a ring of some kind. As he lowers his hand, just before it leaves the frame, I see the design on his ring. It matches the exact same intersecting arrow bracelet I found on Tahira's desk when I first searched her room.

That can't be a coincidence. What could the strange symbol mean?

Finally, Deval signs off, and the television goes black.

Tahira remains seated, staring at the television.

I'm about to get up and go back to the kitchen when sudden, frantic footsteps from the stairs announce the appearance of Susan.

"Tahira!" Susan's eyes are wide. Her face is flushed. "I need you to call 911. Your mother is having a heart attack."

The funeral for Mehar Anand Collins is on a Tuesday. The day is bright, without a single cloud in the sky. Not exactly the right weather for a somber day.

Inside the crematorium, however, the sad mood is a little more obvious.

The material of Maria's black dress is stiff and uncomfortable. The same could be said for Mehar Collins' funeral.

It's not like most funerals I've been to before. No long speeches are made. It's indoors. And there's no casket. There are also very few people in attendance. Gary is here. He chooses to stand next to Tahira. Although, ever since he arrived, the two haven't spoken with each other much. There are three other people in attendance who I don't recognize. They're not family, I know that much, because the last family member in Tahira Collins' life is currently being turned to ash.

Tahira reads a few lines from a book in Hindi. Either she's not fluent or she's having difficulty expressing herself through her masked emotions. So far, Tahira hasn't cried once since her mother has passed away. Even when she's been alone in her room, Tahira has not shed a single tear. I'm sure she's grieving, but not visibly…

After Tahira is finished speaking, we all file out of the cramped room into the lobby of the crematorium. A black suited employee approaches Tahira, and the pair exchange a few words that I can't hear over the other whispered conversations in the room.

Gary approaches me, and our eyes meet. His voice is soft when he speaks.

"I volunteered to pick up Mehar's remains later, but Tahira says she's having them delivered to the house later."

I shrug. What is there to say?

"It was good to see you here today, Maria. It means a lot that you came. Tahira doesn't show it, but she's hurting inside."

I turn Maria's lips up into a slight frown and act sympathetic. Deep down, it's hard for me *not* to be genuinely sympathetic, even toward Tahira. I lost my own mother when I was only a few years younger than she is…

Gary pulls me into a tight hug. My face gets pressed up against his chest. I return his hug. This is weird. Maria's stiff black dress makes it a little difficult to wrap my arms around the tall man, but I manage.

"Tahira says she's going back to the house. I think she wants to be alone. You can probably take the rest of the day off."

A few feet behind Gary, I catch Tahira saying goodbye to an elderly couple. A moment later, she slips out the front doors of the crematorium and into the afternoon sun.

Gary gives me one last hug before he gets distracted by someone else.

Now's my chance.

Making my way toward the exit, I quickly slip out the front door in time to watch the tail lights of Tahira's black R8. She drives north down a busy street.

I shield Maria's eyes from the unrelenting sun and reconsider my "perfect chance." I don't have a car. The bus isn't an option either. Bus routes don't extend to private lakes in the hills. I pull out Maria's phone and request a self-driving car. It's expensive, but it's also my only option.

The silver Accord arrives at my location a few minutes later, and I climb into the back seat.

I don't have an address for my car, so I just tell it to head north. We pass some apartment buildings that look like Maria's. The rundown structures are a stark contrast between the mansions that litter the hills of Las Colinas. Even during a recession, it seems the rich stay rich and the poor get poorer. A job like Maria's would be a blessing to many families in this part of town.

I tell the car which streets to turn down anytime we come to an intersection. After ten more minutes of driving, we finally leave the city and start winding our way through a narrow road up into some hills.

Maria's phone vibrates. The number isn't one she's saved to her contacts. *Status?*

How do they always know when I'm traveling?

I text back. *Following Collins. Mission critical.*

Are they going to tell me not to follow her? They don't like me exhibiting too much of my own free will, but honestly, I'm just doing the job they gave me…

Back before 9.

Not an unreasonable request, but it proves the point that my handlers can still control me.

When I look up from my phone, nothing but rocks and trees line the sides of the road like walls. We climb through the hills for another twenty minutes before my car slows down at a fork in the road. I tell it to go left, and we continue driving for another seven minutes. We're nearing my destination, so I tell my car to pull over to the side of the road to let me out. If I had a human driver, they'd probably think I'm crazy. After all, I'm wearing short heels, a dress…and asking to be dropped off in the middle of nowhere. I shake Maria's head. I *am* crazy.

I step out of the car and gasp as a wave of heat washes over my small body. The sunlight feels too bright, and I blink several times. It can't be more than eighty degrees Fahrenheit today, but it feels more like one hundred. Could I be having a hot flash? That might explain the abnormal heat…and why Maria's body hasn't had a menstrual period. I'd better not faint again.

Tires crunch over some gravel, and I spin around. The Accord performs a perfect U-turn and cruises away.

"Wait!" My voice cracks and does nothing to stop the vehicle. I pull out Maria's phone but don't have reception. Damn. I should've been thinking ahead and had it wait for me. How am I going to get back? What was I thinking?

That's right—I wasn't. Why? I'm usually so good at planning my moves. I haven't been feeling myself lately, that's why.

What a stupid thing to think. I'm *not* myself at all.

I glance at Maria's watch. It's just after 3 in the afternoon. Three hours. I'll give myself three hours to observe and learn what I can about Tahira's lake house before trying to find a way back into town.

Maybe I can hitchhike. Wouldn't be the first time…

The hill off the side of the road looks manageable, even for a short woman in heels. Purse in hand, I sigh and begin climbing. It only takes me about three minutes of hiking to get to the top. At the summit, I have a clear view of the road in both directions. The road north eventually meets a large gate with a sign posted marking everything past it as private property. Good thing I got out of the car when I did. Otherwise, I might have run the risk of showing up on the security cameras flanking the gate.

To the east is the lake. Trees block my vision a little, but the lake looks much bigger in person than it did in the satellite images. The scene reminds me of a time Jeremy and I went fishing on a reservoir near our home. He'd rented a canoe for us. The first fish he caught ended up slipping out of his hands back into the water while I tried taking his picture. I laughed so hard I nearly fell into the lake just like his fish…

As I make my way closer to the edge of the tree line, I spot a lone figure sitting at the end of a pier that extends a few feet out over the lake. Tahira…

It looks like she's alone. The pier is directly in front of the lake house. The lake house is a single story structure with a solar panel roof and large glass windows that make up the exterior walls.

There aren't a lot of trees surrounding the lake itself. Between the tree line and the lake are a solid thirty or forty feet of just grass. Is this all I get for making the effort to come here? Tahira meditating on a pier? What did I expect to learn by coming here?

Her bare feet dangle inches above the water. She looks so peaceful.

Tahira stands up and starts walking up toward the lake house with her back to me. Should I wait for her to leave then investigate the lake house? No. Tahira spends too much time up here alone. It may prove significant to my mission. She *has* to be doing something important up here.

I've come this far already.

I slip off Maria's size five shoes and start running as fast as she can across the grass toward the lake house.

A hundred yards away, Tahira reaches for a door to the side of the house. The lake house has lots of windows, but if I'm quick enough I should be able to reach the house unnoticed. The grass feels good under Maria's feet. When was the last time I ran like this?

I make it halfway to the lake house before I collapse.

Brown eyes with flecks of gold near their pupils are staring down at me when I come to.

Where am I?

My nose tells me I'm outside. There's grass beneath my palms.

Tahira Collins helps me sit up.

That's right…I'm supposed to be spying on Tahira.

Dammit.

My body couldn't have picked a *worse* time to betray me.

My cheeks flush. I avoid meeting Tahira's eyes. I don't have a good excuse for being here. Would Maria have known this place existed in the first place? How can I explain away an unexplainable situation?

"Gary sent you, didn't he?"

"Er…" I nod.

Yeah. Sure. Let's go with that.

Tahira sighs, but she doesn't look mad. She *could* be angry, but Tahira's quite skilled at hiding her emotions when she wants to—like me. "Are you all right? What happened to you?"

"I'm not sure, Miss Collins. I'm feeling better now though."

"Can you stand?"

My head hurts, but I don't think the pain is from falling. The grass is thick and probably softened my fall. Tahira steadies me as I find my legs.

"We should get you inside. You look dehydrated."

Whatever you say, boss…

Tahira keeps a hold of me, and we walk the remaining distance to the lake house. Tahira opens a door for me, and I step into the air-conditioned lake house. I take a deep, refreshing breath.

Tahira waves me toward a leather recliner. The leather is cool to my touch. I sink into the cushions and watch Tahira in the small kitchenette. A few seconds later, Tahira walks around the granite island and hands me a cold glass of water.

The liquid feels amazing as it runs down my dry throat…I mean… Maria's throat.

"How did you get here?"

I mumble something about my self-driving car. It's not hard to fake being embarrassed.

"Why did Gary send you? He knows I just come up here to think."

Great question…why *would* Gary "send" Maria? How come Tahira jumped to that conclusion so readily? I delay answering by taking another sip of water. Tahira keeps talking, almost like I'm no longer here. Invisibility has its perks…

"He's not even family. Why does he care so much? He should worry about his own family."

"Mr. Ryan wants what's best for you, Miss Collins. That's all."

"No one knows what's best for me. Not my mother. Not my…friends. And especially not Gary."

Now Tahira looks a little angry, but not with me. Her eyes are focused outside like her mind is elsewhere.

I've already come this far, and failed this badly, do I even have anything else to lose by trying to ask Tahira a few questions of my own?

"What do you think about when you come here, Miss Collins?"

For a moment, Tahira's attention remains unfocused. Finally, as if she just heard me, her eyes meet mine. She looks at me like it's the first time we've met…I mean…like the first time she's met Maria. She continues to stare at me for a while before she finally responds.

"I come up here because I can think. I feel closer to the universe, closer to the gods."

Tahira's eyes find the windows again like she's zoned out. A few moments of silence passes before Tahira opens her mouth again.

"Father used to bring me up here."

Has her mother's death softened her feelings toward me? She's so much more open than I've ever seen her.

"I guess that's also why I come on my own. This place reminds me of him, even though he's been gone for so long. He taught me to swim in the lake. He taught me how to fish, how to sail, even how to scuba dive."

I have to strain to keep from rolling Maria's eyes. Although, I guess if my daddy owned a private lake I'd do those things too.

"He also taught me about the world."

There's a weight to Tahira's words now that wasn't present a second ago. She speaks slower. "Father taught me all about history, governments, cultures. He taught me that the world needs strong leaders. People who can unite others. Who can keep darkness at bay. Foster peace and progress…and lead humanity into the light. He wanted me to become such a leader."

Tahira's still an idealist? Her words sound an awful lot like the papers she wrote after graduating from university. The conviction in her voice is deep. She *believes* what she's telling me…but the leaders she's describing don't really exist anymore. It's wishful thinking, hoping a leader can unite others and foster peace. Those kind of people only exist in history books.

"He showed me the Path here too. Before he died…"

The Path? Maybe it has something to do with Hinduism? But her mother was the religious one, not her father…

My list of things to learn about Tahira Collins keeps growing.

"At first, the Path seemed out of reach. Like I wouldn't be ready to follow it when the time came. Now that I'm alone though…I feel more confident than ever. The Path feels right. Marrying Deval feels right."

A brief pause ensues. Keep going, Tahira. *Keep. Talking.*

"I don't know why I'm telling you all of this." Tahira turns her attention back to me. Her gaze is electric, penetrating, emotional. "Are you going to report back to Gary? You know I fired him last week."

That's news. But it makes sense.

"I'm letting you go too. I mean, I don't really need you anymore. I'll be leaving for India soon anyway."

Crap.

Did Tahira really just fire me…well, Maria?

"You've helped my family a lot…especially when Mother was sick, but I can't keep you on anymore. I'm sure you understand."

I just nod my head slowly. There's nothing I, or Maria, can do at this point.

Surely this wasn't part of my handlers' plan. If Tahira is firing me so soon before she leaves for India, then my timeline just evaporated. My handlers can't exactly blame me though, can they? Even if I hadn't followed Tahira to her lake house and gotten caught, she still would've fired me sooner than later. It was only a matter of time once Mehar died before Tahira wouldn't really have a need for Maria Antonio. Tahira Collins is a very independent woman.

"I'll give you a ride home so you can collect your things."

Tahira starts to get up from her chair, and I follow. My head is feeling better, but now I have a different kind of headache to deal with—having to explain Maria's unemployment status to my handlers.

We leave the lake house together. Tahira pauses only to make sure the house is locked behind us. I walk slowly to her black Audi and climb into the passenger seat. The interior is as exotic as the exterior, with leather sports seats and red LED lighting around the bottom of the doors that glows when Tahira starts up the powerful engine. It's extremely loud for an electric motor. How have they managed to make it sound like cars that used to run on fossil fuels?

While Tahira is distracted with pulling onto the road, I withdraw Maria's phone from her purse and send the last marked number a text. I just don't include many details on *how* I got fired.

Collins just terminated my employment. Advise on how to proceed?

The drive back is much quicker in Tahira's car. Even though the vehicle has an autopilot feature, Tahira prefers to drive manually. At least that's one thing we have in common.

The ride is a smooth one as we carve our way through the hills down toward San Diego. We don't speak to each other as we drive, which is fine by me.

Why aren't my handlers responding? Are they angry? Usually they want more information, but they're as silent as Tahira Collins. We continue through town until we have to stop at a light. Suddenly, Tahira turns to me and puts a hand on my shoulder.

"I'm sorry for the way I've treated you the past few months, Maria."

What?

Did Tahira just apologize to me? Where did that come from? She's only apologizing to Maria, but still...her apology was sincere. We're still waiting at the stop light when Tahira continues.

"I know I've been a pain to work for recently, so I'm sorry. I don't have any excuses. I hope you'll forgive me."

I hesitate a second before nodding my head slowly. Tahira glances at me before the light turns green, and she visibly relaxes. Her lips form a small smile. Did my forgiveness really mean that much to her?

We pull up the familiar road that leads to Las Colinas; it's much faster in a car than in a slow, electric bus. An abnormal number of parked cars line the street. There are even news vans with dishes sticking out of the tops of their roofs. Uh oh...

I glance at Tahira. Her knuckles tighten on the steering wheel. She starts breathing faster through clenched teeth.

We turn a corner past some trees, and at the end of the road is a mass of bodies. Reporters with their dozens of cameras start moving toward us in a frenzy. Like a tsunami racing towards us, we're consumed.

"Liam..." Tahira curses under her breath.

This is what Liam was planning to do? Go to the media about Tahira?

Tahira is forced to slam on the brakes to avoid running a man over. We slow to a crawl as people crowd around the car, pressing their faces and cameras as close as they can. Their shouted questions range from the absurd to bordering on slander.

"Tahira! When is the big day?"

"Tahira! Why are you being forced to marry an Equalist?"

"Do you consider yourself a traitor to your country?"

"Who will you be wearing for the wedding?"

"How many other wives will you have to share Kapoor with?"

"How many terrorists are related to the Kapoors?"

The media's questions are so…antagonizing. Slandering. It makes sense that they're attacking Kapoor, but Tahira's an American born citizen. Not half like Maria is…er…was.

Tahira keeps her face as emotionless as possible, but beneath her mask she's seething. If Liam really is behind this leak to the media, Tahira isn't just mad…she feels betrayed. Indeed, her hands have begun to tremble as she tries to steer the car through the mass of people blocking our way to the gates.

There's another voice shouting amongst the crowd. It's the guard, Alfonso, trying to make the media personnel move so we can get through. I don't envy his position right now. Poor Alfonso is fighting a losing battle.

Eventually, we manage to inch our way through the reporters. I think Tahira only runs over one or two feet in the process.

The Las Colinas gates swing open, just wide enough for our car to get past. As soon as we make it through the gates, Alfonso shuts them behind us, keeping the pack of ravenous news people outside.

"…as if he thinks this will stop me." Her voice is hardly above a whisper and Tahira's still visibly shaken by the arrival of the media, but she's not trembling anymore. We pull into the circular drive of the Collins home, and head around back to the garage. How am I going to make it out of here without facing the media? I'm sure I'll be recognized as the Collins' maid as soon as I try to leave, and I'll be bombarded with questions.

Tahira seems to be thinking the same thing. "You'll stay here tonight… er…if that's okay with you."

I still haven't heard back from my handlers, so I'm more than happy to take Tahira up on her order. Even if it was disguised as an invitation. Hopefully, by morning the reporters will give up and leave us alone long enough for me to slip out of here.

"You can take the guest bedroom on the main floor." Tahira pulls into the large, detached garage and parks the car. She powers down the vehicle with a simple voice command.

"And Maria? Thank you for listening to me today. I know Gary sent you to follow me, but it's…it's been a while since I've had someone I can talk openly with, so…thanks."

"You're welcome, Miss Collins."

Her gratitude pierces my heart like a needle.

The sun is setting, but the evening air is still warm. I follow Tahira into the house through one of the side doors.

"I was planning on making dinner myself, but since you're here…"

I prepare a classic Maria head nod in anticipation of being asked to make Tahira dinner one last time.

"…do you want to make something together?"

It's like someone has already switched brains with Tahira. She's treating me like I'm her aunt or something, not her ex-maid. Is ex-maid even a thing? I reply to Tahira with a nod. Maybe the death of her mother really *has* wrought this change in her. Death has a way of changing people…

"Awesome. What sounds good to you?"

To me? What *does* sound good to me?

It's been so long since someone's asked me what I want that I don't have an answer. I try to think about what Maria would want to cook, but…I have a chance to be myself for once. Even if it's just cooking food.

"Is Miss Collins familiar with Tex Mex sandwiches?"

Tahira tries to hide her…disgust or confusion…I can't be sure which, but she shakes her head. "I'd give it a go if you tell me how I can help."

We head into the kitchen and I tell Tahira where to find the chuck roast while I get out the slow cooker.

Tahira treats me well as we gather ingredients and start to prepare dinner. She's polite and always defers to me when she has a question about how to cut the vegetables or which spices to use with the meat. Tahira even makes a few jokes as we work. Laughing comes easier for me the longer we spend cooking together.

"So, Maria, where did you learn to cook?" Tahira smiles pleasantly at me.

"Er…*mi mamá.*"

"Nice. Mother taught me to bake. Not so much cooking. Guess that's why we always had a maid."

I smile back. This is so awkward…

After everything is ready except for the meat, Tahira and I find seats across from each other at the dining room table.

Tahira asks me about where I grew up. I give her Maria's answer.

She asks me about my family. I give her Maria's answer.

Then she asks me about my beliefs.

"Do you mean, religion?"

"Sure." Tahira shrugs. "If that's how you organize your beliefs. I guess I mean God, gods, religion, values, fate, higher power, whatever. What do you believe?"

That's easy. Maria was Catholic. But…do *I* believe in anything anymore? I believe in good and evil. I believe in mankind's ability to destroy lives. I believe that roast is starting to smell absolutely incredible. But as far as adhering to a specific religion or value system? I don't know anymore…

Jeremy was always the one with faith in a higher purpose—not me.

I reply with Maria's answer.

Tahira smiles and nods. "I knew a lot of good Catholics. There aren't many of you out there anymore though, right?"

I shake my head.

Tahira goes silent. This is perfect. I have nothing left to lose. Why not ask Tahira her own questions?

"If it's not too personal, um…what does Miss Collins believe?"

Tahira doesn't look at me or answer right away. Maybe I should have started with something less personal…

"Mother was Hindu, obviously. She taught me about her beliefs. But Father…he had different ideas."

Yes. This is exactly what I need.

"I mentioned a little at the lake house, but Father believed in the Path. I still don't understand all of it, but the Path is a symbol for progression, for advancement. My father believed humanity's divine purpose is to learn and grow. To overcome our inherent limitations. He believed the only way to do this is through cooperation, through helping our brothers and sisters. By sharing knowledge and resources. Only then can humanity truly liberate itself…"

"Does Mr. Kapoor believe as you do, Miss Collins?"

Tahira gives me a sharp look but smiles. "Yes. Dev was raised Hindu and believes in the Path too. He's even more of a believer than I am…in some ways."

Tahira fingers something on her wrist. It's the bracelet I found on her desk. The silver rhombus reflects a bit of light.

She notices me looking at her hands and smiles.

"This is the symbol for the Path. It represents unity and cooperation—the basic tenets of the Path."

Could this Path have anything to do with why my handlers want me to kill Deval Kapoor? Maybe. Maybe not. But I have a feeling it's important.

"Were you ever married, Maria?"

Yes…*I* was…

I shake Maria's head.

"Deval and I have never met in person. Our parents knew each other though. People think they know why I'm marrying him. There's the merger of course, and that's a big part of it. When I approached the Kapoors with the idea, initially they were hesitant. It wasn't until the idea of marriage between Deval and I was brought into the conversation that things start to move along. At first I was resentful, but I'm lucky to be marrying a man like Deval. I guess you could say I'm marrying him because…"

Masked men sweep into the dining room like specters.

One of the men smothers Tahira's mouth with a white cloth which keeps her from screaming. Within seconds she goes completely limp. The mercenary lets her fall gently onto the dining table and then proceeds to tie her wrists behind her back.

No.

Why is this happening *now*?

This *can't* be happening now.

I finally find Maria's voice. "What's…what's going on!?"

A pair of mercenaries begin carrying Tahira's unconscious body out of the kitchen and down the hall. I stumble slightly getting up from my chair as I follow. One of the mercenaries meets my eyes. "Timeline is being accelerated. You're making the transfer tonight."

I stop walking. No. It's too soon. I was supposed to have more time. Is this because I got fired? Or because Mehar finally passed away? Or because the media found out about Tahira's engagement?

This was the final result of me becoming Maria Antonio all along, but…

Can I enter another nightmare? I'm finally getting used to the one I'm in now.

And Tahira…

I can't watch her be murdered. But if I don't do as I these men say…they'll murder Jeremy. They'll murder me. What choice do I have?

"Powell is waiting. Get ready to leave. Now!"

As traumatic as watching someone get kidnapped can be, it's even worse being forced to act as one of the kidnappers.

Just like the sun, my sense of control has long since departed.

The mercenaries have a van. The side says *Squeegee Boyz Cleaners* in big, bubbly text. That explains how they got past Alfonso into Las Colinas. They've probably had this part of the operation planned for some time now. But why tonight?

Just like the sun, my sense of control has long since departed.

The five mercenaries lift Tahira into the back of the vehicle, and one of them shoves me toward the open back. I trip on something and nearly fall. Maria's body is sweating. But I'm cold and clammy. My breathing is shallow and my heartbeat…am I having a heart attack? No. My body is in shock.

"Get in the back."

I obey whichever mercenary has spoken and climb into the back of the white van.

The inside looks nothing like a cleaning van should. The vehicle could belong to the FBI. Computer monitors hang along the walls of the van, and several types of weapons are tucked into different, easy-to-reach places. There are no windows, but I can see through the front windshield. The partition between the back of the van and the front is just a wall of metal mesh.

They've laid Tahira down across a metal bench. I take a seat on the opposite side from her. Two mercenaries join us in the back while the other three pile into the front. One of them reaches toward me and slips a white bag over my head. The electric engine starts up, and we begin to drive.

Apart from the ambient sounds of a moving vehicle, all is silent. Tahira still hasn't woken up. Whatever compound the mercenaries forced her to inhale must be strong.

We drive in complete silence. I try to keep track of the turns and stops, but I'm so disoriented I eventually give up.

Somewhere between ten and fifteen minutes later, gravel crunches beneath the van tires as we come to a final, rolling stop.

As soon as we park, the mercenaries pile out. I'm half pushed, half pulled out of the back of the van and ordered to start walking toward the house.

My foot snags on something, and I fall to the ground. Someone pulls me up and removes the bag from my head. A masked man grips me by my upper arm and pulls me along toward the tall, ominous silhouette of a mansion.

I turn around in time to watch Tahira being lifted out. It's dark, and Maria's eyesight isn't perfect…Tahira is beginning to stir. Her eyelids flutter, but they're glazed. Searching. Confused.

I haven't been fond of Tahira Collins, but especially after today, I've begun to see her as…as what exactly? As a daughter forsaken by her parents? A young woman engaged to a man who loves her? A struggling soul trying to find her place in life? All of the above? Yes. I see her as a human being…and a victim.

Like me…

This woman I've come to understand is about to be murdered. And I'm going to take her place in this world.

I want to be sick. Maria's body shivers. I clench and unclench my fists as I march.

I hate myself.

I hate these men.

I hate being Divest.

I can't do this. Not anymore.

An animal rage overcomes me, and I launch myself at the man pushing me toward the building. I punch and kick and scratch, but he's virtually unaffected. Maria's body is too weak. Still, I do my worst and manage to draw blood. He grunts when my small fist connects with his face. The mercenary's grip loosens and I run.

I'm about ten feet away from the pair carrying Tahira when I'm grabbed roughly from behind by someone much stronger than myself. My arms are instantly immobilized. I yell at Tahira to wake up. Someone smothers my mouth with a gloved hand. I bite down hard, but the hand doesn't move. Tahira's voice is cracked and groggy. What's she saying?

I'm dragged through a door into the house and down a hall. Deep shadows mar the walls and carpet like claw marks. It's cold in here, so very cold. The paintings hanging on the walls look ghostly. *The Anatomy Lesson's* soulless, frozen creatures stare unblinkingly at me as I pass beneath them.

Maria's feet churn beneath me to keep up with the pace of those dragging me. We start down a staircase. It's like descending the steps to damnation.

"Bastards! Damn you!" I continue struggling, trying to rip my arms free. Someone hits me sharply in my ribs, possibly with the butt of a gun. I grunt. The pain takes my breath away. They've cracked several of Maria's ribs, maybe even broken a few. Breathing comes in sharp, abrupt gasps. Each inhale fills my lungs with fire.

I can't do it.

It's too much.

I can't…Jeremy…

My will to fight evaporates.

Like a rocket that's spent all its fuel…I grow cold inside. I'm a coward. Pitiful. Weak. How far have I sunk?

We make it down to the basement, and the man carrying me tosses me bodily onto an operating table. I lie there for several seconds before I work up the courage to prop myself up on an elbow. The bile rising in my throat tastes sour as I swallow. Powell's operating room fills me with resignation. I've done this dozens of times. It's become habit. One more time…

But this is the first time my next body is awake and screaming.

Tahira continues struggling to free herself from the men strapping her down to the operating table adjacent to my own. The men are slow and methodical. I can't tear my eyes away from the scene before me.

Tahira…

"Help me! Someone help!"

The drug has worn off completely now. Tahira's eyes are lucid and wide with terror. Her neck muscles are taut, and she continues to cry for help.

I need to look away. But I can't…

"Let me go!"

Tahira's face is wet with tears. She sees me and starts screaming again.

"Maria! What's happening?! Help me! Please!"

I lay on my side in shame and silence. The will to resist has forsaken me. Cheated me. Abandoned me.

These monsters own me.

I look on with cold, bitter anger as the mercenaries gently but forcibly finish tying Tahira down onto the operating table. Tahira strains against her bonds. Her head turns to find me. Her eyes lock onto mine. Her lips move, but no sound escapes. Did she lose her voice? No.

My hearing…

Where is the ringing coming from?

I taste salt. Maria's tears blur everything. I blink and taste more. Tahira's eyes are filled with horror. But beneath it all, there is innocence.

Tahira has never been exposed to this kind of evil before.

The guilt becomes too unbearable. I have to look away. Ignoring Tahira fills me with even more guilt. There's no escape.

Out of the corner of my eye I see him. The conductor for this symphony of evil. Powell stands silently in the shadows, watching the scene play out before him. His face is blank, but perhaps he too is shocked by what's taking place. This might be a first for him too.

Tahira continues her screaming unabated. Surely she isn't in any physical pain; the mercenaries have treated her relatively gently. Tahira's terrified, painful cries bespeak a different kind of agony. Not physical. It's the pain of having one's world upended.

Her screams are like my own. The first time I became Divest.

One last cold tear escapes my eyes for the anguish I see in Tahira's.

A black armored man moves in front of me, blocking my line of sight.

My hearing dips in and out. A high-pitched whine fills the gaps when I can't hear anything around me. I'm too numb to worry about what's happening to myself.

"…wake up you'll…in the Collins home."

"…one, please!" Tahira's voice catches but she keeps screaming.

"…inform Deval Kap…move the date…end of…."

"Help! Ple…!"

"You will…mission depends on…."

Tahira's muffled cries are suddenly silenced. I look past the man in front of me. One of Powell's orderlies has forced a mask over Tahira's mouth. Her hands, which moments before were straining against her bonds, now hang limp. Lifeless.

A pair of Powell's orderlies begin cutting Tahira's clothes away from her body. Preparing her for the cryogenic tube so Powell can perform his surgery.

"…understand?"

I continue staring at Tahira's still body.

Past Tahira, an orderly preps the cryochamber. Blue light bends through the curved glass, casting an ominous glow through the lab. The fine hairs on Maria's neck stand on end. I shiver. I can almost feel the terrible coldness of the cryofluid…

Soon, Tahira's lifeless body will be inserted into the tube…and then my brain…

"Hey!"

The mercenary grabs me by my scalp and forces me to meet his eyes.

I spit in his face.

The man's eyes flash in anger, and he raises a fist.

A gloved hand shoots out of nowhere and stops the mercenary from striking me.

"Not her head!" Powell's voice is high pitched. I've never heard him raise his voice before.

The mercenary shakes Powell off and storms away.

Powell looks at me, and for a second I almost imagine seeing a flicker of pity behind his glasses. But the moment is gone in an instant.

I rest my head back against the cold plastic of the operating table. Powell looms over me, blocking the light above. Metal clinks against metal as he prepares his instruments. An electronic whirring fills the air, and a Meridian laser apparatus descends from the ceiling. Its appendages come to a stop a few feet above Maria's forehead. It's like I'm staring up at the underbelly of a massive spider.

As if my body has a will of its own, I slowly turn my head to take one last look at the *real* Tahira Collins. Her beautiful black hair is being combed and parted by one of Powell's orderlies while another woman prepares a second laser apparatus.

If I take away all that surrounds her, Tahira could simply be asleep. She looks so peaceful. So innocent. Pure...

Powell is motioning for an orderly to tend to me. They inject a thick substance into my left arm and place a monitor just beneath my collarbone.

Someone begins parting my hair, removing strands to make way for the path of the lasers. I don't even wince as the hair follicles are removed one by one. Pain has become an old friend of mine.

I take one last look up at the pale, fluorescent lighting through Maria's eyes as someone puts a clear plastic mask, like Tahira's, over my mouth and tells me to inhale.

I don't even try to count.

What's the point? Whether it's five seconds or five million...any time spent in this hell is too long.

My mind is on a precipice.

The same wasteland that always greets me extends in all directions.

But something is different…

The void.

It's tinged with red.

Amorphous shapes materialize on the edges of my awareness, but the void is diluted with streaks of deep red lines. It can't be my imagination. The void is bleeding.

This place isn't real. Whatever it is, it's not real. I *know* this. Blood in the sky means nothing. I shouldn't be so concerned. But something *feels* wrong.

I'm just a spectator here. Wherever *here* is. Powerless to do anything, I can only observe. Pressure begins to build. Pushing against me from seemingly all directions. I'm pulled toward the edge of the precipice. Slowly at first. Then faster.

The desert below is also dyed red. I've reached the edge. Please. I can't go back. I can't bear it.

I struggle. My concentration has no effect. I'm still being dragged over the edge of the cliff by some unseen alien force. What kind of world awaits me beneath the sands?

Not a world I want to return to. Please. Stop.

The pressure around and within me is unbearable. The plunge is upon me. My consciousness inches forward.

I'm at the edge. For a moment, the pressure releases its grip. I remain frozen. Suspended.

Did I actually think I could stay…?

The void collapses around me. Flashes of red light spark like lightning bolts. The void and I fall together. I am the void. The void is me.

The desert feels hungry. We have to feed it.

In a sudden rush of exploding sand we collide with the desert sands.

Darkness and bloodsoaked light vaporize me.

Pain that I wish would kill me arcs across my awareness.

Worse than being scorched by flame. Worse than electrocution. Worse than dying.

This pain is oblivion.

I'm nothing. All I am is pain. The void groans with me. It's a low, guttural sound that rumbles like storm clouds. The desert wraps its tiny, sharp fingers around me. Constricting me. Burying me. There's no air. But what's the pain of suffocating compared to the pain of being erased?

A breeze. The touch of soft, familiar sheets. I'm in my bed. The sweet scent of jasmine drifts through the air. I could stay here forever. When was the last time I just took a moment to rest?

My stomach growls. I swallow. My throat is terribly dry.

Opening my eyes takes a fraction of a second longer than it should, but my body responds immediately when I sit up.

What the hell? Why am I wearing Tahira's clothes? Why am I lying in her *bed*? Why is my hair so long?

I stare up at the large mirror directly across the room. Tahira stares back at me. Alone.

Her golden-brown eyes are wide.

Tahira raises a hand and touches her face. No.

Tears spring to my eyes, and I bury Tahira's face in my hands. I choke as I gasp for air in between sobs. Salty tears mix with my saliva as I scream. I scream and scream as I dig my nails into a pillow and pull as hard as I can. The fabric rips. My arm and leg muscles cramp. I roll myself into a fetal position and rock back and forth.

No…no…*no!* Tahira…

Eventually, my body doesn't have any more tears to give, but I keep crying. I'm a monster. Ashamed. Unholy. Torn. Divest.

Tahira…I'm so…*sorry.* Wherever you are…I'm so sorry…

Even with sealed lips, Tahira's screams fill my mind. Echoing and reverberating through my skull.

Sunlight peeks through the windows. A bird chirps.

When I look up, I'm the only one in the mirror. My hair is disheveled and my eyes are red. I look just like Tahira did when she was…

I tear my eyes from the mirror like bandages from a wound.

I inhale slowly and release my breath even slower. Over and over until my silent tears finally stop.

Gravity has increased tenfold. The energy it requires to pull myself out of Tahira's bed and toward the bathroom is immense.

My hands fumble with the knobs to the sink. I splash water on my… *Tahira's*…face. I'm so numb I don't even register the water's temperature.

My ears are ringing as I wander downstairs and into the kitchen.

Tahira's body is begging for water and nourishment. I open the fridge and drink a protein shake. I almost choke, and some of the brown liquid splashes onto the floor.

There's a familiar tablet lying on the dining room table. My chest tightens, and heat engulfs me as I grab the nearest thing I can find to smash the screen.

I raise a toaster in both hands. A human face suddenly appears on the tablet's screen. It's a man. One of my handlers? No…

The toaster tumbles from my hands.

My…Tahira's…hands tremble as I pick up the tablet.

Jeremy…

It's just a static image. Jeremy's blue eyes look deep into my own. His handsome face looks unchanged from the last time I saw him. The last time my handlers tortured him for my benefit. For my disobedience.

Then, a single lock of his wavy hair drifts down across his forehead. Just like it did before I ever wore another person's body. Before I became Divest.

"Alex…"

His voice. My name. I fall to my knees on the kitchen floor, still clutching Jeremy's face between my hands. Please be real.

"I don't know what's going on or where you are. All I know is they want me to tell you I'm okay. They've told me they've asked you to do something for them."

My grip on the tablet tightens.

Did they take him out of cryogenics? Or is this just an old recording? He looks all right—but have they hurt him again? How much does he know? Will he still love me if he knows what I've become…the things I've done?

My fears are put on hold when Jeremy continues his message.

"Whatever they're making you do, Alex…I want you to know…don't worry about me. Just…"

Someone off screen forcibly removes Jeremy from the camera, but the audio continues. They're beating him. I scream at the tablet.

"No. Stop it! I'll do whatever you want! Please!"

Can they hear me? They have to hear me.

"Please. Don't hurt him! I'll finish the mission! I'll…"

Three seconds later, the message terminates, and the tablet goes black on its own.

Jeremy.

He spoke to me. He…

The tablet falls from my hands, slides off my thigh, and clatters to the floor.

A reminder…that's what this was. Why else would the bastards allow Jeremy to speak to me? Even if it was prerecorded. They want to remind me my husband is alive. But if I don't do as they say, Jeremy will be silenced. Just like they silenced him from finishing his last sentence.

Jeremy would've told me to run. To save myself. To forget him so they couldn't use him to control me anymore.

But I can't do that.

My handlers must fear I'm becoming unreliable.

I hang my head in defeat.

To resist is to kill Jeremy.

They own me...no...not me. *Divest.*

My eyes drift along the edge of the dining room table until my gaze comes to rest on a phone. Tahira's phone. I reach for it. Attached to the top of the phone is a bright blue note.

Collins' phone. Per your request.

Their hostile sarcasm is barely concealed. I remove the note from Tahira's phone and crush the paper in my fist. Tahira's arms are strong. Much stronger than Maria's had been.

I stare at my new fists. My new arms. My chocolate skin is smooth to the touch. I'm much darker than the color of my real skin, even after a full summer of sun. Her silky black hair falls down past my shoulders. It's well cared for; I don't even find split ends.

I inhale and exhale a few times. Breathing seems normal, and after resting my hand on Tahira's chest I feel my new heartbeat. It's strong and steady. I would expect nothing less considering how active Tahira was.

Tahira's chest is smaller than most of the bodies I've had, with almost no cleavage.

I stand up, and my eye line is much higher than Maria's had been. I'd guess my new height to be around five feet and six or seven inches tall.

Tahira's vision is good. Much better than Maria's had been. Everything is sharp and in focus.

Finally, as is my habit, I reach up to the base of my skull and then to the middle of my neck to find the tiny scars left by Powell's lasers. Tahira's hair is so thick and long it'll be easy to hide the marks of being Divest.

Powell instructed me to always check for unconscious brain functions, like breathing, heartbeat, blinking, and temperature regulation, as well as for conscious things...like being able to walk properly. So far, Tahira's body has responded well to both my brain's conscious and unconscious signals.

I mean...I made it down from the second story without having any trouble. But I *was* just waking up from brain surgery, so I walk around the kitchen and living room to be sure motor control is normal. As I drift listlessly through the house, everything feels so...familiar.

Obviously, my surroundings are familiar to me because I worked as the Collins' maid, but this body feels the space around it in a unique, more relaxed sort of way.

This house feels like home.

But I'm *not* home. Despite what my body thinks. My home just spoke to me through a tablet...

After a minute or two longer of wandering around the empty home, a familiar ringtone echoes through the hall. Tahira's phone is going off. I return to the kitchen in time to answer the call.

"Status?"

I resist the urge to hang up the phone.

"Report."

The image of Tahira bound and writhing on Powell's operating table floods my mind. The memory of her face...my face...filled with terror...

The voice on the other line fades a little like they've taken the phone away from their face.

"Get Powell. She may not have full motor control..."

With effort, I find my voice...I mean—*Tahira's* voice.

"I'm fine...I mean...the body is fine. I have full motor control."

"Good. Now, open the tablet, and you'll find your next instructions. That is all."

The line goes dead.

I lock my jaw but obediently pick up the tablet.

The tablet must be synced to unlock with Tahira's biometrics, because as soon as I look at the screen, it opens. There are a few folder icons, and I tap on the one that says *Open Now.*

My handlers' instructions for my mission are very straightforward. Nothing but bullet points. A list of chores.

- Convince Deval Kapoor to agree to a new wedding date. No later than the end of May.

Why do my handlers want this from me? Why wouldn't the original wedding date still work? I'll have exactly thirty-five days. Not impossible, but changing wedding plans on short notice may prove difficult. How will Deval take this coming from me…I mean, Tahira?

- After the wedding, you must kill Deval Kapoor as soon as possible.
- His death must look like an accident, but you must include enough evidence for authorities to trace his death back to Tahira Collins.
- More instructions will follow if necessary.

I'm going to frame Tahira Collins for her husband's murder.

It certainly won't be the first person I've framed…but it had better be my last.

Tahira didn't deserve what happened to her.

Her life wasn't perfect, but she was robbed of it nonetheless. Tahira's life ended before it even had a chance to fully begin. Whatever goals or ambitions she may have had—they've been erased now. Whatever amount of good Tahira might have effected in this screwed-up world is no longer a possibility. *Tahira* has been erased. What's left of her is nothing more than an empty shell with me inside. And *I'm* nothing but a pathetic imitation of the woman Tahira was…

I still can't get Tahira's screams out of my head.

Maybe they'll never leave.

I need a distraction. Something. Anything.

Otherwise, I'm going to go insane.

I have to focus…have to save Jeremy…

Tomorrow. I'll give myself until tomorrow to call Deval and try to persuade him to move the wedding date.

For now, I need to learn as much about Deval Kapoor's relationship with Tahira Collins as possible. What's their relationship *really* like? I bite my tongue. What *was* their relationship like?

Their texting history seems as good a place to start as any.

Tahira's phone opens just like the tablet did as soon as I look at the screen. I open her messages app and scroll till I find Deval's name. She has him saved in her phone as Dev Kapoor. She has a small ring emoji next to his name too. Should I replace it with a knife?

I start scrolling from the top where I don't have to refresh prior messages and read until I get to the bottom.

Monday 10:45 P.M.

You probably don't want to talk about it but are you ready for tomorrow?

*I think so.
I've already gone through this with dad...*

*You're a remarkable woman Tahira.
I wish I could be there.*

I know you do Dev

Yesterday 7:15 A.M.

What time is the funeral?

Our time is from 8-10

Did you invite Gary?

Yes

Is he going to be there?

*I'm sure he will
You know I can prep the jet and still be there in time.*

*I know, but don't worry about it
I'm sorry Tahira.*

In some ways it's a relief.

She was already gone
a long time ago.

I have a feeling something
bad is about to happen.

What do you mean?
How was the ceremony?

Ceremony was fine.
A few of dad's old friends
from the company came.
It was faster than I thought it'd be

Then what's wrong?

I don't know. I can't describe it.

Do you think it has something to
do with your mother being gone?

Maybe.

Tell me what you need.
What can I do?

Nothing.
I'm just ready to get away.

They know. The media
found out we're getting married.

How did they find out?

Was it Gary?

No.

Well, we knew the story would break eventually.

Yeah

I hope you know I'm not angry. I know it wasn't your fault.

Ever the diplomat ;)

I mean, we wanted the world to know eventually, right? Now people know.

Yeah

Yesterday 6:04 P.M.

Just got out of my meeting. How are you doing?

Yesterday 7:02 P.M.

Tahira?

The couple never talked again. Tahira never replied to Deval's last text. She had her phone out a few times when we were chatting and making dinner together. Her last text must have been sent right before we were taken…

Should I text him back now?

I nearly drop Tahira's phone when it vibrates. Deval.

> *Are you okay?*
> *I'm starting to get worried.*

I bite my bottom lip and feel Tahira's cheeks flush. Why am I panicking? There's no immediate threat. I know Tahira. I can mimic her personality well enough, especially over text. Deval isn't suspicious, just concerned.

> *I'm fine. Sorry I never got back to you*

> *That's okay. I was just worried about you. Especially after our last conversation.*

> *I let my maid go*

> *Maria?*

> *Yeah*

> *Will Gary be by tonight then?*

Damn.

I scroll up and refresh previous messages.

Three days ago Deval and Tahira scheduled a video chat for tonight. Why didn't my handlers warn me? Did they know? I can't do this. Not tonight. Plus, I'm out a chaperone. Should I play the honesty card with Deval?

> *Um, not sure.*
> *I haven't spoken with him since yesterday*

I'll try to get my mother to level.
Her sense of tradition and decency are as
strong as ever though :P

Let me know.

I'll try to find someone.

Great, can't wait to see you again.
I miss your smile.

15

My palms are sweaty, and I can't stop pacing.

It's my own fault. Why didn't I just say no to Deval? Because Tahira wouldn't have?

Why hasn't Gary answered any of my calls?

Who else could I call? Scrolling through Tahira's list of contacts doesn't help. None of the people listed are familiar. And there aren't even that many.

A loud knock at the front door makes me jump.

I cautiously skirt around the living room until I find a window that lets me see who's at the door. It's a man. His crisp purple uniform bears a shipping logo, and he's carrying a package under one arm. The delivery man is also wearing a hat that obscures most of his face.

Just drop the package and walk away. Drop the package. Walk away. The man knocks again. Then he rings the doorbell. Just leave. Please.

Maybe it's Mehar's remains? Already though? They said it'd be at least two days…

I make my way slowly to the front doors. I run a hand through my messy hair, turn the handle, and crack one of the heavy doors open.

"Hey, Tahira."

Dammit.

Liam's eyes search mine. I keep Tahira's face blank.

What do I do?

What would Tahira do?

My slap lands hard and sharp across his face. Yes. That felt right.

I slap him again.

Liam doesn't recoil or even try to soften the blow by turning his face. He takes it. Like he knew it was coming.

"I'm sorry, Tahira. I just..."

"Just what?" Tahira's words come with almost no thought. "Did you think going to the media would stop me from getting married?" Tahira's voice is taut and sensuous. Like a violin.

"Look, can I come in so I can explain myself?"

I shake my head.

He tries to push past me into the house, but I shove him hard with my left arm. "Get out of here, Liam."

"I couldn't watch you throw your life away, Tahira!" Liam is shouting now. He drops the box.

"I'm not..."

"I thought the media would help you realize the mistake you're making. Kapoor is a foreigner. An Indian! Dozens of terror strikes originated from cells in *India*, including the strike on Washington. They can't be trusted!"

A fair point, but Tahira seemed not to care about past atrocities enough to keep her from marrying a foreigner.

"I'll call the police if you don't leave now, Liam. We're done. You shouldn't have come here."

"I'm sorry about your mother too, Tahira. That's...also why I wanted to come. To make sure you..."

"I'm *fine*, Liam. And you can stop pretending like you actually care about me."

My words cut like a knife. His face falls.

"All right, I'll leave. But first..."

Liam takes a step closer to me and pulls me into an embrace. What is he doing? He's kissing my lips. Tahira's lips. Her body freezes.

Perhaps Liam interprets my hesitation as permission to keep kissing me. His kiss is passionate and full of emotions that are dead to me. But Tahira's body is aroused. No. Her mind would *not* agree with her body, and neither does mine. This is *not* happening.

I shove hard with both my hands.

He stumbles and barely misses tripping on the doorstep.

"Tahira. I…"

"Just. *Go.*"

Finally, Liam turns and leaves. His retreat is slow. Defeated, he heads back toward his delivery truck. He must have gone to extreme lengths to get both the vehicle *and* the uniform in order to sneak into Las Colinas. What a nut.

He's left the box he was carrying discarded by the doorstep. I give it a satisfying kick and close the door firmly behind me.

My lips are still tingling. Tahira's body is *not* letting me override its feelings. The body and the mind, connected yet separate. Especially for me…

Tahira liked to exercise, maybe that will help. I drop to the hardwood floor and start doing push-ups. The increased blood flow and small spike in dopamine do wonders.

My breathing is heavier from the exertion, but when I get back to my feet I feel much better. Can't I catch a break? First days in a new body are already disorienting, and that's *without* an ex-lover throwing themselves at me.

A quick glance at a clock makes my stomach sink. I have less than five hours to find someone to act as chaperone for my video chat. Deval hasn't texted me since earlier. I doubt I'm off the hook for finding a chaperone. Tahira probably hasn't been in this situation before. Would it be the end of the world if I skipped the conference? I *do* have to convince Deval to marry me sooner though. I'd have liked a day to at least gather my thoughts, but when do I ever get what I want?

Tahira's phone starts vibrating in her pocket.

It's Gary.

I've been trying to get a hold of him for the past hour. Why am I anxious to answer?

Of all the people in this world, Gary is the one man who knows me… Tahira…the best. Certainly, he knew her the longest.

Still…this is what I was made for…I can do this.

"Hello, Gary."

"Tahira. Why have you been calling me? I thought after our last conversation you made it very clear you didn't need me in your life anymore."

"I let Maria go after the funeral and need someone to chaperone a video chat with Deval."

"I'm in D.C., Tahira, I told you that's where I would be yesterday."

Damn.

Gary exhales on the other line, but it's not a frustrated sigh.

"Have you tried calling Steffany? I know you two don't spend much time together anymore, but I know she's in town. I had lunch with her dad on Sunday."

Who is Steffany? With Gary on the line, I quickly scroll through Tahira's contacts. There' s only one number saved under the name *Steffany Roberts*.

"You think Steffany would come?"

"I'd give her a call."

"Okay. Thanks, Gary."

"Take care of yourself, Tahira. I'm sorry we…"

Gary doesn't finish his sentence. What was he going to say sorry for?

"I have to go now, Tahira. Good luck with things."

"You too. Goodbye, Gary."

Our call ends, and I immediately start contemplating what I'll say to Steffany. I open up Tahira's most used social media app and search for Steffany Roberts' profile. She looks to be about Tahira's age. Once I go back far enough there are even posts of Steffany and Tahira in photos together. They look like they used to go to college together. Maybe they were roommates?

Gary's recommendation is kind of my only option. If I'm successful tonight in convincing Deval to move the date of our wedding it may be the last time I have to worry about finding a chaperone to call him. I cross Tahira's fingers.

Steffany answers on the first ring.

"Tahira! Hey! It's about damn time you called! How are you? I've seen the news. You must be going crazy!"

"Uh…ha-ha, hey, Steffany."

Who did I just call? Steffany has way too much energy. Maybe this was a bad idea…

"I heard about your mom too. I'm so sorry."

"Yeah. It was her time. I'm okay by the way. But um…I have a favor to ask."

"Anything! Your long lost Steff is in town for the whole week. What's up?"

Why is she so eager? Can I trust this woman?

"I need someone to sit in with me on a call tonight. Sort of like a chaperone."

"Oooh! You're calling him, *aren't you? Deval Kapoor? I heard on the news you guys are…well, is it really an arranged marriage?"*

"It's complicated."

"Let's un*complicate it, okay girl? What time do you need me? I can be over in fifteen minutes."*

"Not till five."

"Awesuuuum! See you then, girlfriend!"

I hang up and feel…relief?

Tahira's body mostly just feels even more exhausted now. Can I blame it? My body has been through more trauma, physical and emotional, the last twenty-four hours than most people deal with in their entire lives.

Now what? I've got about two hours to kill.

A nap might be nice…

I make an effort to get comfortable as I stretch out on a couch in the living room. Something feels off. Something is always off. No matter how many times I move pillows or change the angle of my body. Another curse of being Divest…

I set an alarm on her phone to wake me up in two hours.

The doorbell rings loudly.

I nearly fall off the couch.

Why didn't the alarm wake me? I touch Tahira's phone to silence the annoying beeping; it's a quarter to five. I must have slept longer and deeper than I expected.

Through the narrow glass panes that line the door frame, there's an outline of a woman who's either wearing a beach ball on her head or has a killer afro. Who…? Ah, right. Steffany.

She's cupping her hand between her face and the glass. She must spot me because she starts waving a second later.

I blink my groggy eyes a few times to clear the floaties and I make my way toward the front door.

She's dressed in a stylish gray power suit and her black heels are at least five inches tall. Thanks to the help from her heels, she's about Tahira's same height. But her cherry blonde afro gives Steffany the appearance of being taller.

Her skin is pale compared to mine, and a detailed tattoo covers most of her right arm.

Steffany wastes no time standing at the door.

She throws her arms around me in a tight embrace while squealing. "Tahira! Tahira!"

Just before I'm about to suffocate, Steffany releases me from her hug and extends her hand toward me. I pause before I hesitantly take Steffany's hand and shake it. She frowns.

"Uh…what the hell, Tahira? You too cool now for our super secret hand-shake? Ha-ha."

"Er…"

Shit. What's my excuse? Is she going to bring up an inside joke next?

Steffany takes my face in her hands and looks deep into my eyes.

"You have no idea how much I've missed you, girlfriend. It's been too long."

I nod. "It *has* been a long time. It's great to see you."

Steffany beams at me and I grunt as she gives me another tight hug. That was close.

Once she releases me, I invite Steffany to sit down inside. She makes a beeline for a recliner, crosses her legs, and waits expectantly for me.

I take a seat across from her and smile weakly. This is awkward.

"Soooo? What. Is. *Up?*"

"Just check the news."

"I don't believe half of what they're saying about you, Tahira. I want you to know that. But tell me, are you *really* getting married to…you know…an Indian? An actual foreigner?"

"I'm actually going to see if he's willing to move our wedding date to the end of May. So…yeah."

"You aren't nervous or anything? I mean, an arranged marriage…do you even know him that well?"

I shrug.

"What's he like? I mean the media makes him out to seem like…well, you know…"

How *does* the media portray Tahira's betrothed? I can only imagine…

"Well, he's nice, he's smart, he's into cars."

"Oh come on, Tahira. You're describing your two-year-old, make-believe nephew, not your *fiancé*. Real talk with me, girl. Obviously he's handsome, for a foreigner, but knowing you, there's got to be more to this equation than just a kickass ass."

My cheeks get warm all of a sudden. Why am I blushing? This is ridiculous. What would Tahira say?

"He sees the world the same way I do." Yes. That sounds right. Kind of like the conversations Tahira and I had at her lake house and when we were cooking dinner together. Before they took us.

"Who knew an Indian equalist would also turn out to be an idealist." Steffany winks at me.

Equalist. That's the second time I've heard someone call Deval an equalist. Equalists are supposed to share a lot in common with communists. Is this just anti-foreigner propaganda, or is there truth to Deval's political inclinations? Either way, I've never been confident talking politics. Divest or not. I need to change the subject.

"What about you, Steff? What's new with you?"

Steffany throws her head back dramatically.

"What *isn't* new with me? I'm running my own agency in New York now. Technically Dad is funding it…at least until we get a few more clients. You don't need international scandal insurance, do you?"

Steffany interprets my confusion as mock offense and she laughs it off.

"Kidding, Tahira. For real though, when was the last time you looked at your insurance needs?"

I laugh with Steffany, which proves harder than normal. I'm not a bad actress; I simulate emotions that aren't my own all the time. Why is laughter so hard for me? Is it because it didn't come easily for Tahira? Did I ever see her actually laugh? Yes. The last night when we were cooking together…

The television mounted above the fireplace suddenly turns on. In bright text, it warns there's an incoming call from *Deval Kapoor*.

"Oooooh!" Steffany squeals in obvious delight. "What should I do?"

"You can just stay sitting there. I think Deval's mother just wants to know someone else is here with me."

"I wonder what the most inappropriate thing two engaged people could do over a video chat would be…"

I grin. Tahira would think that was funny too, right? I answer the incoming call with a wave of Tahira's hand, and Deval's smiling face fills the screen.

16 16 16 16 16 16 16
16 16 16 16 16 16 16
16 16 16 16 16 16 16
16 16 16 16 16 16 16
16 16 16 16 16 **16** 16

"Hi, Tahira."

"Hey, Dev."

"Heyyyy," Steffany waves.

"This is Steffany." I gesture toward the woman. "She's a friend."

"Pleasure to meet you, Steffany."

Steffany just smiles and nods at the television.

"How have you been?" Deval's attention is back on me. Is he looking at me skeptically? No. I'm fine. Everything's fine. There's no reason to worry. He can't see beneath my flesh. No one ever has.

"I'm fine."

"You don't look *fine. I mean, you look ravishing as always, but…"*

Deval's right. My clothes are wrinkled, and my hair is matted in a few places. Plus, Tahira's makeup is likely smeared all over my face.

"I uh…just woke up from a nap." Deval frowns but doesn't press the issue.

"You should be happy to know I spoke with Samar and Kabir today. They received the final drafts from the board. Everything looks good on your end. Do you have any other questions? Concerns?"

Samar? Kabir? What was on my end? It's got to have something to do with the merger. But I could be wrong, so I just nod like I know what Deval's talking about. As Divest, the phrase *"fake it till you make it"* has taken on a whole new meaning for me.

"What did you think about the post-merger sales projections?"

Er…

"They looked fine to me. No questions here." I smile and Deval visibly relaxes. Was he worried what my reaction would be? Did I respond how Tahira would have? How come I didn't notice how tense he was before?

Without further mention of the merger, Deval proceeds to tell me about his day. I just listen intently and smile every once in a while.

As usual, Deval doesn't seem to expect me…or Tahira…to volunteer her own, unprompted dialogue. Is the topic of Mehar's death specifically being avoided? Perhaps Deval is trying to distract Tahira from the pain he must assume I'm feeling. Which is fine by me. Faking someone else's feelings of loss is tricky. Grief and love, the two worst emotions for Divest.

Deval seems to be running out of things to say; I almost feel sorry for him. He spins a pen in his fingers like he's thinking of what else to talk about. Now's my chance. I can do this. I'm Divest.

"Deval, I'd like to talk with you about something."

"Of course." Deval's eyebrows betray mild surprise. *"What is it?"*

"With my mother gone, and Gary, and Maria, I feel like I don't have much reason to stay here. So…I was wondering if…well…."

Do I sound awkward and anxious enough? I need to inspire sympathy. People are easier to manipulate if they're sympathetic.

"You feel alone. Don't you?" Deval's frown is filled with the compassion I was hoping to elicit. That was easy.

I nod. "All I have to look forward to is being with you. There's nothing for me here in California. Just an empty house."

"I can fly you out tomorrow. Just say the word."

Deval's tone is so soft. So earnest. He really does care about Tahira. He sits forward in his seat, attentive, concerned. Like getting closer to the screen somehow gets him closer to Tahira. Deval's emotions are real. Genuine.

"Well, actually, I was thinking…what if we got married sooner than July? Like…before the end of this month? I just don't see any reason to wait any longer…with my mother gone. It would mean the world to me, Dev."

Deval opens his mouth to speak, but before he can say anything he cocks his head to the side. Someone else is speaking. But too softly for me to hear. Deval sits back in his chair and scratches his head absentmindedly. Whoever else is with him has his attention. Deval holds up a finger toward the screen before getting up and exiting the frame.

I glance at Steffany, who's holding both her hands up with her fingers crossed. Thanks for the support, Steff.

Finally, after less than a minute of waiting, Deval returns to his seat in front of the camera.

Deval winks at me as soon as he sits down.

"Well, I won't lie, Tahira. I'm a little surprised you'd want to move our wedding date. So is Mother. It won't be easy…but as long as the merger continues smoothly, which we have no reason to believe it won't…then we can make something work. You really want to get married sooner?"

"I do. I want to start my new life with you. I have nothing left here."

Deval nods.

"WorldFuse has done its part, so really there's just the matter of making sure you aren't stopped at the border, but I'm not too worried about that. I can fly you out here within the week unless you want to take your jet?"

I have a jet?

"Uh…either way is fine."

"Okay. We can work out logistics by the end of the week."

I force another smile.

"I have some meetings I need to get ready for, but it was a pleasure, Tahira. As always."

"Goodbye, Deval…I mean, Dev." Deval waves goodbye to me, no blowing kisses this time, then signs off.

I should be relieved. I did what my handlers wanted. I'm one step closer to finishing my mission. All I feel is dread.

"Okay, I take it back. Maybe he has a great personality or whatever, but girl, whatever your motivations are, I'd marry him *just* for his looks."

Deval *is* good looking, but I can honestly admit I have zero attraction to the man. I have to kill him, after all. Steffany, on the other hand…

Tahira's fiancé is just another target. Another unfortunate victim in my mission to save Jeremy and get my real body back. Should I fail in killing Deval, I'll succeed in killing Jeremy by default.

"…my new address."

I glance up from my feet at Steffany. She's looking at me expectantly. What was she just saying?

She leans forward in her seat and cocks her head. "Well? Are you?"

"Am I what?"

"Going to invite me to your wedding."

"Oh uh…"

Steffany is silently nodding. Her eyes are wide too. Invite her to my wedding? Um…

"Sure, Steff."

Steffany launches herself from her seat and tackles me. "Oh snap! This is going to be awesome! I'm so excited!"

I pat her back while she squeezes me in her embrace.

"So, where are you getting married exactly?"

"Oh, don't you know?"

"The media has no idea, and you didn't send me an invite over social media, so…"

"Bengaluru."

"Damn. And you're not scared you'll be in danger over there?"

I shake my head. I'll *be* a danger—not *in* danger.

"Well keep me posted. Have you invited anyone else to your wedding?"

Not. A. Clue.

Knowing Tahira as much as I do, I doubt she invited anyone. Her friends are mostly just names and pictures on social media. Even the ones she invited to her home when I was Maria were more like acquaintances than actual friends. I don't have a good answer for Steffany, so I just shrug in reply.

"Is that a no or a maybe?"

"Mostly a no."

"Tahira…I'm just gonna come out and say it…you've *changed*, girl. You're definitely not the same person I knew a year ago."

You could say that again—*girl*. Of course, however Tahira's changed, it has nothing to do with me. I'm just mimicking the personality she had before she died.

"I just don't get it. I mean, you've been through a lot with your mother dying but…the Tahira I knew didn't even like the *idea* of marriage, let alone an arranged marriage."

I purse my lips and remain silent. Tahira wouldn't have bothered to reply. I don't know all of Tahira's motivations, but I *do* know she was confident in her decisions. She didn't care to explain herself to others either.

"Not to mention, the old Tahira would've invited me to her wedding. The only reason I even knew you were getting married at all was thanks to a suit and tie on the morning news."

"I'm sorry, Steff. You're right. I haven't been myself. It's taken me time to sort through some feelings, and I haven't known who to trust with the decisions I'm making. I even let Gary go."

"You fired Gary? Can you even do that? Wasn't he like your…godfather or something? I mean, I know you're sort of Hindu, but Gary was like family. Wasn't he?"

Bringing up Gary was a mistake. These are parts of Tahira's old life that I don't understand yet.

"I'm sorry about your mom, Tahira, really I am. But this is why people have friends. I get that we have separate lives now, but I want you to remember I'm here for you. That's the point I'm trying to make."

I nod and smile in a grateful sort of way. Steffany beams back at me and stands up to give me another hug. Steffany sure likes hugs.

"I'm serious about wanting to be at your wedding though. Text me the details when you and the dream machine work things out, okay?"

"You got it, Steff."

"Good. I've got a date tonight, otherwise I'd stay longer. Dad set me up with one of his client's daughters. Not really looking forward to it, but seeing as my dad is my only investor at the moment…"

"Have fun, Steff." We stand and walk together to the front doors.

"We should hang though before you leave. I'll have to throw you a bachelorette party before you go. I doubt India can match my skills in that arena."

I laugh and try not to scoff. I don't care what Tahira would do, a bachelorette party is *not* mission critical.

We exchange one more hug, and Steffany skips down the steps toward her car. She hops into a bright red convertible that almost matches her hair. I wave goodbye as she gets in and drives away.

I breathe a sigh of relief, and Tahira's phone vibrates in my back pocket. I pull it out to see who's texted her.

Report.

My handlers probably saw Steffany come and go through the Collins' outdoor cameras and want to know the purpose of her visit.

I text back a short reply.

Had to find chaperone for video conf with Kapoor. Wedding date will be accelerated. Waiting to hear back from Kapoor on details.

No further texts come back.

Now what?

My body is telling me it's hungry, but I don't have the motivation to answer. I find myself wandering back up to the second floor into Tahira's room.

Everything is silent. Empty. A fitting atmosphere for how I feel.

I have a dull headache coming on, like a pressure right behind my forehead, well...Tahira's forehead. After a cursory search of Tahira's room, I can't find anything to take for my head pain. Tahira wasn't one for drugs. Maybe Mehar's room might have something. The carpet feels like quicksand, though, and I can't muster the motivation to make the trek down the hall.

I just want to relax. How long has it been since I've had time to myself? What did I do in my real body to unwind? Throw on some sweats? Watch a show? Listen to some music? Get Jeremy to give me a massage...?

What does it matter? None of that will help me now. The itch never goes away. Divest can't get comfortable—ever.

Somehow, I've ended up in Tahira's bathroom.

It's about as big as a normal-sized bedroom, with a shower *and* a full bath that looks more like a Jacuzzi.

Jill Thomas's apartment had a small tub. I used it once, didn't I? Yeah... will a bath have the same effect in Tahira's body?

It's worth a shot.

I walk over to the tub and start filling it with hot water. As soon as the bath is half full, I strip down until I'm naked. I dip Tahira's right foot in up to her knee. The water's hot but not so hot that I need to wait for it to cool.

I slip into the bath and stretch my legs. I dunk my head a couple times, which helps clear my mind and dull my headache. I avoid looking at myself...I mean...at Tahira's body, as much as possible. It's nearly as bad as seeing myself in a mirror...

I soak until the water stops feeling warm. The plug makes a sharp sucking noise when I start draining the water. I grab a nearby towel and wrap it around Tahira's body. Dripping water, I search her closet for a pair of pajamas.

I settle on the first pair of sweatpants and soft T-shirt I can find. A grotesque demon lunges toward me from the T-shirt beneath the word *Metallica*. Tahira was a hard metal fan? I still have so much more to learn about her. I've made it this far though. I also had success speaking with Deval, but it's only been the first day. I still have a long way to go.

Tahira's silky sheets feel cool to her skin as I crawl under. My body melts into the mattress. I figure Tahira's phone will wake me up in the morning.

Frogs take up a croaking chorus outside Tahira's window.

I toss from side to side.

The sounds and images of Tahira's murder are still fresh in my memory. Closing my eyes just makes it worse.

"Are you sure you don't want to keep using her after this mission? Do you remember how hard it was to find someone like her? Do you remember how many subjects failed? The chances of replacing McKenzie are remote at best. She's too perfect to let go."

"*I know how rare a person like Alex McKenzie is, but I've already promised her this will be the last time we expect her to do anything for us. I'm a man of my word. Besides, Powell assures me her brain is continuing to deteriorate. This will be her last mission whether we want it to be or not.*"

"So much for being a man of your word then, Director. You promised we'd give her old life back to her when we were through. Based on the state she's in, will you be able to make good on *any* promises?"

"*Powell is developing a way to stabilize her temporarily. At least until she kills Deval. After that, Powell is confident putting her brain back in her own body will correct whatever is happening to her now.*"

"I still think we should find a way to keep using her. She's too perfect. Too good at what she does. Look how easily she convinced Deval to move the date of the wedding."

"No. You saw how she reacted before and after the last transfer. She's becoming unreliable. Aside from the issues with her brain, her emotions are getting in the way. We try to push her too much, and she may be unusable even for this mission. Why do you think I had you send the message from her husband?"

"To remind her what's at stake."

"Exactly."

"So this really is her last mission."

"Yes. With everything we've made her endure, she deserves what we've promised her. I don't particularly want her to suffer more than she already has."

"Is that compassion, Director?"

"Compassion is our purpose, is it not? Humanity must move forward. Evolve. Advance. Find liberation through struggle. Natural and...forced. Alex is no exception. She deserves to be liberated as well."

"You surprise me, Director. You have such great vision, and yet you still care about one woman. A woman who's nothing more than a weapon, no more than..."

"You best watch yourself, Haight. Where Alex is concerned...you will speak of her with as much respect as the Struggle itself."

"My apologies. I understand, Director."

"No. I don't think you do."

Tahira's phone goes off at 6 AM. My hand fumbles in the dark to try and snooze it, but I can't reach far enough. Instead, I half roll, half tumble out of the sheets and sit up far enough to turn off the buzzing alarm. Even after I turn it off, I'm still left with a faint ringing in my ears.

Why did I get up so early? I check the time again. Oh yeah. This is usually the time of day Tahira goes for a run. Do I bother continuing this routine? It's not like anyone would notice if I do or not. Then again, it's been a long time since I've gone running for the fun of it. Or exercised at all for that matter. Maria didn't have time for exercise.

Maybe this would be good for me...mentally.

I remove Tahira's pajamas and pull on a sports bra I find in her closet. I don some running tights and select a pair of bright green Nikes.

I'm curious just how far I can push this body, so I also find one of Tahira's smart-watches to wear around her left wrist.

Tahira was right-handed, like me.

Tahira's Bluetooth earbuds rest on her desk, but I leave them behind. I'd rather take in all of my…Tahira's…senses, while I run.

Once I leave the house, I start jogging uphill.

The air is already hot and humid even though the sun isn't quite up yet.

Tahira's body doesn't break a sweat until about fifteen minutes into my run. I feel good. There isn't the typical nagging discomfort I normally feel as Divest either.

Running and baths. The only two ways to relax.

I glance at Tahira's smart-watch when I'm about halfway to the top of the hill. The small digital screen tells me Tahira's heart rate is around 150 beats per minute. Not bad for how fast I'm going and how hard my lungs are working.

It's a relief to be back in a younger, healthier body.

What a sick thought…have I really become this insensitive?

The top of the hill rewards me with a breathtaking view. White-tipped waves pulse against the shore where the homes and buildings end. Though Las Colinas is still quite a ways inland, I'm high enough to see the ocean extend all the way toward the horizon where it meets the gray morning sky.

There are no homes up here to interrupt the view. Low, white clouds roll in from the ocean. The sun kisses the back of Tahira's neck. I breathe deeply.

Slowly, an unnerving feeling begins to creep across my skin. I…I've been here before. Tahira's body probably has of course, but…this is something else.

This hilltop reminds me of the precipice. That space between consciousness and nothingness when I'm forced into someone else's body.

So much for enjoying a cathartic experience. Now—I feel like throwing up.

When I finally make it back to the Collins house, Tahira's body is sweaty and needs a shower.

After I've showered, I dress in a typical Tahira outfit. Tight-fitting jeans with frayed seams and a modern, button-up shirt.

I return to the kitchen and make myself some eggs and turkey bacon. I down a protein shake as well.

Okay. I have work to do.

My handlers' tablet still rests on the floor of the dining room. I pick it up and find a spot on a couch in the larger of the two living rooms.

Can I maybe discover why Steffany thinks Tahira has changed? It'd have to be something in the last year of her life.

As usual, the resources at my disposal are limited. But I try to open a search for Tahira Collins using Tahira's phone.

Everything is blocked. Should I be surprised?

My handlers have probably installed some kind of means of blocking my ability to search for things on the internet. I'm restricted to what they've given me on the tablet.

I start with the info on Tahira beginning after she graduated from Stanford University with her international relations degree. Apparently, she enrolled in a masters program online with UCLA. There are no details on her intended masters program, only that she withdrew after a month of classes. At about the same time as total border shutdowns officially went into effect.

My research takes me into the evening; I go without stopping until Tahira's eyes begin to burn. The blue screen of the tablet has started giving me a migraine—on top of my normal headache. I set the tablet aside and squeeze my eyes shut, trying to give them a short respite. Maybe I should turn on some lights...

Crash!

My eyes snap open.

What the hell? Was that glass breaking...?

The noise came from upstairs. I strain to listen for anything else.

Nothing. The Collins home is deathly silent.

Am I going crazy?

Muffled footsteps cross the floor above me.

Nope. I'm not crazy and I'm not alone.

Would Liam break into the Collins home to see Tahira? It's certainly not Gary. My handlers are definitely out of the question too. If they wanted to, they could just order me to let them in through the front door. No one else has access to the Collins home…so whoever is upstairs has to be an intruder.

What should I do?

The steps above begin moving from room to room. Why didn't the alarm go off? I've broken into a fair number of homes myself without tripping the alarms…but that took great skill.

I can't just sit here. I should do something. Either hide or prepare to defend myself.

What would Tahira do?

I walk quickly and silently across the living room floor and down the short hallway that leads to a storage closet. The door creaks as I inch it open. I wince at the sound. The footsteps above me immediately stop. They definitely heard me.

I enter the closet and shut the door behind me. Darkness wraps around me like a heavy blanket. I strain Tahira's ears for any sign of the intruder's movements.

Silence.

Perhaps the intruder didn't know someone else was here. Maybe it was just a burglar and when they heard the closet door they got spooked and fled?

Wood creaks beneath more footsteps from above. They're heading for the staircase. This is no burglar. They're searching for me…

Maybe I'm about to be murdered. This certainly won't be the first time my life has been in danger since becoming Divest.

If someone really is here to kill me, should I even bother stopping them? Death would mean freedom. Though, theoretically, as long as my handlers can get to my brain quickly enough, I can probably survive almost anything. But do I want to put that theory to the test tonight?

Even if I *could* die, I can't imagine my handlers would just let Jeremy go if I allowed myself to die during a mission.

Dammit…

Tahira's tight jeans make it difficult to remove her phone from her back pocket. I move especially slow in the cramped closet where any number of cleaning items could be knocked over.

I pull up the app that matches the logo I've seen on the Collins' perimeter security cameras. Yes! Tahira's phone has access to the security cameras and I can select options like controlling the lights. That might come in handy…

There are two cameras inside the home itself. The only two views are the primary living room adjacent to the kitchen and the large entryway. My breath catches as a dark silhouette makes its way across the living room. It's too dark to make out much detail, but whoever is in Tahira's house is definitely carrying a gun.

Tahira's body panics. My body is telling me to run. To flee. To get as far away as possible. Her skin gets clammy, and sweat begins to bead on Tahira's forehead. Great—I do *not* need a flight response right now.

I fight Tahira's body as best I can, trying to calm her nerves. How is this even possible? The brain controls flight or fight responses. Doesn't it?

The intruder crosses the living room heading right for the hallway. Not good.

Using Tahira's phone, I turn on the lights of a guest room upstairs. Yellow light floods over the balcony and down into the living room. The intruder freezes; they're stalled just at the edge of the camera view. One more step and they would've exited the frame.

I hold my breath until the intruder quickly retreats back up the stairs, running at nearly a full sprint. It's a male intruder. He's wearing dark clothing, and his face is masked. The gun he's carrying is a semi-automatic pistol. Possibly even a smart-gun.

The old home is such that the wood creaks whenever the intruder moves, which gives me a good idea where they're at all times. They make it to the second floor, and the light in the guest room goes out. Darkness returns to the house.

My fingers dance as I send a text to my handlers. They've told me only to contact them in extreme emergencies. I think sharing an empty home with an armed intruder qualifies. Will they come to my aid? What if they don't… then what? Would Tahira call the police?

No.

That's out of the question.

My handlers have expressly forbidden me from ever contacting any government entities. Especially military or law enforcement. If my handlers don't come, I'm on my own. Hopefully the intruder has some sense of self-preservation and decides to leave on their own.

There are no cameras in any of the individual bedrooms except Tahira's, but I can't access that camera's feed without my handlers' tablet. All I can do is follow the faint sound of the intruder's footsteps.

I wait for what seems like forever.

Finally, the footsteps retreat to the edge of the home, and silence ensues.

For good measure, I wait another ten minutes. My handlers still haven't responded. What did I expect? They aren't sending help. I'm just a disposable asset to them…

I check the perimeter security cameras on Tahira's phone. There's no sign of the intruder so I slowly open the door to my hiding place, still careful to avoid making a sound.

The house is bathed in both darkness and silence. I shiver. Why do I feel like…?

Something hits me in Tahira's gut.

I gasp and double over. A deep grunt precedes a second blow, which lands on my back. My knees buckle, and I collapse onto the hardwood floor. The air in my lungs disappears.

I roll over just in time to see a large man towering over me with a gun trained directly at my chest. The barrel is long. Tipped with a silencer.

I freeze.

Shoot me. Please.

Only he doesn't.

He takes a step closer. Then another. He's in no hurry…

The man holds his weapon in both hands with perfect technique. He's wearing gloves and a mask. A necklace dangles just below his collar and catches a tiny amount of light. The silver symbol is just like Tahira's bracelet. The one she wore to her mother's funeral. Only…no…this man's necklace is different. The symbol looks like two arrows pushed together.

"Indian filth."

The intruder's voice is low and harsh.

Tahira's body flinches involuntarily as the man takes another half-step closer.

I almost welcome my murder.

But no…

If he shoots me, there's a strong chance I won't die, and Tahira's body may become unusable. If that happens my mission would be forfeit. Jeremy would pay for my failure. As much as I want to escape this world, I have to survive.

He hasn't pulled the trigger yet. Why is he hesitating? Maybe if I can get him talking…

"Please." My voice belongs to a frightened young woman. "What do you want?"

My eyes meet his for just a moment before I look away again. I have to look afraid. Weak.

"I seek Truth. Truth for humanity."

Uh…say what? Truth?

What does that even mean? It probably doesn't mean anything because I'm talking to a man who's *insane*.

An unpredictable man with a gun is far more dangerous than someone who's sane. This is bad. What if I offer him something…?

"I can give you money. I can even give you a car. I won't call the cops."

"Shut up!"

He takes a step toward me, and I scramble back until he levels the gun at my head. Staring into the barrel of his gun nearly hypnotizes me. It'd be so easy. It'd all be over. But Jeremy…

"I'm going to kill you." The man's voice is as steady as his arm. I don't doubt he means what he says.

"Why? I haven't done anything to you."

"Because!" He growls. "Unitas is death to humanity. Only through the Struggle will we survive. Only through blood and sacrifice can we be liberated. You walk the Path. You want peace. You want unity. So you must die…for the greater good of your brothers and sisters."

That does it. This man is one hundred percent insane. Perhaps my plan to appeal to his humanity was a mistake.

I slowly withdraw Tahira's phone from my back pocket. The man doesn't even notice. I pray I remember the right order of swipes…

"Struggle is life. Unity…is death." The man's eyes are like two gaping holes behind the slits of his mask. I might as well be staring into a double-barreled shotgun. I've seen the look he's giving me many times in the faces of others. It's the look of a person who's about to commit murder. *My* murder…

"Goodbye, Miss Collins."

Lights flood the living room. The gun fires, but the shot goes wide. The assailant stumbles, blinking. Now's my chance.

My ears are ringing as I leap from the ground and tackle the man, shoving him back until he crashes into the nearest wall.

He grunts as I force his skull backward. There's a sharp crack as his head connects with brick. Dazed, the man bellows and tries swinging a fist at me. I dodge and use the man's momentum to pull him forward, bringing his face smashing into my knee with a satisfying crunch. The man stumbles away and levels his pistol at me again. How the hell did he manage to hold onto it? There's too much space between us. I should've made sure he dropped it. I'm a fool.

I dodge to the left just before the gun goes off and land behind a small coffee table. I kick the table into the man's shins. He grunts, and I manage to get back on my feet before he can take aim at me again. Tahira's slender hands grip his gun arm and try to wrest the weapon free. He's strong. Stronger than Tahira. I wish I had my real body.

The man wraps his free arm around my neck and cuts off my breathing.

I twist my hips and elbow him in his gut. He releases me but immediately grabs a fistful of Tahira's hair and pulls hard. I cry out as the man yanks my head away from him.

Taking advantage of the opening, I kick the man hard in his groin.

He let's go of my hair and drops to his knees. I follow up with a round-house kick to his right temple. His gun goes flying as my foot connects with his head, and I quickly retrieve the weapon. When I come up with the gun, his form is prone and unmoving on the ground.

My body is coursing with adrenaline, and Tahira's senses are still hyper…
sensitive.

The man appears to be out cold, but I kick him in the ribs just to be sure.
Then, I force myself to breathe. Short inhale. Long exhale.

Tahira's back aches where the man hit me, and my scalp is burning where
he pulled her hair. Ignoring the pain, I quickly move to the storage closet I
used as a hiding place and retrieve a roll of duct tape. When I return to the
living room, I pull the intruder's limp arms behind his back and bind his wrists
together with the duct tape. I wrap his feet together too for good measure.
Finally, I slip the black mask off his bloody face.

The man has a short beard and mustache. His skin is far whiter than
Tahira's. The ends of a tattoo creep up his neck.

I don't recognize his face. Perhaps my handlers will.

Keeping one eye on the intruder, I locate Tahira's phone. The screen is
cracked a little, but it still works when I turn it on.

I text my handlers and explain my situation. Surely they'll respond
this time.

After twenty seconds, they text back.

Team en route. Do not engage further.

Great. As usual, I do all the hard work while my handlers sit back and
watch. At least they're coming…

How long will it take before my handlers' men arrive?

The man coughs blood and opens his eyes wildly. His gaze rests on me,
and he glares, straining against his bonds.

I squat down low so he can hear me whisper. Gone is the persona of a
scared girl who minutes ago was about to become a murder victim. Now, my
voice is cold and full of the malice I feel in my soul.

"Who are you, and why did you come here to kill me?"

The man turns his head to look at me.

Saliva mixed with blood drips from the end of his wicked grin.

"We have a situation."

"*What now?*"

"A man broke into the Collins home. He attempted to kill her."

"*I'm surprised it took this long, especially considering the things they're saying about Collins in the media. Is she all right?*"

"Yes. I'll also have you know, per your strict orders to keep her alive, I broke protocol and dispatched a team. As always, however, she managed to handle things on her own. She's detained the intruder by herself. My team should be there within ten minutes to clean up."

"*You're lucky she wasn't harmed. I'd have your head is she were.*"

"Yes, Director."

"*I thought we had video surveillance. How did someone get through without us knowing?*"

"Must have come from a neighboring Las Colinas property, or possibly from the south. Video surveillance isn't as concentrated there because of the steep hillside."

"*I don't care how it happened; just ensure nothing like it happens again.*"

"Yes, Director."

"Our agent in Bengaluru reports Kapoor is arranging plans for a new wedding date. Alex will need to be prepared."

"When are we going to start feeding her information on Unitas?"

"We won't be."

"What? Won't she need that kind of information? Tahira Collins knew about the Path and…"

"It won't matter. I know Alex. Even if she doesn't see the whole picture, she'll finish the mission."

"How can you be sure she won't learn things for herself? She might side with Unitas' perspective."

"That's why we're watching her, isn't it? Besides, Alex can't afford to choose sides. For all she knows, her life, her real body, and her husband are all on the line if she doesn't do what we say. Perhaps you can remind her of those things as well."

"Yes, Director. But why go back to threats?"

"She's too good at what we've trained her to do."

"What does that mean?"

"This mission, above all others, we have to remind her she's Alex McKenzie, not Tahira Collins."

"Understood."

"I hope you do."

"You'd better start talking, or you'll be in a lot more pain than you are right now."

My threat falls on disbelieving ears. The man looks like he's about to laugh at me. Except he's lying bound on the floor and I have his gun now. So he holds his tongue. Smart.

Can I even blame him for doubting the validity of my threat? Sure I was able to defend myself, and incapacitate him, but I'm still in the body of a young woman with polished fingernails. Take away the gun and I'm definitely the opposite of intimidating.

Then again, my appearance is probably what gave me an advantage in the first place. This man probably assumed he'd find a lone girl, incapable of defending herself. If those were his assumptions, only one of them was correct.

To emphasize my point, I give the man a good kick to his ribs. He grunts but remains stubbornly silent.

"Why are you here?!" My voice is dry. Hoarse.

The man chuckles, sending drops of blood across the carpet. "I've already told you."

"You've told me nothing."

All I get is a shrug in response.

"Tell me your name."

"My name is irrelevant. I'm Proelium, and you…you are on the verge of uniting a great many people. It will set humanity back years in its pursuit for liberation. For this reason, you must be stopped."

"Enough with the truth and liberation crap. I've done nothing to harm you or anyone else. *Why. Are. You. Here*?"

The man spits more blood and laughs darkly.

"Your plans to marry the Indian devil and unite companies will damage the entire world."

"How do you know about the merger?"

The man grins. "Unity is death. Struggle is life. Unitas must not succeed."

"What are you talking about? What's Unitas? What's Pro…lium?"

The man scowls darkly. "Your lies do not fool me."

I frown and raise an eyebrow. He thinks I'm lying?

"You…how can you not know…? Your father, he…"

"I know nothing about Unitas or this…Proelium. So start talking, or I'll put a bullet in you."

"I've faced the Struggle all my life. Kill me if you wish."

"Who said anything about killing you?"

With a precision shot, I put a round in the man's lower right calf.

The sound of the bullet is only half as loud as the man's scream. He buries his head in the already bloodsoaked carpet. Oops. Did I go too far? I need him sharp enough to interrogate…

To his credit, he manages to bite his tongue through the pain and inclines his head just long enough to bare his teeth. A muscle in his neck spasms.

"Tell me why you came!"

Blood drips from his wounded leg, but I still get no response.

I point my weapon at the man again and finally elicit a reply.

"The Proelium!" His voice is shrill. Have I finally broken him? "It's an ancient order, an even older belief. Humanity can only progress through war!"

More riddles?

Before I can open my mouth the man screams out again.

"Liberation through bloodshed. Suffering. Pain. Death. The Struggle. It's why *you* must die! Your Path, your precious Unitas, all in direct opposition to the Truth. Only the Struggle can be allowed to endure. Unity is death to humanity."

"None of your shit makes sense!" This man still isn't giving me a straight answer. "My mother was Hindu, that's *it*. I'm not mixed up in any ancient...orders."

"You can lie with your words, but your actions cannot. You walk your Path. Just like your father."

I frown. At the lake house...didn't Tahira mention something about a Path?

A door slams.

Six black-clad mercenaries fill the living room. Most are carrying automatic rifles. The only man not carrying a drawn weapon approaches me while the rest of the men surround my captive.

The empty-handed mercenary finally takes his eyes off me and glances down at my silent captive.

"Director wants him alive. Take him to the van."

The other five mercenaries heave the bleeding intruder off the ground. I catch a glimpse of his face as he's lifted from the ground. His eyes are wide, confused. He starts yelling obscenities as he's hauled away. Once they disappear down a hallway his cries are cut short.

I'm left standing alone with the lone mercenary who appears to have been the team leader. His eyes meet mine, and he slowly removes his black face mask. His strong jaw isn't one I've seen before. He's clean shaven and looks to be in his mid-to-late thirties. His eyes drift slowly down Tahira's body. I shiver in spite of myself. Why is he looking at me like that?

He points somewhere below my waist.

"How bad does it hurt?"

What the hell does he mean? I glance down at myself to where he's pointing. A large blood stain spreads slowly down my...Tahira's...right leg.

The pain hits me like a train. My body stumbles as my brain reels from the signals it's receiving. I'm fine. I've taken bullets before. It's not that bad. Tahira's body disagrees with me.

The mercenary grabs me by Tahira's arm and keeps me from falling. The man slowly, and gently, helps me find a place on a nearby couch for me to lie down.

"Looks like the bullet went through clean." The mercenary's deep, commanding voice sounds vaguely familiar. Maybe I *have* seen him before? "There's an entry and exit point. You're lucky."

Lucky is the *last* word in any language I would ever use to describe myself, but I don't have the motivation to retort. Is this a new low for me? Do I really not consider myself lucky for having survived my attempted murder?

Suddenly, the mercenary pulls out a wicked-looking knife from one of his combat boots. For a split second, my face is reflected in the side of the blade. I look like a mess. My eyes are wide and bloodshot. My black hair is in complete disarray. No. Not *my* hair. It's *not* me!

I grip the man's wrist and lock my elbow to keep his blade away. The mercenary reaches behind himself and removes a small pistol. I can't react fast enough as...he places the gun next to my shoulder on the couch?

What's he doing? I must not be thinking straight. I *am* a little light-headed, but I seize the gun and train it right between the man's eyes. He doesn't even blink.

"I promise I won't hurt you." The mercenary's voice is softer now.

His cold brown eyes seem to be telling the truth. He's still holding the knife, but his other hand is raised toward me palm out.

I keep my gun trained on him while he slowly moves his knife down toward Tahira's leg.

Tahira's gun wound is still oozing blood. My jeans are soaked in red.

There's pressure from the mercenary's knife against Tahira's leg, but no additional pain.

"Did he say why he wanted to kill you?"

I give the mercenary a sharp glance. He keeps working. Should I be truthful with this man?

"No. Nothing he said made sense."

"What *did* he say?"

"Like I said. Nothing that made any sense. Ancient religions. Paths. Salvation. Et cetera. If you'd like, I'm sure I could help you find a website on the stuff. While we're at it, we could learn more about the Kennedy assassination, how New Russia is actually being governed by a family of vampires, and why all the first Mars colonists *really* died."

The mercenary makes no comment. Was it foolish of me to be so sarcastic? Especially when he's holding a knife? But so what if he hurts me? It was satisfying to shut him up.

The man proceeds to pull the tight denim away from my skin and cut a horizontal line a few inches above my wound. Next, he cuts vertically down my pant leg.

Two blackish-red holes mark where the bullet entered and exited Tahira's leg. They're less than three inches apart on the very top of my leg. Each has blood seeping out in slow but steady streams.

Moving slowly, the mercenary reaches behind himself and removes a small black bag from his belt.

"I'm going to bind your wound. If you feel more comfortable having a gun on me while I do so, then by all means, but again—I promise I won't hurt you."

I don't trust this man. Why hasn't he harmed me yet? What's he playing at? He's certainly not helping me out of the goodness of his heart. These men don't have hearts. Yes, he's been gentle with me so far. I might even be tempted to use the word kind, but they're all beyond feelings. Beyond kindness. Beyond mercy.

He's just trying to manipulate me.

After a few moments of watching the dark-haired mercenary work on Tahira's leg, I slowly lower my weapon. I resist the urge to shout when he pours some kind of antiseptic on my wound. I also have to bite my tongue when he loops a bandage under and over Tahira's thigh. Finally, with his messy work completed, the mercenary presses a small gun with a syringe for a barrel against Tahira's thigh, right in between the two bullet wounds. I breathe in sharply as the injection shoots into my leg.

"That will help with the pain. It should also stimulate cellular regeneration so you heal much faster."

I will *not* thank this man.

The mercenary probably doesn't even expect me to thank him. Without another word he quickly packs up his gear. The man stands and touches his ear. Someone must be speaking with him through an unseen earpiece.

I try to sit up when the man turns to leave, but he stops me by gently pushing me back down on the couch.

"Stay here for at least another hour. That should be sufficient time for the healing agent to do its work. Don't put too much weight on that leg for the next day or two either."

I still refuse to offer this man any thanks. I scowl at him as he retreats down the hallway his comrades went carrying my...and now their...captive.

Just before the mercenary leaves my sight he calls back to me.

"Keep the gun! Just in case."

What gun...?

Tahira's hands clutch the smart-gun in my lap. Its weight is so familiar... A wave of nausea rolls through me and I toss the weapon onto the ground.

The mercenary's white bandages seem to be doing their job stopping the bleeding. There's also a marked difference in my overall level of pain. Tahira's leg still hurts, but the signals are dull, less consuming. I've got small cuts and bruises in several places from my brief fight with the intruder. And of course, my head still throbs, but that's not exactly new.

All things considered, I've had worse nights. Haven't I?

I stare up at the two-story ceiling and sigh deeply. Tahira's chest rises and falls with each breath I take. The faint sounds of tires on gravel breaks the immediate silence.

Now that I'm alone, I let myself cry.

My sadness sounds just like Tahira's...before she died.

An hour later, I'm still lying on the couch when Tahira's phone goes off. I reach for it on the coffee table; one of the mercenaries must have put it there for me. I'm careful not to move my injured leg too much.

Deval's text is a short one, and I scan through it once before going back and slowly rereading it over again.

Now 9:45 P.M.

I've spoken with Mother. As long as you're confident this is what you want, May 20th will work. I know that's not the earliest but it's still much sooner than we'd first planned. We can arrange everything over the next few days.

I don't bother responding. I will tomorrow. For now, I copy Deval's message and forward it to my handlers so they can start making plans of their own.

I've put in my hour of rest, so I get up and limp my way to the stairs and up to Tahira's bedroom. I strip, which takes more time with a damaged leg, and don't even bother finding pajamas to sleep in.

The sheets cool Tahira's inflamed skin. I wipe a few remaining tears from my eyes and stare out the window.

I quickly find myself falling into blissful oblivion. Is it the drugs I've been given? Or the exhaustion this body feels? Or both?

Why can't darkness keep me folded in its embrace? Is remaining in darkness really preferable to the coming of the morning? Yes. If it means I'm going to spend another day in Tahira Collins' body…

19

"Interrogation didn't give us much. But he was a member of Proelium."

"Proelium? One of ours?"

"No. He was a lone believer. Not very active, or vocal for that matter. Until the other night apparently."

"We were supposed to have the location of every Proelium member. How did we miss this man?"

"I'm still looking into it, Director."

"How did he know Tahira Collins was Unitas?"

"We ran a background check, and it's possible he used to work for her father, John. In the early days of WorldFuse."

"Is it possible this man is the one who killed her father?"

"It's extremely unlikely."

"Hmm…Did he give you anything else?"

"No, we uh…may have gone too far."

"Dammit, Haight…"

"I'll forward you the recordings of the interrogation before his body couldn't take anymore. Maybe you can make sense of something we didn't."

"Fine. And Haight?"

"Yes, Director?"

"How is she?"

"Mild gun wound to her right thigh. Nothing she can't walk off."

"That's not what I was asking."

"I don't have a solid answer. Ask her yourself."

"That's your job. Are you telling me you're having trouble doing what you've been asked to do?"

"I know that's my job. I'm just curious when caring about her became yours."

"We've already had this conversation."

"She's fine. She's handled worse trauma than this before."

"She better be fine. Her physical and mental well-being are both vital to this mission, Haight. Don't forget what's at stake."

"Yes, Director."

<>

I set aside my protein shake when someone knocks at the front doors. A sharply dressed young man from the crematorium hands me an urn made from a simple gray stone. Mehar Collins' remains. I set the urn respectfully next to John Collins' and leave to finish Tahira's morning routine.

<>

We had to book a new photographer. Also a new reception venue. But otherwise, everything is back on schedule.

I'm sorry for creating so much extra work for everyone Dev. But I want you to know I'm excited to be leaving for

India soon.

I'm glad. I know we haven't had much time to chat lately, I've been so busy. But when you get to India. We should have plenty of time to spend together.

Can't wait

Can I really keep playing the part of a concerned fiancé? How much longer can I apologize for any inconveniences I've caused while also acting excited anytime the mention of our union is brought up? Why doesn't Deval go into too much detail with our wedding plans? Is he sparing my feelings? Does he not want Tahira feeling bad for changing plans on everyone? How is this is going to set off relationships with the in-laws…?

At least we haven't had any more video conferences.

May 20th? You sure? Enforcers won't let me re-cross the border unless it's all official. Besides, this Border Travel Visa is going to cost me my half of next quarters commission. Haha!

I thought you said your dad was paying for everything Steff :)

He is. I just wanted you to know how much of a sacrifice it will be to support you and how much I freaking love you girl.

Better be careful your new gf doesn't catch you talking

Meh. Gentri can take a chill pill.
I love her, but you know how relationships
can be sometimes.

Haha, sure Steff.

Steffany isn't my friend. She's not.

Then why is it so easy to pretend like she is?

Is it stupid of me to feel glad that there will be a familiar face besides Deval's with me in India? No. That's all it will be. A familiar face. Not a friend. Just someone I know already…

I exhale heavily and dip into kapotasana. I hold the pose for several moments before releasing and returning to lotus position.

Sweat drips from Tahira's brow into my eyes and I wipe it away with a small towel. The courtyard is eerily silent today. Even the birds seem quieter than usual. Without bothering to shower or change yet, I reenter the Collins home and find a place on a couch next to my handlers' tablet. The screen comes to life when I pick it up and I resume my studies.

Where did I leave off last time? The gods and goddesses. *Vishnu, Shiva, Durga,* and *Brahma.* The list goes on and on. How many are there? Will I be expected to know all of them?

Why do my handlers bother to mention the theological overlap between Hinduism and other religions? I just have to study Hinduism, don't I? Maybe it's because Hinduism isn't so much organized religion as it is a way of life? There are so many sub-sects and diverse beliefs that there doesn't seem to be any one specific way of believing or living one's faith. Jeremy would love learning about this stuff…

No. Stay focus. I need to memorize these things.

Dharma, along with *Kama* and *Artha,* describe the three central pursuits of Hinduism that ideally bring one to *Moksha*—liberation of the spirit.

Each pursuit has its own ambitions, its own…objectives.

Do Hindus truly believe that death is merely the beginning of another life? Possibly even in a different form? All living things have souls? *Atmans*? Would I be an exception?

When someone dies, that person's spirit may be reborn into a new existence. What would one's life be like believing in something like reincarnation? To have multiple lives, over and over with no guarantee of an end?

Will I be expected to know all of their sacred traditions? Rituals? It might be good to learn at least a few. Right? Maybe throw in some *mantras* too?

I manage to fit most of Tahira's clothes, including shoes, into three large suitcases to take with me to India.

After loading everything into the back of Tahira's car, I lock the home automatically using her phone. With a backpack of essentials slung over my back, I tow my carry-on suitcase toward the detached garage. I climb into Tahira's R8 and start the car with a word. Tires screech as I peel out of the Collins property.

Even with an electric motor, the powerful engine roars like a lion as I manually cruise through the streets on the way to Tahira's semi-private airstrip.

The sun is directly above me in the cloudless sky when I finally arrive. There's an unguarded gate that requires a code. I enter the seven-digit password provided via Tahira's phone via her biometrics via me having her actual body.

I park my car in an empty stall as a large twin-engine jet begins pulling out of an even larger metal hangar onto the runway. I grab my backpack from the seat next to me and power down Tahira's car with a simple voice command.

Humid heat greets me as I step out onto the black tarmac. The jet has come to a stop about a hundred feet away from me. A door opens on its side, where a set of stairs unfolds. Large red letters spell out *WorldFuse* along the right side of the plane.

"Good afternoon, ma'am. We can help you with your bags."

I jump.

Two white men in red uniforms appear out of nowhere. They smile politely.

"Oh, uh…yes, please." I pop the trunk to Tahira's car and the men start taking her bags out.

"You can go on ahead ma'am. We can handle this."

I nod curtly and begin walking. I flick Tahira's sunglasses up once I reach the steps to the plane.

"Welcome, Miss Collins. May I take your suitcase for you?"

I glance up at a crisply dressed flight attendant. The woman's uniform matches the red color of the WorldFuse logo. Her red lipstick smile makes me smile back. I hand her the suitcase I've been half carrying half rolling behind me.

She beckons for me to hand her my backpack too. Her skin is pale but she has quite a few freckles. The stewardess pushes a strand of her short blonde hair out of her left eye, and I hesitate.

Is it the movement? The color? It's like…my *own* hair. Not Tahira's silky black mane…my *real* hair.

"Er…Miss Collins?" The woman raises an eyebrow, so I quickly hand her my backpack to draw attention away from my staring.

"Do you remember me?" She flashes me another of her smiles. "I was your stewardess last summer when you flew to WorldFuse headquarters."

"Yes!" I beam back. "Forgive me if I can't remember your name…"

"I'm, Jen. And I wouldn't expect you to remember. It's a pleasure to serve you again, Miss Collins."

Though Tahira's gun wound has mostly healed, my right leg is still tender as I slowly limp up the steps into the plane. If Jen notices my awkward gait, she doesn't say anything.

The inside of the plane is just as hot as outside, but there's a cooler air current through some vents, which I hope means Tahira's body won't be dying of heat for much longer. I need to stop. Can't I go a whole day without a morbid or even *insensitive* thought? I allow Jen to direct me toward the back of the plane.

This plane is much more spacious than the one that brought me to California. There are several seating options, but I end up collapsing on a black, leather couch. Am I starting to have a thing for plane couches?

The palm trees that line the runway slowly start moving backward outside my window as we roll down the tarmac.

I close my eyes during takeoff. The change in altitude exacerbates the migraine I've had since 6:00 A.M.

Five minutes later, Jen comes back to ask if I'd like anything to eat or drink. She catches me massaging Tahira's temples, and the look on my face probably tells her more about how I'm feeling than words could.

I break character for just a second. "Yeah, can I get pretzels and some fentanyl?"

Jen gives me a sympathetic frown. "I know it's not my place—but I think what you're doing is really…exemplary. Our world needs more people like you, Miss Collins. People willing to work together with others."

Maybe I can interrogate Jen too. She may be able to tell me more about the implications of my…Tahira's…wedding.

"Thanks, Jen. But sometimes I don't really see how my actions will really help anyone."

"I think your example is just what people need nowadays. Since the Terror Strikes and the border shutdowns, people have become far less…forgiving. Less unified. My grandmother told me that when she was a little girl, the world used to be so open. Countries traded with each other, and helped each other in times of need. They gave freely of their knowledge and resources to struggling countries. There wasn't so much…division…in the world."

I never had a grandparent to tell me such stories, but Jen is telling the truth. The world was a very different place eighty years ago. Back when globalization was still a thing. Before the strikes. Before the shutdowns.

"I appreciate your support, Jen. It means a lot."

Jen smiles and looks like she's about to say something more, but she hesitates.

Perhaps she feels bad for speaking to me about my personal life, because Jen quickly turns and retreats back to her corner of the plane. So much for getting useful information out of her.

Surprisingly, she returns less than a minute later.

"Pretzels." Jen brandishes a bag of the salty snacks.

She hands me the pretzels, and I thank her. I expect her to leave me alone again, but instead she sits down next to me on my couch.

"Your doctor told me I wasn't allowed to give you anything if you asked for it *but…*" Jen takes my hand in hers and drops three small M&M-sized pills into my palm. She puts her right index finger up to her lips and gives me a small wink.

My doctor told Jen I couldn't take anything for pain?

Who…?

Powell.

I may be left to my own devices, but my handlers are always behind the scenes. Manipulating and scheming from afar.

"It's just an over-the-counter medication, but they *are* extra strength. Hopefully that helps."

Honestly, I'd hug Jen right now…but that'd be unbecoming of Tahira Collins. So I don't.

She hands me a bottled water that feels cool to Tahira's hand. I swallow all three pills in a single gulp. Does my first act of true rebellion in a long time really boil down to taking three small drugs? Pathetic…but just the fact that I'm able to do something rebellious without my handlers knowing feels almost as good as I imagine it'd feel to bury my fist in Powell's face.

Jen's drugs do wonders, and I'm finally able to close my eyes and sleep.

When I open my eyes again, a pilot announces we're less than an hour away from Kempegowda Airport. How long was I out? God that felt good. I should see if Jen can slip me some more of those pills…

I slide open a window and get a breathtaking view of a massive city. Lights stretch for what must be hundreds of miles. A pale sliver of moon shines through a few clouds.

Landing is uneventful.

I barely register disembarking. Men dressed in crisp suits usher me into a black SUV. Doesn't someone need to scan my passport and verify my biometrics? I don't pay attention enough to care if they do or not.

Despite the rest I got, Tahira's body begins to feel extremely sluggish. Maybe it's jet-lag. The sky should be completely dark here, but there's so much light pollution it's hard to tell what time it should be just by looking at the sky.

As we drive, I try to pay attention to my surroundings. The buildings that tower over the streets of Bengaluru are a mix of solar glass, concrete, and stone. Some structures look like they were built yesterday. Others, decades ago. The Hindi on the signs and buildings we pass looks less like writing and more like artwork. It's beautiful.

Despite the hour, there are still quite a few people out. At one point, we drive through a busy market. Are people pointing at me? The glass is tinted, there's no way they can know who's inside.

Eventually we arrive at a large, brightly lit hotel. Someone opens my door when we come to a stop. I feel like a zombie as I step out of the car onto the pavement.

Deval is supposed to be busy tonight. I don't think I could handle meeting him or his family in the state I'm in. An actual bed sounds so nice right now. Tahira's body is begging me for a break. Maybe my nap on the plane wasn't as nice as I thought…

Thanks to being rich, Deval has put me up in the presidential sweet, although my hotel guide is calling it something different. Something in Hindi.

When we reach the top, the hotel employee walks me down a short hall, opens my door, and turns on a light for me.

"Can I get you anything else, Miss Collins?" The man's accent is much thicker than Deval's.

I shake my head and hand him a few brightly colored bills from Tahira's wallet. It's not my money, and I'm sure wherever Tahira's soul is now, her money isn't doing her any good anyway.

The Indian man closes the doors behind me, and I stumble my way toward the master bedroom. I don't even bother changing clothes before I fall face first onto the bed.

I emerge from a black fog. Slowly at first, then my vision snaps into focus. A handsome, dark-skinned man with curly brown hair sits in a chair across from my bed. Black cords wrap around the man, securing him to the chair. He has an expression of horror on his otherwise beautiful features. I glance down at myself. My trembling hands are clutching a gun. What's going on? The hands…they're my real hands. Not Tahira's. My skin is lighter. I have a scar across my left forearm. I'm *me…*

I'm back in my own body. My *actual* body. How is this possible?

I have less than a second to wonder what's going on before I raise the gun and aim it right at Deval Kapoor's heart. My body is my own, but it's acting on its own accord. I can't stop myself as my grip tightens on the gun…then I pull the trigger.

The shot takes Deval in the chest, and his body shudders violently from the impact. There's movement out of the corner of my eye. A mirror hangs on the wall three feet away from Deval. Tahira Collins' reflection greets me. She has her arms outstretched just like my own, and she's holding the exact same gun I am. This isn't real. It can't be real. What's happening?!

My reflection is Tahira's. But I'm wearing my real body. My arms and hands are my own. The strand of sandy blonde hair over my left eye is my own.

But the mirror tells another story.

I'm still in Tahira's body.

This is the mirror's fault. It's causing my mind to play tricks on me. There's no other explanation. But how did I get here? And why can I not make my body do what I want?

Against my will, my arms rise once more as Deval coughs blood. The gun weighs a ton. Kapoor looks at me with terrible pain in his eyes. The pain isn't just physical, it's more than that. I've betrayed him. I've broken him. Killing him is the least of it.

The gun is aimed right at his head. I scream without making a sound as I pull the trigger again.

Somehow, time slows down, and before the bullet crashes through Deval's brain, his face shifts.

His skin becomes lighter. His hair becomes the color of golden sand. His brown eyes become the color of a clear blue sky.

I…I know those eyes. More intimately than anyone else in the world.

Jeremy smiles at me as I scream with renewed horror. I'm helpless to stop the bullet that destroys him.

20

"I've reviewed the footage myself. It's unclear exactly what she was given, but the stewardess likely just gave McKenzie some mild pain relievers. We found an open bottle of pills after we retrieved our surveillance equipment from the plane."

"What does Powell think?"

"Powell says non-prescription pain relievers shouldn't negatively affect her. But he reminded me that inserting an unplanned variable can have unknown consequences in any experiment."

"Kill the stewardess."

"Is that all?"

"You tell me."

"McKenzie has reported that everything's a go."

"Good. Now that she's in India, I want more frequent updates. I want to know how she's performing and if her status changes at all. Understood?"

"Yes, Director."

"Our agent in Hong Kong has managed to confirm the enemy still believes the murders of their Brothers and Sisters have been unrelated."

"I'd expect nothing less. I've always known Powell's research could be used for our purposes. What Alex McKenzie is capable of may just be the tip of the iceberg."

"Indeed. I'll admit I was hesitant when you proposed the idea of recruiting Powell, but you've more than proved your worth to the Proelium. And humanity itself."

"Struggle is life."

"Unity is death."

Sweat pours down my face. Some of it drips on the rubber treadmill track and gets swept away beneath my feet.

Why the hell did I have a dream last night? It was so vivid. So real. But it *wasn't* real. Just my twisted imagination.

The clock on the treadmill tells me it's 5:37 A.M.; I've made Tahira's body run over two miles already. The dreamlike memory of watching my bullet rip through Jeremy's head still haunts me as I jog along the plastic track of the treadmill. My head definitely aches less now as I touch the treadmill screen to help slow my pace, but my mind is still racing.

It was just a dream. I haven't killed Deval…yet, and I sure as hell haven't killed Jeremy. I'd never do that. I'd kill myself before I let that happen.

But his face…Jeremy was so calm. So accepting of the bullet that ended his life in my dream. Whereas Deval looked truly horrified. What does it all mean? Why would I start having dreams now? Maybe the jet lag has something to do with it? Or those pills Jen gave me? A cold fear clutches my heart. What if Powell has commanded me not to take medications for reasons other than vindictiveness?

I wipe away my sweat with a rough white towel and step off the treadmill. My headaches had better not return for at least a couple of hours. I exit the silent hotel gym to find an elevator.

On my way out, a tall muscular man walks down the hall toward me. He's the first white man I've seen since leaving California. He's wearing a tank top and short shorts and looks to be on his way to the gym. He's looking at his phone and barely glances at me as we pass. He does a double take, however, and stops. Damn.

I keep walking.

"Hey." His accent hints at British. "You're Tahira Collins, right?"

He's not really asking. He knows who I am.

Am I really this recognizable?

Ignoring him, I hasten my walk to the elevator.

"Hey, wait up! I didn't mean to startle you."

I push the elevator button ten times. Come on, come on.

"I'm actually a huge fan." I can feel the man standing behind my left shoulder. "How long have you been in India?"

I push the button with the up arrow two more times.

"My name is Paul."

I should have just taken the stairs.

"Look, I'm sorry if I'm bothering you. But you can at least…"

I turn and force myself not to glare at Paul. I'm in no mood to play the part of a rich and famous bride happy to give out autographs and chat with anyone who recognizes me. If it wasn't for my dream last night, maybe I'd be in a better mood.

"Wow. Pictures sure don't do you justice. If you don't mind me saying so."

I probably look like I just rolled out of bed and went for a run, which is exactly how my morning has gone. Paul is either kidding himself or is totally blind. Still, he's looking at me like I'm the first woman he's ever seen.

What would Tahira do in a situation like this?

Paul holds up his phone. "Do you think I could get a quick photo with you?"

"For sure." I smile.

I stand next to Paul, the top of Tahira's head only reaches his shoulder. He leans forward slightly, holding his phone out with his left hand to take our picture. I do my best to give his camera a genuine smile. I also throw in a thumbs up. Maybe that'll compensate for my weak smile.

"Wow! My girlfriend is going to freak. It's such a pleasure to meet you in person."

I try to match Paul's wide grin, but I can barely make the corners of Tahira's mouth move in the right direction. Is Paul's girlfriend is going "to freak" because her boyfriend met *the* Tahira Collins? Or because Paul's right hand was dangerously close to Tahira's backside?

"If you're ever in England…" Paul somehow produces a business card from the back of his phone and hands it to me.

I smile without reading the card. Paul waves goodbye as he turns and heads back in the direction of the gym.

As soon as he disappears around a corner, the stupid elevator finally arrives. Typical.

Once I make it back to my room, I shower, pick at the room service food, and get dressed.

The outfit I've selected is a safe choice. Both formal and stylish, consisting of a pair of tight-fitting gray pants, a white shirt, and bright blue blazer.

It's not like I have too many clothing options anyway. Most of my luggage is supposed to be waiting for me at the home Deval and I will be sharing once we're married.

I'm supposed to meet Deval sometime this afternoon. He's apparently in business meetings all morning, but the rest of the day he's scheduled to be with me…I mean, Tahira.

Meeting Deval for the first time will be the true test of my skills as Divest. Besides Gary Ryan, and perhaps Tahira's ex-lover Liam, Deval Kapoor is the only other person in this world who knows Tahira Collins in an intimate, personal way. I have to convince him I'm the person whose body I'm wearing. Of course, people believe their eyes more than any of their other senses. This has always given me a *huge* advantage being Divest. I can fool anyone. Even the husband of a woman he's been married to for ten years. Just because of the fact that I can slip into her body.

Fooling Deval Kapoor, who has never met Tahira in person should be simple. Easy. No sweat.

Why am I trying so hard to convince myself?

Once I'm fully dressed, I return to the bathroom and do Tahira's hair and makeup the way she usually did when she was alive.

After checking the time, I pack up my meager belongings and wheel my luggage down the hallway toward the elevator. I have the entire floor to myself, so I don't worry about running into any more Pauls, at least until I leave the temporary refuge of my hotel floor.

The elevator doors open on the fifth floor. I glance up from reviewing the Kapoor family intel on Tahira's phone. A stout cleaning lady starts to wheel a cleaning cart into the elevator. Then the small Indian lady sees me. Her eyes go wide. Again? Really? Does everyone know me?

"Oh. *Maaf kijiye.* I'm s…sorry, ma'am. *Maaf keejiyega.*"

"It's no problem; there's plenty of room." I stand to the side of the elevator to make room for the cart.

"No…no, you go ahead, ma'am. *Krpya. Dhanyavad.* Good day."

Before I can protest, the doors slide shut, and I continue to the main floor of the hotel alone.

As soon as the elevator doors part, my stomach drops. I need a baseball cap. Or a pair of dark sunglasses. Something. Maybe if I move quickly no one will stop me…?

Deval said there'd be a car waiting for me outside. I just have to get outside and…

Someone touches my elbow as I'm halfway to the revolving doors.

"Tahira?"

I turn.

Deval Abdul Kapoor is at least four inches taller than Tahira. His hair actually looks much darker in person, but just as curly. He's wearing a dark suit, a pocket square, but no tie. His modern, collarless white shirt is unbuttoned at the top. His dark brown eyes start at my feet and move upward until they meet my own. His face lights up.

He takes one long stride toward me and embraces me.

I freeze. Deval holds me close, and my arms just hang limp.

I remain frozen. Stunned.

After a second or two longer he pulls away, holding me at arm's length while he stares at me.

"Sorry for surprising you." Deval's playful smile is so familiar and so foreign at the same time.

What's wrong with me? Do something. Say something!

Deval's brown eyes capture me. I can't speak. Can't move. He looks just like he did in my dream. Right before I shot him, just before Deval's face was replaced by Jeremy's…

Deval's smile fades a little.

"I know we weren't supposed to see each other until later. But I managed to get away from a meeting early and came straight here. I thought it would be nice to see you before…"

Forcing the image of Deval's bloodsoaked abdomen from my mind takes more effort than it should. It's like pushing the weight of a car all by myself.

I brush Tahira's long black hair behind her left ear and finally force a smile. I can do this. I've been trained for this.

"I'm sorry, Dev. You just startled me is all."

I force myself to look sheepish. Nervous. Like a first date.

Tahira would be surprised at Deval's sudden appearance too. But I try to act *pleasantly* surprised instead of…*un*pleasantly surprised? How do I really feel about my current situation? Awkward? Squeamish? Unbalanced?

Especially after my dream last night. The timing could not have been worse.

"You look amazing." Deval's smile returns in an instant. A slight chill runs down Tahira's spine as Deval moves his fingers down my arm to take my hand.

I shrug and blink Tahira's eyes a few times in response to the compliment. Nope. That was a little too girly for Tahira. I'm already botching this. Deval doesn't notice anything, however.

"You're not wearing your ring?"

I glance down at my left hand. Shit.

"Uh…I was just thinking it might make me more recognizable. I didn't want people stopping me…"

Deval laughs.

"Don't worry, Tahira. Believe me, I don't blame you for wanting to go unnoticed. Besides, you know you don't have to feel obligated to wear it. Right?"

I give Deval a shy smile and set a mental reminder to wear Tahira's ring more often, at least around Deval. Or maybe I won't. He just said I'm not obligated. Dammit. Now I'm confused.

"Have you had something to eat?"

I shake my head.

Deval's eyes light up again.

"I mean…yes. I ordered some room service. Before…"

"…before the fiancé you've never met scared you in the middle of a hotel lobby?"

Deval's grin comes so easily to him when he's around me.

I laugh lightly and cover Tahira's mouth with my hand. The rare occasions Tahira actually laughed around Deval she would always cover her mouth. As if she were embarrassed to be showing emotion.

I can do this. I've had a rough start, but I can do this.

I can be Tahira Collins.

"I really do apologize if I startled you, Tahira. If you want, I can find a taxi and you can take my car?"

I laugh. It comes a little easier this time, not as forced.

"No way, Dev. I've been on my own for too long. I wasn't expecting to see you till later, but I'm glad you surprised me."

This is the first time either of us have met in person, but Tahira's body, combined with my version of her personality, is definitely having an effect on Deval. He's totally enraptured. So far, he hasn't taken his eyes off me once. It'd be a little unnerving if I wasn't engaged to him. Right?

No. It's still unnerving.

"Can I take your bag?" Deval points toward my suitcase.

"Yes, please."

Deval smiles for the hundredth time and extends his elbow toward me, just like Jeremy used to whenever we went for walks together. I wrap my arm around Deval's and follow him out of the hotel.

As soon as I step out of the revolving doors, Tahira's senses are immediately assaulted by sights, sounds, and smells totally foreign to her body. People throng the streets. Most are carrying all kinds of things over their shoulders, stacked on electric mopeds, or piled high on hand-drawn carts. Dozens of sidewalk vendors are selling everything from street food to on-the-go plastic surgery. I'm positive some of the things being sold are illegal in the United States. I swear I can smell ginsemal in the air too. That is *definitely* illegal stateside. The streets look like utter chaos but at the same time there seems to be an underlying order to everything.

Deval tugs on Tahira's arm, which breaks me from my stupor.

People have started to look and point in our direction. Phones appear, and both mine and Deval's names roll through the crowd like a wave.

Like a stone breaking through a river current, a large black sedan pulls up alongside the curb. It's difficult to move. People begin pressing up against me; some are speaking English, but others are speaking in Hindi. I'm sweating. My heart rate rises and I wrap my arms around myself almost instinctively. What's wrong with me today? I need to get a grip...

Deval guides me forward until we reach the side of the car, and he ushers me inside. He hands my suitcase off to a man in a black suit before climbing into the seat next to me.

Once the door shuts, the sounds of the street disappear.

"Sorry about that." Deval flashes me a sheepish grin. "For the most part, my countrymen are excited you're here. I was just hoping we wouldn't be so...conspicuous."

Tahira would probably take this as an opportunity to either tease or complain. I decide to tease.

"What's the matter, Dev? Afraid to officially be seen with me in public?"

Deval frowns and gives me a look I can't interpret. Was teasing the wrong response? Did I offend him?

"I'm just afraid they'll crop me out of the tabloid photos because of how stunning *you* are," Deval teases back.

I could throw up right now. Jeremy and I were never this...sappy. Not even during our honeymoon.

I jump a little when a car door slams shut.

"Take us to the Queen."

The Queen? Deval can't mean an *actual* queen, can he?

Our driver is the tall bald Indian who took my suitcase from Deval. He leans back in the driver's seat and nods. We pull away from the curb and enter the busy street.

"Er...so um...which queen are we going to meet?"

"The Queen of England of course. Well, sort of. The home we'll be living in used to belong to the British monarchy over two hundred fifty years ago. My family purchased it from the Indian government about fifteen years ago."

"Oh." How could I forget? Deval is loaded.

"It's old, but don't worry; we can remodel it however you'd like. You can even start planning now if you want, after I give you a tour, of course."

"Sounds fun."

Our driver slams on the brakes suddenly, and my seatbelt digs into my collarbone. A man yells something at our driver and stalks away, disappearing into the river of bodies flowing to our right. We almost hit him. There are so many people!

"*Band Kare.*" Deval sighs. "President Laghari has started lobbying to open our borders again. If he's successful, the population is expected to grow over three percent in one year alone. We might have to start our own Mars colonies before long."

I nod politely. Does he not know the American Mars Colonies all failed? At least Deval doesn't bring up anything sensitive like why we're marrying each other. If our parents were involved in a religious cult. The economic implications of merging the two companies we control. Or which side of the bed I want.

Deval treats me like I'm nothing more than an esteemed visitor. He's polite and respectful, but the flirting is gone. He hasn't touched me at all since the hotel either. Is it because of the presence of our driver? Or maybe Kapoor family marriage customs? Surely it's not a Hindu-specific tradition, right?

"We'll actually be staying outside of Bengaluru, close to a town called Randpur. It's about an hour outside the city. It should be a little more private too."

I refuse to wonder about all the things "privacy" could mean to Deval. Will my handlers make me wait very long to kill Deval after he marries Tahira? Before sex and the honeymoon would be preferable. Could I request that?

Shoot. It's been a while since I've had a truly morbid thought. I was doing so well...

"So...Tahira, now that you're here, I thought you might like to hear some of our city's history. Did you know as early as the ninth century Bengaluru was an established city? It's perhaps one of the oldest surviving cities in the world. An ancient *vira gallu,* or hero stone, makes first mention of the city. Of course, the Bengaluru we know today used to be called Bangalore. It's actually rather interesting. Many years ago, most of my country's cities adapted to more Anglican-sounding names. One thing you may come to find in Karnataka is…"

A vibrating sound cuts off Deval's lecture, thankfully, and he pulls out his phone from his suit pocket.

"*Namaste maataajee*…Tell them we'll be selling off some of the subsidiaries to fund the rebranding campaign…No…Yes…I'll handle that myself…Yes, I just picked her up and we're headed to the house now…Yes, that would be alright. *Dhanyavad.*"

I glance at him as he puts his phone back in his suit pocket.

"My mother."

I shift in my seat. It's okay if I show that I'm nervous to meet Sanji Ishranth Kapoor, right? Tahira would be, I think…

Meeting Jeremy's mother for the first time wasn't this daunting, but then again, she wasn't the driving force behind our marriage. Nor was she the original founder of a multi million-dollar company. How old was Sanji Kapoor when she started the company? Sixteen or seventeen?

Maybe I'm getting ahead of myself. We haven't even stopped driving yet, and I'm already thinking about the in-laws.

"She's not as scary as the media makes her out to be, you know."

"What do you mean?"

"My mother—Sanji. And just so you know, even though she's technically retired, I'm planning on giving her plenty to help with, for the merger *and* the wedding."

"Why's that?"

Deval shrugs. "Just to keep her busy. A little bit of Sanji can go a long way, believe me."

Does he usually talk about his mother so informally?

After a moment of silence, Deval continues his history lesson. I only half listen. I don't care how many times the government of India has undergone reformation or what city the newest Indian pop singer is from. I content myself with watching the trees outside Deval's window and nodding occasionally when he pauses in his narrative.

Eventually, the streets become less busy and our vehicle picks up speed. The colorful, somewhat dirty streets of downtown Bengaluru are soon replaced by rocky hills, grassy fields, and lush forest. The air is so much cleaner outside the city.

After about thirty more minutes of driving, we come upon a small town. The buildings look older than most of the structures back in Bengaluru, in a quaint sort of way, but there are signs of modern living all around. Solar panels cover most roofs. More than a dozen silent drones zip to and fro overhead. Many of them carry all kinds of things in their small metal arms. In the distance, beyond the town, there's a collection of sophisticated wind turbines. More advanced even than the ones the United States used before the shutdowns.

And the people, they look so…content. So different from the solemn, beaten faces of US citizens struggling through a national recession, the people on the other side of my window are smiling and enjoying themselves.

"I'm sure you're hungry for some lunch, right?"

I glance at Deval and nod.

"What sounds good to you?"

"Uh…Indian food?"

Deval laughs. "Really? You know we can get anything that sounds good to you. Not just Indian food."

"Phew. I mean I can handle the occasional plate of curry, but this California girl needs a juicy hamburger every once in a while."

"The meat might be different than what you're used to, but we can do hamburgers some time."

"Awesome."

We leave the main road that cuts through Randpur and take a narrow dirt path. In the distance lies a large one-story white mansion peaking over the tops of an expansive green hedge.

"The Queen's House." Deval gestures unnecessarily toward the home.

I'm able to get a better view by leaning forward in my seat.

"What do you think? I mean, the pictures I've sent you really don't do it justice, but…"

I pretend to be breathless for a moment as I stare out the window at the Queen's House. "I…I love it."

Except I don't. It's so ostentatious I can't imagine myself ever living in such a place. The home Jeremy and I had was far simpler, and far less…regal.

Deval seems pleased at my reaction. His eyes linger on me for a moment before looking away again.

A knot works its way tighter and tighter around my stomach.

"Take us around back, Faru."

We swing around the side of the large home and pass what looks like a small shrine…a *murti*. There's a stone statue of…*Ganesh*—or is it *Krishna*?

"I'll help you get settled. We can have lunch together, but I'm afraid I'll need to leave you sooner than I thought tonight. Something's come up at Jarrius that needs my attention."

The gravel beneath my feet crunches as I step out of the car. The air is hot. Nearly as suffocating as the smog-diseased cities of the eastern United States. A delicate red leaf drifts through the air, hypnotizing me before landing on the top of my foot.

"Shall we go inside?" I glance sharply at Deval. He gestures toward some concrete steps that lead up to a white set of doors.

I shiver despite the pressing heat.

Is this the place I'll kill Deval Kapoor? If so, he may as well have invited me into his still empty grave. I hold my breath as Deval leads me up the steps by Tahira's hand.

Lunch with Deval is everything Tahira could've hoped it would be, at least…that's how I act.

Deval has my new personal chef work up some thin crust pizzas for us. Deval apparently used to love going to New York when he was young. Before the borders closed.

"Chef Amar is amazing, don't get me wrong, but he's never been able to get the pizza dough to match the authentic New York flavor."

"It's the water. There are unique minerals they use in the dough."

"Interesting." Deval smiles and raises an eyebrow. "But you told me you'd never been to New York, right? How do you know about the water thing? Did you read about it somewhere?"

Shit.

That was me. Not Tahira.

I used to never pass up a chance to provide random facts during conversations. I need to get control of myself. No more character slip-ups.

"You're right. I think I just heard about the water-flavor phenomena on a podcast or something."

When our meal is through, Deval asks me if I'd still care for a quick tour.

"Sure." The moment I stand, a massive pain hits my skull like I've been kicked in the head.

I clutch the mahogany countertop to keep myself from falling on Tahira's face. Not again. Please not again. Not here.

I palm Tahira's forehead and close my eyes. The pain subsides as quickly as it came but leaves behind a dull migraine.

"Tahira, are you all right?"

I blink a few times and nod. "Yeah, I'm fine. Just stood up too fast, you know?"

Deval smiles. It's so easy to lie to him. He's so gullible. Or trusting. Is there a difference with me? Technically, the body he's in love with *is* fine, but the consciousness inside Tahira's body, *my* consciousness, is struggling not to scream.

"Well we've already seen the kitchen, why don't we start with the lounge?"

Deval takes us through nearly every room of the Queen's House. Even though the outside is rich and grand, the interior is lightly furnished, mostly with a lot of intricate rugs and square cushions for seats. Through it all, our chaperone Faru keeps a respectful distance but is always within earshot. At least Faru keeps me from having to react if Deval decides to get fresh with me.

When we arrive at the west end of the house, Deval opens two large wooden doors to reveal a massive master bedroom.

I take two steps inside before I stop altogether.

The chair.

The bed.

The carpet.

The mirror. Don't look at the mirror…

I've been here before.

No. Impossible.

I *haven't* been here before. What am I thinking? The bedroom looks so familiar though. It looks like—my dream.

But no…the comforter is a different color. So is the carpet. The chair has three legs instead of four. I'm just imagining things.

What's going on with my mind?

Tahira's skin is cold, but slick with sweat. Why are my hands trembling? I didn't look at the mirror! I'm okay. I didn't look. I didn't...

Deval is standing beside me talking about curtains or some nonsense, but all I can focus on is the chair. A chair like the one that held both Deval and Jeremy...before I killed them.

Don't look up. Don't look at the mirror. I can't look at Tahira. Myself... divested of my real body. No, no, no.

"Tahira, what's wrong? You look pale. Do you need to sit down again?

"I'm fine." I open my eyes and meet Deval's. I half expect a mass of blood to start pooling across his chest.

"Are you sure? Look, you're trembling. Are you not telling me something? Are you ill?"

"I'm fine." My teeth chatter a little, and I struggle to get control of my mind. Tahira's body.

Deval takes my arm, and I collapse into his chest. He's warm. So warm. So solid. He feels...

Just when my nausea feels like it will pass, I vomit all over Deval's feet.

"You're sure?"

"Yes. I don't want you to miss your meeting. I'm sorry I've made you late already."

"You really don't have to keep apologizing, Tahira. You sure you're feeling better?"

"Dev, I'm *fine*. Really."

Deval sighs. "Okay, I trust you. Can I get you anything else?"

I shake my head and raise my glass of...what did Dev call it? "I'm really okay, the drink is helping. The fresh air is good too. The shutdowns have made it a while since I've had so much jet-lag."

Deval smiles, leans toward me, and plants a quick kiss on Tahira's forehead.

"Call me if I can do anything for you, okay?"

"I will. Promise."

Finally, Deval departs and leaves me alone at my table. The umbrella's shade helps with the heat, and I continue sipping at my drink. A few brightly colored birds flit through the gardens, and I follow their path through the air. So free. So alive.

Stupid birds.

I take another sip of my drink. The carbonation is strong and tastes like limes.

God, I acted like such an idiot. That was so embarrassing, even for me. Deval's face…what was he thinking? Maybe I apologized too profusely? Throwing up on your betrothed the first day you meet him better not be some Hindu omen for seven years of bad luck or something.

At least my head doesn't hurt anymore.

Though, I won't be making myself throw up on purpose just to get a break from my migraines any time soon. Throwing up in someone else's body is *not* pleasant.

Thank *Brahma,* or whoever, I was able to convince Deval I didn't need a doctor. Next to breaking my handlers' orders or going to the authorities, seeing a doctor is absolutely forbidden. Too many questions might be asked. Or I might be given drugs that could interfere with Powell's experiment.

Was blaming everything on jet lag a good enough excuse?

Deval's genuine concern for me…I mean, Tahira…was surprising. Do arranged fiancés usually care about each other in that way? It was just like Jeremy used to take care of *me.* So selfless. His only priority was my own wellbeing. Even when I claimed I didn't want or need his help.

Jeremy always saw through my walls…

Was I acting too independent toward Deval? Too much like my real self? Maybe…but Tahira was independent too.

Tahira's phone vibrates in my hand.

Status?

They must know Deval left for his meeting. Do I tell about my dream? Or throwing up? No. If my handlers think I'm unfit to complete the mission, I might endanger my chances of getting Jeremy back. If I'm sick, they might get rid of me. I can't let that happen. I have to be strong for the life Jeremy and I can still have together.

I text back a quick summary of meeting Deval at the hotel and coming to the Queen's House, and I leave everything else out.

I set Tahira's phone aside on the table and sip at my drink.

A second later the phone vibrates again.

Confirm status?

I bite Tahira's lip. What more could they be expecting me to report? I told them everything they usually want to know. There's no way they can know about my dream, but there's a small chance they know about me throwing up on Deval if they've bugged the Queen's House. Should I just come clean?

Threw up. The pizza I ate for lunch didn't sit well with me. Feeling fine now.

I pause. Waiting to see if they'll buy it.

Fine. You are to keep us updated if your status changes.

Tahira's phone clatters against the glass as I toss it back onto the table. I exhale deeply and rest my head in Tahira's hands. Could this day get any...

"Huh. I thought you'd be whiter."

My eyes snap open. A young Indian girl wearing a brightly colored *sarang* appears by my side. How did I not hear her approach? Her head is tilted slightly to the left, and she's staring at me with big brown eyes. Something about the shape of her nose kind of reminds me of Deval. Her purple sandals match her long sleeve shirt.

"Uh, hello. What's your name?"

"Kaivalya Sadika Kapoor. And yours is Tahira Collins. You're my brother's girlfriend."

I laugh a little; for once it's not hard. She's kind of cute. Kaivalya Kapoor is the youngest Kapoor child. I probably know more about her than Tahira probably did, but I can't give that fact away.

"Actually, I'm his fiancée. We're getting married soon." I smile again.

"I know. You're the one he's been talking about non-stop for weeks."

"Really?"

"Yeah, and believe me, life is going to be easier for everyone once you two finally *do it*."

"Do it?"

"Yeah. *Do. It.* Get married, duh."

"Oh, phew."

"You're weird." Kaivalya scrunches her nose and puts her hands on her hips. So much sass in such a little container.

"Thanks, I try my hardest." Tahira can be sassy too.

It's possible I've earned Kaivalya's respect because a genuine smile flashes across her face before she goes back to pouting.

"I'm supposed to babysit you."

"Are you really? Aren't you a little young?"

"Please, lady. I'm ten—almost eleven."

I nod as sagely as I can. Kaivalya smiles again.

"Well, are you just going to sit around, or are we going to do something together? Deval keeps telling me you're going to be my sister soon, so…"

"Did you have something in mind, Kaivalya?"

"You don't have to say my whole name. Most people just call me Kai."

A taller version of Kaivalya steps out of the house behind her. "Because you're so short, Kai. If you weren't so short people might not have to shorten your name too."

Viti Kapoor is either fifteen or sixteen. Why can't I remember which? Her features are similar to her sister's but much more mature. Viti wears her hair up in a bun. Her black jeans contrast sharply with her modern white *sari*.

She smiles a greeting.

"My name is Viti. Seems you've already met my baby sister."

"You're the baby." Kaivalya sticks her lips out and frowns.

"Nice to meet you, Viti. I'm Tahira."

"Yeah, I know. I followed you on social media before Deval even knew you."

"I got here first, so Tahira has to spend time with me first, Viti."

Viti regards her little sister and shrugs.

"Do you play any sports?" Viti's voice is hopeful.

I rack my brain. Did Tahira play any sports? She did some intramurals in college, but was it for any particular sport?

I shrug. "I like to run."

"That's cool. I'm a soccer player."

"What position?"

"Defender."

She might as well be speaking Hindi for all I know about soccer. Time to change the subject...

"I'd challenge you to a one-on-one, but Kai's kind of been dying to meet you."

"Nuh uh!"

I laugh a little.

"I'll maybe see you later, Tahira. Welcome to India."

I wave goodbye to Viti as she retreats back the way she came.

"Come on, Tahira. Let's go!"

Kaivalya, or Kai as she keeps correcting me, takes my hand and leads me around the Queen's House gardens. While we walk together Kai tells me her birthday is the month after Deval and I are to be married. Her favorite color is black but sometimes it's purple too. Kai loves the flowers and small pools of the gardens and makes a point of telling me so. The grounds *are* beautiful. Peaceful too.

Kaivalya's hair bounces as she skips through the stone paths. If I weren't supposed to kill her only brother, would I be enjoying myself?

It's almost too much for even my hardened mind to handle. I've done some terrible things, but this mission is already taking a toll on me. Can I afford to develop relationships, false as they may be, with Deval's family and still do what my handlers want from me? Are they aware of what they're putting me through? Being this close, this intimate, with a family is a first for me...for Divest.

Why did it have to be Tahira Collins?

How many more values or morals do I have left to bury? How much more of the woman I used to be must I erase to do what it takes to get Jeremy back? Can I kill any more of myself just to keep killing for my handlers? Jeremy might very well end up with less than a shadow of a wife. And I'd be left with nothing...

After exploring the beautiful grounds, Kai leads us back into the house for a snack.

She asks Chef Amar to make her a dish with a Hindi name. All I request is a fruit smoothie. Tahira's stomach is feeling better, but I'm still a little cautious.

I'm itching to be left alone so I can rest both my mind and Tahira's body, but once we're finished with our snacks, Kaivalya leads us into a spacious library overflowing with books. She motions for me to sit on the ground in front of a short table and she pulls out a wooden box from a nearby cabinet.

"Brother says you're excellent, but I'm excellent too."

Kaivalya starts setting up a board filled with black and white squares.

Damn.

I should have paid more attention to Jeremy when he tried teaching me to play chess. I'm definitely on thin ice here. None of the material my handlers gave me said anything about Tahira being good at chess.

"White or black?"

"Uh...black."

Kai moves one of the small white pieces two squares forward.

I mimic her with a similar move of my own but on the opposite side of the board as the piece Kaivalya moved.

Kai grins. "Are you sure you want to do that?"

Nope. I'm not sure about any of this.

Within five more moves each, Kaivalya has me beat.

"Checkmate." Kaivalya giggles.

I throw my hands up in the air and smile. Hopefully Tahira doesn't look as frustrated as I feel.

"I really thought you'd be harder to beat. Guess brother was wrong about you."

Why didn't my handlers let me know Tahira could play chess? What other details about Tahira Collins' life did they overlook?

"Kaivalya, I think we'd best leave Miss Collins now. She looks exhausted."

I turn on my pillow seat toward the voice. Did such a powerful, commanding voice really just come out of such a small woman? Sanji Kapoor has eyes like a hawk and a nose that helps with the same analogy. She may have been considered beautiful when she was younger, and it's true she has a mature elegance about her, but her severe face is easily the most striking feature.

Her black hair is streaked with gray, and she has it tied up on her head in a tight bun. She's wearing a dark green sarang and a sort of shawl around her small shoulders. She's standing as still as a statue with her arms crossed. Is she looking at me disapprovingly? Or skeptically? Both? Sanji Kapoor's gaze almost sends a chill down Tahira's back.

If I had a soul, could she see through to it?

I uncross my legs and stand to face Sanji.

Her expression remains cut from stone as I smile weakly. Should I say something in Hindi? Salute? Bow? Start a staring contest?

I'm leaning toward staring contest when Sanji finally extends a wrinkled hand toward me.

Her grip is like iron as I shake her small hand. Her smile is like Deval's, but in a detached, formal sort of way.

At least I saved Tahira from a mother-in-law like Sanji Kapoor.

I almost cringe at my terrible thought. How many morbid thoughts does that make for me today? Three? Four? Why do I bother keeping track anymore?

"How are you, Miss Collins?"

Sanji's voice is like a mix between a drill sergeant and a school math teacher. Her accent is stronger than all three of her children's too.

"I'm doing well, thank you. Kaivalya has made me feel very welcome."

"Good. Despite the abrupt change in plans, I am glad you are here."

"Thank you, ma'am."

"I trust my son has informed you that you are expected tomorrow at Jarrius headquarters for the finalization of the merger?"

"Er…"

"No? Well, tomorrow you will accompany Deval into the city. I'm sure he will explain more to you on his own. My daughters and I need to be going now, but if you need anything you have my son's number."

"Thank you, ma'am."

Sanji nods curtly and motions for Kai to follow her.

Before they leave the room, Sanji pauses in the doorframe and turns toward me.

"Miss Collins? It's tradition in my family that the bride and groom be accompanied by an adult at all times while they are engaged. I expect you'll observe this until your wedding day."

I nod vigorously. "Yes, ma'am."

"My son has grown up in a world lacking in organized belief systems. As have you. Though I have tried to raise him with firm beliefs, Deval Abdul is not as traditional as myself. I'm sure being near you will offer him many… temptations. I expect you'll be chaste with one another in every sense of the word until you are married."

Way ahead of you, lady. Still…has Sanji Kapoor stereotyped Tahira?

"You don't have to worry about any of that, ma'am. I promise."

"Good."

Sanji hesitates at the door.

"Your father would be proud of you, I expect. He was a good man."

"Thank you." I feel like the mention of Tahira's father would make her both proud and sad at the same time.

"Good day, Miss Collins. I'm sure we'll see each other again soon."

As soon as Sanji is out the door, I take a seat on one of the plush cushions next to a tall window. Sanji and Kaivalya, with Viti in tow, exit through the front doors of the house, and all three climb into the open doors of a blue sedan. The driverless vehicle pulls away, kicking up some dust as it drives down the road toward Randpur.

As they drive off, I get a text from Deval.

Final meeting before the merger is happening tomorrow at noon. Sound good?

I text back a quick yes. He asks me if I'm feeling better, and I respond with a thumbs up emoji.

I assume Amar and my driver Faru are somewhere in the house with me. There's bound to be a maid or two somewhere as well, but the house is so silent now it feels like I have it to myself.

Rain clouds are rolling in from the west, and the first few drops start hitting the windows. Sanji's advice to rest sounds like a fantastic idea.

Navigating my way back to the master bedroom nearly results in me getting lost. Miraculously, my luggage is there when I finally find my room.

Mustering the last bit of energy I possess, I leap onto the massive bed. My body melts into the soft comforter, and I slip Tahira's shoes off, kicking them to the side of the bed.

I reach behind Tahira's back and undo her bra, which I slip through my left sleeve and toss in the same direction as her shoes.

Lastly, I slide Tahira's belt off and pull off her pants, which were getting to be rather warm. My eyes accidentally wander down Tahira's legs. The wound on my right leg has healed, leaving two good-sized scars.

No...not *my* leg. *Tahira's* leg.

My fists clench, and I curl up into a fetal position. Sleep beckons, but what if I fall into another dream? Another nightmare?

But what if it means seeing Jeremy again...?

After I've gotten in a run, and eaten some eggs and hash browns, Deval picks me up around 8:00 A.M. He arrives in a large black SUV. Our driver, Faru, takes us through Randpur and into Bengaluru.

As we get deeper into the city, the number of people packed into the street grows until there are times Faru can't do anything but inch along as we make our way toward the technology district. Massive skyscrapers dominate downtown. So many mirrors…

I tag along with Deval to a few meetings and try not to look too bored. Why am I even here? Tahira already did everything important. Whenever people shove documents at me I just approve everything.

There's excitement over the merger in the eyes and voices of most of the Indian execs. Then there are a few sets of eyes that single me out long enough to give me scathing glares when Deval's looking the other way. Haters.

I ignore them. Tahira would too.

Aside from the covert glares I receive, the morning goes by without incident. Good thing I took time back in California to practice Tahira's signature. It feels like I've signed it a hundred times. My hand is starting to cramp.

Between meetings Deval and I keep to ourselves and make light conversation. As he's telling me about the latest sports car that's caught his attention, Deval moves a strand of Tahira's black hair out of my eyes.

It takes a lot of willpower not to flinch when his hand touches my cheek.

"I'm sorry today's been so boring." Deval rolls his eyes a little. "I promise I'll make it up to you tonight."

"What did you have in mind?" Please don't be anything sexual...

"You'll see, it's a bit of a surprise. I haven't had a chance to officially welcome you to your new home."

I smile and cock my head flirtatiously. Like I'm excited for whatever Deval has planned for us. Only I'm not. I am definitely *not* excited. Now I'm going to be worrying about Deval's surprise the rest of the day. Maybe boring meetings aren't so bad. At least I know what to expect.

One of Deval's underlings informs us our next meeting is about to start. Deval nods then takes my hand.

"There's a small chance they won't expect you to say anything, Tahira. You've already performed beautifully today. But seeing as how you're the primary representative from WorldFuse, you may be asked to comment on the merger."

My stomach drops, but I smile and nod. At least Deval gave me a warning.

Deval leads me down a hallway flanked by large windows that give us a breathtaking view of the city. The smog is only half as bad as most cities back home, but it still stains the streets and buildings with an ugly gray color. We continue walking until we reach a conference room already half filled with suits and ties. There are only a few other females besides myself. It's a miracle there are any women execs in a country like India. Although...maybe I shouldn't judge. American anti-foreigner propaganda has already proved misleading on a number of accounts.

I'm directed to sit across from Deval at the long polished table. The seats are black leather high backs with temperature controls on the armrests. Even with a power suit on I'm still freezing in Tahira's body. The air conditioning in our meetings today has been way too high for my liking. I shiver and crank the heat on my seat.

Tahira's fingers twist my long black hair up into a bun. The rest of the chairs around the conference table slowly fill up, and the meeting starts. Deval catches my eye and winks at me from across the table.

An older gentleman at the far end of the room begins with some opening remarks. A high-pitched ringing in my ears makes it difficult to pay attention. At this point, my presence is mostly a formality at these meetings anyway. I just have to sit back and look pretty while WorldFuse and Jarrius finalize their merger.

The pulsing tension behind my forehead makes it difficult to follow the pace of the meeting. What the hell am I supposed to say if someone asks me to speak for WorldFuse?

Executives continue to discuss things like employee retention, bridging cultural differences, and legal issues they'll face once the merger is completed. When are they going to make me talk? I resist the urge to pull up something on Tahira's phone to keep my mind off my headache. Instead, I get distracted by the clouds outside. Some are gray. I hope it rains.

A lull in the conversation brings my attention back to the meeting. Deval is staring at me from across the table.

I glance around. He's not the only one staring at me.

"Miss Collins?"

My cheeks immediately flush. Idiot. I picked the worst time to become distracted…

I try to find the person who spoke my name. Was it the older gentleman at the head of the table? What was his name again? He's either the equivalent of a CFO or possibly even the CEO.

"I apologize." I cough to clear my throat. "What was the question?"

Several people around the table chuckle.

The older man at the end of the table smiles kindly, but I can tell he's a little exasperated. He's probably not used to dealing with young women like Tahira in these settings.

"I said…do you care to add anything? Before we confirm the final draft of the contract, many of our board members would like to hear about what motivated you to initiate this merger with our company."

"Oh!" Shit. What do I say? I should've thought of this sooner. The throbbing in my head is so distracting. Tahira's motivations behind the merger… what were they? The lake house…Tahira said something about being a leader. She talked about unity, fostering peace and progress…

At least I have something to go off.

"My father, John Collins, believed in a world vastly different than the one we live in today."

I sound so confident. Keep going…

"I believe in that same world. A world where companies and perhaps even governments work together for the betterment of all. I believe, with the merger of our two companies, we can forge a path that others will follow, opening up a future full of possibilities as the companies and the people of tomorrow work together for the advancement of humankind."

Deval is nodding imperceptibly from across the table.

Executives who initially looked like they couldn't care less about what the young woman from California had to say are now leaning forward in their seats. I have everyone's attention.

Deval raises his eyebrows ever so slightly and smiles. Does that mean I'm on the right track? One way to find out…

"Today, too many companies do everything they can to put competitors out of business. Some go so far as to intimidate and terrorize to get what they want—much like world governments. There are rumors of ending the border shutdowns, but the feelings that caused them in the first place are worse than ever. With our actions here today, I believe we can teach the world that unity, not conflict, breeds the greatest results for everyone."

Heads begin to nod, and expressions soften. Deval gives me a discreet thumbs up and turns his attention back to the head of the table. Can I be done talking now?

"Unless any board members have any genuine objections…" Deval's voice is strong and confident. No one interrupts him. "…I believe we are ready to sign off on the final proposal to merge WorldFuse with Jarrius Technologies."

More head nods.

All of a sudden, the table beneath my arms lights up with a soft blue glow. A digital rendering of the merger proposal appears before my eyes. Everyone else seated at the table also has a glowing white rectangle in front of them too.

A few suit and tie aids begin passing out slim styluses to each member of the table.

As soon as I touch the white stylus, the digital contract rendering shifts on the high tech table. A yellow box appears over a black line, indicating where I need to draw my...I mean, Tahira's...signature.

Do my handlers really want me to do this? They haven't ordered me to do anything specific regarding this merger.

The whole process takes me about two minutes to complete. I don't bother reading through anything. I'm not necessarily here to make sure WorldFuse gets a fair shake in this deal. Because I—Alexandria McKenzie—am here to kill Deval Abdul Kapoor. That's it.

When I look up, Deval is still working on his contract across from me, as are most of the other board members who're seated around the long table. I start to spin the stylus in my fingers and zone out again.

Then...movement out of the corner of my eye. One of the suit and tie aids reaches inside his coat jacket. The man is standing up against the wall next to two other aids who're dressed similarly. He could just be reaching for a tissue or something. Am I really this paranoid? No, tissues don't make that shape...

Everyone is oblivious to what's happening. Do *I* even know what's happening? Should I even try stopping whatever's happening? Yes, Tahira would.

By the time the aid's pistol is drawn, my stylus is hurling across the table toward his face.

My stylus lands a glancing blow, right below his left eye. Then he fires.

The gunshot is deafening. A woman screams. Another aids grabs the assailant's arms and pushes upward. A second shot rings out, but the bullet only goes so far as the ceiling.

People are shouting. Panicking. Executives trip over themselves trying to get away from the gunman. One man collides with another and sandwiches him against the ground. I almost laugh out loud. I must be insane...

The conference room devolves into chaos. I'm in some sort of trance. I have no inclination to move, not until I feel hands pulling me backward toward an exit. The gun goes off a third time. More screams follow.

I search for Deval. He's still on the opposite side of the room flanked by two men in suits. Good. He's all right. My handlers would probably kill me if I let someone else kill Deval. The trio is heading in my direction as quickly as they can through the others who're fleeing the conference room. We catch each other's eyes, and Deval points in my direction. He says something to the man on his right. Immediately, Faru breaks away from Deval and pushes his way toward me.

Once he reaches me, Faru takes me by the arm and escorts me the rest of the way out of the room.

Tahira's body remains surprisingly calm as I'm directed out into the hallway, past a team of men in tactical armor carrying semi-automatic rifles, and around a corner. We pass several rows of windows. It's raining outside. A light mist mixes with the smog below us. We come to a stop in an empty room that has four elevator doors. Faru pushes both sets of buttons on either side of the room and asks me if I'm okay.

"I'm fine." Then, considering I'm engaged I add. "Where is Deval? Is he okay?"

"We're evacuating you separately, Miss Collins." Faru's voice is low and calm. Was he a soldier once too?

"What's going on?" My tone sounds off. Tahira should probably sound more scared.

"My orders are to get you somewhere safe, ma'am."

"Was anyone injured?"

Faru ignores me and gently pushes me forward when one of the elevators finally arrives. As soon as we're inside, Faru selects a button for the basement.

Was the would-be assassin from the conference room like the man who assaulted me in California? He didn't have the crossed arrow symbol anywhere on him, but I could have easily missed something like that in the chaos. The Indian aid wasn't aiming for me or Deval though. It looked like his shot had been intended for someone at the head of the table. Possibly the older gentleman conducting the meeting. Did he make it out? If I hadn't intervened…

This is outside my mission parameters. Why should I care who the aid was or what he was trying to do? Then again, my handlers probably won't be happy to hear I'm not the only assassin in play around Kapoor. Even if he wasn't an immediate target, it matters a lot to my handlers that Tahira be the one to kill Deval.

The elevator descends uninterrupted all the way to the basement. As soon as the doors are halfway open, Faru steps out, his gun raised. After he's satisfied the way is clear, he returns to my side and grips my upper arm, pulling me along.

We turn down a few corners and pass through a solid metal door before entering a large underground garage. The ceiling is low. If I jumped I'm sure I could touch the cement above. The air is musky down here, possibly from the rain outside.

Faru leads me toward a row of parked vehicles. He opens the door to the closest one with a quick voice command. Faru holds the door for me while I climb in. A second later we peel out of the garage and up a sharp incline until we reach the main road. Faru waits for an opening before gunning it out onto the busy street.

"It was just one guy. Don't you think Deval is overreacting by having you escort me like this? Where are you even taking me?"

All I get in reply to my questions is an icy stare. No answers. Story of my lives…

I sit back in my seat and cross my arms, frowning.

After two more turns in our car, I get a text from Deval.

Are you okay? Did Faru get you out?

Yes. Faru got me out just fine.
How are you?

I'm fine. Whoever the gunman was is detained and is being turned over to the authorities soon.

When will I see you again?

It could be a while. I need to make sure no one was injured and that the merger is still on track for completion. I'm worried some of the board members will get spooked, even though I warned them there might be opposition from the general public.

I refrain from telling Deval I don't think there's any way in hell the man in that conference room was just some random citizen. Not only did they get their gun through security, but they also managed to pose as a Jarrius employee. Whoever it was had connections. Or training. Or both.

Maybe Deval knows more than he's letting on, but if so he doesn't share anything with me over text.

I'll call you as soon as I figure out what's going on. I'm sorry, Tahira. My family will take care of you until I can return. Text me if you need me.

Sighing, I stretch out on the back seat of the car and listen to the rain fall on the roof of the car. The sound of the rain is soothing. Hypnotic. Like home...

Once the car stops moving I sit up and look around.

We're underground again. I wait for Faru to open my door. The air isn't musty like the Jarrius building. This garage smells like...eucalyptus?

"This is part of the Kapoor family residence. If you'll follow me, I'll show you up to the right floor."

I allow Faru to lead me to a small private elevator. He inserts a short metal card into a reader and scans his face. A second later the elevator doors part.

We ride the elevator up to the fiftieth floor.

Once we stop, the elevator doors open to reveal a massive penthouse. The living room is two stories tall with a balcony extending out from the second floor above. The exterior walls are massive panes of glass that offer a sweeping view of the city below. Not much can be seen through the rain clouds though. The comfortable living room has pleasant green hues and is connected to a beautiful kitchen.

Suddenly, something collides with me out of nowhere. I stumble a little. She can't weigh more than seventy pounds, but Kaivalya almost knocks me over as she grips me in a tight bear hug.

"We heard what happened. I'm so glad you're safe!"

"Yep. I'm safe."

"I was so worried!"

"Were you? Afraid you might not have someone around you can beat at chess?" I grin and pry Kaivalya off me.

"Kaivalya! Leave Miss Collins alone. And how do you even know what happened? Who told you?"

Sanji appears upstairs on the balcony overlooking the main floor. Her light gray sari makes her look like she's made from stone.

Kai shrugs guiltily beneath the gaze of her mother and retreats a few paces from me.

Sanji makes a *hmph* sound and disappears behind the railing. The sound of a door closing follows a moment later. She didn't even ask if I was all right. I could be traumatized, on the verge of an emotional breakdown, and it seems like she couldn't care less. I'm used to people not giving a shit about *me*, but I'm supposed to be *Tahira Collins*—Sanji Kapoor's future daughter-in-law. It shouldn't...but it hurts that she didn't even show me an ounce of concern.

"Brother texted me about everything that happened." Kaivalya's voice is barely a whisper. Is she afraid her mother is still watching?

It seems like you'd want to *avoid* texting a ten-year-old how an armed gunman broke into your company meeting and tried killing people. Although, for all her bubbliness and sass, Kai *does* seem mature for her age.

Kaivalya takes my hand and leads me toward a couch.

Faru remains a silent sentinel next to the elevator door.

"Do you need something to drink? A blanket? I'd let you borrow one of mine. Even my special one."

Oh yeah...a normal person would probably be in shock. I should be acting a little rattled, at least.

"Something to drink would be good."

Her black curls bounce as Kaivalya hops off the couch. She returns with a steaming mug of something that smells faintly like lemons. I sip at it, nearly burning my tongue.

"Anything else?" Kaivalya still looks concerned. I forget traumatic experiences aren't the norm for most people.

"I'm better now. Thanks, Kai."

"Deval told me to take your mind off things. I don't exactly know how to do that, but what do you say to me beating you at another game of chess?"

"Sure." Maybe a distraction *would* be nice.

I last longer than I did my first game, but Kai still beats me handily.

We play two more games before I get a call from Deval.

"I'm on my way right now. I just finished speaking with the authorities."

"How did everything go? What did you find out?"

"I don't know how much I should say over the phone. None of the board members were hurt, though it seems like they had a guardian angel intervene at the most critical moment."

Has Deval already seen some kind of security footage showing me throwing my pen at the assailant?

"I...I didn't know what I was doing. I just saw the gun and I..."

"No need to explain yourself, Tahira. You saved lives today."

"I don't have any of my stuff. Will someone take me back to the Queen's House tonight or..."

"No, you'll stay in the penthouse with me and my family tonight. Things need to...settle down first. I'm concerned for your safety."

"I'm fine, Dev. Really."

"Still, I want to make sure you're safe. My family's home is very secure. Also... it took a lot of persuading from me to keep the authorities from bringing you in for questioning after what happened. It might be best if you lay low for a while."

"What do you mean?"

I keep my voice calm, but my heart rate has picked up without my brain telling it to. Tahira has nothing to hide. Then again, Jill was supposed to be completely off the radar too. Has something similar happened with Indian law enforcement? Did they receive some kind of tip? Why else would Deval need to argue on my behalf to keep the authorities from bringing me in for questioning? What could possibly implicate Tahira?

"It's nothing. I'll explain more when I see you. I'll be there within the next forty minutes."

We say goodbye, and I try not to look as nervous as I feel. Kai's nose is scrunched, and she's eyeing me closely.

"What did Brother want?"

"He was just calling to tell me I get to have a sleepover with you. Is that okay?"

"I guess so. Mother will probably want you as far away from Brother as possible. Our rooms are on opposite ends of the house."

"What's the deal with…Mother, anyway? Why doesn't she like me?"

"She likes you." Kai raises an eyebrow. "Can't you tell?"

Nope. I definitely can*not* tell. Is Kai messing with me?

"Mother treats the people she cares most about with…distance. At least that's how Brother says it."

"Huh." I suppose that makes sense to me. A few people back home, mostly military or ex-military, treated their families the same way. Distance is sometimes easier when you love someone but are afraid to lose them. Or afraid you'll be lost yourself…

An hour later, I'm sitting at a counter next to Kaivalya eating the last bits of some curry and chicken when Deval arrives.

Kaivalya leaps from her stool and rushes up to Deval, tackling him in much the same way she did me when I first exited the elevator.

Deval smiles and hugs his sister in return. Then his eyes meet mine. His features soften. His lips turn upward in a relieved grin. I can feel the masked concern drain from his body. Jeremy. I inhale sharply. Jeremy used to look at me the exact same way…whenever I'd return from deployment…

No.

It's not exactly like Jeremy. Because it *isn't* Jeremy.

I step down from the bar stool and meet Deval halfway.

He's got to be breaking one of his mother's rules by embracing me, but he does so anyway, and passionately so.

He holds me close to his chest like I'm made of glass. Deval's scent smells good to this body. A slight chill ripples down my spine when he whispers in my ear. It's torture.

"Are you all right? Tell me how you're feeling."

"I'm fine, Dev. Nothing happened to me. I'm safe, and so are you."

My words lack the same conviction as Deval's. But it's the best I can do.

"I'm so sorry, Tahira. If I'd known what was going to happen today I never would've endangered you. I…"

A door above us opens, and Deval immediately pulls away from me, repositioning himself so he's at least an arm's length away from me.

"You're back," Sanji says from her balcony. "Good. Did you get all the signatures required to finalize the official merger?"

Her eyes are on her son, and Deval returns his mother's gaze with a short head shake.

"Tomorrow then. First thing."

"Yes, Mother."

"I'm glad you're all right." At least Sanji has *some* emotion. Whatever warmth she may have generated with her words leaves, however, as soon as she turns her back, disappearing from the railing once again.

Deval sighs deeply before glancing up at me, a smile back on his tired, handsome face.

"Well, are you ready?"

"Ready? For what?"

"Our date." Deval grins, and Kaivalya giggles near his elbow.

"I don't see why it would be such a bad thing."

"Your shortsightedness blinds you."

"If the CIA wants to step in and halt the merger, why wouldn't we let them? After killing the CEO, he might have even tried for Kapoor."

"I thought you said our intelligence still can't confirm if the gunman was CIA or not."

"I was CIA myself once. I know their signature when I see it."

"No one else can do what Alex is meant to do. Tahira Collins has to be the one to kill Deval Kapoor. Deval must die at his wife's hand."

"Because…"

"It will rip Unitas apart from the inside out."

"This is all just for Unitas then?"

"Yes and no."

"And the Final War?"

"Soon, yes."

"Unity is death."

"Struggle is life."

I throw my car into sixth gear and roar past Deval on our second to last lap. The engine sounds like an angry lion. Powerful. Deadly. Exhilarating…

Have I ever gone this fast in a car before? The lights lining the track fly past so quickly it's like a strobe.

Even through our narrow helmet visors, I catch a very brief glimpse of Deval's surprised face as I pass him going well over 350 kilometers per hour.

A smile plays on Tahira's lips.

No.

I am *not* enjoying myself. I won't…can't…admit to that. Fun, pleasure, joy, these are foreign concepts for Divest. But racing sports cars on a private track won't be something I forget anytime soon.

Was going on a date the best idea in the first place? After what we witnessed earlier today? Maybe I should've pretended to be more in shock. But the powerful engine beneath me feels amazing…perhaps Deval was just hoping to take my mind off things. Maybe he wanted the same thing for himself too.

The trees surrounding the track are nothing but a green blur as I approach 400 kilometers per hour coming out of the last turn. I floor it and power toward the white line that marks the end of our race.

The straps across my chest dig into me as I begin to slow down. I do one last "victory" lap so I can spend just a little more time in the most amazing car I've ever driven.

Once my speed drops to a manageable level I pull up to Deval's vehicle off the side of the track. My car shudders a little as I come to a rolling stop under the covered parking area.

Deval leans against his car with his helmet off, grinning from ear to ear. He can't see my face through my helmet so I grin in spite of myself. My heart is still pounding, and adrenaline is coursing through my veins as I shut the car off with a verbal command. The car door opens automatically, and I step out onto the asphalt. It feels like the world is frozen now that I'm not moving so fast.

My helmet snags a few hairs as I slip it off my head. I run my free hand through my long black mane and take a deep breath.

"Where did you learn to drive like that?" Deval is still grinning as he walks over to me.

"Where did you learn to *lose* like that?" I wink.

Deval throws his head back and laughs.

I start to laugh a little too. Then I pause.

That was my own joke. Not Tahira's.

I'm sure Tahira could've said something similar on her own, but when I spoke I wasn't pretending to be her. I wasn't thinking like Tahira. I wasn't acting. I was just being myself. For a moment…I was Alex.

Fool.

"Once my pride has had some time to recover I'm sure I'll challenge you to a rematch. What do you say?" Deval pulls off his driving gloves, and I do the same.

I smile at Deval and give him a thumbs up, but I keep my lips sealed. What if I open my…Tahira's…mouth again and say something else that's not in line with the character I'm supposed to be playing?

Deval is still grinning when he takes a step toward me, he's close enough that I can smell him. Tahira's body suddenly reacts with hormones I am *not* willing to act on.

Faru is standing a dozen yards away, near the gate that leads away from the track. Deval follows my gaze toward Faru. His smile fades a little. Does he know about the awkward conversation his mother had with me yesterday… the one about not tempting her son with my sensuous body?

"Shall we?" Deval motions with his hand toward the steps.

"Sure."

"You surprised me today, Tahira. In more ways than one."

Yeah…no kidding.

Deval opens a locker with his thumb to store our helmets before we return to the black SUV. Faru opens my door and I climb inside. The tinted car windows make it seem darker than it is at such a late hour, considering all the light pollution. We're pulling onto a busy street when Deval finally breaks the silence.

"The man with the gun today, he was American."

I glance sharply at Deval. It's so dark I can barely make out his expression. His jaw is set and his eyes are serious. I almost shiver. In the low light he kind of looks like Sanji.

"That's why they wanted to bring you in for questioning. You were the only other American in that room. I thought it was absurd they assumed just because you were both from the States that you might be affiliated. But that's the world we live in, the world we're trying to change. Right?"

I swallow hard and nod.

"Authorities wouldn't tell me much, but after watching the security feed, we think he was after Kabir or one of the other company leaders."

"Do they know why yet?"

Deval shakes his head. "I don't know. I'm sure the police will inform me if they discover anything."

At least now I can tell my handlers that the attacker from today wasn't after Deval. Still, knowing there are other organizations who want to keep the merger from happening badly enough to send a gunman might make my job more complicated.

"Are you still okay spending the night with my family?"

"I don't mind if your mother doesn't."

"She knows. She's agreed it's probably for the best."

I nod.

"I'm sorry if she seems cold or distant. If you haven't noticed, she treats most everyone the same way."

"It's fine. At any rate, Kaivalya kind of balances out your mom."

Deval laughs a little. "True. Speaking of Kai, she tells me she's enjoyed spending time with you. I think she's excited she's getting another sister. Viti feels the same way too."

This mission keeps getting worse and worse. My stomach gets queasy all of a sudden. It takes a lot of willpower for me not to shudder. What am I doing, allowing myself to get close to these people? I hate myself. But to play the part of Tahira accurately, I don't know how I can afford *not* to get emotionally attached to the Kapoors...at least outwardly.

Our car bounces a little as we cross a bridge and reenter the busy streets of Bengaluru. There are less people and less vehicles at this hour, but we still hit pockets of traffic on our way to the penthouse.

We follow a wide street until we pull down into the Kapoors' private garage. The automatic door slides closed behind our vehicle, and lights come on to aid Faru in driving through the narrow tunnel.

Once we park, I follow Deval into the elevator. Faru joins us a moment later, and the three of us ride up to the fiftieth floor. Once we make it to our floor, Deval motions for me to exit first and turns toward Faru.

"*Dhanyavad.* Goodnight, my friend."

Faru says something quiet and gives Deval a quick bow with his hands clasped in front of his chest in a traditional Hindu sign of respect.

Deval returns the gesture, and Faru disappears behind the elevator doors.

It's late now, and most of the penthouse lights are either off or dimmed. Deval puts his index finger to his lips and motions for me to follow him. We walk down a short hallway lit by small lights just above the baseboards. Deval stops in front of a door with two stickers. One is a butterfly and the other of a blue-skinned Kali. The god's skull necklace is more than a little eerie.

"We have a guest room, but Kaivalya said something about a sleepover with you?"

A room to myself would be great, but would Tahira do that to Kai? Maybe…but I don't *think* she would. Should I even care what Deval's ten-year-old sister thinks about Tahira?

Before I can open my mouth, a pair of dark brown eyes appear through a crack in the door.

"You're supposed to be in bed."

"Mother doesn't know; just don't tell her. Please!" Kai's voice is even quieter than Deval's.

"I don't know if Tahira is up for…whatever you had planned, Kai. It's been a long day for her."

Deval is helping my cause, but Kai's big brown eyes are not.

They both turn to look at me.

This isn't fair. All I want is to go to bed and get a full eight hours of sleep. Tahira's body is literally fighting my brain at this point.

"I won't keep her up, Dev. I *promise*. Please, please, please?"

"Tahira?"

Kai turns her big brown eyes on me, and now I can't refuse.

I muster a tired smile. "I can crash with Kai tonight."

Kaivalya grins wide and reaches through the crack in her door to grab Tahira's wrist and pull me into her room.

"Goodnight, Kai. Goodnight, Tahira. I'll see you tomo—"

Kai's bedroom door shuts with a mild click. Kaivalya drags me through her dark room and tugs on my wrist when she wants me to stop.

"Here. This is for you. If you need any other blankets I've got more."

Tahira's eyes can barely make out the shape of a lumpy pile of blankets topped with a few pillows. I smile at Kaivalya. She must be able to see me because her white teeth appear in the shape of a grin in the darkness next to me.

Sheets rustle seconds later.

I'm too tired to care that I'm technically sleeping on the floor. This arrangement is definitely better than other places I've ever slept as Divest though. I start to stretch out and position a pillow for Tahira's head.

"I got you some pajamas too. They're right by your feet. I promise I won't look."

Sure enough, I touch an extremely soft pair of shorts and what I assume is a matching top at the foot of my pile of blankets. Even if Kaivalya were peeking I doubt she'd be able to see anything in the dark. With the last bit of energy I have, I undress and slip into the pajamas. They fit snugly. That was nice of Kaivalya to think about pajamas for me…er…for Tahira.

Tahira's eyes close without my telling them to, and just when I feel like I'm about to drift off to sleep, Kai's quiet voice interrupts me again.

"I'm really excited you're going to be my sister soon, Tahira. I'm glad you and Deval chose each other."

I grit my teeth and shudder at Kaivalya's words. She won't get the sister she wants. The sister she thinks she's getting is likely dead. Not to mention, the entire marriage between her brother and Tahira is a little more complicated than just two people who've chosen to spend their lives together.

"Tahira?"

"Yes, Kai?"

"Shubh raatri bahan."

Her Hindi is a bit too sophisticated for me. *Bahan* means sister, but what does the rest mean? Something like goodnight…or I love you?

I hate myself.

"Goodnight, Kaivalya."

A few moments later, Kai's light, regular breathing fills the otherwise silent room.

Tahira's phone goes off near her head where I set it down. The light glows softly in the darkened bedroom, and I pull it under my blanket to keep the light from waking Kai.

Status?

I blink twice while my fingers tap out a reply.

Body is fine. Spending the night with the Kapoors. I'll provide more info in the morning when I'm alone.

Kai's breathing becomes rhythmic and soothing as I start to drift off. How can I possibly follow through with killing Deval and ruining his family's lives? I've learned through repeated experiences that my murders always have more than one victim. Always.

What the…?

I'm lying on my back. Why am I on my back?

Why am I covered in so many blankets? And why does my spine hurt?

The ceiling above me is a slate gray color. Where…?

I bolt upright and look around. I'm in a bedroom. It looks like it belongs to a little girl. There are lots of bright colors. There's a bed five feet away from me that's small and low to the ground. How did I get here? What's going on?

Hairs stand up on the back of my neck.

Where am I?

Who am I?

My skin is so dark. Whose body am I in? The black hair I'm running my hands through doesn't help me remember anything. My heart begins to beat faster. Something is wrong.

Police…I was running from the police. Somewhere in Virginia? Yes. But this brown body is wrong. I should be Caucasian. My hair is black, not red. I lift my shirt and glance quickly where a knife wound should still be leaking blood. Nothing. No cut. No blood. Just flat abs.

When did I change bodies? Did I make it to the safe house? The buildings outside…I'm definitely not in Virginia. How did I get here? Where is *here*? Was I caught? Taken somewhere? This isn't a dream, right? No. It can't be because I don't dream as Divest. What the hell is happening?

A knock at the bedroom door snaps me out of my trance. I look around for something I can use to defend myself. There are slippers, stuffed animals, a computer, and a long metal lamp that looks solid enough.

Before I can move an inch a small brown girl enters the room. She's wearing a pastel colored dress. She giggles and points at me. "Your hair is crazy."

Who is this little girl? Why is she laughing at me? How does she know me?

"Uh…Tahira? Did you sleep okay?"

Kaivalya. Her tiny voice finally grounds me. She continues giggling at me. Yes. I'm in her bedroom in the Kapoor penthouse. In Bengaluru, India. My body…this is Tahira Collins' body.

Relief and horror clash, and I'm left feeling nauseated.

It's a struggle to disentangle myself from my mess of blankets. I stand up too fast and can't keep from cringing from the blunt, stinging wave that rolls through my head. A fresh migraine greets me along with the sunlight creeping through the clear glass windows.

I barely register Kaivalya complimenting my pajamas. Tahira's body is wearing a rather obnoxious top with matching shorts. The design includes cartoon images of rainbows, three-headed blue people, and stars.

Tahira's clothes have vanished from the place I discarded them last night.

"Shower's in there if you want." Kaivalya points to a door across her messy bedroom. "Oh, and I had Vihaan wash your clothes for you. They should be done soon."

"How long have you been up?" My throat is raw, and Tahira's voice sounds groggy. I rub my sleepy eyes.

"About an hour. Brother left for some meeting or something and told me to let you know he'd be back soon."

I nod.

"I'll be outside when you're done. You can use any of my stuff, just not my blue brush—that one's my special one."

"Thanks, Kai."

Kaivalya skips out of the room, and I lurch my way into the bathroom. It's not a large bathroom by rich people's standards. But then again, it belongs to a ten-year-old. I completely ignore the mirror, though my hands are trembling slightly as I reach for the touch screen to turn on the shower. I can't get my hands to stop shaking. Is it because I'm so close to a mirror? Or maybe because I'm trying to understand what the hell is happening to me.

My memory…This sort of thing has never happened to me before. I fight the urge to scream and pull my hair out. I'm falling apart inside. Tears burst from my eyes as warm steam from the shower fills the room. A shower had better help me pull myself together.

I strip down, fold my pajamas up, and set them next to the sink. Don't look at the mirror…

My eyes are still misty, but the water from the shower soothes my headache a little. Kai has lots of options for my hair, but I grab the first bottle I touch. I massage Tahira's scalp as I apply some shampoo. The suds smell good to me…I mean…to Tahira's body. The bottle says it's lemongrass and thyme scented. Did I like this scent myself? Before?

How many more migraines like this can I take? I'm going to explode or shatter. None of my concerned texts meet sympathetic eyes among my handlers. Powell either doesn't care about my pain or he's being ordered not to help. Which is worse? Thinking about my headache just makes it worse. It's like someone's hitting me repeatedly over the head with a mallet. I'd kill for some pain killers…

The flight attendant Jen did more for me than my handlers ever have. I'll have to see if I can sneak some pain relievers from the Kapoors.

Do I tell my handlers about my memory loss? People sometimes forget where they are when they first wake up, but this was something else. Something much more than disorientation. Then again, if I tell my handlers they might not care at all and I'll have done nothing but weaken their confidence in me. Thus putting both my real body and Jeremy at risk. If I don't tell them, I'll be on my own…but that sure as hell isn't anything new. I start applying conditioner.

I won't tell them. It's not worth the risk. Besides, I have more pressing matters, like keeping myself from having a literal mental breakdown. Come on Alex…Divest…get a hold of yourself.

After I've cleaned Tahira's body thoroughly, I dry off with a pink towel hanging near the shower. As I'm drying myself off, my face looks back at me through the mirror.

My face.

Shit.

No. No. No.

I wasn't being careful.

Oh God. Please no.

I steel myself. Preparing to devolve into a panic attack. My heart beat rises a little, and I start to tremble. My flesh gets goosebumps and…that's it?

Am I okay?

I'm okay…

Maybe the mirror was foggy enough it didn't count.

There are two mirrors. Which one did I look at? The mirror in front of the sink and the one hanging behind me on the closet are just beginning to clear. Maybe the condensation is what saved me. What was that on my back? A birthmark?

I risk a very quick glance.

Just below my…Tahira's…neck, in between the shoulder blades, is a small, blue tattoo. The rhombus matches the same symbol on both Deval's ring and Tahira's bracelet.

Strange…

I wrap the towel around Tahira's naked body and open the bathroom door just wide enough for me to peek outside.

Kaivalya is nowhere to be seen, but Tahira's clothes lie neatly pressed and folded near the foot of Kaivalya's little bed. I tiptoe across the carpet, trying not to get the ground too wet, and retrieve my clothes.

Once I'm dressed, I fold up the blankets that were my bed, and send my handlers a detailed report of everything significant that happened yesterday. I include as much as I remember about the gunman and what Deval told me as we were leaving the race track after our date. I don't mention my memory loss.

Tahira's phone is halfway to my back pocket when it vibrates. My handlers have sent a video file. An icy grip coils around my insides. A lump forms in Tahira's throat.

Calm down.

It's probably just more instructions regarding my mission.

But what if it's Jeremy again…?

I need headphones. There has to be…yes! I find a pair of pink, wireless earbuds next to Kaivalya's nightstand and shove them in Tahira's ears. I connect them with my phone and return to the bathroom. Just in case I need an excuse for being in the bathroom longer, I turn on the sink.

With a touch of Tahira's finger, I open the file and tap play.

Jeremy…

"…ese men are saying you're hurt. That you need to see me and hear me to motivate you to keep going. I'm still not sure exactly what's going on, but they've told me to tell you that I love you and that we'll be together again soon. This will all be over soon, Alex."

Jeremy is seated in a dark room. His hands are bound behind him. The backdrop is an oily black void. They could be holding him anywhere. His face is contorted like he's holding back a grimace. Otherwise, he looks mostly the same as he did in the last video. His hair looks unkempt but clean. There's a small cut near his bottom lip like he's been beaten. His eyes are bright and alive but filled with worry. He keeps glancing to the side of the screen like someone's directing him.

Tahira's eyes begin to fill with tears once again, but they come slower this time. Why? My entire body shudders.

"They still haven't told me where you are or what you're doing, but they've promised we'll be together when you're done. But…"

Jeremy pauses, looks to the side, then focuses right on the camera. Right on me.

"…but Alex, I don't give a damn. Whatever they're forcing you do to, forget about me and you…!"

A gloved fist comes out of nowhere and strikes Jeremy across his face. He grunts in pain and disappears from the screen. My hands are trembling, and I can't keep Tahira's phone level. A second pair of hands drag Jeremy off the ground and sit him up in front of the camera again.

"I'm sorry, my love. I love you to hell and back. I'm sorry…"

The video goes black for a few seconds before a masked man with a modulated voice fills the screen.

"Finish the mission as we've directed, and you'll see Jeremy again. You'll get your old life back. As well as your real body. Just do what we tell you, and this will all be over soon."

The video shifts, and suddenly…the camera is looking at…*me*. I'm looking at myself.

My *real* self. My real body…

My eyes are closed, lips slightly ajar. I could be sleeping…

I'm mostly nude. My short blonde hair floats gently in the bluish substance that fills the cryochamber. It's the same length it was when I "died" in Tokyo. Of course it'd be the same length. Bodies don't age normally in cryo. Even my muscles show no signs of atrophy. Several white bullet scars dot my abdomen and upper right thigh. The marks contrast sharply with my bluish skin.

"Should you fail, or decide not to follow through, you'll lose everything. Two promises. One choice, and it's yours to make."

The video ends and self deletes from Tahira's phone. I collapse onto the moist bathroom floor and bury my hands in my face.

If Kai returns will she hear me sobbing?

I don't care…

Jeremy. My body. So close, but I might as well be on the moon for how close I really am. Why would they do this to me? Are they afraid I won't do what they ask? I suppose every beast of burden needs a good whipping every once in a while…

I don't know how long I remain on the floor, but eventually I pick myself up and exit the bathroom. Kaivalya's door opens quietly, and I walk slowly down the hall.

The smell of something spicy fills my nose as I near the kitchen.

"Better hurry, or I'm going to eat everything."

Kaivalya swivels on her bar stool. There are two plates of scrambled eggs with some thin strips of meat that look like bacon.

There's a maid doing some cleaning in the living room, and I'm almost sorry for her.

"Uh…earth to the zombie lady!" Kai calls from her stool. "You hungry for eggs? Or maybe you prefer brains?"

A dark cloud hangs over me, and I feel like I'm dragging a thousand pounds. I'm in no mood to play Tahira right now, but I raise both my arms out straight, open my mouth like I'm drugged, and emphasize a limping gait.

Kaivalya giggles a little at my attempt to walk like a zombie before I reach the seat next to her and boost myself up onto the barstool. I set Tahira's phone down next to a glass of what looks to be orange juice.

"You look nice." Kaivalya's compliment does nothing to improve my mood.

"You too, Kai." I make a point to compliment her colorful dress and matching bracelets.

"Where's Viti?" I look around in case I missed her.

"Playing soccer or something, I don't know. She's always off with friends."

"Kaivalya…I mean…Kai, you wouldn't happen to have some headache medicine I could borrow, do you?"

She shakes her head. "Mother doesn't believe in drugs."

"Oh."

Typical. No rest for the wicked…*or* weary.

"But we have something else you can have!"

With a little bounce, Kaivalya jumps off her stool and skips to a cabinet set into the wall near the kitchen sink.

She returns with a small bottle filled with a dark liquid.

Without explaining what she has or what she's doing, Kaivalya taps the end of the bottle she's holding against her free hand, depositing a small amount of the black liquid into her palm. Then she sets the glass bottle down on the counter and rubs her tiny hands together.

After she wets both her hands with the mysterious oil, she motions for me to move closer to her.

She takes my forehead in her small hands and starts massaging my temples. At first, nothing changes except for the pungent smell that fills my nostrils. It's not a bad smell, it's just sharp. Maybe some kind of herb?

What is in that bottle? The pounding in my skull gradually dissipates until I feel…nothing. Absolutely nothing. The relief is amazing. Liberating…

"Better?"

"So much better." I close my eyes and hope she doesn't stop massaging my head with her tiny, but strong, fingers. Kaivalya continues with my therapy for a moment longer before my stupid phone interrupts.

"Oooh! Brother is calling you. You'd better take it." Kaivalya looks at Tahira's phone on the counter.

I resist the urge to frown as I pick up the phone and raise it to Tahira's ear. At least there's something I can use for my migraines.

"Hello?"

Namaste, Tahira. How are you this morning? Did you sleep okay?"

Deval's voice sounds level, devoid of any particular emotion. I reply with the same tone.

"Good morning, Dev. I'm doing well, thanks. I slept okay. Your sister sure knows how to make a killer pile of blankets."

I didn't mean to sound sarcastic about my sleepover with Kai, but Deval doesn't seem to notice. If he does, he doesn't call me out.

"Good to hear. I'm sorry I had to leave so early. There were some…things that needed my attention."

"Did you learn more about the gunman from yesterday?"

Deval's brief hesitation tells me more than his actual answer.

"Maybe. I'll explain more when I see you."

"When will that be?"

"Soon. I hope. I'm meeting with Kabir shortly to discuss the merger. It seems we missed a few signatures yesterday, and until we get them, the merger can't move forward as planned."

"Okay. Anything I can do to help from here?"

"Not yet. Although, depending on the reactions some may have after yesterday's events, it's possible we'll need to persuade a few who are rather…faint of heart."

"I understand."

"I'll see you soon, Tahira. I apologize, I have not been a very good host… this merger is…"

"Part of our arrangement."

"Right. Our…arrangement."

There's definitely some bitterness, or perhaps resignation, in Deval's tone. Have I said the wrong thing? Or perhaps it was the right thing but I said it the wrong way?

"I just mean…this merger is important. You've already done a lot to see it work out, and as much as I'm eager to…get to know you…I understand if right now you're needed elsewhere."

"It's okay, Tahira. I think I know what you're trying to say."

Well at least one of us does.

"Talk to you later."

"Bye, Dev."

I hang up the phone and set it back down on the counter.

Kaivalya is looking at me with an odd expression on her face.

"What?" I smile, feeling sheepish.

"Nothing. Just trying to figure out how my brother got someone like you to marry him. Don't tell him I said this, but you're kind of out of his league."

Jeez. I need to change the subject.

"Don't you have school or something?"

"Not really. I'm kind of homeschooled, and Mother scheduled a month-long break for Viti and me just before brother's wedding."

"Ah."

"Brother says you went to an actual university, not an online one. How was it?"

Why did I change the subject? How *was* Tahira's college experience?

"Oh, you know…You get to skip class if you don't want to be there. You learn lots of cool things. You go to lots of parties."

"What kind of parties?"

I'm on thin ice. I can't keep relying on my own college experience.

"Grown-up parties?" What's another topic I can transition to?

Kaivalya gives me a look I can only interpret as sly.

"Tahira, are you a virgin?"

Without warning my cheeks grow warm. I frown and cross my arms.

"Whoa, girl. How do you know about any of that?"

"Tahira, *please*. I'm ten—almost eleven." Kai rolls her eyes. "Besides, Deval doesn't have the guts to ask you himself."

Am I seriously having this conversation with a ten-year-old? She's not even talking about the real me. Why am I embarrassed for Tahira? Honestly, *why* am I blushing? Is it because I don't know the answer to Kaivalya's question?

"You're not?" Kai giggles louder and points at my blushing cheeks.

"Whether I am or not is none of your business, little missy." I push her lightly on her shoulder causing her to spin around on her stool.

Right on cue, the elevator doors slide open, and Sanji Kapoor appears. Today, she's dressed in a pair of sharp black pants with a matching jacket. Her hair is done up in her customary bun, and her face is just as stern as ever.

Sanji's eyes shift from myself to Kaivalya, who I can tell is trying very hard to look as innocent as possible. Sanji's expression sours. Surely she has no way of knowing what Kai was just interrogating me about, but mothers have a sixth sense for such things. I think Kai's attempt at looking innocent is actually working against her. It's hard not to laugh. Kai is struggling too.

"Kaivalya, get your things. We are leaving for several hours."

"But mother…"

"Come. Now. No arguing."

"*Hmph.*"

With her bottom lip turned downward in a poorly concealed pout, Kaivalya hops down from her stool and stomps to her room.

"*Namaste*, Miss Collins. I trust you are well?"

"Yes, ma'am."

"*Accha*. I'm told my son will be joining you shortly. The both of you have some work to do yet if this merger is to succeed."

I nod slowly.

"Do you have any special requests for the flowers?" Sanji still hasn't moved more than three steps away from the elevator. "I'm taking Kaivalya with me on some errands, and we'll be selecting flowers."

"Flowers?"

"For the marriage ceremonies." Her tone is so dry. As if she expects me to be able to read her mind.

"Oh…um…"

Did Tahira care much for flowers? What were the flowers next to her father's urn?

"Jasmine? I like jasmine…"

Sanji nods. "An adequate flower choice."

Can flowers be *adequate*?

Kaivalya reappears carrying a small backpack around her little shoulders. She's also tied up her hair in a tight ponytail and looks markedly less energetic now than before her mother arrived. I don't blame her. The prospect of going out for the day with her mother would depress me too.

"Make yourself at home." Sanji's invitation sounds more like an order as she ushers Kai into the elevator.

As Sanji turns her back to me I give Kaivalya a sympathetic wave.

Now what?

I should have some time to kill before Deval arrives.

Should I brush up on my chess skills?

I could explore the penthouse in the meantime. Maybe I'll find out why my handlers want Deval dead. Maybe something to do with a Path?

I start by exploring the second floor…or is it the fifty-first?

The first two doors I try are locked. I could probably break into either room, but that'd be awkward to explain if I got caught. First, because I have no right to be snooping around, and second, because Tahira probably didn't know how to bypass a biometric lock system.

The next door opens to reveal a small library. Bookshelves line every available space on the walls. The Kapoor's collection is mostly business literature, a few religious Hindu texts, and some history books. Some of the tomes are even kept in glass cases. A few are open, revealing yellowed pages and brownish ink. The language on a particularly old-looking text looks the same as Tahira's copy of the *Vedas*. Sanskrit.

As I turn to leave the library, a sharp glint catches my eye. I stop. It's not a mirror…

A familiar silvery rhombus catches some light from a window. The symbol is engraved into the spine of a maroon book that lies on a shelf at about eye level.

My fingers brush the symbol, then a nearly imperceptible *click* follows. At the same time, my back begins to tingle. Like a current has just gone through me. I quickly withdraw my hand from the book, and the feeling stops. What in the…?

The entire bookshelf slowly swings toward me, and I have to skip backward a step to keep from getting hit in the jaw. Once the bookshelf comes to a rest, I'm left staring into a large…shrine?

Ignoring the mild burning sensation lingering between my shoulder blades, I take a tentative step into the hidden room. As soon as I step across the threshold of the door, dim lights appear, illuminating the room around me.

A subtle waft of incense engulfs me. There are several sticks set into the walls, casting off tiny wisps of smoke. Someone's been in here recently. The walls and floor are a dark red color. Numerous Hindu relics sit atop tables that wrap around the circular room. Some of the figures have candles or incense burning near them as well as *prashad*.

At the very center of the room lies a strange metallic pyramid. It's not very big, only a foot tall at most. An exact copy of the base pyramid hangs from the ceiling, directly above its pair on the ground. Like a stalactite and stalagmite.

A holoprojector. They're supposed to be capable of storing petabytes of information. It must have cost to buy a holoprojector for private use…

My breath catches in my throat. Where have I seen these before? Yes… Samantha Demeter's husband had a holoprojector too…

As if I'm a meteor caught in the gravitational pull of a planet, I'm dragged toward the holoprojectors. My feet make no sound on the carpet as I slowly make my way toward the center of the room.

When I'm two paces away from the base of the first projector, I flinch as a 3D panel materializes in front of me. I can't tell if the image created by the projectors is made from lasers or something else. Either way, it's immaterial and I can pass my hand through the bluish outline without meeting any resistance. There are several illuminated icons on the projected remote.

My curiosity is too strong. Could I learn something about my handlers' motivations? Some secret that might explain my existence and purpose as Divest?

Why hasn't the projector system required a specific biometric match to access? It hasn't even asked for a passcode. Then again, it *is* hidden in a secret room in a private penthouse.

The remote has several buttons to choose from and I touch an icon that looks like a globe. The projectors respond immediately. A column of light appears straddling the two projector units. At first there's nothing except a shifting network of shapes and light. It's mesmerizing. A second later, a representation of the Earth appears.

Countries are delineated by bright blue lines. There are perhaps a dozen red, pulsing dots that surround the globe. There are a handful in the States. One in Japan. Two in China. A faint, dull one in New Russia. And three in India…one of them right here in Bengaluru. It's like a scene out of a scifi movie. I quickly memorize the location of each marker. What do they mean? What would happen if I touch one of the red dots?

Ignoring the pulsing markers for the time being, I reach for the projected remote next to my elbow and select a different icon. One in the shape of a human silhouette.

The globe winks away and is replaced by a long list of names in alphabetical order. Some of the bluish glowing names are bright, others are faded. The projectors' display responds when I reach a finger toward the list of names and try to scroll. I slowly move through the list before stopping on one near the top. *Collins, John.*

Tahira's father.

His name is faded.

Directly below John's name is my body's. *Collins, Tahira.*

Unlike her father's, Tahira's name glows brightly. Strange…

I consider tapping on my current name to see if it pulls anything up, but I hesitate. I wonder if…?

The list of names, some faded some not, whiz upward in a bluish blur until I come to the L's.

What the hell…?

Louis, Camden.

The man I murdered in Chicago using Jill's body…his name is faded just like John Collins' had been.

My heart rate rises. I get goosebumps. What's going on here? This has to be a coincidence. Surely it's nothing more. There are probably plenty of Camden Louises in the world. Right? But I have to be sure…

Like air trapped under water, names of men and women I've murdered bubble to the surface of my mind.

I whip my finger upward and stop once I reach the D's.

Demeter, Broderick is on this list. Samantha's spouse…his name is faded.

So is *Granger, Ian.*

Hashira, Esther.

Faded.

Issmay, Simplicio.

Faded.

Jones, Silvia R.

Faded.

Naraday, Stephen.

Faded.

But *Kapoor, Deval* and *Kapoor, Sanji* glow bright and steady…

There are other names, like the Kapoors, that still glow brightly. What secrets do these names contain?

I scroll back up until I find *Collins, Tahira* again. This time I tap it.

The blue name flashes and materializes into a profile, complete with a recent photo of Tahira. There are four tabs, each with a different title. The one immediately displayed says *History.*

I read the first few lines of Tahira's short bio but don't bother reading through the rest. It's just Tahira's personal history. Similar to the bio my handlers gave me back in California. I skip to the second tab labeled *Calling.*

June 04, 2095

Tahira Collins, daughter of the late Brother John Collins, you have hereby been called to the office of Exemplar. You are tasked with aiding in the reunification of world powers, ending border shutdowns, and fostering peace both politically and economically. Unity is life. Concordia Vitae.

—the Brethren Council

Okay…my body is officially a member of a cult.

I have more questions than answers now. What *kind* of cult do I belong to? It can't be too bad. Uniting countries again is a long shot but certainly not an *evil* goal.

There are still two more tabs…

"*Namaste*, Tahira."

I whirl around, bringing my fists up and spreading my legs apart.

Deval's eyes widen, and he raises an eyebrow. He regards me like I'm a total stranger.

I quickly drop my fists and feel myself blushing. How did I not hear him approach? I'm such a fool.

"Deval, I'm so sorry. I can explain, I…"

"You found our temple; that's nothing to be sorry for. I was going to show this place to you eventually anyway. After our wedding."

"Oh." My eyes meet Deval's. "You were?"

"Of course." Deval's smile is broad and genuine. I relax a little. "We're on the Path together, are we not?"

The Path…

At the lake house, Tahira mentioned her father would take her there to teach her things. Things about history, governments, leaders…and a Path. The man who tried killing me in the Collins home mentioned it too. What does it *mean*?

Deval gestures around the room.

"I imagine this all looks familiar to you. You had your own temple in California, didn't you?"

All I can do is nod. This is bad. What if this is a test?

"This sanctuary is where my family often comes to learn. Also to worship. *Dharma* is so close to the Path, don't you agree? I used to believe that Hinduism was very different from Unitas. Now that I'm older, I realize they're more like two sides to the same coin. Wouldn't you agree?"

Unitas. Tahira is a member of Unitas. Her father was too. Those names on the list, the faded ones…

How many of my targets did Deval know…?

"Tahira…?"

He's acting like I should be familiar with all of this already. What can I say? I'm confident discussing Hinduism or even participating in some of its rituals. But having a friendly chat about a cult my body belongs to? I'm lost.

I need to turn this conversation back on him.

"I suppose they're similar. But how do you mean, exactly?"

"Well, Unitas, Hinduism, they're both ancient, right? We obviously don't know just how old, but it's agreed that both began hundreds of years ago. Both teach of a higher purpose, a reason for existing. Both seek to push humanity forward in pursuit of a higher plane. Truth. Unity. Peace. Liberation. Surely you've had similar thoughts?"

I nod. This isn't helpful. What if I can get Deval to...

"Come on, I can show you more later. Or vice versa, as I'm sure I have a lot to learn from you, Tahira. Plus, Mother would probably kill me if she knew we were alone together up here."

Deval smiles and takes my hand as he escorts me out of the secret room. The wall slides back into position once we're out and Deval leads the way as we begin descending the stairs to the main floor. This is insane. How have I not put these pieces together before? They're all connected. Everyone I've ever been sent to spy on or murder. They're...

"What do you say to some shopping today? You enjoy shopping, right?"

I frown. "I thought you said there was something I needed to do to make sure the merger moves along as planned?"

Deval holds up a finger and turns toward Faru who's standing guard beside the elevator doors.

"Faru, would you be so kind as to make sure the 4Runner is charged? I'd like to take it out today for our errands."

"Of course, *mahoday*. But your mother has left me with instructions not to leave the two of you alone for..."

"It's fine, Faru. We'll be down in a minute. I just need to discuss a sensitive matter with Tahira."

Faru looks torn. Finally, he nods and enters the elevator by himself.

As soon as the elevator doors are closed Deval takes my hand and leads me toward a leather couch.

This isn't the first time I've been alone with Deval…what's the worse that could happen? What "sensitive" matter is he referring to?

"I told you I'd fill you in so…"

Deval meets my eyes. He's still holding my hand in his.

"We think the gunman from yesterday was or is a member of the CIA. Authorities have been unable to officially confirm the man's connection to the CIA, but there's a strong possibility he was sent by your government to kill the Jarrius CEO…and possibly more company leadership if he'd had the chance."

Really? The CIA? This sounds like some foreigner conspiracy…but could it be true?

"The board members we still need signatures from are spooked. They're afraid there may be more retribution if the merger is allowed to continue. I've managed to convince a few of the less reluctant ones that our companies need this merger. We've come too close only to back away at the last second."

"What about the others? The board members who still haven't signed off?"

"That's what I might need your help with, convincing them the world needs this. That the world needs more unity. We can be a powerful example of trust and cooperation. Particularly in light of what's happened with the gunman. I'm confident your words can help change the last few minds that the merger needs to move forward."

What can *I* say that would help the situation? Tahira left me high and dry in this arena.

"But give it a day or two. Kabir and I may be able to convince the last three board members yet."

"Okay. So, in the meantime…"

Deval grins. "Ever been to a *baajaar?*"

26 26 26 26 26 **26** 2

Our drive through Bengaluru lasts about twenty minutes. I struggle to listen to Deval's attempts at conversation.

Those names…in the Kapoor's Temple. It was like I was looking at a grocery list from my handlers. Have all my targets been members of this… organization? Cult? Religion? What *is* Unitas?

A jolt from the car snaps me out of my trance. We pull into a gated lot. The secluded parking area is surrounded on three sides by tall, glass apartment buildings.

"It's about a five-minute walk to the market, is that okay?" Deval searches my face for an answer while Faru opens my door to let me out of the car. Has he noticed how distracted I've been?

"Yep." Maybe a walk *would* be good.

The air smells much like it did when I stepped out of the hotel my first day in Bengaluru. I close my eyes and inhale. Sharp spices mix with different kinds of incense and other, fruity smells.

"Ma'am." Faru's voice brings my attention back.

He's holding a pair of sunglasses and a scarf toward me. I glance at Deval and raise an eyebrow.

"Hopefully those will help us remain, what's the word…incognito." Deval nods at the scarf and glasses. My false fiancé smiles and dons his own hat and glasses. Faru himself is dressed wearing jeans and a long sleeve button-up shirt, rather than his typical black suit and tie. I guess he's trying to help us blend in too? How did I not notice his attire before?

I wrap the thin, colorful scarf around my head and put on the sunglasses.

With our cliché disguises in place, I follow Deval as he waves me toward the lot's gate. Faru follows in tow right behind me.

"Are you hungry, Tahira? Do you want to stop for some food first?"

I shake my head. "I haven't been hungry lately. Might still have something to do with the jet lag." And the fact that I've been killing off members of the same secret group for over a year. *What can it mean?*

"Okay, just let me know if there's anything I can get you. And I mean anything."

That's right. We're super rich…

As soon as we leave the parking lot, we get swept away in a river of bodies. Deval takes my hand to keep us from getting separated as we make our way toward what I assume is an entrance to the market. I glance back after a minute or two. Faru's emotionless face is only a few paces directly behind us.

I'm not a claustrophobic person, but was Tahira? Her body starts to feel clammy. My breathing becomes shallow. I can't get enough air into Tahira's lungs. There are too many people. All around. Pressing against me. With some effort, I ignore the uncomfortable feeling and continue walking, trying to avoid touching people as much as possible. People surround us on all sides, not giving us a second glance.

"This is one of the most popular markets for two hundred miles." Deval has to raise his voice to be heard over the din. "Normally it's not this busy on a day like today. Are you okay? You look a little pale."

I brush away Deval's concern with a lazy wave of Tahira's hand and try not to retch.

Deval still looks concerned, but he doesn't question me further.

We pass under an arch of sorts. *Laxmi*, goddess of wealth, stands atop one of the columns clutching matching lotus flowers in her golden fingers. Her consort, *Vishnu*, stands opposite. Two of his arms are raised and the other two hang at his sides. There's Hindi along the arch, but I don't understand what it says. It's probably something obvious…like *marketplace*.

The crowd thins a little once we're past the archway and into the market. I can breathe easier now too.

We pause for a moment in the middle of a circular stone courtyard. Then, Deval's strong arm pulls me toward a store. Reluctantly, I let him pull me along. The shop front has an artistic, bright blue banyan tree symbol above its entrance.

"You'll like this store."

Why would I like it?

All I can manage is a thumbs up. I'm definitely going to be sick. At least I didn't have a very big breakfast…

Keep it together. No fainting. My gut clenches at the thought of losing consciousness here…surrounded by so many people…

The air conditioning inside the store is absolutely amazing. It was so hot outside. So humid. I was beginning to suffocate.

The store holds a vast array of women's clothing. Some brands were even popular in the United States, at least…they were before the shutdowns eliminated most textile trade. I wander the aisles with Deval shadowing me.

"See anything you like? I feel bad you've had to wear the same thing two days in a row."

I couldn't care less if I had to wear the same outfit for a *month* straight. Wearing someone else's body is kind of like that anyway. Some retail therapy might be a welcome distraction though. Even if Deval's idea of shopping for me isn't really for the *real* me.

I refrain from looking through things that would normally interest me. Do I even have favorite kinds of clothes anymore? No…I've been divested of my taste in fashion. What would Tahira like? What kind of stuff would fit with her wardrobe?

For the next five minutes or so I continue to peruse the aisles. Where are the virtual reality features that allow you to try clothes on without changing? Maybe you have to request a headset?

I find a pair of sleek black jeans and a few tops. A *sari* catches Tahira's eye, so I grab one. A store employee sees me carrying my assortment of clothing and approaches me; I avoid looking too closely at the woman's polished nametag.

"*Kya mein aapki madad kar sakti hoon?*"

The young woman looks up at me expectantly.

I need to learn more Hindi. "Er…English?"

The short, Indian youth frowns.

"Would you like to try those on?" Her English is tinged with a strong accent.

"Yes, please." I hope Tahira's accent isn't a dead giveaway she's American.

"Right this way, ma'am."

Toward the back of the store is a row of pale blue curtains. Do they have fully immersive VR fitting rooms? The young woman pulls back a curtain on the end, revealing an empty space with mirrors on all sides.

Mirrors. Oh God…

I glance away sharply.

I can't do it.

There are too many of them.

"Right in here, Miss…?"

My heart is about to leap out of my chest.

I raise a hand to my breast to try to calm myself.

"Miss…?"

She's asking for my name. My name…

I manage to bite my tongue before saying *Collins*. I don't want to be recognized.

"McKenzie."

I cover my mouth, but it's too late. What have I done?

The employee nods politely and gestures for me to enter the fitting room. My body moves of its own accord. A second later I'm inside, and the curtain closes.

They're just mirrors. They can't hurt me. They can't…hurt me…

I raise both my hands up and push against the mirrors on either side of me. They push back. Closing in on me. They're going to crush me. Their surfaces are ice cold.

I keep my eyes locked on the floor tiles and grit my teeth.

Come on. Pull yourself together. Breathe.

Slowly, I get my heart and lungs back under control.

I'm a fool. What was I thinking using my *real* name? That's right, I *wasn't* thinking…

I'm sure it's harmless. Right? No way my handlers will ever know…but what if they find out? They might punish Jeremy…

This store must be trying to be old fashioned. Vintage. Classic even. Is that why Deval thought I'd like it? Do I even bother trying on any of the clothes? I just want to get out of this box, but does Deval expect me to buy something today? Probably. Some men like it when they can buy you things…

I locate the prices listed on the digital tags. If I get the conversion rate right, and if I account for the extreme devaluation of the dollar, the cheapest item of clothing I grabbed is being sold for $1,800—and it's on *clearance*.

I throw up.

Breakfast spews from my mouth and I gag several times. The acrid mess splashes on the floor, but I keep my eyes locked on the ground.

My throat burns. Tahira's lips tremble, and I wipe her mouth on my sleeve. Immediately, my head begins to hurt and my vision swims. Careful to avoid the pungent mess on the floor, I manage to take a seat on the small bench inside the fitting room to avoid collapsing.

Sitting helps with the dizziness, and after a moment or two, my vision returns to normal. I check my pulse. My heart is beating rapidly, but it's slowing down.

What's happening to me? I need help. Powell needs to know what's going on. He'll know what's wrong with me. He…

No.

I have to be strong. I have to finish my mission no matter what so I can get Jeremy back. I just threw up. It's not like I had a heart attack…

I swallow my discomfort, and some bile, then set about undressing so I can don at least one of the outfits I've selected. I still have an act to play.

The jeans are tight around my thighs, but fit well around my waist. They reach my ankles, which is the current style in India. The first shirt I touch is the color of a smogless sky. It feels fluid but sturdy at the same time. The *sari*…how do I even wear it? The fabric is unbelievably soft and has tiny gold patterns—none of which provide step-by-step instructions of how to don it.

No *sari*. If Deval asks, I'll just say I didn't like the color.

Careful to keep my eyes low, I leave the rest of the clothes in the fitting room but retrieve the clothes I was wearing before. I slip my sunglasses on again before exiting. Outside the fitting room, the air is much easier to breathe. My eyes find Deval seated close by, waiting for me. How long has he been there? Did he hear me throw up?

"Wow. You look…" Deval's eyes find me, and he looks me up and down.

I smile weakly. Do I look as sick as I feel? Maybe my new outfit helps distract Deval in that regard.

"…amazing. You look amazing, Tahira. Do you want to get all that? I think you should. If you like the outfit, of course."

I probably *should* let Deval buy me these clothes. Besides, the clothes I came with have a little bit of my breakfast on them now.

"Do you want to try anything else on?"

I shake my head.

"Okay. I'll go buy everything. You should be able to wear everything out of the store."

"That'd be great."

Deval smiles again and heads toward the front of the store.

As he leaves, I hang back for a moment and catch the attention of the young store employee I blurted my name to earlier.

"I'm really sorry, but I made a bit of a mess in your fitting room."

I hand her a wad of cash and apologize one last time before leaving to find Deval.

He's waiting for me at the front of the store.

"Shall we?"

I nod.

We step back out into the open air of the mall proper, and I let Deval lead me past several more stores. Is he hoping I'll comment on a store I'd like to explore? Maybe—but if I open my mouth again something bad might happen.

People press against me, and I try to stick close to Deval, using him like a windbreak.

We turn down a corner next to a little cart selling some kind of street food. The sizzling and cracking of oil seems louder than it should be. Deval is about to lead us up onto an escalator when Faru appears from behind us and taps Deval on the shoulder.

Faru nods toward a store we just passed.

"Oh yeah, uh…Tahira, there's something I need to pick up. It's for you, actually, and it's a bit of a surprise. So…"

"I can wait here."

"You sure? We'll only be a second, I promise."

I nod.

Whatever Deval's picking up must require Faru's help, because both of them leave my side and walk back the way we came. What is he buying? It had better not be something Deval might expect Tahira to wear the night of our honeymoon…

If it is…I might throw up again.

Standing starts to make me feel lightheaded. I should sit down. A wrought iron bench sits unoccupied a few paces away. Yes. A bench has never looked so inviting.

I take three steps toward it when an intense pressure wracks my brain. It's like someone's hit me over the head with something. I stumble, nearly falling. People and storefronts swim in and out of focus. No. Please no. I can't make my legs move. It's happening. Again.

Tahira's senses are overloaded. People's voices are too loud. The air is too saturated with spice and incense. My clothes too constricting. The pain in my head is nothing compared to the feeling of dread that sweeps through me.

I watch helplessly as the solid ground comes racing up to meet me. My arms are useless.

The initial impact fills my ears with a ringing sound. The stone tiles are gritty beneath my cheek. Someone screams.

Darkness begins to encroach. Smothering me. Dozens of different feet surround me in a distinct semicircle. Get up…can't let this happen…not here…

Blackness consumes me entirely, and I fall into nothingness. As if from atop a precipice…

"She should be fine, Mr. Kapoor. She was most likely suffering from an extreme case of food poisoning. Possibly an allergic reaction as well. We can run more tests if you'd like."

"Thank you, Doctor. Will she be awake soon?"

"Hard to say. It's concerning she hasn't woken yet, but nothing about her condition is an immediate concern. There are a few more tests we could run to be sure, but it seems whatever was causing her such distress has left her system."

"We'll see how she feels about running more tests when she's awake."

"That's fine. We'll keep monitoring her, but at least she's stable now."

"*Dhanyavad.*"

"Of course. Let me know if you need anything else."

"Still nothing?"

"No. Doctors are considering giving her some kind of steroid."

"I'm taking Kaivalya home with me. You should join us. You have been here for nearly twenty-four hours, Deval."

"I won't leave her. Go without me if you must."

"Deval…"

"*Mother.* I'm staying."

"Very well. Let me know if her condition changes."

"Yes, Mother."

The rectangular light above me is blinding.

I blink several times until my eyes adjust.

My throat is dry. The air tastes of plastics…and lemon. There's a hole in my stomach…why am I so hungry?

My body responds slowly as I try to sit up.

Where am I?

I'm naked. No…I'm wearing a light blue gown. Tubes run from my left arm to a series of monitors.

I'm lying in a hospital bed.

The room is empty and silent. I'm alone except for several blinking screens and two gray recliners. The walls are a pale orange color. There's a window with half-drawn shades. It's late.

How long have I been here? My memory isn't responding at all…

Have the arms attached to my body always been so brown? Perhaps it's something to do with the dim lighting? Have I always had black hair? It's like a bottle of spilled ink cascading down my neck. The lines of my cheeks and jaw feel unfamiliar. The touch of my own skin…foreign. Why? I choke. Air isn't getting through my constricted throat. It's too hot. I'm sweating more than I should be.

What…happened to me?

Where am I?

Who am I?

Thoughts come slowly. Images flash through my mind like an antique movie reel. Nameless, blurry faces grin at me. Places and buildings I feel like

I should recognize flash on and off in my head. Gritting my teeth doesn't help my memories come any faster. What's wrong with me...?

Was I in an accident?

I don't have any obvious injuries.

I'm teetering between two chasms. Confusion screams at me to panic and run. Fear whispers that I should devolve into tears. I flounder, trying to keep from falling to either side.

Who. Am. I?

Drunkenly, I scramble to escape from the stifling grasp of the bed sheets.

"Good. You're awake."

I freeze. The doctor is wearing a traditional white coat. Where did he come from? His skin is far lighter than mine. The man's pale blue eyes are devoid of warmth. Those glasses...they kind of make him look like an insect.

My voice won't work properly. All I manage is an unintelligible murmur that barely crawls out through my lips. The man holds up a finger to his thin, colorless lips. "Do not call out. If you do, I'll have to put you under again."

Why would I call out? Why would he have to put me under again? I just want to know what's going on.

I struggle to connect his face with a name. Has he been the doctor assigned to me by this hospital? Is he a specialist?

No.

He...I know him from somewhere else.

Where?

I trust him—but don't like him.

Powell...

Yes. His name is Powell.

Although...he's not the kind of doctor that works at hospitals...is he?

Powell's spectacles reflect the tiny amount of light in the room, and his face is expressionless. How do I know this man?

"I don't have much time." Powell's voice is a whisper. Why is he whispering? "Should anyone approach us while I'm here, do not say a word. Do you understand?"

Why is he treating me like I'm in trouble?

Eventually, I manage to nod. I need answers.

"Who am I?" My lips tremble slightly as I whisper.

"You are Tahira Collins." Powell raises a narrow eyebrow and regards me skeptically.

Yes...

That sounds right.

I'm Tahira...Tahira Collins...

"You've been here nearly three days now. I've managed to gain access to you and have finished with your treatment. Though, I'm not sure if it's enough at this point."

I begin to nod my head, but...Powell hasn't told me what I want to hear. I still have no clue what's going on. Memories are moving about as fast as a glacier...before they all melted.

"What do you mean? What treatment? What happened to me? I overheard a doctor saying I had an allergic reaction."

Powell glances over his shoulder as he picks up a tablet. The blue screen hurts my eyes.

"Please...what's going on? Why am I..."

"There was no allergic reaction. Your brain is failing."

My stomach sinks. I...yes, I *have* been ill. Chronic migraines. A constant feeling like something is wrong with me. Forgetfulness. Nausea. Imbalance. Feeling lost...almost like Mother when she...

"What do you mean *my brain is failing*?"

"I've told you as much as I'm allowed."

Why can't Powell tell me more? I *need* to know more.

He turns to leave, but I reach for his arm. His coat is stiff—and cold.

"Please. What's happening to me?"

Powell shakes his arm free and regards me with a blank stare.

"*Please.*" I'm adrift. Lost. I need something, anything.

Powell adjusts his spectacles and continues to stare at me. Slowly, almost imperceptibly, his posture relaxes. He's no longer standing so rigidly.

"The foreigners do not possess the right technology for diagnosing you properly. Even if they did, I doubt they'd know what to look for, so I cannot give you specifics because I don't have them myself. There is perhaps a myriad of possibilities that may account for your symptoms."

Powell swims in and out of focus; I can't see straight. Still, I stare into Powell's insect eyes, demanding that he continue. I remember being sick, and my chronic head pain, but I have to know more.

"Your brain is developing either a new disease or a new…disorder. Which I fear will eventually kill you."

What…?

Powell pushes his glasses up further on his nose. He sounds like a professor lecturing a class. "You could be experiencing the first signs of a new motor neuron disease. Your body is also expressing symptoms typically found in people with Alzheimer's. Additionally, your body is behaving in ways that might suggest you've received major trauma to the preoptic area or the thalamus itself."

He's talking too fast. Every word is in time with each staccato beat of my heart.

"It's also possible your limbic system is somehow shutting itself down periodically, with increasingly smaller gaps in between episodes. Yet another thought I've had is that you may be suffering from a kind of hyper-traumatic stress disorder, which might explain your nausea and increased heart rate "

None of this makes sense. Why wasn't I aware of any of this before? I just had chronic migraines. Nothing a little medicine couldn't solve…

"Finally, it's possibility that the injections I designed to keep your brain stable are growing less and less effective. Like any drug that loses potency with repeated usage."

Alzheimer's?

Hyper-traumatic stress?

Major brain trauma?

Motor neuron disease?

Injections?

"Of course, it may very well be a combination of *many* of these things. Only time will tell. Either way…your brain is dying."

This is too surreal. A dream…I'm in a dream. I'll wake up soon, and I'll be back in my room. My ailing mother will be there too. Maria will be bringing breakfast soon. None of this will be real. It can't be…but dreams aren't this detailed. Dreams don't wear too-white lab coats and reach over to adjust tubes that pinch.

I'm not in California.

My mother she…there was a…a funeral. I was there.

Fire. Ashes.

Nothing but ashes.

This can't possibly be a dream. It's not even a nightmare. This is real.

"Will I really die?" My dry croak sounds pitiful. Weak. Scared.

"…whatever damage we…or rather, whatever damage *I*…have caused your brain will continue to worsen. There's no reason to hope your brain will fix itself. So yes, in your present state—you will die."

I'm *dying*?

"How soon your brain will fail, I cannot say." Powell is oblivious to my reaction to his words. "But based on the current rate of deterioration, you still have enough time to finish your mission."

My mission? What mission? I still don't even know exactly where I am besides a hospital bed. What did Powell mean when he said *he's* caused the damage that's occurred…or occurring…in my brain? How is he to blame?

Nothing makes sense.

Too many pieces to this puzzle just aren't connecting in my head.

Ice courses through my veins, burning my too-warm flesh. Muscles all over my body begin trembling. Whether from fear, rage, or confusion, I don't know. I'm too scared or too unstable to decide. Maybe it's a combination of all of it. I ball my hands into fists and try to fight the tears that are threatening to explode right along with my emotions. My body feels wrong. My mind feels wrong. Everything feels wrong.

Powell clears his throat.

He keeps talking, but I'm not paying attention.

I can't die. I have…something I have to do first. Someone who desperately needs me. Someone I love more than anything…

The urge to rip my hair out of my head in frustration is overwhelming. Nothing is coming back to me. I'm still adrift. Alone. Frightened.

"…condition worsens. Also—both promises still stand. If you run, if you go for help, you will be terminated. We're always watching. They wanted me to remind you it's your choice; though it doesn't seem like much of a choice if you ask me. Kill Kapoor, or you and the only family you have left will die. Kill Deval, and I can deliver you. I'm the only one who can save your brain."

What?

I'm supposed to kill someone? Someone named Kapoor? And if I don't— *I'll* die? Others will die? My family?

Powell's eyes and body language don't belong to a liar. Why do I trust what this man is telling me? My brain really *is* failing. The never ending headaches I've experienced for the past few weeks are definitely more than the result of an allergic reaction. I'm not allergic to anything besides some pollens…

But…I'm supposed to kill someone? How can I believe that? I *can't* believe it. Something's going on here. Maybe Powell has me mistaken for someone else. I'm not a killer…

Powell adjusts one of the tubes connected to my arm again.

Without another word, like a pale ghost, Powell slips out of my room, taking what little sense of safety or control I had with him.

A scream starts to build from the base of my belly, writhing its way up and through my clenched jaws.

An animal frenzy courses through me, and I reach for a half-empty pitcher of water next to my bedside. It nearly slips, my arm is so weak, but I scream again and manage to hurl it across the room.

It smacks the far wall, making a loud noise and spilling water in all directions.

Just as I'm reaching for the tray to throw next, the door to my room clicks open. Warm yellow light from the hallway pours into my room. A man enters. He's tall and his skin is more brown than mine. His eyes immediately find the pitcher, still spinning slightly on the tiled floor.

Then he turns to me.

I know this man. But why is he looking at me with such…tenderness? Such concern?

This man loves me.

I'm…important to him.

Deval.

The difference between Dev's eyes and Powell's is like the difference between night and day.

A sob escapes my cracked lips. Dev crosses the room in three strides. He wraps his arms around me tightly. He's so warm. "Tahira."

His voice fills me with comfort. Peace. Reassurance…

Yes.

I hold onto him, pulling him as close to me as possible. Deval is the only thing that *isn't* wrong in the world right now. My tears wet his shoulder and chest. Don't let go. Please don't let go.

Eventually, my tears cease, though my hands and arms are still trembling. "Tahira I…I'm so glad you're awake…"

Another sob, full of relief, leaps from my throat.

"I'm going to get a nurse to let them know you're conscious." Dev reaches for a button near my headboard.

"No." I want a few more minutes alone with him. "It's fine. I'm fine."

Dev raises an eyebrow. At least he hasn't asked me about why I threw the pitcher.

"Tahira…you were out for almost *three days*. My family and I…we've been worried sick about you."

"I thought *I* was the sick one."

Dev doesn't laugh at my feeble joke, but he's trying hard not to grin.

"Apparently you've been fighting an allergic reaction. Do you remember eating something or touching something that might have done this to you?"

I shake my head.

"I shouldn't have left you alone in the market like I did. That was foolish of me. *Maaf kijiye,* Tahira. I should've been right by your side the whole time."

"It's not your fault, Dev. I'm feeling much better—really."

He frowns. The image of me lying in a hospital bed hooked up to a bunch of machines probably isn't helping my cause.

"I think I'd just like to go home."

"Home? Like…California? I can't say I exactly blame you. After all you've been through since arriving. I'm sure we can change plans again and get married in…"

"Deval—I mean the Queen's House."

229

"Oh. Right.

"Where are we by the way?"

"Fortis Hospital. It was the closest place to the *baajaar*."

I nod. "Help me out of these tubes?"

"Of course. No—wait. What am I saying? You need a doctor to look at you first now that you're awake."

I wink. "Well you'd better get me a doctor then."

Dev smiles. "I will. Anything else?"

"Yeah, one more thing." I reach for Dev's collar and pull him close to me…but hesitate. What am I doing? Something about being intimate with this man feels…dishonest? That's absurd. We're engaged. Suddenly, Deval leans closer and kisses me. I start kissing him back.

Energy rushes through me. It's incredible. This is better than I've felt in…how long?

After a few more seconds of bliss, Dev pulls away.

"I'll go get a doctor."

He slips out of the room, and I touch my still-tingling lips.

Miraculously, my head pain seems to have cleared for the moment. I'm much more awake. The memory of Dev's lips on mine lingers for a moment, and I savor the dopamine coursing through me. Dev's scent lingers, and I can almost imagine his hands are still around me. Protecting me.

Do I trust myself? Is my mind back to normal? No. A part of me is still missing. I'm incomplete somehow. I've forgotten something crucial. Maybe something that will connect all the disjointed memories bouncing around in my head. There's a nagging from the depths of my mind, like an itch, but whatever it is remains veiled in darkness.

What's my mind trying to tell me?

More memories hit me like a punch to my face.

Biting cold enters my body like icicles being pushed through my veins.

My handlers.

Evil, unknown people. They've ordered me to do something horrific for them. But what?

Oh God…my mission.

I reach for more memories at the back of my mind.

Yes. Powell's voice rings in my ears.

My mission…

The people Powell works for have set me on a journey with murder as the destination—and *I'm* the murderer. But why? Why did this happen to me? Why would I ever agree to something so despicable?

My handlers…they…they're holding something of mine hostage. Something important to me is under their control. What do they have…? What could they possibly have of mine? Mother is gone. I broke things off with Liam. Deval is safe. What else could they use to…

My brain.

Yes.

That has to be it.

The pieces are fitting together better now.

I am my own hostage.

That would explain why Powell is the only one who can save me from whatever is wrong with my brain. My handlers must have worked through Powell to give me some kind of disease, or whatever the hell is wrong with me, to force me to do their bidding. I'm like a modern-day Pizza Bomber.

Sharper, more recent memories begin to surface. I'm in India. My first night was spent in a hotel. The next morning, Deval surprised me in the lobby. We spent the rest of the day at the Queen's House. I met Dev's family. Then there were meetings for the merger. A gunman tried to kill people. Deval took me on a date. I had a sleepover with Kai. Then Deval took us to a mall. Is that when I passed out? It must be…

Why can't I shake the feeling that I've forgotten something?

Is it something to do with the conversation I just had with Powell? Am I forgetting something about my mission? No.

I'm supposed to marry Deval.

And then…I'm supposed to kill him.

But why? Why do my handlers want him dead? Is it because of the merger? Is it because we're getting married? Is it because he's a foreigner?

No. There's something else. There has to be another reason…

Another reason why I—Tahira Collins—am supposed to kill Deval Abdul Kapoor.

"I thought your mother said…"

"We've talked. Mother understands she may have been imposing too strictly. I've promised her we'll still act civilly toward one another though."

"And Faru…?"

"He'll be near, but he understands too. In fact, I think he's decided to just wait for us in the car."

"Oh."

"Besides, the wedding festivities are only a week away. Soon, my mother's wishes won't be as…applicable."

"Right." Dev and I walk hand in hand along a stone path. A brightly colored bird chirps overhead. The air tastes rich and full of life in the gardens of Lal Bagh. The sun is low, approaching sunset. How many days has it been now since I first arrived in India? Have I really lost track?

At least Dev was able to reserve the gardens just for us today. No prying eyes. No flashing cameras. Just us. There are a few groundskeepers, but none of them bother us as we walk through the beautiful palm trees or skirt the edge of the large turquoise lake.

How can I rationalize my feelings for the man holding my hand? Something must be wrong with my heart. I'm drawn to him, but there's a barrier, keeping me from expressing my love the same way he does. I can't possibly love Deval the same way he loves me. But why? Love is a choice…isn't it?

"You want to keep going? Do you need a break?"

I shake my head. "Thanks for asking, but I'm fine, Dev. I'm happy to be on a date with you." Should I even call this a date? It feels wrong to date a man I've been threatened to kill. Even if he *is* my fiancé.

At least our "date" is distracting me from thinking of Powell…er, *was* distracting me…

Think about something else. Anything.

Could I try piecing together the rest of my jumbled, fragmented memories? Remembering my past might help me get a grip on my present. I haven't tried going very far back…

The memories of a younger me are blurry, but continuous. That's normal, right? But why is everything I recall seem to be so…logical? Why are all my memories in exact, chronological order? Like a list. Is this how I've always remembered things?

What are the earliest things I can remember? Yes…I used to spend days at the lake house with my father before he divorced my mother. Mother taught me about Hinduism. Father died when I was twelve. When I was seventeen I began school at Stanford. I met Steffany, one of my best friends. We earned our degrees at the same time but went our separate ways. I found my calling. With Mother's help, I planned the merger of WorldFuse with Jarrius. I accepted the idea of an arranged marriage to provide an example of unity to a damaged world. Everything was going smoothly. Deval and I were ready for the hostility that came. Even after Liam's betrayal.

I just wasn't ready for that same hostility to break into my home and try to kill me…

I accidentally squeeze Dev's hand tight while he's pointing out some flowers. I apologize and act like I'm interested in the plants.

Where is this memory coming from? Why does it feel new? Recent?

It was night. I was alone. Someone broke into my home.

I hid in a closet, but the intruder found me. He attacked me.

Then…what?

Oh God…

I stumble, nearly falling and Dev catches me—barely.

"Whoa, Tahira, are you all right? Did you trip on that root?"

I glance sharply up at Deval and nod my head.

Stepping over the root, Deval and I continue along the path through yet another flower garden.

Kidnapped. The man he…drugged me. Then…

He's the reason my brain is dying. No. That's not right. Powell admitted to that much himself when he showed up in my hospital room.

I woke up in the back of a van. I was taken to an underground lab and tied to an operating table. Then…

An icy shaft descends down through my spine, and I shiver despite the heat of the evening. While Dev is distracted by a pair of birds swimming across the lake, I slowly reach my right hand up to the base of my skull.

The ridges are tiny. Nearly imperceptible.

Laser scarring…

What did they do to me?

The mask they forced over my mouth tasted sour. There were others in the room with me. A doctor. More black clad men with hard faces. My maid was there too. Maria. Did they kill her? I screamed until my voice hurt my throat before I passed out…

What did they do to me?

They definitely did something to my brain down in that lab. The surgical laser scars on the back of my head and neck are proof. But what exactly *did* they do? Powell said he was giving me injections. Wasn't he saying his injections were behind whatever's wrong with me? Maybe that's just part of it. Maybe they implanted a bomb or something? Poison? Nanobots? *What did they do to me?*

Dev taps my shoulder and I flinch. He doesn't seem to notice my anxiety as he pushes the stem of a bright yellow flower over my left ear. He grins and caresses my jaw with the back of his knuckles.

I can barely make my lips twitch up into a smile as I pose for a picture with Dev's phone. He takes my hand and we continue walking. If it weren't for Deval leading me along, I'd be frozen in place. When did it get so cold outside?

After the forced surgery…what happened next? I must have been given my ultimatum. Yes. Like Powell's echoed promises. Marry Deval and kill him, or my brain will kill *me*.

These memories are connecting better than most. Why? This line of events feels right…but it's all so wrong.

Deval is smiling and saying something about a famous Indian general. I've only been half listening to him. Finally, my eyes slowly shift from the ground to Deval.

Who is he to me—really? Isn't he just a way to show the world that unity across lines of hate was possible? Isn't he just a means to an end? No. Of course not, what am I thinking? He's more than that…he's…

Dev laughs at something, and I smile. It feels wrong to smile. But so right at the same time. His voice feels right. His hand feels right. *Dev* feels right. But *I* feel wrong. So wrong.

Deval isn't' just a means to an end. Even if it was supposed to be an unselfish end. He's so much more. But how can I allow these feelings to continue when my life is a sham and my brain is on the clock?

If I complete this mission Powell will somehow be able to save me.

He said I'll be saving my family too.

But, I have no family. I'm alone.

There's no one left for me to care about.

Is there?

If I'm being held hostage, why haven't I gone for help already? Powell said my handlers were watching me. How are they watching me? Is this what has kept me from going to someone for help? Fear of what will happen if they catch me?

Powell said something about two kinds of promises. He said that should I fail to kill Deval—I'll die. Powell also said my family will be killed too. But my family is already dead. Father passed away when I was young. Mother was much more recent. I *have* no family. Just ashes. Surely he doesn't mean Gary…or Steffany.

My heart sinks.

No. I *do* have family.

Deval's family.

Kaivalya's small, innocent face fills my mind. No. They wouldn't dare. But who else could Powell be referring to? My handlers mean to kill the only family I have left. Kaivalya, Viti, and Sanji Kapoor.

But…killing Deval to save his family? What kind of a trade is that? They'd be destroyed one way or another. Whether I fail or succeed, either way, the Kapoor family will be damaged beyond repair.

Are they really my family though?

For the rest of the evening I seal my lips to keep the awfulness inside me from escaping. Deval doesn't call me out on it. Instead, he mostly leaves me to my thoughts.

I wish he wouldn't.

Although we don't use words, there's still a connection. Every time our eyes meet, even for the briefest of moments, I fall deeper and deeper into Dev's eyes.

I'm torn.

Between my body and my mind.

The two are so distinct. Separate. Broken. Why? Why do I feel this way?

My body sends clear, powerful signals to my brain that it wants Dev. While my brain…my brain is struggling to shut down those very same feelings. Logic wars with my emotions. Both sides are equally matched. Which will conquer the other?

Why do my handlers want Deval dead?

Did I ever know?

Have my handlers told me anything else since my surgery? If they're watching me, surely they have some way of…

My phone.

They *have* communicated with me since the lab.

My phone…

No. Don't pull it out now. Not in front of Dev.

Tonight. When I'm alone, I'll check. Please be wrong…

I follow Dev up onto a small bridge that crosses a quiet stream. The tip of my shoe nearly catches on a loose wooden plank. I catch myself on Dev's arm.

He laughs. "Someone's a bit klutzy today, isn't she? Care for a swim, Tahira?"

Can I swim?

Yes…I think. Father taught me. At the lake house…right?

Dev notices my hesitation. I should've smiled at least. He was just making a joke, but I'm unraveling again. Why is it so taxing for me to remember such simple things?

"Tahira, you've been very quiet the past few days. Ever since the hospital. Is something wrong?"

My thumb traces the slim, golden band around my ring finger and I stare at my feet.

"I haven't asked about it much because, well…you've been through so many changes in such a short amount of time." Dev's voice makes me weak in the knees. I'm afraid if I open my mouth, nothing but tortured sobs will escape.

Deval stops us in the middle of the bridge. The soft gurgle of the water beneath us is soothing. Calming.

"I hope I know you well enough now that I can tell when something is troubling you, Tahira. Would you tell me if there was something wrong?"

"Yes." My lie tastes sour, rotten. Perhaps Dev can tell how this word tastes to me as it crawls over my tongue. His eyes are searching, questioning, doubting…but there are things I cannot tell him. The parts of me that are the most wrong are the parts I have to keep to myself. For my sake. For Dev's sake. For his family's sake. If my handlers are watching…

"I care about you, Tahira. Truly. Arranged marriage or not. Merger or no merger. Calling or no calling. I'd marry you without a single string attached. I…I love you."

Dev's eyes are an ocean I could dive into and never leave. Once again, he takes my hands in his. He's expecting me to say something. What can I say? To admit my true feelings would be to twist the knife in my chest deeper and deeper—before I'm supposed to pull it out and kill him.

I have a choice. Not just the one Powell mentioned in the hospital either. If my mind is failing me…I will not hide my emotions behind a wall of fear. If I'm to die, I want to live first.

I choose to be myself.

As for the horrible, terrible choice forced upon me by evil people…I…

"Dev?" My voice trembles. Will I be heard over the sound of the stream? I can't make my voice any louder.

Dev looks at me and smiles, waiting for me to continue. I falter. How can I warn him? How can I say what I need to? Can I even say what I *want* to?

"I…I love you too, Dev. I'm sorry I've been so quiet since the hospital. But there's something I really need to tell you. Something you may not like to hear. Or even believe…"

Deval sighs and nods. "You've been having second thoughts about the wedding."

I blink.

"It's okay, Tahira. You've been so distant, I figured it was only a matter of time before you…"

What? No. How can he not see? Yes, I've been distant, but not because…

"No—no, it's not that at all, Dev! I mean, yes, at first this was all just an arrangement that had to be made. I wanted to show the world division is wrong, that unity is the only way forward, whatever the cost. All I cared about was being a leader to the divided…like my father taught me…and I still want those things, but…I also want *you*."

Dev's eyes soften. His jaw loses its edge, and his shoulders relax.

"You can have me right now, Tahira."

We're so close now I can see the pores of his skin, taste Dev's scent on my tongue, see his heartbeat through the soft white fabric of his shirt.

"No. Not here."

Before Dev can kiss me, I spin away at the last second.

His expression makes me laugh, and I skip away from him before he can grab my hand again.

"Groundskeepers have gone home for the day." I grin and continue to back away from Dev while he remains motionless on the bridge.

"I suppose...but what does that..." The light goes off in his head, and I laugh again.

It's a light, carefree sound that trails behind me through the air as I disappear from Dev's sight behind a flowering bush. The leaves pull lightly at my dress.

The sound of Dev racing to catch me makes me laugh one last time. This time, the sound of my own voice gives me pause. Why does my voice sound so foreign to me? As if I'm hearing a recording of myself. I look around to see if someone else is laughing nearby, but Dev and I are alone. At least, we'd better be.

When he embraces me, Dev's momentum carries us down onto the soft grass. I push the momentary strangeness of my voice that's not my voice out of my mind and instead allow Dev's hands and lips to distract completely.

Is this how *moksha*—liberation—is truly attained?

"Brother says you like the *lehenga* I picked out for you."

"Did he?" I move my rook to take Kaivalya's bishop.

"Ye…hey! You were distracting me. That's not fair!"

"Says the little girl who tried to move my pawn when I wasn't looking."

Kai frowns. "Karma."

I smile. "Karma."

Kai moves a pawn to take one of mine. "Did you enjoy my song at the *Sangeet*?"

"I did, very much. It was beautiful."

"I think Viti is jealous I can sing and she can't."

"I'm also jealous of how short you are…oh wait, why would anyone be jealous of that?" Viti looks up from the book she's reading on a nearby couch. Just long enough to make sure Kai heard her.

"I'm going to tell Mother you're making fun of my height again, Viti. I swear I will."

"Yeah, yeah." Viti grins at me and rolls her eyes.

I move a knight to take one of Kai's.

"I learned about *samsara* from Mother's lessons this morning. She says I'll probably be reincarnated into a rich family, but in my next life I think I'd rather be a butterfly." Kai moves a pawn.

"Oooh, I think you'd make a lovely butterfly, Kai."

"What do you think *your* next life will be like, Tahira?"

I blink.

"Tahira?"

My hand freezes halfway in between moving my rook.

She was just talking about reincarnation. Nothing I haven't heard before. It's a common belief. My own mother certainly believed in it...

My hand hovers over the board, still pinching my rook.

Samsara.

Reincarnation.

My next life...?

"Are you okay, Tahira?"

I shake my head. My mind is blank. Numb. What was I just...?

"You aren't becoming a zombie again, are you?"

I swallow hard and finish my move.

"Of course not. Zombies don't know how to do *this*...checkmate."

"Meh, I let you win that one." Kai shrugs, but she's definitely annoyed. "I figured I'd let you feel good about yourself at least once."

"Hah!" I reach across the board and start tickling Kaivalya.

She squeals and giggles as our chess match devolves into a tickling match.

"Kaivalya. Miss Collins. *Do* stop that."

Sanji Kapoor appears over us like a menacing gargoyle. Her stern glare would've been enough to quiet us all by itself.

"Miss Collins, my son is waiting for you outside. He will drive with you to the press conference."

I nod curtly and get to my feet.

"My daughters and I will be in attendance, but we will be taking a separate vehicle."

"Thank you, ma'am. And...er...ma'am? I also wanted to thank you for your help with the merger. Deval told me you helped sway the rest of the signatures we needed while I was in the hospital."

Sanji nods slowly. "Yes, well, concerns over your health provoked sympathies among the less convinced members of Jarrius' leadership. Kabir and I were able to use that to our advantage. It was a simple matter."

"Your support means a great deal to me."

"Indeed. Now, it's best you get going. The drive into the city will take at least an hour. Deval is waiting for you outside."

"Yes, ma'am. Excuse me."

I pass Sanji and wink at Kai over my shoulder so her mother can't see me.

Kai giggles, and before Sanji can throw me a stern glare or something I exit the library, walk down the hall to the front doors, and step out into the warm spring air.

There are two cars in the gravel drive and the tinted windows make it impossible to tell which one belongs to Deval. As I approach the vehicles, one of the rear passenger windows suddenly loses its tint and reveals a smiling Deval waving me over. I grin.

Gravel crunches beneath my steps and my phone vibrates in my pocket.

I pull it out slowly as I approach the cars.

Not again…

I ignore the text and delete it. It's *them.*

Why do they only ever send one word? Status? How much longer can I keep ignoring them? So far, nothing bad has happened…

Deval opens the car door for me, and I push him lightly on his shoulder. He chuckles but scoots over to make room for me. He knows I like sitting on the right. As soon as we're both buckled in, the car begins to pull away from the drive on its own.

"No Faru?"

Deval looks up from his phone. "He's already there. I sent him ahead to work with building security to make sure they're doing their jobs. Security will be tight. We should be okay."

Our drive from the Queen's House into Bengaluru takes us through Randpur. The town is so calm. So relaxing. Has it really grown on me this much?

The superhighway is packed with more cars than usual. But it still seems like with each kilometer we get closer to Bengaluru both the traffic and the number of people increase dramatically. How can so many people live in one place?

We're forced to maintain a snail's pace when we enter the city. I lean closer to Deval and rest my head on his shoulder. It's just traffic, why am I holding on to each second I get alone with him? We'll have plenty of time alone when we're married…

The knife in my chest suddenly twists. *Will* I have time to spend with Dev after we're married? I clench my fists…what am I going to do? I've been too distracted by…other things.

I clench my fists…what am I going to do? I've been too distracted by… other things.

Deval starts to trace the intricate *henna* patterns on my arm.

"I know I've been busy with things the past few days, I've meant to ask, did you enjoy the *Sangeet*?"

I smile and nod. "They sure don't compare to rehearsal dinners in the States, though, that's for sure."

Deval laughs. "Too much dancing? Was it the singing?"

"I loved all of it, Dev. Really. It was a nice distraction."

"Distraction? Distraction from what?"

I bite my lip. Oh no…

I shouldn't have said that.

I wasn't thinking.

What do I tell him? What do I say? That the *Sangeet* was nice because it distracted me from my failing brain? Do I tell him about the moments I'll become extremely cold but be unable to shiver? Or extremely warm but won't perspire? Do I tell him I'll randomly begin repeating the same task dozens of times for no obvious reason?

What about the sharp ringing in my ears that will last for hours before it goes away? Do I tell him how at least several times a day I'll enter a room or be in the middle of a task and my mind will go completely blank?

Do I tell Deval that my own body is torturing me? That I'm losing my grip? No.

He can't know.

I can't let him know…

243

I can't risk jeopardizing my only source of strength. Even if, at the same time, Dev's also the pulse of my heartache. What am I going to do?

"Er…it's nothing, Dev. I guess I've just been nervous about the press conference. The *Sangeet* was nice because it distracted me from worrying about it. I get nervous in front of lots of people."

Dev pulls me close until our foreheads touch. "It'll be fine, Tahira. I promise I'll do most of the talking."

"Okay."

I rest my head on Dev's shoulder as we drive through the crowded, oftentimes dirty streets, and I try not to cry. My days with Deval are numbered. Whether I follow through with my handlers' orders or not.

I *have* to keep myself together. Mentally and physically. Especially for the press conference…

"We'll be on the third floor of Jarrius Tower. I've limited the conference to an hour. Hopefully, this will just be short and sweet."

"Do you know how many people from the media will be there?"

Deval shakes his head. "I don't, but no more than thirty or forty. We've tried to keep attendance limited."

When we finally arrive at the tower our car pulls into an underground parking garage. The gate lifts automatically upon our approach.

I should be excited…today is the official announcement of the finalization of the merger between my father's company, WorldFuse, and Jarrius… so why do I feel resignation?

Once our car parks itself, we get out and find an elevator.

Dev checks his watch once the elevator doors shut.

"We're right on time. The conference is scheduled to start in the next thirty minutes."

"Sounds good."

Dev smiles at me and leans over to plant a light kiss on my forehead.

The second his lips touch my skin, a bolt of pain shoots through my head like an electrical shock. I hold back a yelp, but the jolt is so sharp I'm unable to conceal my grimace in time for Deval not to notice.

"Tahira? *Kya haal hai?* Are you okay?" Deval's grin morphs into a frown.

I put a hand to my temple involuntarily and quickly nod. "I'm just reminding you there can be none of that on stage." I wink at him, and the stinging in my head slowly dissipates. "Your mother will still have our heads if she catches us doing stuff like that in public."

Deval grins and wraps his arms around the small of my back, pulling me into a tight hug.

"Let her try."

He's joking. Deval respects his mother too much to disregard her wishes completely.

"Just try to behave civilly with the cameras around." I pull him closer. Then my phone begins vibrating in my pocket. I cringe.

"Don't worry, Tahira. I'll be on my best behavior for the cameras. Promise."

The elevator doors open, and Dev leads me down an empty hallway lined with vacant offices until we reach a door marked *Stage Left*.

Dev checks his watch again. "We still have a few more minutes."

"Weren't you hoping to get something from your office?"

"Yes, but that can wait. Besides, I don't want to leave you alone."

"Dev, I'm fine! I won't have a repeat like what happened at the *baajaar*."

"Why don't you come with me?"

"Er…I think I'm actually going to go find a restroom."

"Okay. Just…don't pass out while I'm gone. Meet me back here in ten?"

"Sure."

Dev kisses my hand and heads back toward the elevator.

Maybe I should've asked him for directions to the nearest restroom. Then again, Dev probably wouldn't know. That's the kind of thing a janitor would know.

I move quickly through the halls searching for a restroom. Jarrius tower is like a silent maze. After a minute longer of wandering, I find what I'm looking for and slip inside.

Status?

My thumb hovers over the screen of my phone. Then another text pops up.

We have eyes in Jarrius Tower. You will uphold the decisions made during the merger negotiations. Understood?

Eyes in Jarrius Tower? Cameras? Or literal eyes? Why *wouldn't* I support the merger?

I delete their text and put my phone back in my pocket.

The stall door opens with a soft squeak and I find a sink.

Warm water slowly washes the foamy soap off my hands when a *click* announces the bathroom door opening. I glance up at the mirror.

This section of the building is supposed to be empty. Who…?

Chills run down my back.

I lock my jaw and turn off the sink.

"Liam…I swear. You…"

My fists are trembling. What's he doing here? How did he find me again? How dare he disregard my wishes. What the hell is he thinking…?

"I'll have you arrested. I swear, Liam. You've gone too far. This is becoming…"

"Tahira, just hear me out."

"No! Get out of here. How did you even…?"

"The merger is finished, isn't it?"

Liam is looking at me with a mix of bitterness and relief. His gaze is so intense. It's like he's staring right through me.

I try to slap him but he catches my wrist and holds me firmly.

"You still can't possibly be willing to go through with marrying Deval. I know the last time we spoke you didn't mean everything you said. That's why I'm here. We can run away together. No one will know. You don't have to marry him."

"Liam. You need to leave. Now."

He shakes his head, glances over his shoulder, and lowers his voice.

"Tahira, come on. You can stop the charade. I know you still love me. After everything we've been through…this arranged marriage doesn't have to be your future. We can be happier than you'll ever be with him."

"No, Liam. You don't understand. It was a mistake for you to come here. Now let. Me. Go."

Liam lets go of my wrist and drops his gaze to the floor. "You're wrong, you know. The merger may turn some heads, but the marriage—it won't make a difference. The world is too divided. It won't matter."

"How dare you...?" My breathing is coming in short bursts now. Who does he think he is?

"Just tell me one thing, Tahira. What will you do when the world doesn't follow your example? How will you feel when everything you're doing is for nothing?"

"Liam...I. Don't. Give. A. *Damn*! We are done! I'm marrying Deval. I love him. More than I ever loved you. Now leave!"

"You don't though! You don't love him! You're only doing this because the damn Indians wanted your father's company. You were just the insurance. It's all over. Your marriage is just a formality now. Don't go through with this, Tahira."

"Deval loves and respects me, Liam. The only respect you have is for yourself. If you cared about me, you'd leave me alone!"

Liam takes a step back. His eyes fall, shoulders sagging. His lips move but no sound comes out.

Finally.

Have I broken his resolve?

"You said that if I ever discovered the Path...we'd be together."

What is he talking about? How dare he put words in my mouth?

"There's still time. I can find the Path, I can..."

I shake my head violently. "I'm a different person now, Liam. I'm not the girl you knew in California. Now leave."

He doesn't budge. Instead, he keeps staring at me like this is the first time we've ever met. He looks like a fool.

"I'm leaving. If you touch me, so help me..."

Liam remains motionless as I brush past him. To his credit, he refrains from touching me.

Soon, I'm out the door walking back down the hall. My fists shake and I fight the urge to punch something.

It's not like I've been subtle with Liam. I've been as clear as possible. Right? I don't love him anymore. Did I ever...?

"There you are! I'd worried you'd gotten lost. You ready?"

I look up from the geometric carpet to find Deval smiling.

I nod numbly. Should I tell him about Liam? Security might be able to do something about him...

Before I can speak, Dev takes my hand and leads me through the door to marked *Stage Left*, and up onto a brightly lit, polished black stage.

Angry shouts, and possibly a few cheers, greet us as we step out of the shadows.

There are more people in attendance than Deval suggested there'd be. At least one hundred people. Or maybe it just feels like there's a lot of people because the room is so small? And getting smaller? There are too many eyes on me. The air gets sucked out of my lungs. Keep it together, Tahira. You can do this. You're okay.

Someone hands us microphones, and I let mine hang down by my side while Dev handles the introductory remarks. He shares a quick presentation, mostly bullet points, of what the merger is going to accomplish for our companies...and the world. Then Dev opens us up to questions.

True to his word, Dev handles most of the questions. I only have to speak up on occasion, and when I do my comments are short.

"How does the eminent Sanji Kapoor feel about the merger? Does she feel like a traitor to her country?"

"Have the Americans promised to lift their tariffs? How will your company respond if they don't?"

"Tahira Collins! What qualifies you to have made decisions on behalf of your father's company?"

"Mr. Kapoor, how many members of parliament have you paid off?"

"There are rumors Dalifa Holdings and Mag-Tech are considering reopening trade with the Americans too. Do you have anything to say about this?"

"Mr. Kapoor, when can we expect your divorce with Miss Collins to affect the success of the merger?"

"What sort of methods are you using to force existing Jarrius employees to work with American bigots?"

"Are you expecting to release the official terms of the merger to the public?"

"Will Jarrius be subject to border control laws?"

Deval fields most questions with more respect than the media deserves. He masterfully turns each question around and somehow finds a way to create a positive response. At least there's a wall of well-muscled security guards in front of the stage. They're probably the only thing keeping most people in the audience from hurling things at me.

Don't they understand what this union will do for the world?

I avoid looking too closely at the audience until a pale face slowly makes his way into the center of the room. Liam has made his way to stand directly in my line of sight. Unless I'm forced to speak, my eyes don't leave the pair of hate-filled eyes staring at me from the crowd of people and flashing cameras.

But it's not just hate in Liam's eyes.

There's pain.

Loss.

Betrayal.

Perhaps he's finally accepted that I've moved on.

But in those cold blue eyes, I also see…hunger. Lust.

It sends chills down my spine. Why do I always feel so cold…?

The conference ends with Deval and me thanking those who've come. I lose sight of Liam. Hopefully forever…but that look in his eyes…

"You did well, Tahira. I think everything went as well as could've been expected."

"Yeah…"

The elevator descends rapidly down to the garage.

"You're okay, right, Tahira? People said some nasty things, but you can't take it personally. They'll all understand when they see what this will do for the world. I think we've all been so divided for so long we've forgotten what unity can do for humanity."

"I'm fine, just feeling exhausted is all."

"I know what you mean, but you should get as much sleep as you can tonight. Wedding festivities start tomorrow. I think Kaivalya and Viti have arranged a sort of…bachelorette party for you. You know…so you don't feel like everything about this wedding is foreign?"

"That sounds great."

Only it doesn't.

Days with Deval are running out. Like sand down an hourglass.

I look into Deval's eyes and run my hand through his hair. I'll die before I let myself be used to kill the man I love.

But my family...

Viti, Kaivalya, and Sanji. I still have to warn them somehow. Secretly—so my handlers don't know I've broken their rules. But how?

They know my every move.

Sleep is futile. I toss and turn, trying not to tear my hair from my skull.

How do I warn Deval? How can I keep from putting his family in further danger? How have I let things get this far?

The rising sun turns the dark sky a warm purple color. Beams of light from my windows do nothing to warm me. Wrapping more sheets around me doesn't help. It's so cold…

I unclench my jaw, but only when my teeth feel like they're about to break. A muscle in my neck won't stop twitching. My breathing becomes increasingly labored as the sun continues to rise. The stress is getting to me. Just as I'm about to try to find a bag to breathe into—I get a text from Dev.

Mind if I join you this morning for your jog?

This could be my chance.

This could work…Yes…

We could use the lake path. No one ever comes out that far from Randpur. It's basically in the middle of nowhere. I could tell him on the pier…

An hour later, Dev pulls up to the Queen's House in one of his many sports cars. He's already dressed and ready to go when I step outside to greet him. The crisp air is perfect for a jog. Before we leave, I force Dev to leave behind both his phone and his smart-watch. I do the same.

Despite the intangible weight across my shoulders, the wind on my face, the burn of my muscles, and the time spent with Dev is liberating. Or is it just distracting? A temporary diversion?

With so many plants all around, the air is thick and rich. The sky is gradually painted a rich blue color. The color of the deep ocean.

Dev and I continue running side by side along the dirt path. What exactly am I going to say? And how am I going to say it? Assuming I can warn them, where could the Kapoors go? Would Sanji believe me? Maybe if it came from her son? Deval…will he trust me and flee someplace my handlers can't find them? Even if it's safer for him and his family to leave me behind, would he go?

I'm breathing heavily, and sweat runs down my body when we stop beneath a large tree to rest. Is my heart rate so high because of the exercise or the stress? Or both? Maybe I shouldn't be running so hard…

The lake is close now. The smell of the water drifts through the air. Clean and fresh. How many times have I jogged here since I've been living at the Queen's House? Why am I drawn to this particular lake?

"I'm impressed, Tahira. You run this far every day?"

"Most days."

Deval is bent over, breathing heavier than I am.

A laugh begins to swell in my chest, but the dark, crushing weight on my shoulders keeps it from reaching my lips.

Wooden beams creak beneath our feet as we step out across the small pier. Insects buzz through the air, though they don't bother us much. I lead Deval down the long platform until we're maybe thirty feet out across the lake. The undisturbed surface of the water is ringed by dense, green jungle. There's no other living person in sight.

This as good a place as any; we're certainly far enough away from Randpur. Dev will know how to help me. He'll know what to do. I just have to tell him what's wrong. There's no way my handlers can spy on me here…

"You ready to go back now? Before I pass out?" Deval grins and wipes his forehead.

"Actually Dev, there's something we need to talk about…"

Dev frowns. "*Accha*. What's on your mind, Tahira?"

"I…"

Suddenly, a faint buzzing sound worms its way through my ears. The noise is coming from somewhere…overhead. There. Above our heads is a tiny black speck. A drone. Barely noticeable in the sky, it's probably rather large, but because it's so high up it appears no bigger than a winged insect. How I've managed to both hear it and see it is nothing short of miraculous. Or perhaps not. The drone isn't moving…it's as if…

"Tahira?"

I glance back at Deval, only now he's looking up at the sky too. It takes Deval longer than me to spot the drone.

"Is that a drone? They never come out this far from Randpur. Maybe it's malfunctioned? It's just sitting there…"

No. It's too much of a coincidence. That drone is *definitely* not malfunctioning. A horrible feeling sweeps over me, like someone is standing right behind me. Breathing on the hairs of my neck.

"You said you had something you wanted to talk about?"

"Yes, I…"

No. Stop. Words are no longer safe. I can't risk it. Not here. Not with a drone perched and watching like a hawk. It can hear us. See us. Even from so far away. My spine continues to tingle, and the breeze off the surface of the lake chills me to my bones.

"Did you want to talk about it now, or…?"

"It's nothing. I'm just…having trouble remembering tomorrow's plans." Deval laughs.

"Truth is—I'm a little nervous, too. I mean…I'm dying to marry you Tahira, but…well, I don't know. I've been looking forward to tomorrow for a long time now. It's crazy that it's finally arrived."

"Right. I know what you mean."

"Come on, I can go over the itinerary with you on the way back." Deval's smile reaches his eyes. His beautiful, honest eyes. "Walk with me? I could use a breather."

"What about this one?"

"Sure."

"Tahira, you said the same thing about the last three."

"I like them all."

What gave Kaivalya and Viti the idea that an American bachelorette party mostly consists of shopping? At least we aren't going to any clubs...

The stores are beginning to blur together. How are my cheeks *still* warm since the last store? Because Kai and Viti just giggled the whole time? Or because the store sold nothing but undergarments and lingerie? What's the big deal?

Vrrrrr. Vrrrrr.

"Are you gonna get that?"

"Huh?"

"Your phone." Viti nods toward my pocket.

"Oh."

I pull out my smooth, glass phone. My stomach drops to the floor. My heart beats against my chest as if it's trying to flee my body. This is the first time they've called. I shouldn't have been ignoring their texts...

Why are they calling me?

"If it's Dev, you can't answer. That's against the rules of the party. Kai, I told you to take her phone."

"It's not Dev." I shrug, and my phone continues to vibrate.

I slip the phone into my back pocket and look busy eyeing the jewelry.

Focus. I just have to do what Deval said and let Kai and Viti buy me at least one pair of earrings and my *mattha patti*. Then I'm off the hook.

My eyes rest on a pair of bright red earrings. Rubies. They look like drops of blood...

"Oooh!"

I flinch. Viti appears next to me, staring at the ruby studded earrings.

"Those are awesome. You should try them on. Here's a headset."

Viti hands me a pair of VR goggles. I try to smile as I slide them over my eyes.

After a brief second of darkness, a three dimensional rendering of myself lights up in front of me. The virtual me is standing in a bare room with lighting coming in from different angles against a white backdrop. My virtual hair is even done up in a tight bun. Do I really look that depressed?

"I'm putting in the codes now. Do you want to see yourself with the *matha patti* too, Tahira?"

I nod in the general direction of Viti's disembodied voice.

A second later, I'm wearing both the ruby studded earrings I was just looking at and the *matha patti* I picked out earlier. The image of my body spins when I wave a finger, and I can see all angles of myself. The jewels look a little bigger on me than I thought they would…but Kai and Viti seem to like them a lot.

"Well? What do you think?"

"I love them." The 3D rendering of myself winks away as I slip the VR headset off. I muster a quick smile. "Thanks for helping me decide, Viti."

"I helped too! Why does Viti get all the credit?"

I pinch Kai's cheek, and she frowns.

Vrrrrrrr.

My phone…not again…

What do I do?

"Hey…uh, Viti? Dev put me under orders that I couldn't pay for this stuff myself. Do you mind buying everything while I go to the restroom? I'll be right back."

Viti nods and I hand her Deval's card.

"Go fast! We have one more stop." Kai winks at me.

"Okay, Kai. I'll try to be quick."

I walk quickly toward the back of the store, find the restrooms, and enter a stall.

As soon as I lock the door behind me, I withdraw my phone.

My fingers tremble as if I'm handling something that might explode. I suck in a breath and return the last missed call.

What am I thinking?

I'm thinking I'm afraid what will happen if I don't give my handlers what they want.

This is insane.

"Report."

The single word is cold. Modulated. Threatening. Familiar…

I keep my voice just above a whisper. "What do you want from me?"

"You've been avoiding us. Why haven't you maintained contact?"

"I've been getting your texts. I…"

"Need I remind you what's at stake?"

The voice on the other line is so sharp…so devoid of warmth. The person's tone by itself is more than enough to remind me—everything I know and care about is at stake…

"You will reply in detail when we ask you for information. Do you understand? You will also respond in the affirmative when we give you instructions. Do you understand?"

"Yes." I want my voice to be strong…but it's nothing more than a whimper. Why do I sound so weak? I'm not weak…I'm…

"We own you. Don't forget what you have to lose. Now—tomorrow you will perform every aspect of the marriage ceremony as directed. Following the ceremonies, you and Kapoor will travel to the coast, where you will board a yacht. You are to find a time to kill him at your discretion. In your room will be a vial of poison. Do you have any questions?"

"How…how do you know we're going to be on a yacht?"

"You don't think you're the only person close to the Kapoors that we control, do you?

What? Who else could this voice be referring to? Certainly not Sanji or her daughters. A maid perhaps? Amar? Faru? This is too much…

"What will happen to me after I…"

"You will be taken into custody. If you're asked to give a statement you're to say you killed him because you are a patriot of your country. You wanted sole control of both WorldFuse and Jarrius Inc."

"…understood."

"After you've been interrogated by Indian officials, we will collect you. If you disobey us, you die too."

The line goes dead.

I drop my phone to my side.

Tears threaten to spill from my eyes, and I choke back a sob. I can't kill Deval. But I don't want to die either…

I grip my phone tightly, muscles tense. My nails dig into the screen, and I wish my phone would crack. I'm so powerless…

If Jeremy were here he'd know what to do.

I blink.

My phone clatters to the ground.

I just…

What was…?

A name. I just recalled a man's name.

Why isn't my memory doing what I want?

A sudden pressure builds sharply behind both my eyes and spreads to the rest of my head.

That name…

A bitter taste fills my mouth, along with a sharp, throbbing pain across my forehead, which slowly begins clawing its way through the rest of my skull. I scramble to collect my phone as anxiety grips my chest like a vice, choking off my breath. The bathroom stall whips open as I make my way out of the restroom.

Kaivalya and Viti are waiting for me near the front of the store.

"You okay, Tahira?" Viti cocks her head to the side. "You look a little pale."

I'm fine. I'm okay. Just answer Viti. Breathe…

I bob my head. "Thanks for buying the jewelry."

"Still up for one more stop?" Viti's smile does little to lift my spirits. Neither does Kai's.

"Sure." I take Kai's hand and let her lead me out of the store.

We drive as if we're headed back to the Queen's House.

"Where are we going?"

"You'll see." Kai winks.

Our car takes us toward the outskirts of the main city. Trees eventually replace the buildings altogether. Fewer and fewer vehicles accompany us on our journey. Our road winds through hills covered in lush vegetation. Clouds above us appear to be on fire due to the setting sun. It's a beautiful drive, to wherever it is Kai and Viti are taking me…

"We're here." Kai's voice betrays her excitement when our car finally comes to a stop.

"What do you mean?" There isn't much light, but we haven't arrived anywhere in particular. There's nothing around. Just rocks and trees.

"Let's go, Tahira!"

Shrugging, I open the door next to me and climb out of the car.

Our vehicle has parked itself in a circular gravel lot of some kind. Just off the side of the road. "Come on, Tahira! Hurry!"

Shrugging, I open the door next to me and climb out of the car.

Viti is already walking toward a group of trees off the side of the road. Kaivalya appears at my side and takes me by the hand.

"Come on, this way."

I follow Kai's lead as we hurry to catch Viti. Gravel crunches beneath our feet before becoming hard packed soil. There's a small wooden trail marker of some kind. We're going for a hike? I did *not* bring the right shoes…

We pass through the first of the dense trees into the forest, following close behind Viti on a dry dirt path.

"Something's not going to jump out and scare us, right?" I step over a large root and help Kai do the same.

Kaivalya giggles. "I don't think so. Besides, we're almost there."

"Almost where?"

"You'll see."

We continue hiking through the ever-darkening wood. A handful of birds chirp pleasantly above us. Their calls mix with those of insects as well. My modern cut *kameez* has long sleeves, but I'm still a little chilly. At least my garments will keep me from being too bothered by any bugs.

After another minute or so of walking, the trees part. We're standing at the edge of a gradual cliff that overlooks all of Bengaluru.

It's amazing.

The city lights are spectacular but don't compare to the beauty of the setting sun. The glowing orb is blood red, lazily dipping below the horizon.

"Look, Tahira! The sun is red tonight. That's the bride's color. Right, Viti?"

I glance at Viti who has her eyes fixed on the horizon. Her eyes glow red. Creepy.

Eventually, she nods. "The bride's color signifies purity, fertility, and prosperity."

Viti sounds like she's repeating something from a script. The symbolism of the color is familiar knowledge. I read about it before coming to India, didn't I? Was it so recent though? Didn't I also know this stuff when I was young? Didn't Mother teach me these things?

My sisters and I stay together on the top of the hill until the sun goes down, and then a while longer to enjoy the glow of the city lights.

It's a beautiful, peaceful moment. Like the calm before a storm.

"We should go. Mother said not to be back too late."

"But Viti…!"

"Hush, Kai. Let's go."

"It's okay, Kai. Viti is right. We should get going. I had a wonderful day with you though."

"Best bachefo…batchemor…bachelorette party ever?"

I laugh. "Without question."

I take Kaivalya's hand in mine, and we follow Viti back to the car, using the flashlight from Viti's phone as a guide.

The entire drive home I'm sick to my stomach. What is tomorrow going to bring? For the man I love? For my family? For me…?

More pressure, more stress, is building within my chest that could explode any second, causing me to disintegrate into a million pieces. How nice would that be? If I could just…fade away? I wouldn't have to hurt anyone, through my action or inaction. Sanji, Viti, Kaivalya, and Dev…their lives would be better if they'd never met me. If only I could erase myself from this existence and begin a new life.

Perhaps I would be a butterfly like Kaivalya.

Such a life would be far simpler.

Butterflies don't have to kill the ones they love.

I get up earlier than usual to run. The more I push myself, the less it helps with the pounding in my head. Yoga in the gardens doesn't help at all.

I'm getting married today…I shouldn't feel like this, should I?

After showering, I dress in simple black shorts and a beige tank top before making my wat out into the living room. The furniture has been pushed up against the walls, probably to help accommodate more guests. How many of Kapoor relatives are supposed to be coming? I should have asked…

Members of Deval's extended family trickle in slowly. Viti and Kaivalya mostly hang next to me, introducing people as they arrive. I smile, bow, and shake the occasional hand, all with a forced smile plastered on my face. Remembering everyone's names is a challenge. Why am I even bothering trying to memorize names? It won't matter after today anyway…

Eventually, once at least a dozen Kapoor relatives have congregated, an older woman dressed in a dark blue *sari* calls everyone's attention to begin the *Haldi*.

I sit cross legged on a brightly colored rug while everyone surrounds me in a circle around a small, natural flame. A younger cousin, or second-cousin, brushes my arms, legs, and face with a yellowish paste intended to purify me and surround me with blessings. I close my eyes and...nope...I don't feel pure...or blessed. Sacred mantras are spoken and I utter a few prayers myself. Even with Viti feeding me the words slowly, I still stumble over the Hindi.

Once the *Haldi* is complete, I'm gifted a series of colorful bangles. *Choora*. Viti and two other relatives help put them on my arms. They hang loose and make delicate clinking noises whenever I move.

Next, Viti and Kaivalya tie matching *kalire* to both my wrists. They're heavier than they look. What are the *kalire* supposed to symbolize again? Prosperity or something?

I fight the urge to frown. These ceremonies are nothing but distractions. It's almost like they're designed specifically to keep me from thinking of a new way to warn Deval.

Once all preparatory rituals are complete, Viti and Kaivalya escort me back to my room so I can change into my wedding dress.

Is this all actually happening? It's too surreal to be...real.

Didn't I always imagine that I'd get married in a white dress in some kind of traditional Christian church. Or at least in front of a judge? Was that before Mother began teaching me about Hinduism?

No. That doesn't make sense, I've always expected to have a Hindu wedding. Right?

I enter my bedroom alone and Viti closes the door behind me after flashing me a quick smile. Once the door clicks shut, I turn toward my bed and—my dress.

Oh my...

My breath catches and I touch a hand to my chest.

The base material of my *choli* is a gorgeous, lively red color. The sleeves are a softer cream color. Like the color of desert sand. The garment has tiny red jewels sewn into patterns of gold thread running down it like rivulets of water...or tears.

I pick up the *choli* by the shoulders and hold it at arms length. It's short for a top, and doesn't look like it will cover my midriff. I guess this is why I've worked so hard to maintain such great abs...

The *ghagra* skirt seems excessively long. Will I be able to walk properly? The skirt is also a vibrant red color with pleated edges and more jewels sewn into the fabric along with beautiful golden patterns. Some of the patterns on my wedding garments even match the *henna* designs still covering my hands and forearms. I'm going to look like a work of art.

In the bathroom, I remove the *kalire* and *choora* and quickly wash off the yellow paste from my head and arms in one of the sinks. Dressing myself takes no longer than ten minutes. The beautiful silk garments are incredibly soft. Is it possible that they feel even better than they look?

Once I'm finished dressing, I regard myself in the full body mirror next to my bed. A total stranger stares back at me.

She has my face, my tightly sealed lips, my hollow eyes. But the rest of her...

I can't believe this magnificent, dazzling woman is *me*.

I can't believe I'm getting married.

I can't believe I haven't found a way to save Deval and his family...

How can I look so beautiful on the outside, but feel so miserable on the inside? My reflection shimmers as tears threaten to spill down my numb cheeks. No. I can't let the storm clouds behind my eyes begin again. Viti and Kaivalya are waiting outside so they can help me with my makeup and hair. They'd kill me if I ruined their canvas.

"Tahira! Oh my goodness, you look amazing!"

I spin around as Viti and Kaivalya come rushing toward me from across my room.

"You look amazing!"

"I hope I look like you some day."

"The colors really look great on you, Tahira. Really."

I fight to keep my smile from turning into a grimace. How can someone even *threaten* to harm such wonderful, innocent girls?

I need to warn Deval that his family's in danger. But when? The rest of the day will be filled with friends, family, and celebration. Will Deval and I have any time alone? Maybe when we leave for our honeymoon, but not before. If my handlers are capable of planting a vial of poison in Deval's yacht, they're probably more than capable of bugging it to spy on us. To make sure I do what they want…

I need to warn Deval *before* we make it to the coast.

Once Kaivalya and Viti have finished fawning over my *ghagra choli*, they help me put on the rest of my jewelry. My gold *matha patti* runs down along the top of my hair and ends in a ruby-studded pendant that rests against my forehead. The cold metal has a strange calming effect, like the touch of Deval's lips…

Viti places a gold necklace around my neck that extends just past my collarbone. Next, she twists my hair into intricate braids before winding it all up into a tight bun. While Viti works, Kai's little fingers expertly apply my makeup. I look even more alluring and alien than before. Lastly, I put my engagement ring on.

Once they're finished with me, Viti and Kai pull me out of my room, and for the next hour I pose for dozens of pictures. We start inside then move outdoors. The photographers have an endless list of poses, and we cover nearly every square inch of the Queen's House gardens. At least the weather is pleasant…

My smile feels more like a mask. Beneath my mask, beneath my makeup, beneath even my flesh…I feel false.

Shouldn't it be much harder for me to hide my real emotions? Why is this coming so easily? It's like second nature. Even my voice, with its bubbly, breathless joy, sounds nothing like it should.

Viti and Kaivalya join me for a few photos. They're wearing matching red *saris* that are slightly less vibrant than my own ensemble. My two sisters-in-law are all that I have as far as a bridal party.

After my photoshoot is finished, I'm ushered back into the Queen's House to await Deval and the rest of his family.

The Kapoor relatives mostly keep to themselves so I find a seat next to a window and absentmindedly start to play with the tassels of a pillow. My eyes are down. I can't react fast enough to the person who collides with me, nearly knocking me off my seat and onto the ground.

"Tahira! Girl, you look incredible! I'm totally going to have an Indian wedding now."

A genuine smile finds its way to my lips. She came! I hug back, waiting for Steffany to stop trying to suffocate me. "Steff! You're actually here!"

She's dyed her hair a bright shade of blue that looks like it would glow in the dark, but otherwise she looks the same as the last time we saw each other in California.

"Of course! I promised I'd make it, didn't I? Damn Enforcers can't keep me from seeing my best friend get married!"

"It means a lot that you came, Steff. Really." It's like having a real friend at my wedding. But she *is* my friend…isn't she?

"I'm glad Dev got the official invitation sent to you in time. Where are you staying?"

For the next ten minutes, I catch up with Steffany. Apparently, things are going great between Steff and her girlfriend Gentri and she asks if a Hindu wedding would work for a bisexual couple.

Steffany's voice is interrupted by others exclaiming and laughing. Someone calls out Dev's name. He must almost be here. My heart starts to beat faster, and Steffany gives me one last hug before whispering that she'll find me later in the day after the rest of the ceremonies.

Birds swim above in the gorgeous blue sky and sing melodies that drift through the air. Even the flowers seem extra vibrant.

Anyone else couldn't have asked for a better day to get married…

People have begun to congregate outside on the front lawns of the Queen's House. Everyone is smiling and laughing.

Is there someone amongst all these unfamiliar people who, like myself, is secretly under my handlers' thumb? Perhaps they were lying to me…

Would they lie to me about something like that? To manipulate me?

A smile springs to my lips when Deval finally arrives. What is he doing? What's he…?

I squint my eyes and laugh.

Is that an actual *elephant*?

How much did it cost to find an elephant? The species has been on the brink of extinction for so long, haven't they? Then again, money is no object for the Kapoors. Deval is just so…normal. So humble. Is that why it's hard to remember he's a rich billionaire? Aren't *I* a rich billionaire too though?

Deval's tall mount easily rises above the crowd of friends and relatives. He's smiling, dressed in a crisp, formal *sherwani* the same cream color as the sleeves of my *choli*. His curly brown hair is wrapped in a majestic, red *sehra*.

He's supposed to be symbolically leaving his native village and coming to my own...but my "village" is thousands of miles away. The cavity in my chest widens. I'm alone. No one from home is here except Steff...

Dev and his elephant slowly make their way through the sea of dancing family and friends.

Cameras are pointed up at Deval as some men help him dismount from his elephant. Dev disappears amongst the crowd.

Who had the cameras? Did Dev end up inviting people from the media? What will the world think about us? Will Liam's words turn out to be true? There will definitely be those who oppose the idea of our marriage. Those who condemn us. But people need to see unity. The world needs unity...

It takes a while, but eventually everyone outside on the lawns files into the broad, ceremonial *mandap*.

After a few more minutes of waiting, Sanji Kapoor appears as I'm picking at a thread on a pillow and tells me they're ready for me.

It's time...

Do I have butterflies in my stomach? Or am I going to throw up again?

"You look beautiful, Tahira." Sanji's eyes soften. She's never looked at me with such tenderness before. Has she ever even called me by my first name? "My son is fortunate to be marrying a bride such as you."

"Thank you, ma'am."

"I feel I owe you an apology."

I cock my head. Really? Where is this coming from?

"When you and your late mother approached Deval and me with the idea of merging our two companies, I confess my first instinct was not unity. Since then, I have judged you too harshly. The boundaries I set between you and Deval were too harsh. I did not believe your intentions to be selfless. I was wrong to act as I did. You are fulfilling your calling admirably, my child. You are a true Exemplar. I hope you can forgive me."

My throat constricts, and tears begin to well. Should I say something? What *would* I say?

Sanji continues before I can come up with a response.

"When I started Jarrius, I was so focused on my own calling, my own journey along the Path, and the success of my company that I took no husband for myself. Seeing you with Deval...I wonder if I made the wrong decision in not pursuing my own family."

"Your *own* family, ma'am? But..."

"While I consider them my own, Deval, Viti, and Kaivalya were my sister's children. I adopted them when she and her husband died in a car crash many years ago."

"Oh...Dev never told me..."

"I expect he was waiting until you were married. Very few people know this. We try to keep it that way."

Before I can ask more questions, Sanji extends her wrinkled hand toward me. Her grasp is firm as she takes my hand and leads me out of the sitting room.

We exit the Queen's House through a set of back doors that leads to the gardens. Four men dressed in the same cream-colored *sherwani* as Deval wait for me to take my place under a *chadaar*.

Once I'm under the awning, the men supporting it begin to slowly walk me toward the front entrance of the *mandap*. The tent is quite large, almost the size of a house.

People are clapping and chanting things when I enter. Beneath the canvas canopy of the *mandap*, the air is far cooler on my skin.

Flower petals are thrown in my direction. Jasmine. A mild, sweet-smelling incense burns and makes the air taste thicker. The men supporting the *chadaar* over my head walk slowly. My heart beats faster with each step. Deval smiles at me from atop a small rectangular stage at the end of the runway. His eyes melt the ice surrounding my withered heart. I hold back a sob.

I step out from under the *chadaar* and have to lift the bottom of my skirt to keep from tripping on my way up the short steps. My dress suddenly feels ten times heavier. I take my place beside Deval.

He looks at me. Dev has never been this emotional. The degree of love and joy within his eyes threatens to betray my own emotions. As confused about them as I may be...

Someone hands us each a beautiful red and white garland. Deval gives me a slight nod, and I reach up to place his garland over his head and around his neck. He bows slightly so I don't have to reach as far. People cheer and clap.

An older woman in a dark blue *sari* directs Deval and me to take seats next to each other on the stage.

Two of Deval's cousins pinch the ends of a rectangular silk sheet, our *terasalla,* and use it to create a barrier between Dev and me. The surface of the *terasalla* ripples slightly and obscures everything except Dev's silhouette. As soon as I let go of Deval's hand beneath the sheet, my whole body becomes cold. So cold…

The woman in the blue *sari* reads from a Hindu text. *Mantras.* The Hindi goes in my left ear and out my right without leaving any meaning behind, so I content myself with looking through the faces smiling back at Deval and me. Can they see my turmoil? My discomfort? My falseness?

There's so many people. All so close. It's like the walls are constricting, pushing them nearer and nearer…

Someone taps my shoulder and I flinch. A soft laugh ripples through the crowd. A young girl hands me two bowls, each filled with something pungent.

Right. *Jeelakarra bellam.* Stop getting distracted, Tahira. You're getting married.

Deval and I utter simple prayers and reach our hands under the *terasalla* to touch each other's foreheads with bitter and sweet herbs. What is this for again? Yes…Viti said the herbs are supposed to symbolize the bitter and sweet moments we'll experience together as husband and wife. I fear the bitter has already taken precedence…and the worst has yet to come.

When the *terasalla* separates us again, I look back out into the crowd. There's a Caucasian man…he's staring right at me. Where did he come from? Why am I just noticing him now? There are plenty of other people looking at me, but this man…his gaze is different. Intense.

Steffany is the only other person here who doesn't have brown or olive-skin. This other man stands out like a flash of lightning in a storm. Is he a friend of Deval's? I've certainly never seen him before in my life, but something about him seems so…familiar. His face? Or maybe his bright, electric blue eyes? Something in the recesses of my mind begins screaming something unintelligible at me. Like an itch that won't go away. Was the man already looking at me when my eyes found him? There's no recognition in his eyes either. He's just…staring at me.

Or is he staring at Deval?

The man isn't smiling like most everyone else. His jaw is set, his brow furrowed, but not in anger. Determination?

I flinch when the *terasalla* is suddenly removed.

My eyes break away from the mysterious man for no longer than a second, but when I look back—he's gone.

Like a phantom. Or a memory…

Deval helps me to my feet. What's going on? Is there another ritual? Who's speaking? It's English. What are they saying?

"…husband and wife."

I blink.

Cheers erupt around us, and Dev embraces me. The jewels of his *sherwani* press into my cheek, and I breathe in his scent. My lips twitch up in a smile. Deval and I hold each other for a second longer before we break apart with the happy sounds of our guests still ringing in my ears.

I'm married…

I'm his wife.

He's my…

"*Shabash!*" Friends and relatives swarm around the stage to congratulate us. People are chanting. Dancing. The air becomes far too dense. Dizzy…I'm so dizzy…

Someone touches something wet to my forehead. An older man holds me by my shoulders, and something brushes through my hair and braids. A reddish-orange powder dusts the air around my head, and I hold back a cough. Some of the bright red powder gets on my hands.

The instant the chalk touches my flesh, it mutates…becoming darker, heavier, and wet. Blood.

My hands are covered in blood.

What the hell is happening?

It's dripping. Blood is getting all over.

No.

I need a towel, a tablecloth—anything! Something to wipe the blood off my hands. It's getting on the floor. Why haven't people started screaming at the sight of me? Why are my hands and arms covered in so much blood?

Someone taps my shoulder; I flinch and spin away. Dev tries to reach for me, a frown on his face. He sees the blood...

I hold my hands out in front of me. Stay away. I can't get any blood on Dev's beautiful garments. My own dress is already ruined. Why is he meeting my eyes? Why isn't he gaping at my bloodsoaked hands? Why is Dev holding onto my elbow? Don't touch me!

I can't get the words out. "Don't...!"

"Tahira! Hey, you're all right. Here..."

An orb of blue hair bounces toward me through the crowd.

Steffany pulls Deval's arms away from me by both his wrists, getting blood all over herself in the process.

"What are you doing?" Dev is yelling at Steffany. My heart beat pounds in my ears, and I gasp for air.

"She's having a panic attack." Steffany's voice is much softer than Deval's. Her lips move again, but no sound reaches me. Dev nods. He looks back toward me and approaches, palms raised. I back away, shaking my head from side to side. He can't touch me. Dev...

"It's okay, Tahira. Let's get you someplace quiet. Okay?"

I bite my lip and nod.

Maintaining his distance, Deval motions for me to follow him.

With the eyes of hundreds of people on my back, I want to run, but my legs are barely working. I stumble toward an unmarked door just behind the stage. Dev opens the door.

Finally—I can breathe again.

The air is cooler. Thinner. The lights are dim, and I shudder as I collapse onto the floor, wrapping my arms around my legs.

I squeeze my eyes shut and just focus on breathing without choking. The door to my small room closes. I'm alone.

So alone.

Knock, knock, knock.

My eyes snap open.

I suck in a deep breath. Getting to my feet is a bit of a challenge in my gown.

The cold metal door slides open at my touch. Deval looks worried. I fall toward him. He catches me and pulls me close. We're standing behind a wide swath of canvas. Metal stage supports peek beneath the wall of fabric. Muted voices from the other side tell me at least a few guests are still here. How long was I alone?

We hold each other, and I squeeze my eyes shut.

"Steffany told me you were having a panic attack. She knew what to do."

A panic attack—since when do I get panic attacks? I suppose that sort of makes sense...my body was *definitely* attacking me. If I hadn't gotten to the room away from everyone when I did...I don't know what would've happened to me.

"How are you feeling now?" Dev's eyes meet mine, and I smile. Shame can't keep my emotions at bay with Dev's arms protecting me.

"Better."

"You sure? I almost had Faru call for a doctor, but Steffany told us you just needed time alone. She said this sort of thing used to happen a lot? When you were in school?"

I have to tell him. We're alone. I have to warn him.

"Really. I'm feeling much better. But Dev...there's something I need to tell you..."

"No need. I already filled him in for you, girl. Don't worry."

Steffany appears around a corner of the *mandap*.

No! I just needed five more minutes alone with Dev.

Deval nods and holds me at arm's length. An exasperated frown plays on his lips. "You could've told me you dealt with severe anxiety, Tahira. It's nothing to be ashamed about."

I cock my head and give Steff a sideways glance. Is this true? I don't...remember...

Steffany glances at Deval before looking back at me. "She was getting better. By graduation she could handle crowds and spaces just fine."

"I'm fine now. *Really.*" I don't sound too convincing. Dev's eyes continue to search my face.

I look down at my hands. They're still covered in…No—it's just the *henna* patterns, lightly dusted over with a red chalk. The blood was just in my head.

"Do you need something to drink, Tahira? I can get you some water."

I nod. A slight breeze ripples the walls of the *mandap*, and my whole body shivers a little. The canvas flaps in the wind. It's darker outside, the sun is probably setting.

The rest of the guests look up from their table conversations when we reemerge from behind the stage. People begin clapping. I give the few guests who've remained a sheepish wave, and my cheeks grow warm.

"I've already told everyone that they're welcome to head to the reception hall, but some wanted to stay and make sure you were all right."

"That's nice."

Deval grins weakly. "Let's get some food in you before we have to take more pictures."

After I pick at a plate of food, Deval and I are directed around the Queen's House gardens by the same photographers who took my bridals. Being with Dev…my husband…makes me feel less fake as the cameras capture our happy faces. But even Deval's presence can't keep the coldness at bay for long. I did *not* just have a panic attack…did I? I've never hallucinated during one of my episodes before…

What's going to happen to me?

Sanji, Kaivalya, and Viti join us for family portraits before Deval and I escape back into the Queen's house to change clothes for the reception.

Deval opens the door to the master bedroom for me, and once I'm inside the door clicks shut. I start removing all my jewelry and set it all on a wood dresser. What if I write something for Deval? I slip out of my *ghagra* and let the skirt fall to the floor. A note might be easier to conceal. I remove the *choli* one sleeve at a time and…Dev's reflection is staring at me through the mirror above the dresser.

My cheeks flush.

I clutch my skirt to cover myself. Dev blushes—then he laughs. A kind, rich laugh that sparks a laugh from me in return.

We're married...

Slowly, I let my skirt fall back to the ground.

Dev crosses the room, and we devolve into a world entirely our own. I unbutton his shirt and lose myself in his embrace.

Sheets and pillows are scattered when we finally emerge from our reckless emotion.

No words are spoken between us. They don't need to be. While Deval changes into his tuxedo, I find the gown Viti picked out for me. The silvery fabric is smooth and supportive. The dress falls to just above my ankles, making it much easier to maneuver in.

"Are you ready?" Deval finds me in the bathroom, and I finish touching up my makeup.

"I think so." I smile into our mirror at Dev's glowing reflection.

Arm in arm, we leave our room behind and find the vehicle waiting to take us to our reception.

As we pull away from the beautiful grounds of the Queen's House, I glance back. Will I ever return to this place?

We drive north. The setting sun to my left glares angrily at me. I ignore it. Deep, looming clouds in the distance spell a coming storm.

If Faru weren't with us, would I tell Deval everything that's going on right now? No. They might have bugged the car. Plus, I can't trust Faru…I can't trust anyone…

It's dark when we finally arrive. Muffled sounds of singing and music emanate from the reception hall. Guess the party started without us.

The reception hall is a beautiful, ornate building surrounded by gardens. It's almost as if someone dropped the building right in the middle of Lal Bagh.

Arm in arm, Deval escorts me up the steps.

"I promise we don't have to be here longer than necessary. Besides, I can always make the excuse that you're about to faint and need to rest." Dev winks at me, and I punch his arm. He frowns. "I'm sorry. That was rude of me, wasn't it? I didn't mean to poke fun at your fainting, Tahira."

"It's okay, Dev. Couples are supposed to tease each other, aren't they?"

Jeremy used to tease me too…

There it is again!

Who the hell…?

The name is gone. Vanished. Like a faint whisper abruptly carried away by a breeze. Is my mind playing tricks on me again?

Why can't I remember?

The name won't come to me. Gritting my teeth does nothing to help my concentration, but slowly…faintly, a man's face materializes in my mind's eye. It's a face I've seen recently. Before…

We pass through a set of wide, glass doors that slide open automatically. The inside of the reception hall is quite packed. Lights are dim. The ceiling is easily at least twenty feet tall. People are distracted with the music and dancing and no one notices our arrival.

Dev leans in close, probably so he can be heard over the noise. "What do you say we stay for a few dances, I'll make a quick speech and we'll leave? We do have a boat to catch anyway. A storm is supposed to be coming too, but we should be fine as long as we…"

"Ah! There's the happy couple!"

Steffany appears out of nowhere gives me another one of her tight, slightly uncomfortable hugs. She shakes Dev's hand and I suppress a laugh. Steff is currently attracted to other women, but the look she's giving Deval…

Dev smiles pleasantly. "Thank you again for the help earlier, Steffany. Are you enjoying the festivities?"

"Hells yeah. But what's this drink I can't seem to put down?"

Steffany brandishes a slim glass cylinder filled with a light pink liquid.

"*Solkadi*." Deval smiles. "Don't worry, it's not alcoholic."

"Oh." Steff frowns. "I was kind of hoping it was."

We chat with Steffany for a minute longer before we say goodbye. Steff embraces me tightly one last time. "You better keep in touch with me better than the last time we said goodbye."

"I'll try. I promise, Steff."

"Good. And no more panic attacks. I won't always be around to save your ass."

She gives me a kiss on my cheek and waves goodbye.

"Steffany is rather…intriguing, isn't she? Seems like the type of person you'd want to have at a party." Deval's probably too nice to say what he really thinks.

I smile. "One learns to love her."

We only stop a few times to chat with some of Dev's friends or family on our way to the front of the reception hall. Once we reach the small, elevated stage, someone hands Dev a microphone.

I try clinging to the shadows while Deval thanks everyone for coming. My heart rate is normal, but I still avoid looking too closely at the crowd. No more episodes. I have to stay strong. Time is running out. Could I drag Dev to a restroom? Onto the roof? Surely my handlers can't be watching every inch of this place, can they?

A fresh round of dancing begins after Dev's brief speech. Can I just stand and watch?

Then, two pairs of small hands find my own.

Viti and Kai look up at me with expectant eyes. How can I say no?

For the next two songs, I dance with my sisters to drums, flutes, and *sarod*. The music is elegant, swift, and lively. At least there aren't a ton of other people dancing close to us. Do they know I apparently don't do well with crowds? Did Deval tell them?

A slower song begins to play, and Deval makes his way through the guests toward me. He takes my hand, and together our bodies move to the music in a rhythmic pattern of steps and twists. It's almost like my body knows what to do of its own accord.

We sway along the path the music makes, and I fall deeper and deeper into Deval's eyes…until a pair of bright, blue eyes find me through the bodies of other dancing guests.

His hair is cut short. Lips pursed, he's almost as pale as a ghost compared to everyone else. He's dressed all in black, arms folded across his strong chest, and looking right at us. It's the man from before…

Dev spins me in a tight twirl, and then…the phantom man is gone. Where did…?

I'm still seeing things.

Hallucinating.

Losing my mind…

When the song ends, I'm breathing heavier, and Deval grins at me. My own smile feels weak. He raises his eyebrows, and I nod my head. Dev takes my hint.

If only time would break its relentless march forward. Time is just as much an enemy as my handlers. I can't escape it.

"I haven't planned any sort of grand exit, so we can leave without too much attention. Is that okay?"

I nod. Apparently, receiving attention isn't my forte. Even on my wedding day.

"Good, let's get going. We should make it to the coast in time that we shouldn't be too bothered by the storm."

"Okay."

Dev grins, takes my arm, and together we escape into the night, leaving the sounds of the party behind us.

We cross the street to where our car is parked just as the first few drops of rain begin to fall. Deval closes the passenger door behind me, careful not to catch my dress. I look across the street and freeze.

It's him. Sitting in a car on the opposite side of the street is the man. The phantom. My hallucination.

Jeremy.

Yes! The name matches the face staring at me from fifty yards away but—that's it. There's nothing else. No other memories, no other associations come to mind. Just a name that belongs to a face. What the hell?

Deval opens the driver side door and climbs into the car. When I look back across the street, the man is gone. So is the car he was in…

My heart begins beating faster. My lungs heave, compensating for my panic. I *have* to be hallucinating. There's no other alternative. What if my brain fails completely before I'm able to help Dev?

The car comes to life with Dev's short verbal command. I need to tell him what's going on. Before I lose my mind completely.

But…Dev has had this car for at least as long as I've been in India. My handlers have had ample time to bug it with sensors or cameras. My eyes dart across the dash of the car, but there's nothing suspicious. Do I risk it?

No. What if I'm wrong and there are cameras watching? I can't put Kai and Viti in danger...

Am I really this powerless?

Two other vehicles follow us from our reception toward the coast. Our security detail. Once we reach the superhighway, our car reaches a cruising speed of 250 kilometers per hour. Deval talks while our car drives. I mostly just listen, nodding and making an occasional brief comment. His joy is so apparent it hurts.

A light rain begins to fall. The clouds overhead bear down on me like an endless void, threatening to crush me. I shiver.

Lights from the buildings hugging the coast illuminate the undulating ocean. The white cresting of waves and the smell of the sea breeze fills me with...homesickness? No...something else?

We drive down a narrow road past some weathered buildings. The road brings us close to a large dock, filled with several expensive looking pleasure boats. Most are swaying slightly in the water. The wind is picking up.

"The crew already has everything prepped for departure. I even arranged for our luggage to be sent on ahead."

I nod, but I'm not really paying attention. We continue along an asphalt platform before turning down a wide, private pier. A three-story yacht sits at the end of the long pier.

Apart from the open deck, the walls of the craft look completely seamless. Not a single break anywhere. As if it was made from a single piece of silvery metal. Does it even have windows? It looks like a knife lying on its edge. Beautiful and dangerous at the same time.

I catch Deval's eye, and he winks at me as our car descends a small ramp. A gate opens, and we drive all the way up to the side of the yacht. I look over the edge of the pier and the reflection of white lights dancing off the black surface of the shifting water momentarily hypnotizes me.

Once our vehicle parks, a man dressed in a crisp, white uniform opens my door. The man holds an umbrella for me as I exit. Water sloshes over my feet as I step in a puddle on my way to meet Deval at the end of a metal ramp extending between the yacht and the pier. I nearly slip crossing it up onto the main deck of the boat.

We enter through an open hatch attended by another man in a white uniform. My eyes are heavy as Deval leads us through a series of soft carpeted hallways. How big is this boat? The walls are made from a rich wood that's so polished I can see my own reflection.

Finally, we come to a set of doors that slide open at Dev's touch.

The master cabin offers a sweeping view from the aft of the ship. It's like the walls are made from glass, but from outside they appeared to be solid metal. "How…?"

"Cipher-tech." Dev smiles, gesturing at the walls. "The metal's composition is quite similar to smart glass and can still shift opacity, but it's twenty times stronger."

"Oh…"

Menacing clouds blend with the night sky, and a pale glow from the moon barely makes its way through the weeping void.

Somehow, my leaden feet get me to the king-size bed and I collapse, sinking into the bone-white comforter.

"Who knew getting married feels like having just run a marathon?" Deval sits on the edge of the bed and begins removing his shoes. I close my eyes and try to force myself to stay awake. How am I going to warn Deval *now*?

Something tugs on my right foot, and I glance up sharply. Dev removes my left shoe. Then the right. He grins.

"Dev I…I don't know what you were expecting from me tonight, but I'm so tired, I…"

Dev blushes, and his eyes fall.

I've said the wrong thing.

"It's not that I don't want to…it's just…"

"Don't worry, Tahira. It's late, we're both tired."

My hands find his face, and I pull him closer. His cheeks feel so warm against my icy lips. He kisses me back. Each brush of his lips is like fire against my too-cold skin. Dev helps me slip out of my gown, and I crawl under the sheets, trying to keep myself from shivering. He doesn't join me but remains standing next to his side of the bed.

"I'm going to have a quick word with the captain. I'll be back in a minute. Can I get you anything?"

I shake my head.

He can't get me what I want.

Dev bends over and kisses my forehead before leaving.

As soon as the doors to our room click shut, I wrap a blanket around myself and start searching the walls for cameras, microphones, anything.

There's nothing along the sides of the doors so I start running my fingers over the edges of the windows. They're clean too. Where else would someone put cameras? The desk? The bathroom door? What if Dev comes back and sees me like this? What kind of an excuse could I use? That I'm checking for dust? Or that…

I stop. My fingers brush over a tiny ridge, just above the headboard to the bed. It's transparent and less than a centimeter in diameter. No larger than a coin. The camera is probably positioned to give whoever is watching a complete view of our room. Should I cover it with something? I'm so… naked. This place isn't safe.

Is *anywhere* truly safe?

I'm running out of time.

Is this all just futile? How am I going to convince Deval I'm telling him the truth in the first place? Assuming I can even find someplace private…

Everything seems so surreal, but I have no choice.

I *must* try.

I love Deval too much to do nothing…

"The mission is over. Her mind is lost."

"What the hell do you mean her mind is lost? Be more specific."

"Powell has been monitoring her condition even closer since she ended up in the hospital. He thinks McKenzie has...well, it's difficult to describe..."

"You'd better start trying."

"Powell seems to think McKenzie's own memories have fused with the life history of Tahira Collins. Everything we fed her on Collins and everything McKenzie learned on her own has become real to her. McKenzie thinks she *is* Collins. Body, mind, personality, everything. She doesn't remember who she really is anymore. Totally body dysphoria."

"How can you be sure? She's the best at what she does. Alex could just be playing the part better than..."

"We sent Jeremy in with a team."

"What? Without my authorization?"

"You've been difficult to reach. I made a judgment call. We were planning on giving her one final warning anyway. To make sure she'd follow through with the last steps of the mission."

"Well? How did she respond?"

"McKenzie is good, but she hasn't seen her husband in person for a very long time. As you know, in the past, the mere mention of his name causes her to lose composure and fall apart. Video recordings have had an even stronger effect on her emotional and psychological state. She…"

"Get to the point, Haight."

"Today, she looked right at him. On three separate occasions. Analysis of her micro-expressions proved there was no recognition. There was no significant emotional response, only mild confusion—that's it. She might as well have been staring at a stranger. Tahira Collins had never met Jeremy McKenzie, and now…Alex hasn't either."

"Damn. How is something like this even possible? Everything was going so well…she was so close. Can Powell reverse these effects?"

"I've already asked. He's doubtful anything can be done at this point. He keeps repeating this is 'unexplored territory.' That's also why we sent her husband in with a team. To see if we could snap her out of…whatever she's experiencing."

"What the hell…how is it she's still been doing what we tell her?"

"I don't know. Powell spoke to her at the hospital. It's possible he broke protocol and told her what he thought might be wrong with her brain. If she thinks we have the only cure to what's happening to her…the promises we've made might make it seem like…"

"Like we can save her life if she does what we want. Like her brain is our hostage. Not her husband."

"That's just a guess, but whatever her motivations currently are, I don't think we can trust that she'll carry out the mission. She's been compromised."

"Hmm…"

"Director? Do you want me to send in an extraction team?"

"No. We'll wait."

"For what?"

"For Alex to do her job."

"And if she doesn't? If the Alex McKenzie we know doesn't exist anymore?"

"Leave it to me. I'm taking control of this operation."

I'm exhausted. Mentally, physically…emotionally. It takes all my strength to focus…I have to find some way to tell Deval we're in danger, that his family is at risk too.

But our room isn't safe.

There has to be another way.

I flinch when our doors slide open and Deval enters. He smiles at me. I take a deep breath, adjust the blanket around me, and stand before he can fully remove his jacket.

"Hey, um…Dev? I'm not feeling very well. Do you mind if we get some fresh air?"

"Of course. Here, I can open a window…"

"Actually, I was thinking the deck might be a little bit better."

Dev's frowns and raises an eyebrow.

"I'm not going to faint or have a panic attack or anything. I've filled that quota for the day. I just need some air is all."

"You know it's still raining pretty heavily, right?"

I nod.

Dev's frown slowly shifts to one of his charismatic grins. "Whatever you say, Mrs. Kapoor. Let's go get some fresh air."

Mrs. Kapoor? That's right…I'm his wife. I'm Tahira Kapoor now…

"Let's get you something to wear first. You can't go around with nothing but a blanket. Even if it *is* extremely sexy. Maybe we can both dress like this tomorrow."

Try as I might, I can't keep from grinning.

Once I slip into a pair of sweatpants and pull on a shirt, we exit our room and make our way through a short hallway toward the bow. We only pass one other crewmember. How many are there total?

The initial breeze that blasts through the open hatchway is salty and chills me to the bone. Dev steps out first and takes my hand as I follow. The bow is empty save for a few deck chairs. Perfect. The sea wind dances through my hair as we make our way further out onto the open deck. The rain is bearable, but it's definitely picking up. It has to be safer to talk out here. Even with cameras, it'll be impossible to overhear us. So why won't my heart stop beating against my chest...?

I can do this. It's the best chance I've got.

Deval follows me as I lead him by the hand to the very end of the bow. The wind makes his shirt ripple across his broad shoulders. A few lights built into the floor provide illumination. Waves crash against the sides of the yacht as we cut through the inky black water.

"So...what is it you...?"

It shouldn't be this hard to hear, even with the rain and the waves. Is my hearing failing me right along with my brain? I point to my ear, and Deval pulls me closer.

"I said—what's troubling you, Tahira?"

He knows me so well. I should give him more credit. Not much gets past Deval. I just wish he could read my mind. It'd make this so much easier...

Standing on the tips of my toes gets me even closer to his right ear.

"How did you know I wanted to talk...?"

Deval gives me a knowing look. "What's on your mind?"

"A disease."

Deval frowns and cocks his head. "What?"

"My mind, my...brain...it's diseased. It's what made me pass out at the *baajaar* and why I had to go to the hospital. It's why I haven't been...myself."

Dev shakes his head and moves a wet strand of hair out of my face.

"Tahira, where is this coming from? You're fine. Besides—the doctors cleared you before you left the hospital. What do you mean you haven't been yourself?"

I've started off poorly. He doesn't believe me. I have to go back further.

"Dev—I was kidnapped, in California."

The faint grin on Dev's face disappears. His eyes narrow. "Tahira, what are you talking about? What do you mean you were *kidnapped*?"

"It was just after my mother's funeral. After the American media found out about our marriage, a man broke into my home and...kidnapped me."

"I don't...what...why haven't you said anything about this before?"

"Just listen...please, Dev. This is important. And I don't think we have much time."

I can't keep my voice steady, and I'm fighting back tears. I have to go on. The knife in my chest twists even deeper.

Dev purses his lips but lets me continue.

"After I was kidnapped, they took me to some sort of laboratory. Then they did something to my brain. Look…"

I grab Dev's hand and pull myself closer to him, as if I'm going in for a kiss. It's not graceful, but if anyone is watching…

"Tahira. The rain is getting worse. We should go back inside. What are you…?"

"Here!" My voice is sharp. Angry. Why am I angry?

I guide Dev's hand up through my scalp. Next, his fingers brush over the scar where my spine meets my skull. A sob escapes my throat. With my hand guiding his, I trace the ovular line of the second scar that goes all the way around the very top of my head. When I'm done, I release his hand. It falls back to his side, limp.

Deval's expression has changed. His eyes have hardened. Is he starting to see I'm telling the truth? Surely he can at least see something is wrong with me, right?

"Tahira, I don't…what was that about? Does your head hurt?"

"They did something to my brain, Dev! It's dying. *I'm* dying. The scars… didn't you feel them? Give me your hand again, I'll…"

"What's going on here, Tahira? I don't understand…"

"Please, just listen. You *must* believe what I'm telling you."

"You're not making any sense, Tahira. Why would someone kidnap you then let you go? "

"To use me! To force me to do what they want! It's like my brain is their hostage. They told me they're the only ones with a cure for whatever they've done to me. Even if there *is* a cure elsewhere, they said if I ever went for help they'd kill me…and your family."

"But who're 'they,' Tahira? What do you mean you have to do what 'they' say?"

My vision blurs suddenly. Tears are starting to swell. Deval's own eyes have become misty. Does he see the pain I'm in? The emotional turmoil? He doesn't know that the worst is yet to come…

"I don't know, Dev. I don't know who they are. My memories are so...so confusing." I can't hold back my tears any longer, and I begin to weep. My whole body seizes. The cracks in my soul widen. I'm breaking...

"I don't know who did this to me or why, Dev. But they told me I have to...I have...to...*kill* you."

A wave crashes against the yacht. Water sprays me in the face and I blink.

At first, Deval doesn't react.

He just looks at me—unmoving.

"I know how this all sounds, Dev." My throat burns. I lock eyes with him. *Please* believe me.

"It sounds crazy, Tahira." Deval turns his back to me and runs a hand through his hair.

Rain continues to fall, and the floor beneath my feet rocks with the waves. Is my balance off, or is the rocking intensifying with the storm?

I remain frozen to the metal beneath my feet. Dev's knuckles whiten as he grips the handrail surrounding the bow of the ship. Should I say something more? Would adding more details to my already bizarre, disturbing story make things better or worse?

"I want to believe you, Tahira. Really, I do."

I look up from my feet. Deval only a foot or so away from me, but it might as well be a mile. I still can't read his expression.

"Do you trust me?" I take Deval by the hand.

"Of course I trust you." Dev's voice catches slightly. He squeezes my hand in his. "But if what you're saying is true..."

"It *is* true! All of it. We need to find a way to warn your family too, Dev. And soon..."

"Why soon?"

"I was supposed to kill you tonight."

"So..."

"So when I don't, my handlers are going to know, and your family will be in even more danger."

"Is it the Proelium?"

"The...*what*?"

Proelium…where have I heard the name before? The way Dev sounded when he said it…

"The Proelium? Dev, what do you mean?"

Deval's eyes get a far off look. "There've been rumors…Brother Andrews was convinced there was a plot against certain members of Unitas. But we've always believed they were unorganized, lacking any kind of formal leadership. Each member was supposed to be independent…but if Andrews was right and the rumors are true…"

"Dev? What rumors? I don't know anything about the Proelium."

"What do you mean? Surely you've heard the rumors too. Brothers and sisters dying or being murdered all over the globe? The Brethren Council was convinced they were unrelated. Each investigation pointed to a unique, unrelated culprit. Each with different motives."

Why is he acting like I should know what he's talking about? I…the man…the one who kidnapped me in California mentioned the name. Proelium. He said he was one of them…

No.

Proelium. CIA. Evil mercenaries. It doesn't matter. Saving Dev and his family is all I care about.

"Dev, whoever sent me to kill you doesn't matter right now. We don't have much time. We need to warn your family. They told me if I ran, or went for help, or failed, then they'd kill your family."

Deval is searching my face.

Does he believe me? Finally?

His eyes narrow. Lips pursed, he stares deeply into my eyes, only he's not looking directly at me. His mind is elsewhere.

He believes my story. He has to…

"It's the Proelium. It must be. I've always warned the Brethren that the Proelium might forsake aspects of their doctrine to pursue the Struggle on a grander scale."

"Listen to me. Proelium or not, we need to get you someplace safe. Do you have a way of contacting your family? We can't use any of our own phones or devices. I'm sure they're being tracked."

Dev nods distractedly at me.

"Dev? What are you thinking?"

"I…"

A man's scream pierces the night like a thunderclap.

Together, Deval and I spin toward the noise.

The lights on the second story bridge cut out. A second later the bow of the ship is bathed in darkness.

The world around us moves in slow motion. My stomach drops. I'm dizzy. My perspective tilts. Dev.

He's already moving. Pulling me with him.

"Dev! What…?"

He holds his index finger up to his lips to silence me.

We reenter the ship. The hallway lights are out too. Where the walls meet the floor, thin red emergency lights flash on and off lazily like a strobe. Half blind, I follow Dev. My breathing sounds much too loud in the eerie silence. Where is he taking us?

We turn a corner, and Dev reaches for a door. It slides open with a soft click. It's so dark inside. What…?

"Get in. Hurry. You'll be safe here."

"I…what? No. No, I'm not leaving you."

He frowns and puts a finger up to his lips. I'm shouting. Why was I shouting? My hearing is off…

"Tahira. Listen to me."

I shake my head violently.

Heavy footsteps on the deck above cause Dev and me to freeze.

Deval jerks his head and pulls me down the hallway in the opposite direction the footsteps are moving. We run, as quietly as possible. I swear the pounding of my heart is far louder than my shouting had been. Are the red pulsing emergency lights getting brighter? Or is my mind playing more tricks on me?

We reach a staircase, and Deval motions for me to wait. He points up and mouths the word *bridge.* Slowly, he ascends the steps. I bite the inside of my cheek until I taste blood. Why did he leave me here? What's he doing?

The ship is so silent. Where is the crew? There's only the sound of muffled waves against the yacht. I wait thirty seconds, and then I begin climbing the stairs toward the bridge.

Shadows warp and dance across blacked out screens and control panels.

Wide, sweeping windows provide an expansive view of the ocean around us. Were it not for the moon's soft light, and the thin glowing coastline, everything would be shrouded in complete darkness.

There are bodies. Several of them. Their white uniforms stand out like stains in the darkness.

"...Dev?"

Suddenly, a shadow detaches itself from the ground and rushes toward me. I start to scream, but a hand clamps down over my mouth.

"Shhhh. It's okay, Tahira. It's me."

I exhale deeply as Dev takes my hand and leads me to a hunched over figure on the ground. He releases my hand and kneels down.

Emergency lights continue to pulse, illuminating the man's face. Faru.

"I'm...sorry, *mahoday.*" Faru's propped up against a control panel. His voice is weak. Something's wrong with him.

"What happened? How many?"

Faru shakes his head, and his chest shudders. He holds up a finger covered in something thick and wet.

"One man?"

Faru nods. "Take this...and go."

Faru extends something black and angular toward Deval. A smart-gun. Deval shakes his head. "We're not leaving you. I'm going to get you help. I..."

"The ship is compromised. Get to the lifeboat…you…"

Faru coughs and goes silent.

"Faru…my friend…" Dev takes Faru's head in his hands. Their foreheads touch. Whatever Deval says to Faru is too quiet for me to hear.

When Deval stands, his face is contorted. His eyes look almost black in the minimal light. He tucks Faru's weapon between his belt and the small of his back. Deval's fingers are covered in warm blood when finds my hand.

Then we run.

We flee down from the bridge and back down a long hallway. The flashing red lights are so strong I have to squint my eyes to keep from being blinded. Deval's hand is slick with blood, and I have to hold on tight to keep from slipping out of his grasp.

We turn a sharp corner and freeze.

A shadow, clad entirely in black, stands at the far end of the hall.

I blink. Once. Twice. This specter is no hallucination. He never was…

His hands hang empty by his sides. Somehow, the absence of a visible weapon makes this man twice as intimidating. Deep shadows make his eyes look like gaping holes. He's staring right at us. No, not *us*—just Dev.

The grim, red emergency lights accentuate Dev's set jaw. His grip on my hand tightens painfully. Run. I have to run. No. What is my body thinking? I have to protect my husband.

"Were you sent by the Proelium?" How does Dev sound so calm?

The shadow takes a step forward. Instinctively, I edge in front of Deval.

"Tahira. What are you doing? Get…"

I ignore Dev and brush his hands away.

"I recognize your face." My voice is quiet. "You've been following us. You were at our wedding. Who are you?"

The man removes something from the inside of his jacket. The red lights reflect off a long, wicked knife that's slightly curved at the end. A low humming sound fills the air. Is it coming from the knife?

The man's motions are fluid, confident. His angular features and intelligent gaze are so…intimate. The way he stands, how he holds himself…he's as familiar to me as my own reflection. How?

Yes.

I spit out his name before it slips away again.

"Jeremy!"

His focus is broken. Jeremy's eyes narrow, and his face betrays surprise. Doubt. Anger.

"How do you know my name?" His deep, confident tone is more recognizable to me than my own.

"I...I don't..."

"I *said*..." Jeremy takes another step forward, "...how do you know my name? Did *they* give it to you?"

Why don't I have an answer for him? Why isn't my brain giving me what I need? Why...?

"Sir, drop the knife or I'll shoot you. Tahira, get behind me. He..."

Images, whispers, and memories begin bubbling to the surface of my mind like air trapped under water. Cryochambers. A beach. Gunfire. A courtroom. Spindly arms tipped with Meridian lasers. My house. Mirrors...so many mirrors. A pale woman with blonde hair. Deval. Jeremy. Everything's a mess. What does it all mean? Jeremy he...he knows me too. He...cares about me?

"Jeremy." I'm pleading now and brushing Dev's arm off me. "I don't know how I know you, but I do! I know you're not a...killer. Not...anymore. Please. Don't hurt us."

"You're lying. I don't know you." Jeremy's voice is piercing. Sharp. "And you sure as hell don't know me."

"Jeremy. Please."

Jeremy shakes his head and advances a step forward. His voice is frightening. It used to be so rich. Now, he sounds dead inside. "I'm sorry. You don't know what's at stake for me."

"You don't have to hurt us, Jeremy. Just put the knife down." I raise my *henna*-laced palms toward Jeremy. One step takes me closer to him. Then another. What am I doing? Can I even trust what my heart is telling me? Or is it my brain that's telling me I can trust this man?

"Jeremy...you—"

"Stop saying my name, woman. You don't know me."

But I *do. How* though?

"You can stop this, Jeremy."

I take a third step forward.

"I can't." Jeremy's voice shakes. He's angry…at me? At Deval? "If I don't do what they've sent me to do—they'll kill her. My Alexandria…"

Time freezes.

An arc of blinding pain sears my mind like a hot iron.

It's agony.

I scream and hold my head, crushing my palms against my temples from the pain.

Countless images flash before my eyes like rain in a maelstrom.

A thumping, my heartbeat, pounds inside my head. A screeching sound fills my ears, and I can't do anything except close my eyes and shudder. What's happening to me?

My sense of balance disappears. I sink to my knees before collapsing to the ground. An endless desert flashes through my vision. I start to suffocate. A swirling black void consumes me. My body burns like it's being licked with flames, then I start to freeze. Burning. Freezing. Over and over. I sink beneath the beige carpet. Sand smothers me. I inhale, choking on the tiny crystals. Tahira's limbs begin to shudder uncontrollably.

Is this it? Am I dying? Like Powell said I would?

No…

Tahira's limbs!

Tahira's limbs are shaking. *Her* body is on fire. Freezing.

My body…*her* body.

Her mind…*my* mind.

I'm *not* Tahira Collins.

Who am I?

What am I?

Divest…

Tahira's eyes snap open. Why is everything moving so slowly?

Deval towers over me. He doesn't see Jeremy moving toward him with his knife…heading straight for Dev's neck.

Jeremy.

Deval.

No. No, no, no!

I can't let this happen.

Dev's name flies from my lips, and I kick myself up off the ground.

I crash blindly into Jeremy. Our momentum carries us sideways past Deval. We crash into the wall, and I smash Jeremy's knife hand against the panel. He drops the knife.

Jeremy's eyes are wide. I smash my left fist into his bewildered face. Jeremy's head snaps back, hitting the wall with a dull thud. I punch him again.

Before I can land a third blow, Jeremy grabs my wrist and spins me into a chokehold. I elbow him in the stomach. He's wearing some kind of armor. Jeremy's embrace tightens.

He's holding me again...

Just like he used to...no...not like he used to...

"Mmmm...!" My air is cut off. He's killing me. I push off the ground and try twisting.

I stiffen.

Jeremy's knife is inches away from Tahira's neck.

"No, Tahira! Don't touch her! You..."

"Shut up or she dies."

Dev looks horrified. His gun is raised but there's no confidence in his stance. Shadows mar his otherwise handsome face.

The air around Jeremy's blade is hot. I grunt. The knife hums with some kind of energy. It's burning Tahira's skin without even touching me.

What do I do? I'm slipping. My vision is dimming. I can't breathe...

"October 2, 2093." Tahira's voice is hoarse, barely a whisper.

Jeremy's arm around my neck loosens a fraction. I suck in a breath.

"What did you just say?" The blade moves even closer to Tahira's skin. The tip is a hairsbreadth away. It burns!

"That's the day we were married." My breath is shallow. Tahira's lungs burn with each labored inhalation.

"It was stormy. It'd been raining for three days straight, and you told me you couldn't have asked for a better day to get married."

"How do you..."

"We got married in front of a judge."

"Who...?"

Jeremy's face is a mess of rage, but I keep going. Memories spew from my mouth like vapor.

"After you kissed me you said we should leave the military."

"Stop it."

"That first night we slept on the beach under a tarp."

"You don't know…"

"We were soaked by morning, I thought we were going to get pneumonia."

"Dammit, I said *stop it*!"

I cringe.

He never used to yell. Or curse. Never…

Jeremy's entire frame is shaking. I've made a mistake. I should've known how this would seem. I'm not his Alex…not completely.

Suddenly, Jeremy's arm spasms. I slip under his hold and out of his reach. I step away just as he collapses to the ground in a heap.

What just…?

Two small silver barbs protrude from Jeremy's chest.

Deval has me by my hand, and I'm stepping over Jeremy's unconscious form. He leads us down the hall until we reach a small door. I'm seeing double. The red, glowing letters across the hatch door dance left to right.

The hatch slides open, and a gust of wind pushes me back a step. Have the yacht's engines been killed or are we just drifting? Emergency lights from the ship cast shifting reflections across the choppy waves. The storm has worsened. Rain is falling in sheets. Only four meters away, a set of steps leads up onto an emergency raft. Dev steps outside the hatch and tugs on my arm. No.

"Wait!" I dig my feet into the ground.

"What? Tahira, I have to get you out of here!" Deval's voice is steady but with an edge of urgency.

"I can't leave him."

"Tahira, what are you saying? I need to get you someplace safe."

I shake my head violently.

"That man…Jeremy…he…he's my…"

I can't read Deval's face. His expression reveals nothing. How much of what I said, about Jeremy, did he believe?

He opens his mouths to speak but stops and glances behind me.

I spin around. The hatch hangs open. Jeremy is stirring. Surely the electrode barbs are still conducting electricity. Not enough, apparently.

"Tahira, hurry. We have to move!"

Deval takes my hand again, but I hesitate.

I'm torn.

Slowly, I raise my right arm. The beautiful, brown skin, covered in patterns and swirls of *henna* isn't mine. Deval isn't my husband. The life I've been living for the past two months is not *mine*.

But Jeremy doesn't know any of this.

All he sees is a stranger.

To him, I'm not Alexandria…I'm just the wife of the man he's trying to kill. What do I do?

Run. Fight. Give up. Save Deval. Save Jeremy. Save yourself.

I fight the urge to scream.

Both of them…I can save both of them.

I glance at the life boat then back to Deval and nod.

In a matter of seconds, Dev is behind the helm and powers up the small vessel. We quickly begin descending off the side of the ship toward the churning blackness below us. From his seat at the helm, Dev removes his phone and hands me a lifejacket at the same time. I approach Dev and get close to his ear.

"Dev…I'm so sorry! This is all my fault. Get back to the coast. Warn your family. There may still be time."

He looks away from his phone's glowing screen and twists toward me sharply. "What…!?"

I hold Dev's face in my hand and kiss him for as long as I can. He kisses me back. Tears fall from my eyes, mixing with thick raindrops and sea spray. God…what's happening to me? These emotions…are they even mine? Do they belong to Alexandria…or Tahira?

No. I'm Divest…but am I my mind? My body? Both? Neither?

Does it matter?

I don't care. It *doesn't* matter. I love Deval. I love his family. I care for their safety.

But…Jeremy…

I pull away.

Before Dev can stop me, I turn my back on him, drop the lifejacket, and leap.

I crash against the side of the boat and panic. The edge of the main deck is wet and slippery, but I get both hands on it and grip it tightly. I wrap my fingers around a metal bar and hug the side of the ship.

"Tahira! What are you *thinking*?!"

Grunting, I exhale deeply and pull. Tahira's arm and ab muscles strain as I yank myself up and onto the deck. I duck under the railing and turn on my side to watch as the crane wires lower Deval into the choppy waves below. He's almost to the bottom. The steel cables drop him closer and closer to safety. He grips one of the cables, nearly slipping and falling into the ocean below, and tries to climb. He slides back down and tries again.

There's confusion, pain, and worry in Deval's beautiful eyes. He shouts. *I'm sorry, Dev.*

Deval points at something. I twist, and a sharp blow lands across my face, knocking me over.

Scrambling on my hands and knees, I try to crawl forward across the cold, wet deck, but something heavy lands on my back.

Sea spray splashes me in the face, stinging my eyes as I struggle to throw Jeremy's weight off me.

I roll to the side and scissor my legs.

Jeremy growls, and the pressure of his body lessens slightly. I throw an elbow back to where I hope his face is and manage to connect with something hard. Jeremy grunts, and I push against the ground, flipping him up and off of me.

I leap to my feet and spin around. Jeremy is already on his own feet, his knife is gripped like he's about to throw it. The yacht shudders beneath my shaky feet. Jeremy wipes blood from his nose and lips. Did I break his nose? I didn't mean to hurt him.

Jeremy's eyes burn with hatred. He's never looked at me like that...

"My orders have a hierarchy, you know?" Jeremy's yelling. A trickle of blood runs down the side of his face.

"I know, but you don't have to do..."

"They told me not to harm you but to kill Kapoor at all costs. One of those costs just might have to be you. Unless you get out of my way."

Tears continue to stream down my face.

I'm trembling, and my vision is swimming. Up and down with the rocking of the ship.

No.

Not now.

My brain can't be doing this to me right now.

Jeremy approaches me and pulls his arm back, ready to strike.

"I'm sorry, Mrs. Kapoor…I have to do this…to save her."

I want to speak my name, but my voice isn't working. My lips move, but no sound comes out.

"I'm sorry…"

A wave crashes against the side of the ship, and a deafening ringing reverberates through my skull. My shoulder connects sharply with the yacht's metal bulwark, and Jeremy clutches the outer railing. His knife is gone. Probably swallowed by the sea. A second wave smashes our vessel, sending water crashing up over the side.

I blink and rub the seawater out of my burning eyes, and…Jeremy… where is he? No. No, no, no. Oh God, no!

He's gone over the edge.

Slipping, I get to my feet and stagger forward a step.

A head appears, then an arm. He slips. His fingers barely manage to cling to the metal edge of the deck.

"Jeremy!"

The ground beneath my feet sways, and I slip my way toward him. Laying flat on my stomach, I reach for his arm. He glares at me then…grasps my wrist. The black ocean reaches its own fingers toward him, threatening to take him from me. The ocean moans and throws water at us. Tahira's arms feel like they're about to pop out of their sockets. I begin sliding over the edge myself when, finally, Jeremy pulls himself the rest of the way up, over the edge of the deck. He rolls onto his back and closes his eyes.

I tug on his arm.

"We need to get inside."

Jeremy coughs seawater that mixes with the blood from his nose. Whether he hears me or not, he gets to his feet, and together we make our way toward a hatch.

"Why did you help me? You could've sent me off the edge completely."

Jeremy eyes me from his position on the couch opposite my own. The bleeding from his nose has stopped, but a nasty gash across Jeremy's forehead still leaks blood. He frowns but something's changed. The fire in his eyes has been doused. Maybe nearly drowning can do that to a person.

The red emergency lights are our only source of illumination. All of Tahira's senses remain on high alert. Is that why the pounding in my head is so intense? Or because I'm four feet away from Jeremy...?

Numerous books line the shelves on either side of the tall Cipher-tech walls. This must be some kind of library. Tahira's fingers touch the point on her neck where Jeremy's strange knife singed my skin. The wound is tender. It will probably leave a scar.

Without taking my eyes completely off Jeremy, I pull a blanket off the leather seat next to me and approach him, skirting around the glass coffee table that separates us.

He flinches. I pause.

"You're hurt. We need to stop the bleeding."

I point to his head, and he touches the wound gingerly.

The leather couch is stiff as I take a seat next to Jeremy. He doesn't take his eyes off Tahira's hands as I slowly raise a wadded corner of the blanket to his bleeding head. His own hand replaces mine as he presses the fabric against the wound.

"You didn't answer my question." An undertone of anger has reentered Jeremy's voice. Did I ever hear him talk like this when we were together? No. At least not around me.

"Jeremy...I..."

What can I say?

Nothing will make a difference. I'm not Alexandria. I'm in another woman's body. I'm not the person he knows and loves...or loved. I'm still Divest. Still a monster.

Aside from the muffled storm outside, the water dripping from my hair is the only sound that breaks the deathly silence.

It wasn't supposed to be like this.

Jeremy wasn't ever supposed to see me this way. One last mission. That was it. Then I'd get my real body back and Jeremy would never have to see Divest. I was supposed to keep him from seeing what I'd become...

Tahira's voice cracks. "The men that sent you here. What did they tell you about...your wife?"

Jeremy's free hand becomes a fist. A spark ignites behind his eyes. What am I doing? How must this sound to him? I'm a stranger...but I can't stop now.

"That's none of your concern."

"Please."

"*They* have her. Frozen in a tube."

"Cryogenics, right? With bullet wounds across her legs and abdomen?"

His eyes narrow. "How the hell do you know that? Are *you* one of them too?"

"No! I'm not...I mean...not anymore."

Jeremy suddenly gets to his feet, dropping the blanket and taking a step toward me. Shit. That was the wrong thing to say, but how can I lie to the man I love more than life itself? I scramble backward on the couch. I'm a fool.

"Jeremy, please! I want to help you. I can explain everything. It's me. Your wife. It's…"

No. I can't say it. I'm *not* Alex. Just Divest.

"I don't know how the hell you can possibly know the things you've said, but you are *not* my wife."

My lower lip trembles. No. He has to see I'm telling the truth. He has to know it's really me—inside this body. But…what did I expect? If I were in his shoes…would I believe my own story?

Jeremy's voice is cold. Dangerous. "What. *Are*. You?"

"I…"

Jeremy's eyes break from mine, and he looks up sharply at something over my shoulder. I turn.

"Deval? No! What are you…?"

Silhouetted against a pulsing crimson background, Deval steps cautiously into the room. Soaking wet, he brings his hands up together. He's holding something…Faru's smart-gun…

"Dev. You were supposed to…"

"What's going on here, Tahira?"

"I can explain."

"I wish you would."

"I can. I will. Just put down the gun. Please. No one has to get hurt."

It's too dark. I can't read Deval's expression. Is he shivering? "Don't move!"

Instinctively, I raise my hands, palms out. But no, he's not aiming at me. The angle of Dev's weapon has shifted slightly. Just past my right arm. Jeremy.

I step in front of Dev's aim, and he immediately lowers his arms.

"Tahira. What are you doing? Get out of the way."

"No. I won't let you hurt him."

"He tried to kill us."

"Because he's trying to save me!"

"Save you?! Tahira…do you even hear yourself?"

This is all wrong. Deval was supposed to leave. Save himself. Now *he's* the one pointing the gun.

"Deval…Dev, I'm not who you think I am."

"What do you mean?"

301

"I'm not Tahira Collins."

"What does…no. This is ridiculous. Get over here, Tahira. We're leaving. Authorities are on their way right now."

"I'm not…" Goosebumps cover my skin, and I wrap Tahira's arms around myself. Shaking my head doesn't clear the fog in my mind; it just makes me dizzy.

"We're getting out of here. Together."

"I'm not leaving without Jeremy."

"*Tahira…*"

"I'm. Not. Tahira!"

Tears stream from Tahira's eyes. What do I do? What do I say to end this nightmare?

I glance over my shoulder at Jeremy. His hands hang limp by his sides. The cut on his forehead has stopped bleeding so profusely. The bitter scowl scarring his features slowly dissipates to a frown. Turmoil clouds his eyes.

My eyes slowly find Deval's. He has to know. I have to be the one to tell him. "Deval…the Tahira you knew is…gone. Probably dead. I'm so…s… sorry. This is just…what's left of her. Her body."

I gesture to myself. I'm a demon. A horrific creature.

The shame is unbearable.

Confession was supposed to be good for the soul. Does this prove I don't have one?

Deval looks at me with a mix of horror and confusion. His face breaks my heart.

"Tahira…is this some kind of schizophrenia? Dissociative identity disorder? Another panic attack? What…?"

"No…I…*no!* Don't you understand? This isn't some kind of personality disorder, I'm…"

Deval shakes his head and takes three short steps toward me. I remain motionless. Dev keeps his eyes and his gun on Jeremy.

"Don't move, or I'll shoot you. My wife and I are leaving."

Deval reaches for my hand. I recoil at his touch and take a step back.

"Dev! Listen to me, please. My name is Alexandria McKenzie. My brain, my consciousness, is inside this body. It's just a shell for me to wear. Something I used to get close to you…I…look! Remember?"

Gathering Tahira's hair, I expose the side of my skull where he'll be able to see the scars again. Even in the dim light, surely he can see…

Jeremy edges slowly around the side of the coffee table. No. Don't.

Deval stiffens. "I said don't move!"

"Listen to him, Jeremy. Please." Warm tears slide down Tahira's cheeks. When did I start crying again?

Jeremy shakes his head without taking his eyes off Deval. "My mission… they said all I have to do is kill Kapoor…to save my wife."

"But I *am* your wife!"

Jeremy lunges toward Deval. The gun goes off.

Glass shatters as Jeremy tackles Deval, and the pair crash against a bookshelf.

Pieces of glass tumble down Jeremy's head and shoulders. Deval has something sticking out of his arm. A small knife hilt. The pair struggle, neck muscles straining.

The gun fires again. The shot ricochets off the metal walls. Echoing endlessly in my head. *Clang. Clang. Clang.*

Jeremy shoves Deval hard against the bookcase. The gun falls to the floor and gets kicked under a lamp. Everything tilts violently to one side as the yacht pitches forward. Jeremy grunts and throws Deval to the ground.

I leap for the gun, but Jeremy wraps his arms around me. He has no trouble swinging me around by my waist and tossing me across the room. Fiery pain erupts across my head and back as I smash into something sharp. Stars. I'm seeing stars. Deval clutches the end of a couch next to me, trying to get back to his feet.

Jeremy is bleeding from his shoulder, but his expression is calm. No, not calm. Determined.

"Please…" Will he even hear me? My voice sounds so faint. "You're not a monster. Not like me."

Jeremy shakes his head, slowly. He turns, searching. The gun.

The whole room rolls away from me, but a rush of adrenaline spurs me to my feet. I leap onto Jeremy's back and manage to get my right arm under his chin to crush his windpipe. He gasps.

Jeremy strikes at me. I let the blow land sharply against my shoulder. He tries to hit me again. I flex Tahira's muscles harder, choking him. Jeremy collapses to his knees, and we fall.

He leans back, and I crack my head against the floor. My grip around his neck loosens for only a moment, but he still manages to wrest my arm free.

Before I can do anything, Jeremy jumps upright, just in time for Deval to punch him in the face.

I have to dodge Jeremy's boot as he takes a step backward. Deval swings a fist again, but Jeremy blocks and follows up with his own punch to Deval's abdomen. Then his face.

"Jeremy, stop!"

Deval drops to the ground. His eyes flutter. If I had my real voice Jeremy would listen to me! But I don't have my real voice…just Tahira's.

"Please…Jeremy. Stop this…"

Jeremy ignores Tahira's pleas and reaches for the pistol next to his foot. He raises it toward Deval's prone form.

The gun inches toward Deval for the kill shot.

My body moves as if possessed.

Yes.

Can it be that for once…in all my lives…my mind is at peace with my body?

I tense Tahira's muscles, *my* muscles.

Then I leap.

Bang!

…

It takes me far too long to hit the ground.

My body is limp, and the ground hits me like a car. My vision turns off and on, pulsing with the rhythmic, crashing waves. I'm not cold anymore. My chest is on fire. Oh my God…

Like a slow-moving venom, finally hits me. It grips my mind and tightens, consuming me. I can't scream. I can't breathe. Can't do anything.

I'm so sleepy, I could lay here forever…

Deval shouts something.

Jeremy stares down at me. Shocked.

My lips move. He has to know.

I love you, to hell and back.

Jeremy's eyes fill with doubt, confusion, and…what else?

My vision cuts out, and then he's gone. My Jeremy…gone. Was he ever really there? What new hell have I fallen into? Please. Jeremy. Come back…I need you.

An immense pressure begins crushing my abdomen.

I open my mouth to scream but nothing comes out.

Deval is kneeling by my side. There's a wad of something in his hands. The bride's color is everywhere. On his hands, his arms, the blanket.

Red all over.

His lips move. My ears aren't working properly. Everything sounds like I'm underwater. Dev. Oh Dev…

I blink and he's gone too.

Darkness encroaches from every direction. Something cold and icy claws at me from the inside out. I'm going to die. Will this time be the last?

Someone is cradling my head. Deval. He came back for me. Something wet is falling from his eyes onto my cheeks.

I lift a finger. Then another. Dev takes my hand. I sob. What am I doing? Comforting this man in my last moments? Trying to feel some semblance of peace, some affection, from him in return? This is just me pretending to be Tahira. I can't possibly trust myself, or my memories, or my feelings.

But…love is a choice. *Not* a feeling.

I love him.

Oh my God…I love him…

Tahira Collins or not.

I love Deval for myself.

Darkness begins to consumes me completely. Deval's face is burned in my mind as my vision winks out.

The real hell can't possibly be worse than this living hell.

Or what if there's no such thing as hell? What if there's nothing?

Or what if the Hindus are right and death is just a transition?

What if I'm reincarnated?

What if I come back as a butterfly? Kai would like that.

What if…?

"I've just sent a team to recover the body."

"And Alex?"

"It's taking longer than we anticipated to reach her. The chances that her brain…"

"Haight—just tell me what you know."

"Ideally, given time, we should be able to repair the body. The bullet…"

"I don't care about the body. I want to know if Alex's mind will still be intact."

"Depends on the type of doctor you ask."

"I'm asking you."

"I'm not a doctor."

"Haight. So help me…"

"Powell will be analyzing her brain as soon as we retrieve the body. After we get some results, we'll know if we made it to her in time or not."

"Fine. And Kapoor?"

"He hasn't left her side. But there are too many people. We can't exactly…"

"Where is he now?"

"Waiting outside the operating room."

"And his family?"

"We don't know. They've disappeared."

"What a mess."

"We might still be able to salvage the situation. If…"

"No. Get Alex back, then this operation is over. Where is Jeremy?"

"He's um…well…we don't know that either."

"What!?"

"We lost him. He made it off the yacht but his tracker stopped responding shortly after."

"Did he drown?"

"Possibly. We can start searching for his body if…"

"No."

"No? You don't want us to look for…"

"There's no point. The rest of our plans will continue as outlined."

"But we've shown our hand."

"True, but this may be something we can use to our advantage. The Struggle teaches us that all challenges are given to us for a reason, does it not? Besides, the rest of the pieces are in motion. It will be difficult for Unitas to stop us now. Despite Alex's failure."

"So it's true then?"

"War is upon us, my friend."

"Struggle is life."

"Unity is death."

"I know how it sounds, but it's not Tahira. It's her body, but her mind…"

"How is this even possible?"

"I don't know."

"Where are you now?"

"Waiting. The surgeons are operating on her—*it*—as we speak."

"How much do the surgeons know?"

"Nothing. They've just assumed it's undergone a recent brain surgery. They think they can save it. I'm not even sure why I bothered taking it to…"

"Do not be hard on yourself. From what it sounds like, she—whoever she is—saved your life."

"I suppose we saved each other. I don't owe that creature anything now."

"Well…you did a noble thing. For good or ill. Though, I fear you are still in danger. I'm sending someone to you."

"Who?"

"A brother. One of our Chosen."

"I do not fear for my safety."

"*Be that as it may, the Brethren Council fears for your safety.*"

"What about the monster who killed my...who killed Tahira?"

"*Do not be so quick to assume, my son. You don't know the woman in Tahira's body is also guilty of her murder. How can we even be certain Sister Tahira is truly dead?*"

"The unholy creature who stole her body seemed very sure..."

"*I am sorry, my son, truly. But troubling times are ahead. We need you, now more than ever.*"

"I understand, but what do you expect me to do when the Chosen gets here? Abandon Tahira's body? The doctors have already recognized her."

"*The Chosen will assist you in recovering Tahira's body.*"

"So we can burn it?"

"*We will discuss our next steps after you've reached a safe location. I am sorry, Deval. Truly. The crimes you have witnessed are unspeakable.*"

"The Proelium must pay."

"*Ours is not the Path of violence, my son. Or revenge.*"

"Perhaps. But unity wasn't supposed to be possible for the Proelium either."

"*This is perhaps the most disturbing revelation of all. If the Proelium have united under a single banner...*"

"We will need to be ready for anything."

"*I will warn the rest. You focus on getting someplace secure.*"

"What about my family?"

"*They are safe. But I cannot disclose their location. If the Proelium have joined forces...we cannot trust this form of communication.*"

"I understand. Thank you for your help, Brother Aarav."

"*Of course, my son.*"

"I have to go. A doctor is looking for me."

"*Be safe, Deval. Unity is life.*"

"Struggle...is death."

I should be dead.

I deserve to be dead.

It's the only thing that makes sense.

But hell isn't supposed to be high above the clouds. Is it?

There are no buildings, no trees, no mountains, no people—nothing.

I'm alone.

The landscape is faded, like it's covered in smog…

Is this heaven? Paradise? Nirvana? Limbo?

Maybe it's just me. Alone forever?

My consciousness feels funny. What's wrong with me?

Why can't I move?

Why do I feel so disoriented? So lost?

Where is up? Down? Is there even a horizon?

Are those distant clouds? Or…no…

It's like I'm locked inside a massive sphere.

My consciousness trembles, and the ground beneath me shakes. It can't be. Please. No.

No, no, no!

Not here. Anywhere but here. This isn't possible. I *died!*

Energy courses through me and my awareness is pushed forward.

Sandy dunes stretch endlessly beneath me.

My mind is on a precipice…

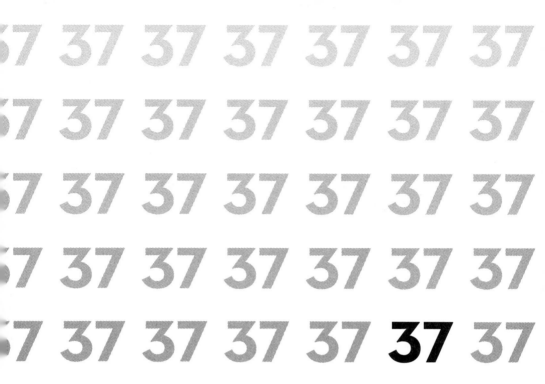

No.

I'm lying down. It's warm but not uncomfortable. Something, sheets or a blanket, covers most of my body. My body…!

Warm light blinds me. I blink several times.

What's going on? Whose body am I in? Is it mine? Whose heart is beating within my chest? Why am I alive? *How* am I alive? Am I back in the clutches of my handlers? I was with Deval. I saved him. And Jeremy…

Jeremy!

I try to sit up but don't make it more than a few inches.

My ankles and wrists are being restrained.

Whoever's body I'm in is completely covered by a thick, gray sheet that rises all the way up to my chin. I bite it and try tugging. I have to know. Whose body am I in? The sheets are too tight. I can't get them to move. I strain against my bonds. This body feels lethargic. Weak.

I'm in a hospital. No. The bed looks like it belongs in a hospital, but my room…the walls are brick. Old brick. Cement seams are cracking in places. It smells old too. Where am I?

Soft yellow light pours through a single glass pane window. It must be close to midday. Opposite the window, across the room, is a solid-looking wooden door with a dark handle. The rest of the room is bare. Where are their cameras?

Something between a sob and a grunt escapes my lips, but I resist the urge to scream. I'm pulling so hard against whatever is wrapped around my arms that my skin begins to chafe. I don't stop struggling. Back and forth. I have to get free. Why didn't I die? Why couldn't I have ended when Jeremy tried to shoot Deval? Is Deval even alive? Did Jeremy return to finish him off? I bite my lip, and my eyes start to water with sharp, stinging tears.

Something slips. An animal frenzy takes over, and I rip my wrist free. The sheet comes untucked. Yes!

My arm is slender. Faded patterns of dark ink blend with smooth, brown skin. *Henna.*

No.

Tahira.

I'm still in her body.

This isn't happening.

I *died!*

The bedsheet feels terribly heavy as I rip it off the rest of my—*Tahira's*—body. I'm wearing a black, skin-tight compression suit that covers everything except Tahira's arms and feet. The material is like plastic on the outside but is soft and supportive on the inside. I fumble with the fabric cuff tying my right arm to the bed until Tahira's other arm is free. A pounding in my head begins, but there's no pain. I reach for the bonds around my ankles and undo the straps.

I leap from the bed and dash toward the door. The handle is cold to Tahira's touch and won't budge. Throwing her weight against the door does nothing except hurt my shoulder. I'm trapped.

The window.

It takes me three long strides to cross the room. How high up am I? Two or three stories? A swath of short, smooth grass lies directly below the window. Interspersed every few feet are potted flowers and exotic plants. A low-hanging stone wall rests a dozen yards away. Some kind of garden? No other people are in sight. Beyond the perimeter wall is dense, green forest for as far as I can see. Where am I?

Could I still be in India? I'm definitely not stateside. This has to be some kind of base my handlers were using during my mission. Do my handlers have Jeremy here too?

Jeremy...

I have to know. He has to be alive. He has to be here.

Tahira's body is leaden. What kind of drugs has Powell pumped into me this time? I return to the bed and examine the monitor attached to the wall. It's a simple metal mount held into the bricks with four metal bolts. After five tugs, it dislodges from the wall completely. Reddish brick dust fills the air. I rip the wires free and test the weight of the monitor by swinging it back a forth a few times.

Finally—I hurl it at the window.

The glass shatters easily on impact. The monitor soars through the air, followed shortly by a dull thud as it hits the ground below.

I approach the window.

I'm definitely at least three stories up. I have to get out of this cell to find Jeremy. What if I break a bone though? If I was in my own body...

Jump. Just do it.

I put both hands on the window sill to hoist myself up. There's a soft click of metal on metal from behind me. The door. Someone's coming.

A second lock clicks open. There are muffled voices on the other side of the door. Shit.

Just before the door swings open, I slide under the bed, flat on my stomach.

Two pairs of legs enter the room. The first is dressed in dark pants with black boots. Mercenary. The second person...is barefoot and has dark skin like mine. No. Like *Tahira's*.

"What...*where is she?*" The soft voice belongs to a man. An older man I'd guess. "Look, my son! The window..."

The black boots make their way over to the window. Pieces of glass strew the ground. Tahira's heart is beating so loudly. Can't they hear it? How much longer can I hold my breath?

"We must find her. Quickly!"

The first man leaves the window and exits the room in a hurry. The man with no shoes follows close behind.

I wait thirty seconds…then roll out from under the bed and dash through the open door.

I'm in a hall. The walls are made of the same stone as my cell. Everything looks so…old. Bricks and stone are yellowed with age. Is that incense in the air? The stone floor is gritty beneath Tahira's bare feet. I shiver.

What do I do now? The hallway to my left ends in a solid wall two doors down. To the right, it extends maybe fifty yards before connecting to some kind of larger chamber. The place seems deserted. Where did the man and the mercenary go? How am I ever going to find Jeremy in this place? How can I be sure he's even here? That he's even alive…?

The wood door to my left swings open. A short bald man with a thick white beard dressed in yellow and orange robes exits the room. He looks up at me with wide eyes. Before he can open his mouth, I throw myself at him. We tumble to the ground, and I strike him sharply across the face. His eyes roll backward in his skull.

I stand over his unconscious form and glance into the room he just left.

It looks identical to my cell; though, instead of a bed, a simple rug lies at the center of the room. The hell is this place…? Why is this guy dressed like…? No. No time to wonder. I need to find Jeremy. I need to escape.

Tahira's bare feet make it easier to move silently as I dash down the hall. I pass three doors, none with windows, and I don't dare try barging into any of them.

This is hopeless. There are too many doors. I'll never find Jeremy. I need a plan. I'm an assassin; what do I normally do…?

Get to the security hub. Yes. Find their cameras. It's got to be centrally located. Possibly well guarded. I'll know it when I see it, I just need to keep moving.

I keep to the shadows and reach the end of the hallway. Before me is a very large, very open rotunda. The chamber is a perfect circle with several other hallways extending off in different directions like spokes on a wheel. The red stone floor matches the walls. Candles burn from their mounts, illuminating intricate, colorful wall murals. Some look Hindu. Gods and planets surround me on all sides. The ceiling is immense and curves up to a single point, easily fifty feet tall. The dome is unlike anything I've seen before. Am I in some kind of temple? A *mandir* perhaps?

Where are all the guards? The mercenaries? Surely they can't *all* be looking for me outside? Was my ruse really that effective?

"There she is!"

I spin toward the sound. Another robed man has appeared directly across the large chamber, seemingly from nowhere.

A second man, younger than the first, exits the shadows behind the robed figure. He's dressed in black pants and a matching shirt. His skin is dark. Far darker than my own.

I'm momentarily frozen as he starts walking quickly toward me.

Before I can take a step in any direction, a hand grips my shoulder from behind. "Ma'am, you…"

Tahira's elbow connects with a jaw. The hand releases its grip from my shoulder, and I start running. The black man in front of me slows. His eyes betray confusion. When I'm maybe four feet away from him, I jump. For a moment I'm weightless as I lean backward in the air and wrap my legs around the man's neck. I twist with my momentum and bring the man crashing to the ground.

I get back to my feet quickly and take two steps toward the robed man. He stumbles backward, up against the wall. His brown eyes are wide. Mouth agape.

Pathetic. But…my handlers *should* be afraid of me.

"Stop!"

I grab the robed man by his forearm, pull him toward me, and spin.

A Caucasian mercenary regards me from across the rotunda. His nose is bleeding. Maybe it wasn't his jaw that I hit. Oh well. I'll settle for a broken nose.

"I said *stop*." Blood and saliva drip from his mouth as he speaks.

I glare into his green eyes and try to ignore the gun pointed toward me and my human shield.

"Go ahead. Shoot." Tahira's voice feels and sounds different. It hurts. Like it hasn't been used for a while. "I guarantee you'll kill him first."

I take a step forward, locking my arms around my hostage's neck.

No one speaks. The white man either can't or won't. My hostage definitely *can't*.

"Where is Jeremy?" My voice cracks. I cough and repeat myself. "Where *is* he? Tell me!"

The mercenary's lips remain sealed. His companion I tackled to the ground begins to stir.

My hostage makes the effort to speak. I'm crushing his windpipe, so nothing but a weak murmur leaves his lips. I relax my grip ever so slightly and the robed man sucks in a breath. "He's…here…"

"What do you mean, here? I want to see him! Where's my husband!?"

The commotion has drawn the attention of others. A dozen robed figures and black-clad mercenaries begin to appear from doors and hallways surrounding the rotunda. They're coming for me.

"Where is my husband!"

Tears sting Tahira's eyes. I'm fighting for breath. It's like *I'm* the one being choked. Why does no one else draw a weapon? I'm an easy target now. So outnumbered. I'm a fool. Did I really think I could escape?

"Tahira…"

The name is whispered. Eyes stare at me from all directions. Too many. Who spoke?

A man breaks from the crowd and approaches. He's tall and dressed in a loose white *sherwani*. His curls seem longer than usual. His eyes darker, more sunken. Full of sadness. Pain. Anger…

Deval.

What's going on?

Why is Deval here?

Where is *here*?

Nothing makes sense…

"Please let go of Brother Aarav." Deval's voice is soft, but…he isn't looking at me like he used to. He's detached. Avoiding my eyes.

He knows what I am.

My arms suddenly lose all their strength.

I release the robed man, and he stumbles away. His breathing comes in ragged gasps.

I sink to my knees and curl up into a ball against the rough brick wall.

They'll definitely kill me now. This was probably all just a cruel trick anyway. I've broken their rules. I tried to escape. Worse…I failed in my mission. Now they're punishing me in the worst way possible.

But why is Deval here…?

People are murmuring. They might as well be shouting. I just want to close my eyes and never open them again.

Deval's touch is familiar. I don't recoil. His hand feels so warm against my bare shoulders.

"Tahira? I mean…*Alexandria*…?"

Dev's fingers trace my arm until his hand finds mine. Our fingers interlock. There's no spark, no affection in the way he holds me.

I lift my heavy eyes to meet his. He's so close, but an invisible barrier keeps him from moving any closer. Ask him.

"Where. Am. I?"

Deval sighs and gestures around the room at the mix of people.

"This…is Unitas."

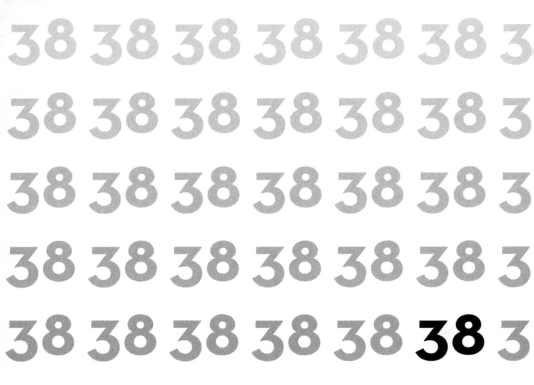

The sun is high.

A slight breeze tugs at Tahira's hair. How did it get so long? It's down to the small of my back now. How much time has passed since the storm and the yacht? A leaf falls from a tree above and lands on my lap. I brush it off, and it drifts to the ground.

I run Tahira's nails through her hair and sigh. What am I doing? They said they have Jeremy here...somewhere. I should be with him right now. We should be running away together. Trying to restart our lives and regain some semblance of normalcy. But...

Robed men approach me, heading toward a *murti*. Their voices grow quiet as they pass me. They don't trust me. They're afraid. Probably for good reason. I'm a monster. A wild animal. A freak...

I cross one foot over the other. The ground is warm against Tahira's soles. I pull her knees up against her chest and rest my forehead against them. A bird chirps somewhere overhead. Otherwise, the stone courtyard is utterly silent.

Something touches my shoulder. I flinch.

Deval takes a step back and frowns. Oh Dev...

Even *he* doesn't trust me. Not anymore. Why does his trust mean so much to me? I don't deserve trust. Not after what I did to him…

"May I sit?"

After a moment I nod and scoot a few inches to make more room on the stone bench. He sits at the edge. There's only two feet that separate us…but it might as well be two thousand.

Sunlight dances through Dev's curls.

"They want me to ask you again if we can offer you real clothes?"

I shake my head.

"Shoes? Food? Water? Anything?"

I bite my lip and stare at Tahira's feet.

He sighs. "You know…you'll have to eat and drink eventually."

A bit of stone from the bench comes loose beneath my fingers and I pick at the chasm, widening the crack.

"Tahira…I…"

"I'm *not* Tahira." Tears begin to well up in my eyes, and I look away so Dev can't see.

"I…you're right. I'm sorry. It's Alex, right? Alexandria?"

I shrug. What does it matter what my name is anymore?

"At first, no one believed me when I told them what you said. About… everything. But while you were recovering, we did some tests, a few scans…"

Another leaf falls on my lap.

"So now you believe me?"

My voice is barely more than a whisper. Dev moves a little closer. I feel his eyes on me. What is he thinking?

After a long pause, Deval sighs. "Yes. I believe you."

I nod.

"Did they kill her? Did they kill…Tahira?"

I squeeze Tahira's eyes shut and grip the edges of the bench. Of course he wants to know. What can I say?

"I don't know…"

"What do you mean you *don't know*?" He's angry. Dev's voice is filled with pain. "How can you not know if she's…!?"

"I don't know what they do with…with…"

I can't do this. I bury my head in Tahira's hands. Don't cry. I'm done crying.

"I'm sorry. I just, I have to know. This whole time, I thought you were really her."

"That's what Divest is best at."

"What?"

"Nothing. It's…what I am. Divest. Just something I call myself."

"I see."

I can't stop now that I've started. He has to know the truth. *My* truth.

"They took everything from me."

"You mean you weren't recruited? You aren't part of the Struggle? The Proelium?"

I shake my head. "I was an American soldier. My team and I were ambushed by a terror cell. I was shot. The next time I opened my eyes, I was wearing another woman's body. Divested of everything that used to be mine."

"So, they made you into Divest? And forced you to…"

"They kidnapped Jeremy. My husband. They said if I'd do what they wanted…they'd let him go. When I was given my very first mission, I thought killing one person for my handlers would end my nightmare. But they kept giving me more and more assignments, threatening to destroy my real body and end Jeremy's life if I didn't cooperate. I obeyed."

I pause and shake my head. "At first, I did what they wanted because I was afraid. Terrified really. Months went by and things changed. After the first few murders…what did one more matter? They made me into a monster."

"I'm sorry, Alex."

"I'm sorry too."

I meet Deval's gaze. He's hurting; I can see the ache in his dark eyes. Terrible truths are sometimes worse than terrible lies.

"Are they all right?"

"Who? The men you attacked? They'll be okay. Brother Aarav is…"

"No." I shake my head. "Kaivalya. Viti. Your mother…"

"Ah…yes. They're safe."

I nod. Deval scoots a little closer to me on the bench but still not close enough to touch. "I'm sure you have other questions."

"How am I still alive?"

"We had a helicopter fly you to the nearest hospital. For a few moments, you actually *were* dead. You went into surgery. Once you were stable enough, the Brethren thought it would be wise to transfer you here. Especially after the Proelium tried to recover you…"

"They came for me?"

Deval nods.

"Was anyone hurt?"

"Sister Karima…she'll spend a few more weeks recovering."

"Dev…can I ask you…*why* am I still alive?"

Silence. Deval looks away.

"Deval? Why did you save me? Why not let me die?"

"Because…we need your help."

"Who's we?"

"Unitas."

"What *is* Unitas? Some kind of religious cult? A secret society?"

Dev cracks a thin smile. "Perhaps it's a little of both. But…they never told you?"

"My handlers never told me anything they didn't absolutely have to."

"I see." Deval frowns. "Essentially, Unitas is a global network of people. We're dedicated to uniting humanity in the search for Truth. We call our efforts the Path. You understand, in Hinduism we believe in *moksha,* correct? Liberation of the spirit?"

I nod.

"We believe it's humankind's destiny to achieve true liberation of the spirit. To not be bound by physical limitations. Not necessarily the way Hinduism describes it, but close…"

Weird.

"And…the Proelium?"

"They believe in the Truth too. Although, instead of a Path, they believe in something they call the Struggle. They think that war, conflict, and division are the only ways humanity can reach true liberation. For thousands of years they've practiced the idea of division so devoutly they've never united to pursue their own common goals. The Brethren and I believe that's changed…

we think they've joined forces and are planning something. Something to deeply divide humanity."

"How can the world be *more* divided than it already is?"

"We're not sure."

I frown. "And you think I do?"

"No. Well, maybe. But that's why—"

"Why you need my help? To figure out what they're planning? To discover their big, bad plot?"

Deval hesitates then slowly nods. "We need your help...and you need ours."

I shake Tahira's head violently. "Unitas. Proelium. Whatever. I don't want to be used anymore. I don't want to be a weapon...I just want my life back."

"Help us stop the Proelium, and we'll help you get your life back. I promise."

"No. This isn't my fight. I'm done. I've robbed too many people of their lives chasing the promise that I'll get mine back."

"Don't you want revenge!? Don't you want to destroy the people responsible for turning you into a...a...?"

"A monster?"

Deval swallows and looks embarrassed.

"Killing more people won't change what I've become. I can't help you, Dev. I'm sorry. Truly."

"Don't you want your...you know...your *real* body back?"

I purse my lips and make fists with both of my...*Tahira's*...hands.

"If you help us, we can help you get your body back. We think we know where the Proelium are located. All we ask is that you help us in return. For the sake of humanity. What we're fighting for is bigger than just you and me."

"Yeah? You'll help me get my body back?" Tears begin welling in my eyes, stinging, burning, angry tears. "Is that before or after I kill a bunch of people for you? Or infiltrate some government? Or sleep with people to learn their secrets? *What?*"

"We're not asking you to do any of that; we just need your help trying to find out what the Proelium are planning."

Deval moves even closer to me on the bench. There are less than six inches between us now. He reaches for my hand. I let him hold it.

"Alexandria...I'm sorry...for everything. You're as much a victim in all of this as anyone else. I understand if you don't want to help."

Without my brain telling it to, Tahira's body slowly leans toward Deval and I rest my head against his chest. He doesn't recoil. Doesn't push me away. Instead, he wraps an arm around my bare shoulder. I could stay here forever. His heart beat is so soothing. Why?

Dev holds me but doesn't pull me closer. Not like he used to. What am I doing? I'm a mess. A broken, pathetic excuse for a person. Everything is so wrong. Except Deval. He doesn't feel wrong.

But...Jeremy...

Doesn't Jeremy deserve to hold the *real* me? Like Deval deserves to be holding the real Tahira right now?

I can never be who Deval deserves me to be. But I might be able to be Alex again. For Jeremy's sake. For my own sake.

What would Divest do?

What would Tahira do?

What would...Alex...do?

"You really know where my body is?"

Deval nods. "There are two likely locations. Bases that the Proelium are using for whatever they're planning. One here in India. Another in New Russia. We've been monitoring both."

"And you'll help me get my body back?"

"Yes. We have members, Chosen, who can help you. We have people trying to figure out how the Proelium managed the transplants too. We only ask that you help us in return. It's not an understatement to say that the fate of humanity is at risk."

"Okay..."

"Okay?"

"Okay—I'll think about it."

He nods. "Okay." Dev's voice is reassuring. Calm. Steady. Grounded.

A reddish-brown butterfly glides through the air and lands on my knee. After a few moments, it flaps its wings and disappears over the edge of the low-hanging wall surrounding the courtyard.

Eventually, Deval clears his throat and pulls away. "So...do you want to see him?"

"Jeremy?"

Deval nods.

"I..."

My heart suddenly starts beating heavily and my stomach sinks. Surely he knows exactly what I am, if he didn't before...on the yacht. They must have told him. Do I really want to see him like this? Wearing someone else's body?

"Yes..."

"All right, follow me."

The heavy wooden door opens with a click and I step into the room. The stone walls are bare, and the only source of light comes from a small window.

A lone figure sits in the middle of the room on a flimsy looking aluminum chair.

Jeremy looks up and glares at me. Then, recognition sweeps over his features and his mouth goes slack.

"You..."

I hesitate at the door. Why can't I look at him directly? My body takes a step backward. I shouldn't be here. He shouldn't have to see me like this. I'm a...

"Alex."

My eyes finally meet his and within seconds I cross the short distance separating us and embrace him.

My momentum nearly tips over his chair, but it settles and I pull him even closer as he stands upright.

I hold him as if I'll never get to hold him again. His chest and arms are so familiar. His scent is invigorating. Jeremy exhales on my ear and it sends chills down my back. I'm home.

But…why isn't he holding me in return?

It's true. He *does* know what I am. A freak. A murderer. A despicable, horrible creature.

My body reacts as if I've been electrocuted and I step away from Jeremy.

He's dressed in simple, cotton pants and a loose *sherwani* with sleeves that stop at his wrists.

His wrists…

Jeremy's hands are bound behind his back.

That's why he didn't embrace me too. Not because he doesn't love me anymore. Not because he's sickened by me. Because his arms are tied… that's it…right?

"Is it really you?"

His deep voice penetrates to the center of my being. I shrug and stare at my feet.

"Alex…it's okay."

The ground blurs and I rub my eyes with Tahira's arm.

"No. It's not."

"Well…truthfully, I'm still into blondes. But the next time we go backpacking you probably won't need nearly as much sunscreen. Right?"

I laugh before choking back a sob. "I've missed you. *So* much."

Jeremy takes a half step toward me and leans over to rest his forehead against mine. "I…I've missed you too, Alex."

We stand awkwardly for several moments with only our foreheads touching. I have to tell him.

I have to tell him there's a chance to get the real me back.

A chance he can hold *me* in his arms again.

I have to tell him…

Tell him…

…

What am I doing?

Who is this man? Why am I holding him so intimately?

I release the man and take a quick step backward. Chills run down my spine and turn my legs to gelatin. His pale skin and wavy locks are familiar…

he's...the man from my wedding. The phantom. The one who tried to kill us on the yacht.

I need to get out of here.

Deval. Where is he? He's...okay, I was just with him. Wasn't I?

Where is my husband?

The man takes a step toward me, a look of concern on his face. "Alex? Is everything all right?"

I scream as I spin, pull the door open, and flee.

The man's calls echo down the dimly lit hallway as I run. "Alex! Alex...!"

Why? Why was he calling me Alex?

I'm Tahira.

Tahira Collins Kapoor.

ABOUT THE AUTHOR

McKay grew up in Springville, Utah, where he swam competitively year-round, took piano and art lessons, and read every sci-fi and fantasy book he could get his hands on. After graduating high school, he spent two years in Santiago, Chile, serving the people and falling in love with the country. After returning to the States, he married his wife Jessica and they're currently living in Provo, Utah, where McKay is finishing his Personal Financial Planning degree at Utah Valley University. *Reincarnate* is McKay's first published novel.

ACKNOWLEDGMENTS

A very special thanks to my acquisition editor, Jess Cohn, who not only gave my story a chance but went above and beyond to help *Reincarnate* become a reality. Also, Daniel Wheatley, my production editor, who was key in making this book polished and ready for publication. Another special thank you to Jeff J. Peters, who acted as an impromptu mentor and provided invaluable advice.

Thank you to my incredible beta readers: Jessica, Nichole, Travis, Austin, Marisa, Mara, Bethany, Gurleen, and Brady. You were all phenomenal!

Finally, thank you to all those who pledged the highest tier rewards with Kickstarter:

Mike M.

Derrin H.

Merle S.

Samuel C.

Nichole M.

Tyler O.

TJ T.

Angela & Mark R.

Siera M.

Brad & Shauna M.

Ondra M.